driftwood DAFFODIL

LOUISIANA MADE MEN BOOK ONE

I couldn't be bothered
Novalee

AUTHOR WARNING

This is a dark romance and is intended for a mature audience. Reader discretion advised. This book contains but is not limited to, violence, profanity, tobacco and alcohol use, references to childhood trauma and loss.

For Sherry and Kasey

Name Pronunciations

Novalee: Nova-lee
Giovanni: Gee-oh-vaughn-ee
Atlee: At-lee
Darious: Dare-ee-us
Memphis: Mem-fiss
Veda: Vay-duh
Kato: Kay-toe
Romeo: Row-me-oh
Cesare: Sea-zar
Chuck: Chuck
Carissa: Car-iss-ah
Ezra: Ez-rah
Sutton: Sut-ton
Kendall: Ken-dall
Alex: Alex
Atlas: At-lass
Saul: Sal
Antonio: An-tone-ee-oh
Mancini: Man-chee-knee
Fiore: Fee-or-eh
Barone: Bar-oh-n

Playlist

'Way Down We Go' by Kaleo
'38 Years-old' by The Tragically Hip
'The Hanging Tree' by Jennifer Lawrence
'Hold On' by Wilson Phillips
'Cheap Thrills' By Sia
'Last Night's Mascara' by Brynn Cartelli
'Daffodil' by Florence and The Machine
'Basket Case' by Green Day
'What It's Like' by Everlast
'House Of The Rising Sun' by Lauren O'Connell
'Wolf In Sheep's Clothing' by Duality
'Disarm' by The Smashing Pumpkins
'You're Going Down' by Sick Puppies
'Do I Wanna Know' by Artic Monkeys
'Ready Or Not' by War Hall
'Daylight' by David Kushner
'Come Out And Play' by Nirvana
'Numb' by Linkin Park
'The Sound Of Silence' by Disturbed

DAFFODIL MYTHOLOGY

The daffodil is a brightly colored flower that's often associated with sunshine and good luck, but this flower has a dark past that starts with its name.

Daffodils are members of the flora species Narcissus, which derives from the same name in Greek Mythology. When Narcissus was rejected by his romantic interest, he became so obsessed with his own reflection that he refused to eat or drink and died.

Along with being a symbol of selfishness, vanity, and self-obsession, the daffodil can also draw penury and ill fortune if a single flower is given as a gift.

In medieval times the daffodil was an omen of death. It was believed if someone saw a flower drooping, it was a foretelling of their end. They are also extremely poisonous. The toxin in their alkaloids can cause death if not treated in time.

Even with all of this, the only thing most people see when they gaze upon a daffodil is beauty.

Chapter 1

NOVALEE

2 YEARS AGO,

My arm strained to push the door open. It wasn't weight or a lock that made the task difficult. It was the dread heavily sinking in my heart that made everything arduous. Simple actions were now utterly exhausting. Getting out of bed, brushing my hair, and even opening my eyes felt like a chore.

It was as if an indescribable weight was pressing down on my chest, constricting the world around me. But it was the helplessness that was the worst. My entire life was about to be flipped upside down, and there wasn't a damn thing I could do about it other than watch the floor fall out from under me.

With a sigh, I stepped across the threshold and was met with a myriad of stares. Some were filled with pity, but most held nothing but hatred and disgust. The courtroom was crowded today.

Well, one side was.

The crime of the year is what the newspapers called this, and no one wanted to miss that. Provided they didn't have to sit on the defences side that is. Then they might be associated with my family. And God forbid they actually knew my brother's name.

"That's the younger one," an older woman said in a hushed tone as I walked past. "Poor thing probably had no idea who her brother was."

Oh, I knew exactly who my brother was, and why he committed his so-called atrocity. Kato was kind and loving. Not that any of them would know that. All they cared about was the murderer that the media sensationalized.

Hushed comments and curious stares followed me as I held my head high and marched over to the empty side of the room and sat down. Let them watch if they wanted. I didn't care what they thought. Each and every one of them could rot in hell.

"I hope you prayed for your brother's soul, little girl. Justice will be served today."

I didn't see who said that, but snorted anyway.

Justice? Really?

Is that what they called this mockery of a trial? There was nothing fair or equal about this bullshit. Just the important, unimportant, and the media circus that surrounded us. No one heard or cared about our side of the story.

Guess I shouldn't be surprised.

Sorrow and loss seemed to follow me around. Yet I still managed to see the value in life. Until the night my sister went out and everything changed. One little decision tipped everything upside down.

Now food had no taste, colors weren't bright, and that hole in the woods we were afraid of as kids now seemed like an awfully inviting place to crawl into. It was as if the universe itself was reflecting my pain.

Or mocking it.

There were no dark clouds hanging in the air, or light drizzle to dampen the mood. What the universe gave in my moment of tragedy was a bright, clear afternoon sky and smiles filled with giddiness.

Here I was trying to stop my family from crumbling apart while all of my friends were filled with cheer. Summer vacation tended to do that. It was the time for freedom, fun, parties, and apparently resentment. I should be with them, swinging off a rope. Not sitting here wishing I could sink down to the bottom of our swimming hole.

But I couldn't even do that, because I was the only one left to hold it all together. It was a losing battle. Like trying to put a broken glass or vase back together with a piece missing.

Even the Louisiana heat was against me. It was especially thick and heavy. The kind of muggy warmth that seeped through the walls and saturated every surface. The taste in the air along with the sticky feel of the wooden bench on my thighs, was inescapable.

I looked over at an older woman as she fanned herself with a notebook while the man next to her wiped the sweat off his brow.

This room was filled with annoyed, overheated people, and I wished with every fiber of my being that I could be just like them. What I wouldn't give for air conditioning to be my biggest worry. But the only thing I could feel was my heart dropping as the locked door on the right swung open and a prisoner was brought in.

Kato.

He shuffled forward with his shoulders slumped while I tried not to cry at the shackles around his ankles. My brother wasn't this broken down shell of a man with scruff on his face and disheveled hair.

What happened to the man who woke me up every morning with a bright smile. The one who was vibrant and full of life. Where was the guy who taught me to face my obstacles head on, without anger or regret, because the only thing that could stand in my way, was me. Had he given up?

Had I?

Tears threatened to trickle down my face while my lungs warmed from the overheated air, but I still forced myself to smile. The Kato I grew up with would want me to look on the bright side. Hope was all we needed to find a light in the shadows. That was something he was constantly saying.

I had hope. I hoped that my sister would survive her attack. When she finally opened her eyes on that hospital bed, I hoped the bright sparkle that used to light up her hazel orbs would come back. Then I hoped that the cops would take pity on us and release our brother so I wouldn't have to tell her he was arrested.

I even held onto that hope during the trial. But the instant that guilty verdict was read, any spark of hope I had died. Pain and numbness was the only thing I felt now.

Veda would never be the same and Kato's fate was about to be sealed. All I could do was sit here and listen. The fact that Kato chose to wear his prison issued grey jumpsuit instead of his suit told me that he'd already accepted defeat.

Veda was broken, Kato was gone, and I was what… A witness? A bystander? The clean-up crew?

My brother didn't take me with him to the bar that night. I didn't hear Atlas Mancini bragging about what he'd done to our sister. I wasn't there to stop Kato from beating him to death. But I had to live with the repercussions.

Happy fifteenth birthday Nova.

Disappointment flooded Kato's face when his blue eyes landed on me. How I longed to see just a hint of the smile he used to wear.

Not many people in town knew who my sister and I were, but Kato… His charm was an infection that drew people in. It didn't matter if he'd known them his entire life, or if they just came into his garage for a quick oil change. Kato made everyone feel special.

It's funny how fast supposed friends would turn on you. Not one single person was sitting on the defense's side of the courtroom – aside from myself and the reporter in the back. Not a single one of his friends or coworkers bothered to ask how he was doing, or check in on us. We no longer existed to them. Even my brother's fiancé had moved on.

So here we were, once again left with no one but each other.

Kato and I should be out on the bayou with our rods in the water. Not sitting in a stuffy courtroom. Guess I could kiss that birthday tradition goodbye. Memories were all that was left.

Veda whining and complaining that she needed to get up so early while Kato teased us about becoming gator food.

"Stop rocking the boat," he'd sing. *"Those gators are waiting for lunch."*

That boat was currently docked alone and unused, while Veda was stuck in a hospital bed barely able to move on her own. All because Atlas Mancini and his friends decided they wanted to have fun with our sister.

Two guards led my brother over to where his lawyer, Harry Tucker, was sitting. Though I'd argue that Harry wasn't worthy of that job title. He didn't even attempt to put up a decent defence. The only thing he did well was wear a suit. And even that was iffy.

"Nova?" Kato huffed out a breath. "What are you doing here?"

"Where else would I be?"

As much as I wanted to crawl into a hole and disappear, I would never abandon him. I was going to sit right here in the blue summer dress Kato bought me for my birthday, and smile for the both of us.

I'd be the light in his shadows.

Kato slipped into his chair and whispered, "I told you not to come."

"I know." I just didn't care.

Kato sighed and pinched the bridge of his nose, though I wasn't sure why he was surprised. I was thirteen when our mother died and he took over the parenting role. He should be used to me disobeying him by now.

Not many twenty-year-old's would be willing to raise their sisters. Teenage girls were a pain in the ass. I was one and could barely handle myself. Yet Kato didn't so much as hesitate. He stepped up without a single complaint.

"Go home, Nova."

I rolled my shoulders back and looked him dead in the eye, "I am home."

Kato was my home, and so was Veda. She was still recovering and couldn't be here, so I would be here for the both of us. I was going to keep my ass on this bench and support my brother until they took him away.

The thought of that made me sick.

"Stay right there, Nova." Harry said while flipping through some papers.

"Why would I leave?"

"Because I told you to," Kato growled while giving his lawyer a dirty look.

Harry sighed, "you need someone to make a statement on your behalf, Kato."

A statement?

"So," I leaned forward to rest my arms on the banister between us. "Can I say anything in this statement?"

Like how Atlas Mancini and his asshole friends raped my sister and left her for dead.

"Yes," Harry rolled his eyes my way. "But the point is to appeal to the court for leniency."

Oh I'd appeal to the court.

"Don't piss the judge off." Harry warned as if he could hear my thoughts.

"I won't." Why would anyone get upset about the truth, especially a judge?

I could feel that reporter's eyes boring into the back of my skull. Why wouldn't he be trying to listen in? This was the story of the year after all. Not that anyone actually told the full story.

Veda's name wasn't in any of the papers. There was no grand expose on the horrors that almost took her life, because she didn't have the last name Mancini. The Ford siblings were nobody to them. Hell we were nobody compared to the nobody's.

The Mancini's however, that was a family everyone talked about. I shouldn't be surprised. The rich always won the media race. Though according to the rumors floating around, one could argue that the Mancini's were the cause of most news.

I suppose I should consider myself lucky that Kato was arrested at the scene of the crime. Otherwise he might've just disappeared. Wouldn't be the first time someone mysteriously vanished in this town.

My best friend Memphis called Soiree the town of cement shoes. Everyone had a pair, the question was whether or not you got to try them on.

"Nova," Kato tipped his gaze over his shoulder and hissed, "Just go home."

"No."

"It's your birthday." He argued.

"And I want to spend it with my brother."

"Jesus Christ," he grumbled. "Can you just listen to me for once in your life?"

"I do listen to you. Family sticks together, remember that?"

Every time Veda or I would feel alone or abandoned by our parents, he would say it was fine because we still had each other. And no matter what, family stuck together.

"Yeah well, I fucked that up, didn't I?"

"You were protecting Veda."

This wasn't his fault. It was Atlas Mancini's. Our sister was fighting for her life, when Kato overheard Atlas bragging. Beating him with a tire iron in a bar full of people was a light reaction as far as I was concerned. And exactly what Atlas deserved.

Unfortunately, the court wouldn't allow that to be used as evidence. Technically he was never convicted of rape, therefore legally, it never happened. Atlas wasn't even accused. Veda didn't regain consciousness until a week after our brother was arrested.

The Justice system sucked.

Kato shook his head, "What am I going to do with you?"

He knew it was useless arguing. Just like I knew there wasn't anything I could say to comfort him. That didn't stop me from reaching out to give his shoulder a reaffirming squeeze.

"It's okay. Whatever happens we'll get through it. Together."

Those were the exact same words he told me when mom died. For two years it was us against the world. That wasn't going to change.

Not now. Not ever.

"Fifteen to twenty years isn't something you get through, Nova."

I sucked back the sorrow burning a hole in my heart, "Yes it is. We just move through it one day at a time."

His nostrils flared with a quiet snicker. "Who taught you to be so optimistic?"

"My brother." I smiled. "He's a good guy. You should meet him sometime."

"Sounds like a chump to me."

"Nah," I waved my hand dismissively. "He just got a raw deal."

We all did.

Shadows crept across Kato's face, darkening his expression. I knew what he was going to ask before he spoke. "How's Veda?"

Even now he was worried about her. Kato always protected us. It was our turn to protect him.

"Better. Maw Maw is with her. She's starting to walk again."

I didn't have the heart to tell him that one of her attackers left behind a little piece of himself that was currently growing in her belly. That was mostly because I didn't want to try and explain her decision to keep it.

Kato nodded as if that piece of information made everything alright.

For a split second I could pretend that things were normal. That Kato and I were having a conversation instead of waiting for the world to be ripped out from under us.

Then the bailiff spoke. "All rise."

Everyone stood up causing a loud scuttle to ring through the room.

"The honorable Judge Kenneth Lamont presiding. God save the state and this honorable court."

"Pfft, honorable," I snorted.

Kato shot me a warning glare.

I rolled my eyes back at him as the Judge took his seat and clacked his gavel.

"Be seated."

My stomach dropped as I sat back down. This was it. Judgment hour had come.

"Kato Levi Ford…"

Don't throw up… don't throw up…

"You've been convicted of manslaughter in the first degree…"

His words were cut off by a loud bang.

It took me a second to realize that the door was thrown open and the judge had stopped talking. I kept staring at him waiting for the word years to come out of his mouth. Fate was about to rain down on us in heavy pellets of dread. I couldn't move or breathe. Until I saw the look on Kato's face.

That's when I heard the hushed murmurs and footsteps that made me turn my head.

My anxiety instantly morphed into anger.

Three men in suits were strutting through the door. The older one I recognized as Cesare Mancini – father to Atlas aka rapist asshole. The other two I assumed were members of the 'family'.

Cesare waltzed past and my fists balled, causing my nails to dig into my palms.

Why were they here? They didn't bother to show up for the trial. So why now? Did they just want to revel in my brother's fate? Watch as my family fell apart?

It should be Cesare up there, not my brother. If he controlled his family, then none of this would be happening.

"This is all your fault."

I didn't realize I'd said that out loud until the last one stopped and cocked a brow.

"What was that?"

The deep baritone of that growl reverberated through my ears as my eyes rolled over a black suit jacket to a pair of the most piercing green eyes I'd ever seen.

This guy was tall, well over my brother's six foot frame. And if that wasn't enough of a reason to hate him, he had a head of thick black hair and a five o'clock shadow that made him look older than he was.

The guy couldn't be much older than me, yet he looked like an adult. Know how old I looked? Fifteen, and I still had to argue my age with some people.

"I wasn't talking to you."

"Really," a dark cloud moved across his gaze as he leaned in closer, "because I could have sworn you said something?"

My father used to get that same expression. Kato called it the thousand yard stare. I didn't remember much about our father – he was in the military and died overseas when I was six. But I remembered that cold emotionless look.

I was convinced my father was a robot. I'd feel a cold shiver for hours after he tucked me in. Then he was gone and that look in his eyes was all I could remember.

"Now," one of his hands grabbed the back of the bench while the other flattened on the banister on the other side of me. "Why don't you repeat what you said."

A voice in the back of my mind told me to duck my head and keep quiet. My mouth didn't get that memo.

"I said, this is all his fault," my head tipped towards Cesare. More specifically Atlas's fault, but he wasn't here to receive my wrath.

"Is that right?" His eyes narrowed. "You should be careful how you talk to people like us."

People like us? I didn't know who this guy was but fuck him and his fancy suit with his holier than thou attitude.

"I'll…" was all I got out before Kato cut me off.

"Take a seat, Mancini."

Mancini? Did that mean…

"Get lost Gio," Kato growled when he didn't move.

This man wasn't just any Mancini, he was Atlas's younger brother. Well that explained the look of death. It also explained why I didn't recognize him. We didn't go to the same school, or run in the same circles.

"I said fuck off." Kato snarled with more authority.

Still Gio didn't move.

He didn't so much as glance in Kato's direction. His sole focus was on me. It was disturbing how intrusive his stare was.

"You should sit down." I suggested. "You're holding up court."

I was much more concerned with the bailiffs preparing to move in on my brother.

Gio tipped his head. "And you're sitting on the wrong side of the room."

Kato immediately shot out of his chair, causing the bailiffs to move closer.

They weren't the only ones on edge. The fanning in the crowd had stopped. Everyone was too busy watching with their mouths open to care about the heat. I could hear them all holding their breath in anticipation.

The only one who wasn't phased in the least was Gio Mancini. Or maybe he was? I couldn't tell. There was nothing but coldness on his face.

This was not good.

"I'm his sister." I quickly explained, hoping that would calm things down.

It didn't work. If anything Kato got more worked up.

Especially when Gio responded with, "I know who you are."

"Leave her alone!" Kato barked.

"I wouldn't worry about your baby sister. I'm sure she can take care of herself." Gio's eyes stayed fixed on mine. "Isn't that right, *Novalee?*"

Why did he know my name? A better question was, why wasn't anyone doing anything? The only person they seemed worried about was my brother.

Figures.

No, don't pay attention to the full grown man intimidating a teenage girl. What the hell was Kato going to do? He had shackles on his feet for Christ sake. That didn't stop the guards from moving in preparation to tackle my brother.

"If you don't stop disrupting my court Mr. Mancini, then you'll find yourself in contempt."

Now the judge said something. Not that it mattered to Gio. He continued to glare at me as if nothing was wrong with this situation.

There were so many things wrong that I couldn't even begin to count them, but I could focus on one. I could sit here and channel all of my hatred right back at Gio. There was only one problem... he was better at it.

I never thought I'd be thankful for Cesare Mancini. But when he gave his son a small wave and said, "Sit down Gio," I breathed a sigh of relief.

For a second I thought Gio wasn't going to listen.

His jaw ticked as he glared down at me like he wanted to beat me to death. None of this was for me. The only reason Gio kept pushing was to get my brother worked up. Every time the guards moved in, the corner of his mouth curled a little. He wanted to see Kato get hurt.

Thankfully Gio gave into his father's demand, and shot Kato a dirty look before walking away. Allowing me to let out the breath I'd been holding in.

Chapter 2

A hangover is defined as a severe headache or other effects from drinking an excess of alcohol. The other effects may include nausea, memory loss, and blurred vision. Of course this all depended on how much alcohol one consumed. If they had a couple drinks, then maybe a headache.

However, if they were like me and stupidly decided to suck back a healthy sample of everything in the bar, then a full blown '*I want to kill myself*' hangover was definitely in the cards. The only thing worse than living through that feeling, was being woken up in the middle of it.

There I was, lost in oblivion while drooling on my pillow, when a shrieking pierce cut through my brain with the force of a lightning bolt. Okay that might've been a slight exaggeration, but like I said, symptoms may vary depending on the amount of consumption.

Considering I had no idea how I got home or where my pants

were, it was pretty safe to say, healthy sample was probably not the right term for the amount of alcohol I drank.

At one point I remember walking around with a bottle in each hand with what I think was a pot on my head. There may have been a gator and some kind of mud fight?

My recently exified boyfriend Simon was to blame for last night, but the award for most annoying person on the planet went to my best friend, Memphis. He was no doubt the culprit behind my new unwanted ringtone.

The high pitched voice of Christina Aguilera assaulted my brain on a good day let alone when my head felt like it was being split open. I would murder him for that later. Like when I had more control of my limbs, or when I had the ability to roll out of the bed.

In the meantime I was stuck where I was, listening to Genie in a Bottle with my cheek pressed into a pool that smelled like bourbon and swamp water.

By the way, that was not a good scent to wake up to when my stomach and I were on friendly terms – which we weren't – but it wasn't the worst scent either. Nothing topped the day Memphis and I decided to go digging in the bog for buried treasure.

My mother spent a week trying to get the stench out of my clothes. Then ended up throwing them out. Memphis did try to cheer me up when she cut my hair though. He was always doing stuff like that. He had this frustrating need to see me smile. Hence my new ringtone.

On a side note, Genie In a Bottle was not my first choice for feel good song of the year. It wasn't even a feel good song the year it came out. I appreciated good music, and I'd even admit that Christina had an amazing voice.

If I could sing one one thousandth as good as her then I might not have been kicked off the church choir. My rendition of highway to hell was not well received, but I was seven and hadn't found my voice yet. I still hadn't found it ten years later.

Christina on the other hand, was singing along and belting in my ear about guys rubbing her the right way.

"Ugh." I grabbed my other pillow and slapped it over my head, in an attempt to muffle the sound.

It didn't work.

My head throbbed as the song pierced through the fabric covering my ears. I was definitely going to get Memphis back for this. Just wait. The day I painted his room mustard yellow would be nothing compared to my revenge for this.

'Rub me the right way.'

Why would anyone write a song about this? Who in their right mind thought these lines would make good lyrics? And why the hell would anybody want to sing it?

Keep your rubbing to yourself lady. No one wants to hear that shit.

Except for maybe Simon. Apparently he was all about the rubbing. At least that's what I assumed after walking in on him and Cindy Fassbender last night – who I lovingly referred to as Fries. As in *'would you like some fries with that'.*

The girl had absolutely no shake. Neither did I for that matter, but you didn't see me adding my side dish to every meal that happened by. She did have a nice chest though, which was more than I could say for myself.

Seventeen years on this planet and my boobs still hadn't shown up. I wouldn't mind a couple extra inches either. I was tired of using a stepping stool to reach the top shelf.

Speaking of stepping stools...

I'd kill for that little blue one MawMaw had right now. I could throw it at my phone and maybe even break it, so my vision wouldn't be assaulted by the horribly painted yellow flowers on it when I went into the kitchen for a snack. Two problems solved in one go.

I got that my nephew was only one, but what little boy wanted flowers on his stool? I'd be doing the kid a favor.

Unfortunately the stool was all the way in the kitchen. That was way too far. If I wanted to throw something, I'd have to use what was at my disposal.

God damnit, that means I have to move.

Or did I?

If I laid here long enough the phone would stop ringing, and I could go back to sleep in silence. That sounded like a great plan to me. And one I was more than happy to follow, if the person trying to get a hold of me, didn't immediately call back.

Fuck my life.

Didn't they know I was trying to die in peace? If I could move without the room spinning, then my first choice of activities to do wouldn't be answering the phone. It'd be to have a shower. I smelled like a mix of bayou water, French fries, and baby powder.

What the hell did I do last night?

Not sure I wanted to know the answer to that, but I did want my phone to shut up.

Grumbling, I slapped my hand down on the pillow over my head and chucked it across the room – which was an epic fail on my part.

My phone wasn't across the room. It was on the bedside table right next to my head.

The only thing I accomplished was breaking the lamp on my dresser.

"Damnit." I groaned and rolled over to creak my eyes open.

Vision was not my friend. I had no idea eyeballs could hurt like that until I tried to inspect the broken orange ceramic. My lids scraped across my eyes as if they were made of sandpaper.

Then there was the dryness. Every time I smacked my mouth my lips would get stuck and do this weird joker smile thing.

Why weren't there sinks in bedrooms? It would save so much

time. The first thing I was going to do – once I could think without pain – was invent the bedroom sink. Or tell someone else with more motivation so they could invent it.

The pillow flopped off the dresser and landed on the pile of broken ceramic, causing a quiet chink to ring through the air.

Sighing, I rolled my eyes back that way.

I liked that lamp. Had to wrestle it out of Maw Maw's hands last week. For a woman well into her seventies she was seriously strong. Or I was amazingly weak. Both options had their merits.

Going back to sleep also had some serious merits. Like not wanting to gouge my eyes out.

It would be nice if whoever was calling would just give up. Clearly I wasn't in the mood to talk. Yet my phone was going on the third or fourth round of genie in a bottle. Then again it might just seem like that.

Again, no one wants to hear about someone getting rubbed the right way.

Grumbling in defeat, I reached out and snatched my phone. The only thing that stopped me from throwing it next to the pillow was the Darth displayed on the screen.

Veda, I should've known.

By the way, light was also not my friend.

I clicked to answer, dropped the phone down on the bed next to my head, and closed my eyes.

"Finally."

I loved my sister, but did she have to yell? "Why do you hate me?"

Sisters were supposed to be nice to each other and let them sleep when their head felt like it was cracking open.

I was never drinking again.

That thought was so cliche I wanted to throw up. It was also a complete lie. But I most definitely wasn't going to drink for the next twenty-four hours.

Simon's screwed up face flashed in front of me. Lips all twisted up while his eyes rolled in the back of his head. His eyes used to light up for me. Not last night. All the bastard did when he saw me standing there was smile. Cindy Fassbender's head was bobbing in his lap and he thought it was funny.

Prick.

I could always tell everyone how small his dick was. Not that I'd seen it – that train I managed to avoid – but it seemed like the thing girls did when they were scorned. Simon and I hadn't been dating long. Only three months, during which he never got more than a kiss. If blue balls were a thing then I hoped his ached the entire time.

Cheating asshole.

Guess I shouldn't be surprised. Life was full of disappointments. My brother Kato was proof of that. He was two years into a fifteen year sentence for killing one of the guys that raped our sister. And did the cops try to find the other two? Of course not.

Why would they waste their time on trailer trash like us? One of them did ask what Veda was wearing that night though. So there was that judgment.

"Nova," my sister squealed, making me wish I still had that pillow on my head.

Was I in hell? This had to be the plane of the damned. Why else would my entire body be punishing me? My arms felt like they were weighed down and my left leg was doing this weird twitchy thing, where all the muscles in my calf would tense as my foot jerked out.

"Are you listening to me?"

Not in the slightest.

I snorted. "Of course I am."

What the heck was up with my leg? Did it want to audition for river dancing or something?

"Good, so when can I expect you?"

What? I cocked a brow at my phone.

"That depends, if we're going out for supper again I'm gonna need time to empty the hot water tank and about three bars of soap." I paused and glanced down at the grass stains on my once white tank-top. "Maybe five bars of soap."

"Jesus Christ Nova you didn't hear a thing I said, did you?"

"Stop being overdramatic." I sighed. "You asked if I was listening to you."

See I was totally paying attention.

"And before that?" Veda challenged.

Well, if she wanted to make things difficult.

"Something about gumbo?" It was worth a shot. I figured I had about a fifty fifty chance, and I liked those odds.

The breath that my sister let out told me that I did not land anywhere near the bullseye. "I need you to come and pick me up."

I rolled my head towards the clock, who's blaring green digits felt like lasers being burned into my orbital sockets. It was two in the afternoon. Way too early for this bullcrap. Besides…

"Aren't you at work?" Normally Veda had the weekends off – she worked for a domestic company called Sunnyside Maid Service. Their slogan was *'save your time and let us mop your grime'.*

"Where do you think I need you to pick me up from?"

"Well I don't know Miss. I'm gonna take a couple extra shifts." I didn't make that choice for her. "Why don't you call Maw, Maw?"

"Trust me, I tried." she muttered, "She's at golf."

Yup, that's right my Maw Maw played golf. That wasn't typically an activity for an older southern lady, but the last person that called Maw Maw older got smacked with her nine iron.

"So take the bus." I grumbled.

"I need to leave now!"

"That sounds like a you problem." Honestly I wasn't even sure if my truck was here. I didn't drive to the party last night, but that didn't mean I didn't decide to go for a ride later.

"Nova, please, I need to get out of here."

Veda had to get out of everywhere. To say my sister had some trauma from her attack would be an understatement. The only reason she left the house at all was to earn money to feed my nephew.

"I'm sorry I can't help you. There's this amazing place called bed where I plan to spend the entirety of my Senior year." Not to mention I'd have to find some pants.

My eyes fell down to my bare legs. *When did I put on socks?*

"I really need your help here." She whined.

"Again, that sounds like a you problem." They worked in teams of three, why couldn't one of them bring her home?

"I'm not kidding."

Neither was I. "Get Rita to drive you."

"She had to leave early."

Veda's voice quaked with an oncoming panic attack. Part of me wanted to let it happen – my sister needed to start living again. And it wasn't like she'd be walking home in the middle of the night. But I couldn't do it.

If I had gone with her that night then none of this would've happened. I couldn't leave her alone again. That didn't mean I was happy about it.

"Fine," I groaned and pushed myself up. "But know that I hate you."

I didn't, but that was beside the point.

"I'll text you the address, just... Hurry up. There's someone watching me." Veda said and hung up.

There was always someone watching or following her. Veda saw danger everywhere. I got it. She survived something that should've killed her. Can't say I'd be any better. That's why I didn't understand her decision to keep my nephew.

Don't get me wrong, I loved Knox, but he was a living reminder of what happened. Yet, Veda clung to him as if he was her only lifeline. She claimed she was being a good parent, but Veda gave helicopter moms a bad name.

It wasn't healthy. She needed a life of her own that included her son. Not one that revolved around him.

A text vibration drew my attention back to my phone.

Darth: Have you left yet?

Geeze give a girl some time to find pants.

Then again, if I showed up in a dirty tank top and underwear she probably wouldn't ask me to pick her up again?

Ugh, but then I'd have to hear Maw Maw's modesty lecture. I took one naked run down the street and I never heard the end of it. I still owed Memphis for that dare.

Grumbling a curse under my breath, I swung my legs off the bed.

Standing up wasn't so bad. At least the room wasn't spinning, which considering I had to operate a motor vehicle was probably a good thing. My stomach however did not agree. For a second I thought I was gonna blow chunks. Thankfully, I managed to hold it back.

My sister was the one insisting that I come and pick her up, so if anyone was going to witness my entry into the toilet bowl Olympics, it would be her. I would, however, grace Veda with the honor of splashing some water on my face. Mostly because I needed something to help wake me up. But life was about the little things.

The sight that greeted me in the mirror was not one anyone wanted to see. All the makeup on the left side of my face was smeared. Mascara had run under my eyes, causing this punched in the face effect that movie make-up artists would be jealous of, and a bright line of red swept from the corner of my mouth and curved over my left cheek.

My clothes weren't any better. My tank top looked like I drug myself through a pile of dirt, while Elmo smiled at me from the pajama shorts I found on the floor. My homeless look was topped off with a nice sweaty arch on the right side of my hazelnut hair.

I looked fabulous.

At least that's what I'd tell the cops when they pulled me over assuming I jacked the truck I was driving.

"Hold on to your zippers men," I snatched a pair of sunglasses off the hook by the door and grabbed my keys. "the next swimsuit supermodel is about to grace the general public with her presence."

I was almost disappointed when I stepped outside and saw the afternoon sun glinting off the blue hood of my otherwise brown Ford.

I might be a little upset if it was gone – the truck was Kato's work in progress before he got locked up – but if it wasn't there, then I'd have a reason to crawl back in bed. Couldn't pick my sister up if I didn't have a vehicle to do it in.

On the upside I found my pants.

One of Maw Maw's garden gnomes was wearing my jeans like a hat. I preferred to call them yard gnomes because that's where they were. All over the yard. In the grass, in the garden, under the tree, and behind our cheesy plastic white picket fence. Why a plastic fence I had no idea? Maw Maw was classy like that.

She also had a thing for those creepy little statues. Personally I could do without them. They were always watching me with their beady little eyes and colorful hats. I suppose it was better than the rusted out car frame our neighbor Mr. Garibaldi had on his lawn.

He was currently in the midst of an ongoing war with the local racoon population. By my count the racoons were winning. Last week they stole his broom.

Welcome to Sault Saint Marie Estates. Where the people are almost as run down as the road.

The fact that they put estate in the title was laughable. It was a trailer park, or mobile home court as Maw Maw called it. I called it tornado magnet.

Who in their right mind would put something like this on a hill? Didn't they ever watch the news? We even had someone that was constantly baking people casseroles, who could complain that she never got her dish back.

I quickly threw the sunglasses over my eyes and dragged my feet forward.

My plan was to escape the heat but then I remembered my truck was too old to have air conditioning. So I settled for driving with the windows down, which did wonders for my current 'just pulled my ass out of bed' hairstyle.

By the time I pulled up to the address my sister texted, I looked like one of those glass balls filled with electricity that followed your hand around. A look that I was pretty sure would not be appreciated in a place like this.

I peeked over my sunglasses at the house I was parked in front of. This place looked like one of those picturesque estates in magazines. Complete with a wrap-around porch and fountain to the left, who's trickling sounds were aggravating my headache.

The only reason I got out of my truck and walked up to the door was because I wanted to get out of here as quick as possible. My bed was calling my name.

I opted for the doorbell, rather than exert the effort it would take to lift the heavy looking handle on the large golden lion door knocker.

A classical song dinged through the air, making my lip curl. Was that Mozart? What kind of pompous ass designated that for their doorbell?

That question was answered when one of the large black double doors swung open.

My brow arched at the older man. He was probably in his early forties and definitely looked better than I did. The black three piece suit he was wearing fit his large frame so well that I wondered if it was made specifically for him.

I questioned every choice I'd ever made when he arched his brow, "Can I help you?"

"Probably not." Pretty sure I was beyond help at this point.

He sighed, "is there a reason you rang my doorbell?"

I had to lift my chin a little more than normal to meet his gaze, and I almost scoffed at how well his dark hair was styled. This man reeked of money and power.

I just reeked.

"Obviously." Who would ring a doorbell without a reason? Other than Billy and Kyle. I'd get those little pissants one day. "I'm here for my sister, so if you could run along and fetch her that would be great."

"Why would your sister be here?"

I was not in the mood for this. There was a perfectly good bed waiting for me at home. "She works here."

One would think that would've been the end of his game of twenty questions, but no.

"Doing what?"

I rolled my eyes, "Does it matter?"

"Yes."

Things would go easier if I answered his question, but I didn't like the way he was staring at me. "Why?"

"I don't like the looks of you."

Wow, way to kick someone when they were down. News flash asshole, I didn't like the looks of me either right now.

"Aren't you pleasant." I scoffed back at him.

"That depends," he crossed his arms. "Are you going to answer my question?"

Ugh, fine. I'd answer, but only because it was too bright out here. "She's a maid. Her name is Veda."

He eyed me for a second before saying, "why didn't she drive herself?"

"That's a fantastic question, why don't you go ask her?" And what business was it of his?

Who the hell cared how she got to work as long as she got there.

I waited for him to move but he just stood there glowering at me while the afternoon breeze tickled the back of my legs, reigniting the nausea churning in my stomach.

God damnit Nova, don't throw up. Then again...

Weighing my options, I eyed his crisp, clean suit. How quick would he move if I hurled chunks all over that expensive looking fabric.

His head tipped a touch to the side, "I'm not sure *you* should be driving."

Well I didn't ask for your opinion.

"See, I see your lips flapping, but I don't see your legs moving to go and get my sister."

That made both his brows rise. "Do you know who you're talking to?"

"Yeah," that was obvious. "you're the guy preventing me from crawling back into bed and dying. So if you don't mind..." my fingers made a run along motion.

"Little girls shouldn't be so rude."

Little girls? Okay, this guy was starting to piss me off.

"Look Fabio..." That's as far as I got.

As I raised my hand to point at him, my sister appeared from around the corner and grabbed my arm.

"What took you so long?"

Why the hell was she in such a hurry? God forbid she was two minutes late to pick up Knox.

Veda dragged me away while the asshole in the door called out, "you might want to let your sister drive."

I glared over my shoulder, "And you might want to get a better suit. No one wears black anymore."

Did I care about the current fashion trends, hell no. I couldn't have cared in the least, nor did I know what color was in right now. But he seemed like the type of guy who would care.

"Nova," Veda scolded while pushing me towards the driver's door. "Just, get in the truck."

I grumbled under my breath and hopped in behind the steering wheel, but not before I flipped doorway asshole off.

Chapter 3

GIOVANNI

There was one thing most people in this world had in common, a lack of respect. Take a gator for example. They were fierce creatures that could tear apart a two hundred pound man in minutes, yet people still infringed on their domains.

So many deaths could've been avoided by that one simple word. A man could be rich, poor, or the baddest motherfucker out there. None of it mattered if he didn't have respect.

My eyes followed the tip of a dark green tail as it flipped, then disappeared in the water. This particular gator had been staring at me for about fifteen minutes. Still as he was, I could see his eyes popping up above the waterline. He didn't come up on shore or anywhere near me. He just stayed where he was, watching. It was as if he could already smell the blood in the air.

Shifting my gaze, I looked towards the right at the second story of a house barely visible through the trees.

Why would anybody build their home this close to the bayou? It might have something to do with the two guys I'd seen earlier carrying rifles. Hunters would be my guess. Or poachers. Didn't really give it much thought after they took off on their boat. Nor did I care to.

There was only one reason I was sitting in my Range Rover tucked in the trees. Business. Simon Fisher owed my friends and I money. How he cleared his debt didn't matter to me. He was the one that placed the bets and he was the one that was going to pay them off. If he had to do that with a broken leg, well, so be it.

Wouldn't be the first time I beat someone down, and it certainly wouldn't be the last. Simon had more than enough time and I was done with his excuses. At this point it was a matter of respect. Something that slimy little weasel clearly didn't have.

Sighing, I glanced down at my watch.

Where the fuck were they?

We said ten o'clock. It was almost ten thirty. If Atlee was wasting my time because of pussy again, I was going to kick his ass.

"Fuck this," I growled and pulled out my phone just as bright beams of headlights cut through the darkness.

A familiar silver Audi rolled through the trees.

Fucking finally.

I shook my head as the hood bobbed with a dip in the road. It wasn't a surprise that they came in Darius's car, but Atlee's truck would've been a much better choice for this run down dirt plane. Darry called me a control freak, yet he insisted on driving. He was not on good terms with motor vehicles. Cursed was more like it. I stopped counting the accidents he'd been in.

The ironic thing was not a single one was his fault. I think the car gods just had it out for him. Or someone else did? I was looking into it.

I climbed out, walked around to the back of my Rover, and folded my arms across my chest.

Darry responded by giving his dark eyes an exaggerated roll, before opening the driver's door and stepping out.

"Sorry," his chin tipped towards the passenger side, "Apparently Atlee had something to do."

I just bet he did.

My glare snapped over to the head popping out through the open window.

"Hey," Atlee lifted a wooden bat and pointed it at Darry, "no one gets handsy with my sister."

Well I wasn't entirely wrong. It might not be pussy in the typical sense, but it was still pussy. "Kendall can take care of herself."

"And stop climbing out the window," Darry added in a snarl. "There's a fucking door for a reason."

"Yeah," Atlee nodded, "but it's your door."

I couldn't argue his point. Last week I just touched Darry's hood and one of the hubcaps popped off. It was the strangest fucking thing I'd ever seen and yet it wasn't. If anyone I knew needed their own personal driver, it was Darry. That shit would probably save his life one day.

"And you," the bat in Atlee's hand swung in my direction. "You should be thanking me. Someone needs to protect your brother's interests."

"Romeo can handle his own shit."

My brother was not happy about his future wife. Can't say I blamed him. Kendall was supposed to marry our brother Atlas, until he was murdered.

Kato Ford would pay for that one day. In the meantime I was perfectly happy to watch him rot in prison, with the occasional beat down of course. Killing was too easy. I wanted that prick to suffer.

"That's not what you said last week." Atlee argued.

"That was different."

Last week we weren't talking about some chick. We were talking about the family. While Romeo was off doing his own thing, I'd dedicated my life to the mob. And who was going to get the throne? The brother I wished died instead.

"I mean," Darry shrugged. "He is the oldest."

"Atlas is the oldest!"

Or he was, until he was taken away.

Neither one of them said anything, because there wasn't anything to say. Just like there was nothing we could do about it. We weren't boss. We weren't even made yet. Romeo took the oath when he was sixteen, and here I was, eighteen years-old with not even so much as an offer or job to enhance my position. It was bullshit.

"How about we just do this." Darry said while looking over at me. "You ready?"

I shot him a dirty look. "I've been ready since ten o'clock."

My annoyance was obvious, but they should've been here on time. I had better things to do than wait around.

"You, my friend, need to get laid." Atlee piped in. "I know this cute little blonde…"

That was not one of the better things I had planned. "I don't want your leftovers, Atlee."

I just wanted to get this shit over with and get on with my night.

"You sure?" Atlee asked. "Because I'm seriously starting to worry about your dick."

"My dick's fine."

That wasn't entirely true. My dick was bored as fuck. All I had to do was snap my fingers and some bitch would drop and open her mouth. It was too easy. Was it too much to ask for a little fight, or a snide comment?

Fuck at this point I'd take a dirty look. Anything that would give me a reason to take her over my knee, and not because she was playing a game. I was tired of the fake crap. I wanted something real.

Someone who would give back just as good as they got. I wanted a woman, not some demure, submissive bitch that did whatever I wanted because of who I was. The last place I'd find that was with Atlee's leftovers.

"Whatever." Atlee pushed his fingers through his dark hair. "But I think you should least let her suck your dick?"

I shook my head and pushed off my Rover, "Let's just get this over with."

Darry nodded and followed me into the trees while Atlee jumped up and whooped to the sky.

The only thing Atlee liked more than pussy was ruining someone's day. Judging by the bat he was merrily arching through the air, Simon was about to get his shit fucked all the way up. Worked for me. Until Atlee started clacking the edge of his weapon off Cypress trunks.

Darry and I both stopped to cock a brow back at him.

Atlee shrugged at our glare. "What?"

"There was a reason we didn't drive up to the house." I whispered in a growl.

Wouldn't want Simon running out the back door before we even got there.

Atlee muttered under his breath and hung his head like we'd just taken away his favorite toy.

"He's a little pent up." Darry leaned in and added, "Kendall wouldn't let him fuck up the quarterback."

My brow rose. "That's who tried to feel her up?"

That surprised me a bit. Randal wasn't the sharpest tool in the shed, but he knew his place. The whole team did. They learned that lesson when we tried to fix the first game of the season and the running back wouldn't play ball. He wasn't on the team anymore. I was pretty sure he left town.

"You know, Atlee," Darry's coal eyes gave a lazy roll. "The guy probably looked at her for too long."

That was fair. Atlee once broke someone's arm because he accidentally brushed against one of his sisters. Kind of ironic considering he'd already pounded his way through half the pussy in school. And that was before adding in his obsession with virgins.

Mind you his baby sister Alex didn't help. That girl flirted with anyone who smiled at her, which didn't go over well with their father. He shipped her off to boarding school last week.

As far as Antonio Fiore was concerned, his daughters were only good for one thing. Marriage. In order for that to happen they had to be virgins. No self-respecting made man would lock their son into an arrangement for used goods. Unless those goods were used by the prospective husband of course. At that point it was more about maintaining the girl's honor than anything else.

That didn't mean it didn't happen. I was just waiting for Atlee to fuck the wrong girl. Then again his father would kill someone before letting his son marry into what he considered a second rate bloodline.

And God forbid she wasn't Italian. Atlee's dad was old school. Sometimes I wondered if that was why he fucked around so much. Sooner or later he'd be tied down to someone he didn't want.

Thank fuck I didn't have a sister. A Mancini would've been the first on Antonio's list. Not to mention, I might have to kill one of my best friends. I knew the sick shit Atlee was into. Just the thought of his knife going anywhere near someone I was related to made me want to smash his skull in. How he was handling this Romeo and Kendall crap I'd never understand.

At least it wasn't Darius. The stuff he did to chicks made Atlee's little blood play games look like nap time at preschool. I wasn't entirely sure what he did to girls, but every chick he'd ever fucked went white when they saw him after.

A blue two story came into view as we broke the tree line. Usually places this close to the east side of town were run down, and especially if they were this close to the bayou. But all in all this was a decent little piece of land. The yard was clean, the grass was neatly cut, and the garden to the left of the house appeared well cared for.

The roof however could use some work. A few of the shingles were flapping in the breeze, causing a small ticking sound to ring out as we marched across the grass.

Atlee practically skipped up the steps, where he tapped the tip of his bat off the door while Darry and I joined him. If his goal was to mimic a knock, he failed. This eerie, hollow beat was carried in the breeze brushing past.

Needless to say the door didn't swing open to welcome us inside.

Darry blew out an agitated huff and ran his fingers through his blonde hair. "Why did we bring him?"

"Siiiimon," Atlee sang while clacking the bat on the door again.

I nodded at the sparkle in Atlee's bright whiskey eyes. "That's why."

Fear didn't become an issue when Atlee Fiore was involved. He was a horror movie all on his own.

Movement in the left window caught my peripheral view. I turned just in time to see a pair of wide eyes duck behind a faded green curtain.

"Fucker's trying to hide."

That caused a spark to flash across Atlee's already gleeful face. "Aw come on Simon. We just want to talk, Buddy."

Technically he wasn't lying. I had a lot to say to Simon while my fist slammed in his face. Like where the fuck is my money?

The worst imitation of a female voice I'd ever heard came from the other side. "I sorry, no Simon here."

Darry and I both dropped our heads in a shake.

Atlee on the other hand, that fucker's entire demeanor brightened up. "Oh, he wants to play, does he?"

That was the only warning we got before he stepped back,

lifted his leg and gave the door a hard kick. A splintered cracking rang through the air as the door broke, and not cleanly. That shit cracked in half, causing the left half to swing inwards while the part with the knob stayed latched in the frame.

All I could do was pinch the bridge of my nose.

So much for inconspicuous.

Guess I shouldn't be surprised. Subtlety wasn't Atlee's strong suit. Let's just hope whoever was out on that boat didn't hear his not so quiet entrance. That would cause way more cleanup than a couple thousand dollars was worth. Not to mention the fact that my father would get involved. Unlike my older brother I didn't cause problems. I solved them.

"Don't worry," Darry gave my shoulder a squeeze, "I'll stay out here and keep watch."

"That's probably a good idea."

Atlee was already kicking pieces of wood out of his way to storm in the house.

The scream came before I could take a step and follow. By the time I managed to jimmy my way through the entrance, Atlee had Simon pinned to the ground with the tip of the bat digging into his neck.

"Atlee," I warned.

Dead men couldn't pay debts, and Simon was starting to turn blue.

"What?" Atlee shrugged, "He tried to run."

Sure he did.

I looked at the bat, then back at Atlee, who groaned and eased up on the pressure. Simon immediately started coughing oxygen back into his lungs.

"Simon, Simon, Simon," I tsked while walking further in the house.

Other than the chunks of wood littering the floor, the place was fairly tidy. It even kind of smelled good. But the thing that caught my eye were the various gator parts sitting around like trophies.

"Look Gio, I'll get you your money," Simon coughed out. "I just need a few days."

That's what he said last time, and the time before that, and the time before that.

I came to a stop where he was sprawled out on the floor and tipped my gaze down to his paling expression. "Does it look like I have a pussy to you?"

No words came out of Simon's mouth as it opened and then closed.

This apparently agitated Atlee, because he slammed the bat down on the ground next to Simon's head. "He asked you a question motherfucker. Does it look like he has a pussy?"

"No," he answered quickly.

"Then why are you trying to fuck me?" I shot back at him.

There was a moment of silence where I could see the thought flash across Simon's face. He was gonna bolt. And that's exactly what he tried to do. His shaking frame shot up and booked it for an open door to the right. I didn't chase him. I didn't have to.

Atlee was all over that shit. Instead of making the grand escape Simon thought he would, he wound up slammed back against the wall with a forearm pressing into his neck.

Atlee arched a brow. "Did you just try to run?"

"No," Simon wheezed out.

"Only little bitches run, Simon. You're not a little bitch are you?" I wasn't the only one who grimaced when Atlee's hand swung through the air to smack down on Simon's groin. "Nope, I don't feel a pussy. Just some sad ass fucking balls."

And Atlee didn't stop there. He stepped in closer and squeezed his hand, causing a pathetic screech to echo throughout the room.

"There's some money in my wallet!" Simon shrieked out.

That's more like it.

Atlee yanked his wallet out of his back pocket and tossed it my way.

My mood went down a degree when I opened it up and counted the cash inside. "Sixty isn't going to buy you shit Simon."

"That's all I have," he whined.

Alright. I nodded at Atlee. "Break his legs."

One would think I just gave Atlee the keys to the kingdom by the way he called out, "Fuck yeah!"

He stepped back and lifted the bat, preparing to swing, but Simon held up his hands. "Wait… I'm sure we can come to some kind of agreement."

"Such as?" I said while signalling Atlee to hold up.

"Um… I uh…."

I sighed. Usually when someone offered an agreement they had one in mind. I wasn't in the mood to wait around anymore.

Just as I raised my hand to wave at Atlee, Simon spurted out, "I have a girlfriend."

Did this piece of shit seriously just offer to trade his girl for a debt? The reasons to keep him alive were dwindling by the second.

"Don't lie to us." Atlee snorted. "What girl in their right mind would fuck you?"

He had a point. The only thing Simon had going for him was his hair. Besides, "I'm not interested."

Imaginary girlfriend or not, if I didn't want Atlee's leftovers I sure as fuck didn't want his.

The next thing Simon tried, did make me pause. "I'll pay you double."

Atlee and I shared a look. More money wasn't a bad thing. Not that any of us needed it, but that was beside the point. There was only one question.

"When?"

"One week." Simon said a little too quick for my liking.

"I'll give you five days." I raised my hand and pointed in warning, "But I want my money on Friday Simon."

He nodded.

I spun around and walked towards the door, pausing long enough to look back at Atlee and say, "Make sure he understands."

How my friend accomplished that didn't matter to me. The smile Atlee gave me in return was all the explanation I needed.

Chapter 4

The street lights in Sault Saint Marie Estates were about as well taken care of as the pot holes in the road. It was like a sporting event anytime someone with a low to the ground car drove in here. I'd sit outside on the deck and smile as they went by.

It didn't matter how slow they drove, the undercarriage always got scrapped. Sometimes Memphis and I would make a game out of it and bet how much damage would happen.

The best was the guy with the low rider. It took two days for him to drag his car out of that hole. Consequences of living so close to the swamp I suppose. Wet ground did not make for great roadways, or foundations. Hence all the mobile homes occupying this area.

Knox pushed over a blue hatted gnome and clapped his little hands as the streetlight in front of our place flickered. Shadows danced across his face making the thicker patches of dark hair on the sides of his head look like curled horns. Turning my nephew from a cute one-year-old into some kind of creepy gnome killer with like four teeth and an innocent giggle.

There was a sight to make someone shiver. Mind you it could also be the remnants of my hangover. My headache was gone, but every once and awhile the world would spin.

I'd still be in bed if Veda hadn't decided to turn into the cling master 3000 when we got home. She'd been holding onto Knox ever since she picked him up from Sue and Winnie's down the street.

I felt bad for the kid. He needed some air. Especially after spending the day with those two busy Betties.

If there was an official gossip column for this part of town then it was Sue and Winnie LeBeau. But it had its bonuses. Mrs. Devereux's affair with the milkman was important information to have. It gave me a reason to badger Maw Maw. I didn't even know milkmen were still a thing. Why the hell was I being sent to the store if we could have milk delivered?

Knox chomped down on the gnome's hat and burbled, "Gnaw flinx.

"That's right Knoxy," I gave him a small nod. "You show those beady eyed bastards who's boss."

"Novalee Nadine Ford."

Oh crap.

I tipped my head back to see Maw Maw's unimpressed face eyeing me from the other side of the screen door.

"Did you just cuss at that baby?"

Technically no.

"Maw Maw, I hate to inform you of this but the days when bastard was whispered in secret died long before the first phone booth."

Not all phone booths were gone. Not on the east side of Soiree anyway. Though the last time we drove past it I was pretty sure I saw a family of squirrels sacrificing a crow, but hey, we still had one. How many towns could say that?

Maw Maw's response was one I'd heard so many times that it played in my mind along with the words that came out of her mouth. "Not in my house, it didn't."

The lecture continued as I rolled my head back to watch Knox happily continue to chew on the gnome.

"This is a God fearing Christian house…"

"I go to church." I argued.

Every Sunday I was dragged out of bed at the crack of dawn, except for today. Mark Winslow had to fill in for Father John and Maw Maw didn't like him. His shifty eyes disturbed her. Or so she claimed.

"You need to take your prayers more seriously young lady."

That line was always followed with…

"God sees everything, Novalee."

"Great," I grumbled. "Maybe he'll see the answers to my calculus exam."

Having to spend my senior year in St. Agatha's was bad enough, then Maw Maw had to go and sign me up for advanced calculus.

"I'm tired of watching you waste your potential…"

That was her reasoning for sending me to the private catholic school.

"If I were you, I'd be questioning the merits of this so-called educational institution."

"Don't sass me missy," she waved her finger at me. "You used to be an honor student…"

"My point exactly," I interrupted. "Clearly they have low standards."

Why else would they give me a scholarship? I was not the prime candidate. The highest mark I got last year was in art, and that was only because I got bored one night and actually put some effort into my year end sculpture.

A heavy breath came from Maw Maw as she tipped her head and gave me a scowl. "What am I going to do with you, child?"

I leaned back, shot her a smile and sang, "wish me well in my mediocre life of waitressing and divorces?"

Maw Maw shook her head, "Do you take anything seriously?"

"Yes," I was completely serious about the divorces. I figured somewhere around three.

"Pastor John called."

"That wasn't my fault." All I did was point out how illogical it was to fit two of every animal in one boat. Was every breed of dog in there and if not where did the other ones come from? "I warned them against having me teach Sunday school."

"Those children had nightmares for a week, Novalee."

I shrugged. "One of them asked about hell."

So I put on a movie. Looking back, horror probably wasn't the best genre to go with.

"Please tell me you didn't make them watch Show Girls?"

I rolled my eyes as Memphis walked up to the gate.

"My goal wasn't to scar them for life."

His blonde hair glinted in the streetlight as he chuckled and shook his head. Tall jackass didn't even bother to open the gate. He just swung one of his long legs over the two foot fence and strutted in the yard.

I tried that once – the latch on that plastic piece of crap was a pain in the ass to open – I ended up knocking half the fence down. Maw Maw was less impressed with that than she was my language.

"Memphis," She sang with a happy tone. "What a nice surprise."

My best friend was the angelic grandchild Maw Maw hoped I would be. I swear sometimes she thought the sun shone out of his ass.

His light eyes brightened as he smiled back. "Hi Mrs. Broussard."

"Good lord child, how many times do I have to tell you to call me Billy-Jo?"

I swallowed down the need to remind my dear sweet grandmother that Memphis preferred the less fairer sex.

It was sickening how girls fawned over him. If angels were a thing I imagined they'd look a lot like my best friend. His big honey eyes were far brighter than they should've been and there was the exact right amount of wave in his golden hair.

Tie that in with his fair complexion and pleasant smile and even I might've found him attractive. That is if I didn't know he peed the bed until he was five, or that he ate a worm when he was eight. Somethings you just can't forget.

"Sorry mam, but I believe in respecting my elders."

Gag.

"Aren't you sweet," Maw, Maw shot me a look. "Novalee could learn a thing or two from you."

Oh I learned a few things from him, like don't drink three cups of water before going to sleep.

"Don't you let her corrupt that baby anymore."

Seriously? The kid was busy trying to devour one of her precious gnomes and she was worried about me corrupting him. It was pretty clear which one of us had murderous tendencies in this scenario.

"I won't." I rolled my eyes as Memphis lifted his hand in a salute. "Scout's honor."

"Pfft scout," I scoffed. "I think you need to go to more than one meeting to be considered an official scout."

He was all for the Boy Scouts until he found out that they camped in tents and went fishing. Why Memphis's father was so surprised when he came out, I never understood. Our childhood was filled with obvious signs.

Like the delight he'd get out of a good game of dress up. Or his need to religiously watch project makeover, and there were the posters of Jensen Ackles plastered all over his room. I'd seen that man's abs more than any other man on the planet. Not that I was complaining.

Memphis shrugged. "It's not my fault they didn't have better uniforms."

"And how long did it take you to get ready this morning?" I asked while rolling my eyes over his crisp and clean black t-shirt and unwrinkled jeans.

"There's nothing wrong with looking good. You should try it sometime."

Ugh, no thanks. "I prefer the extra sleep, thank you very much."

Memphis cocked a brow at my Elmo shorts. "Did you raid Knox's closet?"

"Hey, Elmo is the in thing in some circles."

He huffed and crossed his arms. "Preschool playgroups don't count as circles."

"I happen to think Elmo is cute." Maw Maw said from inside.

A smug grin spread across my face. "See."

I could practically hear my best friend's thoughts when he shot me a look. He was wondering if god was punishing him. Though I would argue that without me he wouldn't know how to duct tape a muffler back on a truck.

Speaking of which, I should probably apply a couple more strips. I wasn't exactly paying attention when I picked Veda up, but I was pretty sure I heard something scrape.

"Well, I'll leave you two alone." Maw Maw paused before walking away. "Remember young lady, this is a God fearing Christian house."

"Okay Maw Maw." I sang back.

"What did you do?" Memphis cocked a brow and climbed the stairs to join me on the deck. "She doesn't give you the god fearing Christian house speech unless you really messed up."

He wasn't wrong. Usually those lectures are reserved for when

I argued the materialistic value of holidays like Easter and Christmas. Or when Maw Maw felt one of us needed to cleanse our sins, which lately was every other day. And by one of us I meant me. My sister's idea of rebellion was saying damn instead of gosh darn.

Once upon a time Veda was normal. One night was all it took to blow up our entire world. We were doing fine until then. Kato worked hard to provide for us. Both Veda and I were doing well in school. Now my sister was a single mom, caring for the product of her attack, and we were living with our grandmother.

Maw Maw said this was just one of life's steps down. Sure, if that step down was off a thousand foot cliff.

I waved my hand through the air, "she's just mad because she lost at golf."

Maw Maw took golf seriously. A little too seriously if you asked me.

"Did she manage to keep all her clubs in one piece this time?" Memphis asked while taking the wicker chair next to mine.

Last time Maw Maw lost she broke her nine iron.

"I think so." I gave him a quick point of my finger, "but her bag has seen better days."

Lighting bugs flew around the yard while we sat there quietly watching Knox. He was happy as a clam sitting in the grass in his own Elmo outfit, with the tip of a ceramic hat in his mouth. As calm and normal as this was, I knew what was coming.

The party last night was at Memphis's boyfriend's house. The last thing I wanted to do was talk about my failed relationship with someone who had the perfect one. It was sickening how in love Memphis and Chuck were. I wanted to throw up every time I was around them. There was such a thing as too much public affection.

"So?"

Here we go.

"Last night happened?"

"Which part of last night are you referring to? My amazing consumption of alcohol or finding Simon in a room with Cindy?"

"Actually I was referring to the bathing suit fashion show you gave everyone… Wait…" Memphis tipped his head my way. "Simon cheated on you with Cindy."

I was surprised he didn't know. "If you consider Cindy slurping back his dick cheating, then… yeah."

"Don't you consider that cheating?"

My eyes rolled over to his. "I think the fashion show answers that question."

"Asshole." He muttered then added, "Well, at least you didn't like him."

"I liked him."

"No you didn't."

I added a lip curl into my next argument. "Yes I did."

"All you did was complain about him."

What did that prove? I complained about everything. Just last Monday I spent all day bitching about the way the shirt I was wearing felt. Sure I found it in Veda's room, but that shit was itchy. A little consideration would've been nice. She knew I was allergic to wool.

"That doesn't mean I didn't like him."

"Yeah right," Memphis leaned back and folded his hands behind his head. "That boy has absolutely no good qualities."

"Simon has plenty of good qualities." Like his ability to shove his dick down someone's throat, or insult a group of people with one word.

On our first date he managed to make the table next to us get up and leave. Our second date wasn't much better, but at least it wasn't at the diner where I worked.

Then there was his kissing technique. It took some serious skill to make someone fear that their face might get eaten. His best quality though, was that there was no possible way I could fall for him.

Memphis snorted, "Name one."

"He has nice hair." I was actually kind of envious of the way Simon's hair seemed to fall perfectly into place.

"You went out with him for nice hair? That's the dumbest thing I've ever heard."

"In case you forgot, we're teenagers," I pointed out. "Dumb is kind of in the job description."

There were plenty of other dumb things I'd done. Whatever happened last night for instance. Or the time I thought my bike could ride over water. Oh and can't forget the time we thought it would be a great idea to shove hot peppers up our nose. Neither one of us smelled right for like a month after that.

At this point bringing up a slight misjudgment on my part was redundant. Memphis had been there for every stupid decision I'd ever made. I was there for his too.

"Besides, I wasn't the one that tried to convince our seventh grade class that Corey Hart was a god among men."

That was during his eighties pop phase. He even tried to bring back wearing sunglasses at night.

In typical Memphis fashion, my best friend lifted his chin and said, "I stand by my judgment. At the time he was a god among men."

Wish I could be so sure of my choices. I kind of just went with the flow. What was the point in fighting, disappointment was inevitable.

"And," he drawled out, "we were talking about your choice in men. Not mine."

Not this again.

My eyes rolled. "I think we've established that my judgment skills are lacking."

"What, no. All your *boyfriend*, choices have been great." he said emphasizing the lack of plural on the boyfriend part.

"Hey," I swung my finger through the air. "I've had other boyfriends."

"Tucker Gerald doesn't count."

Ah, Tucker Gerald. We had our wedding on the playground next to the swings. It was a beautiful ceremony with a toilet paper veil and my mom's nightgown. He dumped me the next day because Cindy gave him her Fruit Roll Up. But he was still my husband for almost twenty-four hours.

"You know what I think?"

We shared a crib every weekend, of course I knew what he was thinking. "That chokers are an underrated accessory."

Memphis huffed out a breath and slid his unimpressed gaze my way. "I think you should get revenge and make-out with someone in front of Simon. Show him what he's missing."

What he was missing? Really. I cocked a brow down at the Elmo shorts hugging my thighs. To which Memphis rolled his eyes.

"As much as you like to pretend you're nothing special, I know different." He crossed his arms. "And so does Simon. It wouldn't take much to make him jealous."

He did have a point. I wasn't really into girls, but... "Cindy is kind of easy."

Memphis huffed, "Nova..."

To which I huffed back, "Memphis."

"You could do so much better than Simon."

"I don't know if Cindy is better than..."

"Oh my god, not Cindy!"

I shrugged, "it was your suggestion."

"That was not..." Memphis took a long deep breath, after which he calmly added, "St. Agatha's is different."

Memphis's parents weren't rich by any means, but they made

enough to send him to private school. At least I wouldn't be alone, that was one good thing. Plus I was kind of curious how the Memphis and Chuck thing worked? Did they hold hands, or make out in the cafeteria? I couldn't see that going over too well in a catholic environment.

"There's an entirely new breed of men in that school."

I didn't think about that. "Okay… but isn't the janitor a little too old for me?"

"Oh my God," Memphis threw his arms up, "you're impossible to talk to when you're like this."

"But, I'm always like this."

"Exactly my point." He rose from the chair and sliced his hands through the air in an I'm done motion. "Don't call me."

I waited for him to storm off the deck and up to the gate before calling out, "Can I text you instead?"

Memphis's honey eyes rolled over his shoulder.

"Yeah," he nodded.

I nodded back, "Cool."

My best friend always managed to make me feel better. For a minute I forgot what Cindy sounded like slurping on my boyfriend's dick. Sorry ex-boyfriend. I should probably let Simon in on that little piece of information. He tried calling me like twenty times today.

At least I wouldn't have to see him at school, or Cindy. So there was that. I just had to walk around with a bunch of rich pompous assholes. One thing was for sure, I was taking all the Fruit Roll Ups with me tomorrow.

"Come on Knoxy." I skipped down the steps and scooped Knox off the ground. "Time for bed. Tomorrow I'll teach you the importance of having bribery material."

Chapter 5

GIOVANNI

Everyone had something they did to unwind. Like a crutch of sorts. If you watched someone long enough, you'd see what their crutch was. My father liked to read, Darry took a drive down a place we called rollercoaster road – though considering his luck with vehicles I didn't see how that was relaxing – and Atlee lost himself in a sea of pussy. It didn't matter who it was or how powerful or rich they were, everyone had that crutch.

I had two, one of which I was staring at right now.

Turning the boat, I steered towards the left. The only light out here were the soft silvery beams of the moon bouncing off the murky water, but I knew exactly where I was going. The hum off the motor and various dips and plunks of bayou wildlife were like home to me. As was the small island that was hard to see in the middle of the afternoon, let alone at night.

The bow of the boat dipped up as I reached for a post to the left. I assumed that's what was left of a dock. I knew every tree and structure in this part of the swamp. I had since I was a kid. There were no roads or trails leading to this island. Just moss and water.

Honestly I couldn't remember how I found this place. Did I swim, or was there a bridge or trail that washed away? Then again I didn't remember much from that day other than my mother's coffin and smell of death.

I finished tying the boat off and stepped out into the tall grass.

Sometimes when I closed my eyes I could still hear the search party calling my name.

It took almost two days for anyone to find me. I wasn't sure if it was hunger or guilt that pulled me towards them, but whatever it was they were happy to see me.

My father was not.

That was the first time I got the you need to man up lecture. I was six-years-old when I learned how to bottle up my emotions, because made men couldn't show weakness. One had to be strong to be in this life, or else you'd be cut off at the knees.

Atlas got that. While he taught me what it meant to be a Mancini, Romeo was off doing his own thing. I didn't even see him at the funeral.

That was when I decided I'd be like Atlas. Strong and powerful. The kind of man who didn't take shit from anyone. A real leader. That didn't stop my mother's screams from haunting my dreams, or the guilt from filling my chest when I caught my father crying alone at night.

My mother's death fractured our family.

Atlas destroyed it.

Ducking down I cut through the Spanish moss hanging off two cypress trees and walked into a small clearing. On the far right edge stood what was left of a stone cottage, surrounded by daffodils. Nothing else grew here. There was no grass, or moss covering the ground. Just the patch of yellow flowers circling the broken structure.

Despite growing up in Louisiana, I was never one to put much stock into things like curses and voodoo. But sometimes I couldn't help but wonder about this place.

In 1843 a woman named Darya LaBelle lived here. According to the journal I'd found she was a voodoo priestess who had fallen in love with a plantation owner, Mathew Atkins. His wife decided to take her anger about the affair out on their child. Darya repaid her cruelty with a curse derived from the poison of a daffodil.

I didn't know what happened to Darya, there was no record of her or her death. The only record of her existence was the leather bound book I found buried in the ruins. There were a few signs that someone lived here. A few broken dishes, a picture so faded with time that I couldn't make out what it was, and a grave marked with a small wooden cross.

The entire Atkins family was wiped out by a mysterious plague in 1845. Not necessarily unusual for that time. A common cold could take someone down.

The daffodils however…

I ran my hand over the soft yellow petals that shouldn't be here. Flowers like this didn't grow wild here, let alone thrive. Yet, there they were, standing bright and proud in the broken place. I think that was why I kept coming back here. Seeing those daffodils almost made me believe in magic again.

Magic didn't exist of course, but it was nice to think that some of the stories my mother told me were real. Even if it was for just a second. She would've loved this place. My mother was a conundrum. She always saw the beauty in things, despite the life my father lived.

The mob was dangerous. There was no guarantee what the next day would bring. Life, death or something in between. Yet my mother always smiled. I even saw it on the day she died. That smile was the last thing she gave me before pushing me in the cupboard. Like it was another fairytale she was telling.

Unfortunately reality was much darker, and it always came crashing back.

My phone dinged with a text that made me pinch the bridge of my nose.

> Carissa: Are you coming over tonight?

That was vise number two.

Carissa Barone, Darius's mother.

> Carissa: I haven't felt you in so long.

My cheeks puffed with a grumbled huff as I sat down on what was left of the house's broken steps.

Atlee wasn't wrong when he teased me about a dry spell. I told myself it was because I wanted something real, and I did. But I was also trying to cut ties with bad habits. And Carissa Barone was about as bad as they came. If Darry knew what I'd been doing with his mother, let alone how long it had been going on… he'd never look at me the same.

Hell, I didn't look at me the same.

When this shit first started it was kind of cool. I was fourteen and she was the sexy older woman guys fantasized about. The taboo factor only made it hotter. Carissa was up for anything.

A quick blow job in the back of the school, jerking me off under the table when my father invited them over for dinner. Once I fucked her outside her bathroom door while her husband was in the shower. It was all fun with no attachments.

Then Atlas died, and things changed. She became something I needed, instead of something to do.

> Carissa: Are you there?

Yeah I was fucking here, I just couldn't tell her that.

I wanted to. My thumbs were ready to type in a response, but I just sat there staring at her messages. Carissa was sick and twisted. What kind of woman would seduce a teenager? But she helped me regain the control I lost when I lost my brother.

I was drinking and picking fights with anyone I could. It was Carissa who pulled me back. Anytime I felt myself slipping, I'd just have to picture how she looked down on her knees, ready to do whatever I said. It was addictive and I needed to stop.

Darry was my friend. Every time I stuck my cock in his mother, I was betraying him. Not to mention what my father would do if he ever found out.

> Carissa: Do you know what I'm doing right now?

Oh I had a pretty good idea and so did my dick. But I managed to stay away from her for two months. If I engaged now…

> Carissa: My fingers feel so good. Want to see?

Yes.

> Me: No.

> Carissa: Are you sure?

That text was followed by a picture of delicate pink flesh held open by two manicured fingers. I licked my lips as memories of how she tasted on my tongue caused my mouth to water.

Fuck. Why the hell did I text her back?

> Me: I'm fucking busy.

I should've put my phone away. It would've been easy to tuck it in my back pocket and forget she ever texted. But I didn't. I sat there and watched as a string of pictures showing Carissa finger fucking herself flowed across my screen.

This needed to stop.

> Me: I told you we can't see each other anymore.

> Carissa: Don't you miss me?

Yes and no. I fucking hated her, but I needed what she could give me. I itched for that sense of domination.

> Me: No.

> Carissa: I miss you. I miss how good you stretch me.

God damnit.

> Me: Stop it.

> Carissa: I'm aching for you.

> Me: Stop it Carissa.

> Carissa: You make me cum so hard. I need your thick cock.

> Me: God damnit! We can't do this anymore.

> Carissa: Why not? Don't tell me you're worried about Darry finding out?

Of course I fucking was.

> Me: You should be worried about it too.

If Darry found out he'd probably beat the crap out of me, which would be well deserved. I wouldn't blame him if he put a bullet between my eyes. But it was more than that. I was tired of feeling this way. Broken and dirty. I wanted to be better than what I was.

> Carissa: We've had this talk before, besides, you need me. No one knows you like I do, Gio.

She did have a point. It was her that showed me how good it felt to have complete control over someone. I didn't even know I had that side. Sex was just sex. I'd bust my nut and move on. She was the one that taught me it could be more.

It could be all consuming, addictive, and more satisfying than any therapy on the planet. And I tried a lot of therapy. I spent years seeing a shrink after my mother died. It didn't do shit.

> Carissa: I know what you need Gio.

> Me: I can find it somewhere else.

I had too.

> Carissa: Sure, you might find some little girl who will play along, but that's not what you want.

My free hand fisted as the next text came in.

> Carissa: You need to punish someone.

It bothered me how well she knew me. Did I want to own a girl so completely that I controlled her next breath, yes. But I also wanted her to fuck up and fight back, so I could reign her back in.

Watching someone bend to my will was the only way I could find some peace.

It was a game I played in everyday life. Carissa saw that. That was how she lured me in with her little games. And I hated how easily I fell for it. I still wanted to fall for it.

Carissa: You know you want to punish me.

She got that one right. I wanted snap her fucking neck.

Me: Don't push me.

Carissa: You like it when I push you.

This bitch…

Me: Cut the shit, I'm not in the mood.

Carissa: Well, I am.

Me: Good for you. Go fuck your husband.

Carissa: He's asleep.

I rolled my eyes.

Me: And how's that my problem?

I was done with this game. That is until the next text came through.

Carissa: I'll use the Manhandler.

My brow arched down at the words on my screen. The

Manhandler was a giant dildo she hated using. She must be pretty desperate to pull that offer out. Or she was bluffing.

> Me: Prove it.

A second later my phone was filled with the image of a big fake dick. Behind that I could see Darry's dad, with his eyes closed and mouth open. I personally didn't have anything against the guy. As far as dad's went he was decent.

He showed up to school meetings and coached Darry's younger brother's little league team, which was more than most made men. I should probably feel guilty for fucking his wife. But I didn't.

> Me: Did Dom take his pills?

Dominic Barone had problems sleeping.

> Carissa: Yes, an hour ago.

Sucking in a deep breath, I tipped my head up to the sky. I couldn't do this. Carissa needed to fuck off and go bother someone else. Then again, it wasn't like I was actually touching her. I'd just be watching. It would be like a quick fix. How smokers cut back before stopping. There wasn't anything wrong with that.

My phone vibrated in my hand drawing my eyes back down her lips wrapped around the head of the Manhandler.

Don't do it Gio, don't respond.

> Me: Just the tip? You can do better than that.

Fuck.

I told myself I wouldn't reply this time. Then a video came through.

Carissa was sucking it back like a pro, while moaning how good I tasted. But it was the gagging that made me pull my cock out and start stroking.

Carissa: Do you want more?

Yes I wanted more, I fucking hated myself for it.

Me: What the fuck do you think?

She must've been waiting because the instant I hit send, her next text came through.

Carissa: Well, I want to see you.

Fuck that. Sexting was one thing. I was not getting on a video call.

Me: Too bad.

Carissa: Fine, then I'm not sending anymore.

Fuck her. Concentrating on the video, I jerked my shaft. I didn't need her to finish.

Carissa: My pussy's so wet, I wish you could see.

God damnit.

My cock ached at the possibility of seeing what she was doing. Was she riding her hand while sucking the toy, or was she shoving that thing deep inside her.

"Fuck!" I snarled and hit the video button.

Almost instantly Carissa's bright blue eyes fluttered back at me.

"Are you fucking happy?"

"Yes," she sang way too innocently. "You look frustrated."

"No shit." I barked back.

The tone of her voice pissed me off more than the fake pout on her lips.

"Don't worry baby, Momma take care of you."

"Don't fucking say that."

The last thing I wanted to think about while I had my dick in my hand was momma anything.

"What's wrong, did Gio have a bad day? Well maybe if you would stop blowing me off…"

I cut her off… "I swear to fucking God Carissa."

"Alright," she giggled. "hang on."

I cursed her existence under my breath while she propped her phone up on the dresser, then crawled back on the bed and spread her legs. I stroked myself as she grimaced and shoved the Manhandler in her cunt, but something was wrong. Everything was there. Her soft moans and pussy swallowing the large dildo while her husband slept beside her.

Normally I'd be all over this shit. But no matter what I tried, I couldn't get into it. My eyes kept rolling over to Darry's dad. He had the same cleft in his chin as his son.

There were two people in this world who always had my back. Atlee and Darry. They'd been there for me since we were little kids. It didn't matter what happened. Death, sickness, or a lecture from my father, they were there supporting me. And I was doing this.

Where was the line? What was next? Would I fuck one of Atlee's sisters just because it would make me feel better, even though I knew what their father would do to them? If my father found out about this shit he'd kill Carissa. Yet here I was stroking my cock like it didn't matter what happened to one of my best friend's mothers.

"Stop," I said and tucked my dick away.

"What's wrong?" Carissa asked without so much as pausing.

I scrubbed a hand down my face to try and wipe the image of her getting off from my mind. "I can't do this."

"Yes you can." She just kept on fucking herself like I didn't say a thing. "Come on Gio, I'm so close. Come with me."

My eyes rolled over to the man sleeping beside her.

"Come with your husband." I said and hung up.

I was no better than the prick who knocked up Darya LaBelle. I should be cursed too and join the scum of the earth like Mathew Atkins in the depths of hell.

Sighing, I looked over at the daffodils blowing in the breeze. Maybe their poison would come for me one day.

Chapter 6

Before my sister became an introvert that hid behind her child, Veda was a normal teenage girl full of useful pieces of information. Like how not to get caught sneaking in the house drunk, and why girls should stay away from football players. Yes, my sister was that girl in school. The one that waved her pom poms and dated football players.

While those lessons weren't things she'd necessarily taught me per say, I did learn from her mistakes. So in my mind they still counted towards her sibling quota. As did the time she told me how important one's entrance could be to their overall reputation and memorability. And let me just say my entrance into St Agatha's was a grand one.

When I pulled my truck into the parking lot, more than half the student body ducked for cover. My favorite were the two girls who dove into a nearby bush, can't say I blamed them. Backfire roaring out of the muffler could easily be confused for a gunshot.

Let's just say when I pushed open my squeaky door and stepped out, I had a bit of an audience. I couldn't wait to see their reaction when I started it up and covered all these pretty cars in a cloud of smoke.

I slammed my door shut – a tad harder than I needed to – flipped my ponytail over my shoulder, and headed for the front entrance. A few people whispered as I walked past and I got a death glare from one of the girls in the bushes. That one hated me. On the upside I definitely nailed the memorable part of the entrance scenario, and I beat my old record for making a nemesis.

Cindy and I were friends until the second day of kindergarten. How was I supposed to know mud fights weren't her thing? She was less than appreciative of the glob I smashed in her face. It wasn't my fault she didn't have a sense of humor. The other kids thought it was hilarious.

Speaking of other kids...

I looked up at the girls eyeing me from the top of the four steps to the entrance. Every girl here was wearing the same blue plaid skirt and white shirt I was, but these three stood out. Based on their manicured nails and perfectly styled hair, I was going to assume they were either here for some kind of photo shoot, or they were the it girls.

Every school had them. A group of three or four girls who walked around like they were queens and every one should bow down before them. The sad fact was, some people did bow down.

Personally I didn't see the appeal. Looking that good had to be exhausting, and I didn't have time for that shit. I barely had time to tie my hair back before Maw Maw was pushing me out the door.

There was only one question now… which one was the leader. There was always a leader. Queen bitch so to say, and she was usually the worst.

Walking up the steps, I scanned the two blondes then looked

over at the dark haired one with her arms crossed. She looked a little more entitled than the others.

"You should put a warning on that thing." One of the blondes said as I reached out for the door handle.

"I could," I glanced over my shoulder at my truck, "but I feel like the blaring siren and flashing lights would distract from the beauty of my paint job."

Her lip curled, "that thing needs a lot more than a paint job."

"Yeah," the other blonde snorted, "Like a wrecking yard."

That one was obviously a follower.

"Your laces are untied," I said and walked in the school knowing full well that she looked down despite not the fact that she was wearing high heels.

A shoe I seriously considered investing in when I was met with the crowd in the hall. Was everyone this tall, or was I just that short? There were only about five people who I could see over. One of whom was an older woman wearing a nun's habit and robes.

I went to church every week with Maw Maw, but watching her boss around people bigger than her was just eerie. Add in the fact that everyone appeared to be doing what she said, and I was definitely not going anywhere near her.

If I was going to get punished for my blasphemous ways, it would be at church like everyone else. At this point I wouldn't be surprised if Father John had an hour reserved every Sunday just for me. I tried telling him that some people just couldn't be saved, but he didn't listen.

Thankfully I didn't have to stand there avoiding eye contact with the holy sister of the hall for very long, because Memphis popped out of a door on the left and skipped up to me.

"There you are, I've been looking for you everywhere."

He did realize that school didn't start for another ten minutes?

"What are you talking about, I've been here for an hour. But I could see where you would have issues finding me. This much plaid would blind anyone."

Did I mention how much I hated this uniform? I had to iron it. Who the fuck does that? Seriously? Who in this day and age cares about wrinkly fabric? That just meant it was comfortable, which is something I think everyone could appreciate.

"Stop complaining," Memphis smirked and gave my skirt a tug. "I think you look cute."

"Fantastic, maybe my dream of getting knocked up in the storage room will finally come true."

He cocked a brow, "the last thing you need is a baby."

"Hey, don't knock the life of a teenage mom." I watched that show. They seemed to have a good time.

"You do realize you have to actually have sex to get pregnant."

"Ugh, technicality." I rolled my eyes, "and you might want to watch what you say. I doubt sister Mary of the hallway will be appreciative of your language."

"Who?" Memphis leaned to the side and looked over my shoulder. "Sister Anne."

"Shh," I hushed. "Don't say her name, you might invoke her."

It was his turn to roll his eyes, "she's harmless."

"Says the choir boy." Literally. Memphis was a choir boy. So not only did he look like an angel, he also sang like one. It was annoying.

"Come on," he looped his arm in mine. "I'll show you your future baby daddy storage closet on the way to your locker."

"And where is your future baby daddy?" I asked as Memphis pulled me down the hall.

"At practice, and would you keep your voice down," Memphis said in a hushed tone.

"Ah," I sang. "Sister Anne doesn't seem so harmless now, does she?"

Catholicism and homosexuality didn't go together so well. As far they were concerned it was a sin. Well, most of them. Father John welcomed everyone, so he wasn't entirely bad. Though I did sometimes wonder how the church felt about his open door policy.

"Wait…" I tipped my gaze towards my best friend. "Does this mean that I won't be subjected to your annoying public displays of affection?"

He shot me a dirty look in response.

Hmm, this place might not be so bad after all. Memphis and his boyfriend Chuck gave new meaning to the word nauseous. They were so cute it physically hurt to watch them. They also never fought, which in itself was wrong. Every couple argued.

I tried countless times to start something. Like leaving open condoms wrappers in Memphis's car, or sending sexy texts to Chuck with an unknown number. I kind of gave myself away on that one though. I got all my pick up lines from Maw Maw's stash of books.

On a side note, historical romance probably wasn't the best place to go for seduction material. I still didn't know what a vicar or rake were, but apparently both were desirable. Just not in sexting form. Chuck had absolutely no interest in sucking my vicar.

After showing me where my locker was, Memphis took me to my first class, which I argued I should be fashionably late for. Had to make an entrance after all. But my best friend was all about punctuality. Meaning I was five minutes early because he needed time to get to his class.

That I blamed on the school. This place was way too big, and clean, and it smelled way too good. High schools should smell like bad decisions and guilt. Not fresh flowers and incense. And don't even get me started on the stained glass windows and shiny wooden desks. I had yet to see one name or doddle carved in anything.

Just when I was starting to think this place wouldn't be so bad, I walked into Spanish class.

Sitting on the right side of the room was the blonde I met outside.

Judging by the gleam in her dark eyes, she was about as happy to see me as I was to see her. And of course the first empty desk I saw was right in front of her. She must've sensed what I was thinking because next thing I knew she was leaning back and narrowing her eyes. As if she was challenging me to do it.

As tempting as it was to inconvenience her – and it was awfully tempting – bush girl number one had already claimed my open nemesis position.

I took a second to glance around for another open spot. That's when the universe gave me another gut punch. The only other unoccupied desk was in the right corner of the room, next to the cocky smirk of an insanely good looking guy. My hormones literally amped up a notch just looking at him.

He was tanned and big, but not so big that he looked like he could crush someone with his forearms. That didn't mean he wasn't built. There were visible firm edges pressing against the fabric of his shirt.

Then there was his smile. It was the kind of small corner of the mouth curl that made the devil dance in the depths of his whiskey orbs. Which by the way sparkled all on their own. I didn't even know they made guys like that.

I hated him already. Bastard probably also had those washboard abs that could cut glass.

Pfft, prick.

Sighing, I weighed my options. Did I want to sit beside evil demon spawn Barbie, or Greek Olympiad – who I wouldn't doubt had seen every girl in this room naked.

Decisions, decisions.

Evil demon spawn Barbie did kind of look like Cindy, and Cindy had my boyfriend's dick in her mouth this weekend. That was a reminder I didn't run the risk of next to the Greek god. Then again who the hell knew what Greek gods did behind closed doors.

Memphis was the gossip queen – not that I paid attention to any of his claims. That ship sank when he tried to convince me Medusa lived in his backyard.

Grumbling under my breath, I stomped over to the right side. At least the Greek god would ignore me. Someone like that didn't pay attention to someone like me. I was wearing cookie monster socks for Christ sake. That was my way of rebelling against the uniform.

I flopped down in the desk – which was annoyingly comfortable for something made of wood – and dropped my chin in my palm.

This was all Simon's fault. How hard was it to keep your dick in your pants? There was a zipper there for a reason.

My lip curled at the girl whispering in Greek God's ear. I highly doubted he was reaching under her desk for a pencil. Great, Spanish and a show. I could've gotten that by staying home and watching telenovelas. If there was a god up there he'd strike me down right now.

"Hey," The girl tipped her head and slowly eyed me. "Did you know you have a sock on your ass?"

I looked over my shoulder and sure enough there was one of Knox's little blue socks clinging to my skirt.

Fabulous. Served me right for throwing it in the dryer before getting dressed. Guess the girl with a sock on her ass wasn't the worst identity I had.

"Yup," I sighed. "I sure do."

Greek God's brow rose. "Why do you have a sock on your ass?"

"Clearly, I'm trying to start a new fashion trend." I flopped my eyes his way. "You want in?"

"Oo," he leaned in a little closer. "You have jokes."

"I also have a lot of problems." Anyone could see that.

One of said problems was this conversation. Why was he talking to me anyway? Didn't anyone ever teach him to stay in his league. Don't dip below that line. Like say, he could keep talking to the girl that was whispering in his ear – who seemed suddenly very annoyed with my existence.

"Are you new here?"

And yet he was still talking to me.

Lovely.

Would the teacher be mad if I sat on the floor? There was lots of space down there. I could open all my books and spread out my notes. Maybe even take a nap?

"You look familiar." I tried not to think about what was on the hand he used to prop his head up. Not to mention the finger he was tapping on his chin. "Do I know you?"

"Nope."

His eyes narrowed. "Are you sure?"

"Yup." I'd never been more sure of anything in my life.

"Well then, allow me to introduce myself." A charming grin spread across his face as he held out his hand. "I'm Atlee."

"I know who you are." I didn't. I had no idea who he was, but I did know that there was no way I was touching his hand.

"But you just said…"

I cut him off. "I said *you* didn't know *me.*"

Which was one hundred percent true.

Did my snide comment make him drop it, of course not. Why would the universe start liking me now?

"You're sassy." The devil started dancing in his eyes again. "I like it."

Oh boy, Greek God liked me. My life was now complete. God could bring that smite on anytime.

"I bet you're a virgin too." He purred while raking his eyes down my side.

Seriously, just slit my throat. I'm totally cool with it.

Atlee shifted in his desk and took a deep, heavy inhale. "You smell like a virgin."

Oh please. "I smell like fabric softener and depression."

Why was he looking at me like that? Did he not see the dozen other girls who were well put together?

I should've worn the Elmo shorts.

The girl behind Atlee was about as impressed with my unwanted attention as I was.

She curled her lip while twirling her finger through the air. "You might want to think about running a brush through your hair."

"Hey," I shot back. "Not everyone can afford a brush."

Or the time to find one. The shower I took was way too long. But I didn't smell like bourbon anymore.

Atlee's brow rose. "You can't afford a brush?"

Okay, that lie might've been a little out there.

"What's your name?"

Ugh, what was with the twenty questions? "I don't have one."

"You don't have a name?"

"Nope."

"Uh huh," he muttered. "So what do your parents call you?"

"I don't have parents either." That one wasn't a lie.

"See," he threw his hands up in the air. "That's your problem right there. You can't buy a brush if you don't have a name."

What? "That doesn't make any sense."

His brow arched, "neither does not having a name."

Touché Mr. Greek God, touché.

"I bet you have a name now," he said with a coy tip of his head.

Alright, that was enough.

"Let me save you some time," I turned in my desk to look at him. "This, whatever you're trying to do, isn't going to happen. I don't have daddy issues..." I totally did. "I'm not into football players or whatever you are. I'm not interested. And you smell too good."

He really did. I'd been secretly breathing in his scent since I sat down.

"I smell too good?"

I nodded. "That's right."

"You're not interested because I smell good?"

"Correct."

"Okay," he sat back and eyed me for a second. "What should I smell like?"

"Cheap cologne and regret." Like all teenagers.

The smile on his face widened. "I like you."

I practically groaned out loud. Clearly my goal was to deter him. Not egg him on. And to make matters worse the giggle from across the room was grating on my nerves like sandpaper. I had to grit my teeth against it. Evil demon Barbie even sounded like Cindy.

I didn't realize my fists were balled until Atlee dipped his eyes down. "You okay?"

"I'm fine." I hissed while unfurling my hands. "Some people just have annoying voices."

"Oh, I get it." He tipped his head to glance over my shoulder. "What'd she do, fuck your boyfriend?"

"No," I sneered. "Someone who looks like her did." *Why did I tell him that?* "And she didn't fuck him," *and why was I clarifying?* "she just sucked him off."

Seriously, god could bring on that smite anytime.

"Okay," Atlee nodded as if he had some sudden sense of understanding. "I'll make you a deal."

Couldn't wait to hear this.

"I'll slap the shit out of her, if you tell me your name."

I rolled my eyes. "Sure." Like that was ever going to happen.

Next thing I knew he was up and darting across the room. My jaw dropped as his palm swung through the air, cracking off the side of Demon Barbie's face so hard that she flew out of her chair.

Well shit.

Chapter 7

GIOVANNI

I walked into the cafeteria and looked around at the checkered floor filled with different cliques sitting at clean white tables. This wasn't my favorite place to be. In fact I kind of despised this room.

People talked too much and the first day of the year was always the worst. Everyone wanted to catch up after summer break, so no matter where I went someone was talking.

Thankfully most steered clear of us. It wasn't as if Atlee, Darry or I went around advertising what our families did, but rumors still went around. More than a few students here had a parent or relative that spent some time at my dad's casino, and not always to gamble. Even still there were a few that didn't care who our fathers were. Some might call that brave.

I called it stupid.

My footsteps slowed as I passed a group of football players. The starting quarterback Randal Stevens was a cocky bastard who had yet to learn his place. This was my school, not his.

Even now the prick was grating on my nerves. Leaning back in his chair with his feet propped up on the table like he didn't have a care in the world.

"Why are you staring at me Mancini," Randal tipped his head my way. "You want to suck my dick?"

"Isn't that Carter's job, he has his nose shoved so far up your ass he could taste your balls." I shot back, making the rest of his table laugh.

Randal on the other hand wasn't as amused by my retort, but I wasn't the only one who thought something was going on between him and Jake Carter. I just had the balls to say it out loud.

I smirked at the tick in Randal's jaw and headed over to my table, where Atlee and Darry were waiting. Though Atlee had this look on his face that didn't sit right with me. More specifically the glimmer in his eye. A glimmer that lit up when I sat down.

"What the fuck are you so happy about?"

He smiled back at me, "nothing,."

Nothing my ass.

I grew up with the guy and knew what that curl in his lip meant. Atlee had a smile for everything. Picking up chicks, getting out of trouble, sweet talking a teacher or cop, and amusement like the one he was wearing now. There were only two things that amused Atlee Fiore, pussy and someone else's suffering.

"What are you up to?" The last time Atlee smiled at me like that was the day Romeo came home.

"Why would I be up to something?"

He was always up to something. Atlee lived in this perpetual state of fuck. Who can I fuck with, who can I fuck up, and who can I fuck. Since he didn't have bloody knuckles or a chick draped over him, I was going to assume it was the first. And I was more than likely the target.

"I'm not in the mood for your shit, Atlee. Run your game on someone else."

He slapped his hand over his heart, "Would I run a game on you?"

Yes he fucking would.

I shrugged, "don't blame me when you get punched in the face."

"Oh, I don't think you'll be hitting me."

Huffing out an exasperated breath, I looked over at Darry, "Do you have any idea what he's up to?"

Darry just shrugged and continued eating.

For some reason the scowl etched across his face bothered me today. It wasn't an unusual expression, especially on Darius Barone – fucker probably came out of the womb with his brows knit – but today that scowl seemed to accentuate the cleft in his chin. Reminding me of how his father looked when Carissa called last night.

My encounter with her should've ended when I hung up. I should've got up and went home to sleep, instead of staying there and jerking off three times to the pictures she sent. At one point I even considered driving over there. And the worst part, Darry didn't make me feel guilty. Just pissed off that I didn't watch his mother come all over that dildo.

I was a shitty friend.

"So," Atlee said, drawing my gaze back to him. "How was your morning?"

How was my morning? What the fuck kind of question was that?

"It was fine."

His brow rose, "Just fine?"

"It's school Atlee, what the fuck do you want me to say?"

"I don't know," Atlee braced his elbow on the table and dropped his chin in his palm. "Something interesting must've happened."

Alright, he was definitely up to something.

Dropping my fork on my plate, I said, "what did you do?"

He must've done something. That was the only explanation for his annoying behavior.

"You mean besides slapping the shit out of Catherine Hall?" Darry muttered.

Of course he did, though I couldn't say I was surprised. Half the student body wanted to slap that cunt. Honestly, I was amazed she made it through the doors without getting smacked by someone.

Atlee pointed a finger at Darry, "I had a good reason for that."

"Right," Darry rolled his eyes. "I forgot about the elusive new girl."

"What new girl?" I didn't hear about anyone new.

My question caused Atlee's face to light right up. "Oh, you haven't met her yet?"

Was he being coy on purpose? I couldn't be bothered to learn the names of the people I'd been going to school with for years, let alone give a shit about some new chick. Besides…

"No one cares who your next flavor of the week is."

"First off," Atlee held up one of his fingers, "A week is way too long, bitches be getting clingy and shit. Way too much of a hassle for me."

I rolled my eyes. Typical Atlee.

"And… something tells me you'll want first crack at this one."

I snorted, "Doubtful."

I'd fucked a total of two girls in this school. Both of which were unsatisfying one night stands that lasted a night too long. High school girls couldn't handle the shit I wanted. Or they tried to fake it, which was worse. I was not interested in going down that road.

"Well, you can judge for yourself." Atlee tipped his chin towards the door. "Here she comes now."

He wasn't going to let this go until I at least looked. So against my better judgment, I turned around and immediately cocked a brow. She was cute, I'd give him that. Mind you I just had a back view, but there was no denying those curves.

The girl was a tiny little thing too. The top of her head barely reached the guy beside her shoulders. She'd be nice and easy to control. All I'd have to do was wrap that hazelnut ponytail in my fist and she wouldn't be able to go anywhere. Plus I did appreciate how her ass looked in that skirt.

Wait...

"Is she wearing cookie monster socks?"

"Yeah," Atlee nodded. "She had one stuck to her ass earlier."

What the fuck? "She had a sock stuck to her ass?"

Atlee sat back and snickered, "that girl gives new meaning to the term hot mess."

Great, another chick with issues. Well, there goes that idea. Then again...

I gave her another quick scan, raking my eyes from top to bottom then back up again.

"So, what do you think?" Atlee asked.

It could be fun, or messy and I didn't like messy. Nah it was better to stay away. Besides, why would this girl be any different than the others? All I'd be doing was wasting my time. Atlee could have her.

"Thanks," I sighed. "But I'm..."

She turned around, cutting my words off. There was something about her. Something oddly familiar but I couldn't place what it was.

"Something wrong, Gio?"

"I don't know," I muttered back at Atlee while searching her pink lips and button nose. "She looks..."

"Familiar?" He finished for me.

Yeah, but I didn't know why.

"What's her name?" Darry piped in.

That's when I got smacked in the face with a pair of hazel eyes.

My fists balled as my jaw clenched. "Novalee Ford."

"And there it is." Atlee sang, making me want to punch him.

He knew the whole time and didn't say shit. That alone consti-tuted a beat down. Now I knew why he was so goddamn annoying.

My fists balled as Novalee skipped over to a table where two guys were seated. One I think was on the basketball team. Chuck maybe? I was too busy plotting a murder to give a shit. What the fuck was she doing here?

"Did you say Ford?" Darry tipped his head. "As in Kato Ford?"

Yes, I fucking did.

"She's his sister." I hissed.

The last time I saw her was at her brother's sentencing. She'd grown up since then, which explained why I didn't recognize her right away. But it didn't explain why the fuck she was here. Kato killed my brother and now his sister was in my school, laughing and talking with her idiot friends like she belonged here. The entire Ford family could burn alive and I still wouldn't be satisfied.

"Fuck this." I shot up and stormed across the room.

Somewhere behind me I could hear Darry curse under his breath as a chair screeched across the floor. My friends could do what they wanted. My focus was laser locked on one target. And she didn't see me coming until I slammed my hands down on the table in front of her, causing the trays on top of it to bounce.

"What the fuck are you doing here!"

When she looked up at me it took a second for recognition to flicker across her face, but the deep lines that pulled across her forehead told me she knew exactly who I was. If Novalee was upset by my presence it didn't come out in her tone.

"You must not have gotten the handbook, but this room here," she waved her hand through the air. "Is called a cafeteria. It's where people come to eat."

Was she getting smart with me? "Is that so?"

"That's right, hence," her eyes slid over to the tray in front of her. "The food."

I responded to her snide comment by snatching the tray and tossing it across the room.

That's when everything got quiet. Aside from the blonde guy sitting across from her.

"That's enough, Gio." Apparently he didn't like me picking on his friend. Fucker stood up and puffed his chest out. "Leave her alone."

My eyes snapped over to his. "Sit the fuck down. This doesn't concern you."

Not to mention I'd destroy him. My forearms were bigger than his neck, I'd snap him like a fucking twig.

The other guy seemed worried about what might happen and tugged on his sleeve, "Leave it alone Memphis."

At least he wasn't an idiot.

"Yeah Memphis," Atlee walked up behind me and dropped his arm on my shoulder. "Leave it alone."

"Why don't you make me Fiore."

"You see this shit," Atlee kept his gaze fixed on Memphis while he leaned in closer to me and added, "fucker wants to play."

I could see Darry out of the corner of my eye. He was creeping up, getting ready to grab the blonde bodyguard if he tried anything. His friend saw him too. I assumed that was why he stood up and positioned himself between the two.

Novalee on the other hand seemed unfazed.

"It's okay Memphis," she held up her palm. "Gio just saved me from throwing up later. There's a lot of fat in fried food and girl's gotta watch her figure."

My jaw ticked as I glared down at her. "Do you think you're smart?"

"Well… I did know what a cafeteria was so… one could argue I'm a notch above you in the intelligence factor."

Every muscle in my body tensed as I growled, "get out of my school. We don't allow murderer's sisters here."

"So you draw the line at rapist's brothers then?"

If I wasn't pissed off before then I sure as fuck was now. My hand shot out wrapping around her neck, which caused her little bodyguard to come at me. Atlee was ready for him.

He jumped up and sprang across the table kicking trays and food everywhere. Memphis didn't get a chance to touch me before Atlee tackled him to the ground. Darry had his hands full holding the other one back.

All the hatred I had poured down at the girl I had pressed back into the table.

"My brother wouldn't touch your sister with his dick." I growled while nodding towards Memphis who was on the ground struggling against Atlee's hold.

Novalee's eyes darkened, and for the first time I saw a hint of hatred burning across her face.

"No," she hissed back. "He used his own dick when he held my sister down and raped her."

My fingers tightened and I could feel her pulse against my hand. She might look calm, but she was scared. I could feel the fear coming off her and so could my dick. The pink tint of exertion flowing down her neck had me harder than stone.

I was thrown off by the sudden urge to tear her clothes off, but it went away as quickly as it came. One look at the sneer on her face was all it took to reign myself back in.

"This is your last warning. Get the fuck out of my school." I folded over her small body to growl in her ear. "Or, I'll fucking destroy you."

Chapter 8

As far as first days went, this wasn't the worst. That award went to grade five when I tripped over the art teachers desk and accidentally dyed my face blue. This day had nothing on the two weeks I spent looking like a Smurf. Sure I may have made a few enemies, and was attacked by Gio Mancini in the cafeteria.

But I didn't have a sock stuck to my ass anymore and my face was still it's original fair – I refuse to tan so I'll be the whitest girl alive – complexion. And the freckles on my nose and forehead didn't count. They weren't cute, I don't care what anyone said. Those dots were as annoying as Gio Mancini.

Was I bothered by the fact that I was in the same school as him? Of course. Gio was an asshole, his brother was an asshole, his friends were assholes – especially Atlee. Now I knew why he smiled when I told him my name.

I knew that Gio went to this school – Memphis had a boy crush on him in tenth grade – But a little heads up from Atlee about his friendship group would've been nice. I'd devise an evil plan for payback later. Right now I just wanted to go home.

"I should walk you out."

Memphis had been following me around all afternoon. It was getting kind of creepy.

"I'll be fine," I closed my locker door and slung my backpack over my shoulder. "Why don't you go stalk your boyfriend, he's probably all nice and sweaty."

I assumed that was why Memphis went to all of Chuck's practices. He claimed to like the game, but I knew more about sports than he did. And I actively went out of my way to avoid them.

Memphis crossed his arms. "My sweaty boyfriend can wait."

"I said that once. Then Cindy found Simon."

"Don't change the subject," Memphis sneered. "This is a serious problem, Nova."

"I agree. But Cindy has stuck worse things in her mouth." I couldn't think of any examples right now.

"Need I remind you that you were attacked this afternoon?"

I was well aware of that. The bruises on my neck reminded me every time I turned my head. How I was going to explain them to Maw Maw, I hadn't figured out yet.

"I'll be fine." I repeated when Memphis started following me down the hall.

Gio was more bothered by our shared school status than I was, which gave me a new appreciation for St. Agatha's. Besides, what could he possibly do to me that I hadn't already done to myself? Hit me? Big deal. I wrestled a gator in my underwear – or so I was told. Still couldn't remember everything that happened at that party.

Memphis paused and glanced past me at the exit. "I can't…"

Knowing where this was going, I decided to cut him off. "Listen, bodyguard of the century. I know the trek through the parking lot is a dangerous one, but I've got my safari gear. No lions are going to sneak up on my ass."

"I'm more worried about the wolf."

Wolf? I don't know if I'd compare Gio Mancini to a wolf. Sure he was tall and intimidating with arms that could snap my neck with a flick of his wrists. And he did have this dark, menacing 'I want to eat your face off' glint in his deep jade eyes. But he was nowhere near furry enough to be compared to a wolf.

"You need to come up with a better animal than that." I could cuddle with a wolf and not worry about being smothered by their hulking mass of muscle.

Memphis crossed his arms and cocked a brow. "Haven't you ever heard of the wolf in sheep's clothing?"

"I'm pretty sure Gio ate the sheep… and the wolf… and both their clothing." He probably ate their families too after burning down their house.

"Nope," he shook his head. "I'm walking you to your truck."

My head fell back with a groan. "I told you I have my safari gear."

"A three year old condom and pack of gum don't count as safari gear."

He said that now but when he was trapped in the forest with no food and nothing to collect fresh water, my gum and condom would start looking really good.

Ugh. "Will you just go and support your boyfriend already." I threw my finger up in his direction. "Don't make me get back together with Simon."

Technically I hadn't officially broken up with him yet. I'd been ignoring his messages for two days, so one would think he'd gotten the hint. Then again Simon wasn't the brightest bulb. I once saw him try to eat a wax piece of fruit.

"You wouldn't do that. The guy cheated on you."

Did he have to point that out?

"You underestimate my stubbornness."

It was a common mistake and one that he'd made a few times over the years. My championship title of worm eater proved that. That dare came from a book we read in second grade. *How To Eat Fried Worms* which by the way had no recipes in it for said dare.

"And you underestimate Gio Mancini."

Oh the fear was real. I knew he hated the very ground I walked on and wanted to fuck me up in any way he could. I also wasn't going to let him dictate my life. Mediocrity took work. I had places to go, people to see, and future divorces to plan. Besides…

"If you start following me around like a bodyguard then he's just going to think he got to me."

Memphis arched a brow, "He did get to you."

"But we don't want *him* to know that."

There was only one way to handle someone like Gio, and that was to ignore them. The second they knew they could push your buttons, they'd never stop. I'd dealt with enough bullies to know that. Nothing pissed them off more than a non-reaction.

"And what are you going to do anyway?"

Memphis puffed his chest out, "I can take care of myself."

"You cried last week for thirty minutes when you stubbed your toe."

I wasn't even exaggerating with that one. He literally cried for thirty minutes while holding his foot like he broke it. I timed him. Memphis and pain did not go well together. It was sweet that he wanted to protect me though.

"It hurt," He whined.

"I'm guessing Gio's fist will hurt more."

As comical as I thought it would be to watch him try and accessorize a broken nose, I couldn't let him get in the middle of this fight. My best friend may think he was protecting me, but he'd just be another victim. And that I wouldn't allow.

Memphis looked up and pondered his options before letting

out a sigh, "fine. But don't think I'm not walking you to every class tomorrow."

"Great," that was an amicable compromise. For now anyway. We could renegotiate terms tomorrow.

"Now," I said while backing down the hall. "If you don't mind, I have an important appointment to get to."

Memphis's expression dropped into a deadpan look. "You're going to go home and cry on your bed while listening to Total Eclipse Of The Heart, aren't you?"

"Pfft, no."

I totally was. Sometimes I hated how much he knew me.

"You better not waste a single tear on that idiot. Simon isn't worth it."

Way to ruin my night's plans Memphis.

"In case you haven't noticed I'm a girl. We're supposed to be emotional and needy."

"Girls wear make-up and don't smell like their nephew's baby shampoo. You might want to try that tomorrow."

I gave him a salute, "Yes drill sergeant."

He answered me with a firm middle finger, before spinning around and darting down the hall in the opposite direction. Towards the gym where Chuck was at practice, I assumed.

Once I was free of my unwanted shadow, I spun around and suddenly noticed how empty everything was. I did admittedly spend some extra time at my locker, but I didn't think it was that long.

Did everyone rush out the doors when the bell rang? Where was everyone? This was seriously eerie. There should be a couple of people still in the halls to muffle the sound of my footsteps.

I told myself that I was just being paranoid and pushed the door open to step outside.

The parking lot didn't help my nerves any. It was just as vacant as the school. There were maybe five or six cars plus my truck. On the upside there didn't appear to be anyone waiting for me, and I checked. Peeked around corners, searched for shadows and found nothing but me, the breeze tickling my calves and my truck. Now that was different.

I stopped to cock a brow at the bright red *hore* painted across my hood. Well, it was good to know originality was still alive and well.

Sighing, I unzipped my backpack and dug around inside for a marker. After which I stepped on the front bumper, reached out, and added a w.

Much better.

If I was going to drive around with a slur sprawled across my truck then it sure as hell was going to be spelt right.

Opening the door, I climbed in my truck and stuck the key in. It was a little disappointing that no one was around to dive in a bush, but I guess I'd have to get that entertainment tomorrow. Because I was coming back, despite Gio's threats.

I was looking forward to seeing his reaction. Unlike everyone else in this town, I wasn't scared of the Mancini's. What more could they do to me?

That thought should've comforted me on my way home. Instead it caused my imagination to run wild. Every possible nightmare scenario played through my mind. And Gio was there in each and every one, laughing in the background. Decapitating me, stabbing me in a dark alley, and of course burning me alive. That one sent a shiver up my spine.

By the time I parked in front of our trailer, I'd come to one conclusion. I watched way too many horror movies. Tonight might be a good night to dive into some feel good cartoons with Knox.

Two steps out of my truck made me reconsider the horror movie thing. One could get a lot of murder ideas from a horror movie, which was exactly what I wanted to do to the driver in the red car, pulling up behind my truck.

Maybe I could make it in the house before he saw me?

"Nova." Simon called.

Apparently not. Fuck my life.

I didn't bother closing the little plastic gate behind me when I headed up to the front door.

"We need to talk."

The only thing I needed to do was get inside. Why did Maw Maw insist on locking up? We didn't have anything worth stealing.

"You can't keep ignoring me."

I begged to differ. I was doing a fabulous job so far. *If only I could get this damn door open.*

"I know you can hear me."

There was no proof of that. Maybe I had earbuds in, or maybe I wasn't paying attention. It was quite common for people to be distracted. For instance, I didn't see Cindy running her hand down Simon's arm that night. Nor did I hear her annoying as fuck giggle. I was too busy sucking back alcohol.

"Come on Nova," He walked up behind me and whispered in my ear, "the silent treatment is a little childish, even for you."

I wasn't childish. His stupid red sneakers were childish.

"Sorry," I sang while continuing to fight with the lock. "I didn't recognize you without the girl on your dick."

He let out a frustrated sigh, "Look, we both did things we aren't proud of."

Seriously? That was the excuse he was going with?

"You looked pretty proud to me." Or did he forget about the smile he gave when he saw me standing in the doorway?

I didn't.

I saw it every time he sent me a text. *Nova, answer me. Nova stop hiding. Nova answer the damn phone.* Ugh, give a girl some space, and by space, I meant move away, never talk to her again, and possibly die in a car crash on the way out of town.

Okay, that might be taking things a little too far, but would the world really miss someone like him?

"We've been dating for three months."

Wrong. "It's been three months and four days."

Trust me that extra bit counted. Every day with Simon felt like a year. Was I surprised that someone I invested my time in betrayed me? No. But I could still be pissed off about it. And I had a right to be.

"What did you think would happen? Guys have needs, Nova. It's not my fault you're sexually anorexic."

Oh fuck him.

"You know what Simon." I spun around prepared to rip him a new asshole.

That's when I stopped.

From far away Simon looked a little banged up, but up close he looked like a bag of shit. Actually I think a bag of shit would have a better appearance than he did. His left eye was almost swollen shut, there was a deep purple bruise along his jaw, and...

"Are you limping?"

Simon straightened his shoulders and rolled his neck. "I fell."

"Down what? A cliff?" And did he hit every single rock on the way down? Because that would be great.

"I'm fine." He sighed. "It was just an accident."

My brow rose, "Were you playing crash test dummy? I've heard that's a dangerous game."

And did he record it, because I would love to watch it?

"I know a few ways you could make me feel better." He teased with an eyebrow waggle.

My face dropped. "Unless one of those ways involves my knee meeting your balls, I'm not interested."

"This is what I'm talking about Nova. I put the time in, I should get the prize."

"You seriously think I'm going to let you touch me?" Was he delusional, or just stupid?

The look he gave me in response, said that yes he was indeed delusional.

"I've put in the time."

And apparently stupid.

"I'd rather bathe in acid, then wrap myself in salt with a spritz of lemon juice, then dry off with sandpaper."

Pretty sure that would be less painful then feeling his grubby hands pawing at me.

"Jesus," Simon's lip curled. "Do you have to be so descriptive?"

"I don't know," I shot back. "Did you have to put your dick in Cindy's mouth?"

I thought it was a fair argument.

Simon, did not.

He rolled his eyes. "I hope you get over this before our date on Friday."

He had to be kidding? Was he always this dumb and I just didn't see it? No girl in their right mind would go out with someone who cheated on them. Now, I may not be in my right mind, but I still had self-respect. Kind of.

"Consider your Friday night wide open."

Disbelief tugged at his brow. "You're breaking up with me?"

"*You* canceled any relationship obligations I had when you let Cindy suck you off."

"Come on Nova, you're a mess." His hand swung over me. "Who else would want you?"

"Well when you're working on a two day hangover, one doesn't really have time to accessorize." I was doing pretty good all things considered.

"So you're obviously upset about what happened."

You think.

"I'm sorry, alright. Now can we move past this."

Every fiber of my being wanted to rip that perfect hair out of his head. "Sure Simon, let's move past this. How about you move that way," I nodded at the open gate, then looked back at the door with my keys hanging out of the knob, "and I'll move this way."

Simon didn't like my suggestion. He stepped in, forcing my back up against the door, and slammed his hand down on the wood above me.

"You don't get to dismiss me."

"I believe I just did."

The shadows moving across Simon's face warned me to keep my mouth shut. "Who the hell do you think you are?"

"You're ex-girlfriend." That probably wasn't the best thing to say, but why would I start doing the smart thing now?

"I decide when this relationship ends," his hand rose and I closed my eyes, waiting for the inevitable smack.

It didn't come. Instead of a slap and stinging cheek the click of a gun being cocked rang through my ears.

"Step back."

I cracked my eyes open to see our neighbor Mr. Garibaldi standing on the other side of the house in his green housecoat. Simon's hand was in the air ready to strike, but his eyes were locked on the barrel of the shotgun pointed at him.

"I mean it boy. Go home."

Simon took one last look at me then began slowly backing away.

I'd never been more happy for the local raccoon war than I was at that moment.

Chapter 9

GIOVANNI

ovalee Ford was in my school. Mine! The same one I'd been going to since high school started. People like her weren't supposed to get into St. Agatha's, yet there she was. If I wanted to get kicked in the face I'd hit on Atlee's sister, or tell Darry I was fucking his mother. Was being the operative word.

Maybe this was karma, or someone's idea of a joke. It sure felt like a fucking joke.

Here Gio, welcome to school. Now sit there and stare at the bitch whose brother killed yours.

There was a joke with a killer punchline. Because killing someone was all I wanted to do. Her brother for fucking with my family. My brother because Romeo was a dick who didn't deserve to be boss, and Nova's blonde bodyguard for being her friend, because why the fuck not.

But the person I wanted to kill the most was my father. The prick knew she'd be there – he was on the committee that signed off on her scholarship – and he didn't say shit. Well that wasn't true. He did say a few things when I confronted him about it. Like: *'the girl's IQ tests were off the charts,'* and *'maybe you'll learn some patience from this experience'.*

Patience? Motherfucking patience. Was he kidding me?

"God fucking damnit!" I threw my fist into the dash over and over again, and didn't stop until blood was trickling down my cracked knuckles.

"Gio…"

Fuck, I forgot Carissa was on the phone.

"Are you okay?"

I was great. Everything was fan-fucking-tastic. Or at least it would be when I slit Novalee's throat.

Looking down at my bloody hand, I flexed my fist, tightening the skin around my sore knuckles and hissed, "I'm fine."

"You don't sound fine."

No shit Sherlock.

"Are you at home?" Carissa asked in a tone that could easily be mistaken for worry.

I knew better. I'd seen firsthand how good her acting skills were.

"No, I'm not at home."

I didn't like being there. There were constant reminders of Atlas everywhere. Pictures on the wall, the mug he used in the morning, and the crack in the corner of the kitchen table from when he came home drunk. Not a single room in that house held any kind of escape. And the ones that did were stained with my mother's blood. It was a wonder I could sleep at all.

"So this girl…"

"Novalee," I finished for her.

"Do… you like her?"

My brows knit at the speaker where Carissa's voice was coming from. "No I don't fucking like her."

Did I like Novalee? What kind of question was that? I'd like her a lot better after I plucked her eyes out of her skull.

"So… you don't want to punish her."

Oh, I wanted to punish her, and her whole fucking family.

Just when I was starting to move past Atlas's death, there she was. Like a goddamn nightmare with a face I couldn't get out of my head. That was the part that really pissed me off.

Those pouty fucking lips and bright hazel eyes were like a punch in the gut. Kato's sister had the same sneer as him. I wanted to rip it off her face and fuck her at the same time. For two years not a single chick in school could get my blood roaring, and now my dick wouldn't fuck off. I'd been hard since lunch.

All this time I'd been telling myself that I'd find someone who could fill the need Carissa met. And who was it that finally called to that dark part of me? Novalee fucking Ford. Not some cheerleader or random pick up that I'd be more than happy to use, but the sister of my sworn enemy.

What kind of backwater, bullshit irony was that?

I should kill her. Or better yet kill her brother and make her watch.

"Gio, are you still there?"

"Yeah," I sighed. "I'm still here."

Though I don't know why I called Carissa in the first place. I was so pissed off at my dad that I needed to hurt someone, or fuck my frustration away and I found myself calling her.

"I know exactly what you need."

I just bet she did.

"Why don't you come over and I'll help you forget all about this girl."

Letting out a long exhale, I hung my head and pinched the bridge of my nose. "I'm not interested in getting in your pants."

My dick wasn't going anywhere near her. Not that it agreed.

"I'm not wearing any pants."

Of course she wasn't. "Listen Carissa…"

"Gio," she cut me off. "I know what you're going to say, but… this wouldn't be anything other than one friend helping out another."

That was a PG way of putting things.

"Carissa," I sighed. "It's not a good idea."

"You called me for a reason. I can hear how frustrated you are."

Frustrated didn't even begin to cover it.

My mind was set on murder, all I could see was red and my dick was screaming for release. And not the kind that I could give myself. I could try, but I'd been trying for two months and nothing seemed to satisfy me.

Don't get me wrong I came, but that didn't stop the dark need from crawling up my spine. I was managing it just fine until today. Now that urge was so heavy that I could feel every muscle in my body tense with need.

"Darry will be home soon." That excuse was more for me than her.

"He just took Ezra to his baseball game."

Both Darry and his dad were heavy supporters of his little brother's sport. They'd take him out for ice cream after and maybe a movie. That gave us at least three hours.

"We could just talk?" She suggested.

No we couldn't.

"Come pick me up and we'll go for a ride." When I didn't answer she added, "you sound like you need someone to talk to."

Did I really want to open that door? Then again, talking wasn't so bad. Only two people had seen me cry. Atlas and Carissa. The night he died she didn't say a word. She just held me for hours while I sobbed.

Fuck it.

"Alright, fine." Sucking back a deep breath, I started the ignition and backed out onto the street. "Be outside in five minutes."

This was a bad idea. Every road I turned down, I told myself to go the other way. Right up until the moment I pulled to a stop at the end of her driveway. My hands gripped the steering wheel as I stared through the windshield at Darry's house.

We used to play in the shed to the left. It was our clubhouse. The sign we made out of cardboard and crayons was still hanging on the door. The words were worn off but I could still see them. *'No girls allowed.'*

I needed to get out of here.

My foot just started to lift off the brake when the front door opened and Carissa came out. The second I saw her I knew I fucked up. She was wearing a tight little black dress that barely covered her ass and pushed her tits up, into mouthwatering mounds that had me licking my lips.

She flicked her blonde hair over her shoulder as I tipped my head to the side and ran my eyes down the length of her. The last thing Carissa was dressed for was talking. Not that I gave a shit right now. It took everything I had not to pull my dick out and jerk off right then and there.

I'm here to talk and nothing more.

That was the chant I had running through my head as she skipped up and hopped into the Rover beside me.

She propped one of her legs up on the dash and smiled, "Hi."

I couldn't stop myself from rolling my eyes down her leg to the sweet spot between her thighs. Her position caused the dress to ride up, giving me a perfect view of a pussy I told myself I didn't want to touch, despite my fingers twitching to do just that.

Carissa knew exactly what she was doing. Trickling a coy finger over her knee and down her thigh while singing, "do you like my dress?" in that seductive tone.

No. I fucking hated that dress.

"I like it." My head tipped to the side while her finger grazed closer to her pussy. "But, Dom says it's too small."

I could see where he was coming from. If my wife was prancing around in some shit like that, somebody would end up dead.

"Can we not talk about your fucking husband."

"Okay." She dropped her leg and slid a little closer to me. "What do you want to talk about?"

Anything that would take my mind off the sweet scent of her perfume.

"I see you're still in your uniform." Her palm flattened on my thigh igniting a fire in my veins. "Did you come right from school?"

"No," *Don't fucking touch her. Keep your hands on the wheel Gio.* "I was too pissed off to change."

"Because of Novalee." she sweetly purred while sliding her hand up my leg. "Is she pretty?"

She was fucking gorgeous with an ass that I'd love to spank raw. God damnit, now she was in my head again.

"Can we not talk about her either." I said while gritting my teeth against Carissa's touch.

Her fingers continued inching closer to my dick, making me tighten my hold on the steering wheel. I needed to get control of myself.

Closing my eyes, I rolled my neck and took a deep inhale through my nose.

Not sure why I thought that would help. If anything it made things worse, because all I could see behind my closed lids was the fire burning in Novalee's hazel orbs. She fucking hated me, possibly more than I hated her. Why the fuck did that turn me on?

"You're so tense," Carissa whispered, ticking my ear with her hot breath.

"What happened to just talking?"

Her lips pressed against my neck, "we are talking."

"Doesn't feel like talking."

She hummed and slipped her hand under the waistband of my pants to grab my cock.

"Fuck," I hissed and let out a groan as she began stroking my shaft. "Stop it Carissa."

Her grip tightened, making my head fall back against the seat. I kept telling myself that if I kept my hands on the steering wheel then I wasn't doing anything wrong.

"Do you really want me to stop?"

No.

"Yes."

She laved her tongue up my neck and whispered, "are you sure?"

A half a second later I hauled her on my lap.

I FUCKED HER.

God damnit, I promised myself I wouldn't go down that road again. Darry deserved better. And I couldn't even last five minutes. Yeah, I could blame it on Novalee, but that would be a lie.

It was my decision to go there. No one held a gun to my head. No one forced me to stick my dick in one of my best friend's mothers. That was all me, and it damn sure wasn't going to happen again.

This mistake I could chalk up to a goodbye fuck. I'd go to bed and forget all about it. Tomorrow shit would go back to normal and I could pretend I'd never met Carissa Barone.

The second I opened the door, that plan went out the window.

My brother Romeo was standing on the second floor balcony smoking a cigarette.

He looked down when I walked in the house and blew out a cloud of smoke. "Where were you?"

I dropped my keys in the green bowl on the table next to the door and grumbled, "went for a drive."

What the fuck did he care anyway?

He bent over, rested his arms on the banister and looked down at me, "That was a long drive."

Was he timing me?

"Where'd you go?"

I started walking up the steps and glared at my brother. "Nowhere special."

Aside from the green eyes that Romeo inherited from our mother, we all took after our father. Dark hair and olive complexion. But sometimes when the light hit Romeo in the right angle, I could've sworn I was looking at Atlas. They could've been twins. Romeo even had the same suspicious quirk in his brow.

"That was a long time for nowhere special."

"You said that already."

He shrugged, "I supposed I did."

Why the sudden interest in my life? Growing up, I barely saw him,and now it felt like he wouldn't go away.

I rounded the corner at the top of the stairs and crossed my arms. "What do you want, Romeo?"

My brother didn't do anything without a reason, that much I did know about him. Well that and that he took the oath to join the family at the age of fifteen. I'd be eighteen in a week and my father hadn't so much as mentioned the *Omerta*.

"I'm just checking in on my little brother."

"Go check on someone else." And he could get rid of this Persian rug running down the middle of the hardwood while he was at it. Why did my father insist on keeping it? I fucking hated that thing. Every time I saw it my jaw tightened.

I didn't have many memories of my mother, and the ones I did have kept me up at night. The things that were done to her haunted my dreams. I could hear her scream every time I closed my eyes. And everything that happened to her was done on the twin of this goddamn rug.

The gold, green, and blue swirls entwined in the fabric weren't pretty. They were a fucking nightmare. One, it seemed like I was constantly trying to escape. I blamed my father for that. Who he was, put the target on her back. He should've protected her better.

Atlas's death, that one was on Romeo. He should've been with him that night. I should've been with him.

Romeo straightened up and flicked an ash off his cigarette. "I worry about you Gio."

That made me snort. "Sure you do."

"Carissa Barone is bad news Gio," he pointed the lit end of his cigarette at me. "Stay away from her."

"What?" There was no possible way he could know about that. We were careful. "Are you fucking crazy? Why should I be worried about Darry's mother? She's harmless."

She might be addictive and seductive but she wasn't a threat.

"You're a shitty liar little brother." Romeo kicked off the banister and strutted my way. "I could smell her on you the second you walked through the door."

When he paused and leaned in closer, I had to stop myself from punching him in the face.

"She wore the same perfume for me."

Chapter 10

NOVALEE

Last night wasn't one of my better nights. Maw Maw was stuck in the past when the word bastard was whispered in secret, so it wasn't a huge shocker when she was upset about the whore scrawled across my truck. Ever try to explain something like that to a god fearing Christian woman – it didn't go well.

She didn't buy my story for that, but she did buy the explanation I gave her for the bruises on my neck. Apparently accidentally strangling myself with a scarf was more believable than a gang of misfit sailors vandalizing cars in a school parking lot. Not sure what that said about me. I didn't even own a scarf, but it was a half win, and I'd take it.

Besides, it wasn't like I could say Gio Mancini strangled me. Maw Maw might try to beat him to death with her nine iron – that was her weapon of choice. Then there was Veda. She never did confirm whether or not Atlas was one of the men who attacked her. According to her, she couldn't remember what happened that night.

I called bullshit on that one. We lived in a three bedroom trailer, the walls weren't that thick. I heard her crying in the middle of the night. I used to ask her about it, but she would just say that I was hearing things.

Lying wasn't one of Veda's strong suits. She was that kid who would bust themselves, and say something like 'I didn't eat the cookies' when their parents called them down.

And those skills didn't get any better with age. If anything they got worse. So I knew Veda remembered everything, but I didn't press the issue. It wasn't like it would do any good. Kato was already in prison, and her rape was deemed inadmissible. Pushing her would only make her relive it. And honestly, I wasn't sure I wanted to know what they did to her.

Hence why I refused to bring up Gio's involvement. The last time the name Mancini was mentioned around Veda, she hid in her room for three days. It wasn't worth traumatizing her again because some guy decided to be an asshole in school. I could take care of myself.

At least I thought I could.

I looked through the windshield at the people walking around.

Not nearly as many people ducked for cover this morning when I parked, but I was getting quite a few angry glares. Huh, either my confrontation with Gio Mancini made me popular, or my nemesis had some serious competition.

Grabbing my bag off the passenger seat, I hopped out and headed for the school.

There were a few whispers and a couple of finger points as I passed people, but nothing too bad. I know I didn't have a sock stuck to my ass, and I took the time to put on some make-up and do something with my hair. Maybe it was my normalcy that was throwing them off.

It threw me off, but I needed to look half decent when I saw Gio in the halls. Telling me not to come back, as if I had a choice in the matter.

Maw Maw would kick my ass and I was more afraid of her than I was him. Plus, I'd been practicing my *'awe did the baby lose his bottle'* look all night. It was a hard expression to pull off. There had to be the right amount of condescending with just a touch of fuck all the way off. And let me just say, I had that look down pat.

No one was going to rattle me.

Or so I thought until I saw Memphis waiting at my locker, which had the same word written across it as my truck. Misspelled and everything. Well at least my hater was consistent.

"Hey," Memphis grimaced as I sighed and stuck my hand in my bag. "I tried to wash it off…"

"Don't wash it off," I said while walking up to add the w. "They need to see their mistake."

There was someone wandering around this school who thought that hore was the proper spelling. Didn't say much about the educational abilities of this institution. A fact that someone needed to point out. I had better things to do than waste my time correcting shit. I didn't know what those better things were yet, but something would come up.

"I don't know who did it…"

I waved Memphis off dismissively, "It doesn't matter."

I was just going to assume it was my nemesis. She came in here all mad because I made her dive in a bush and took it out on my locker. God I hoped she had an evil laugh, that would be awesome. I should probably find out her name. Bush girl didn't sound quite right.

Memphis crossed his arms and leaned against the locker next to mine. "You're oddly put together this morning."

I shrugged, "I found my brush." And curling iron.

His eyes narrowed, "What are you up to?"

"Why would I be…" My words were cut off when I opened my locker and a bunch of boxes fell out, clinking off the floor.

Memphis immediately started scolding the people laughing around us while I picked up one of the boxes still in my locker. *Miss. Suzie's edible panties.* Well, every whore needed their tools I guess. And it was cherry flavor. Couldn't ignore the irony in that one, though… "Some condoms would've been nice!"

Whores needed to practice safe sex too. What the hell was I supposed to do with a bunch of edible underwear?

My brow rose. *They are edible…*

Quickly stuffing the box in my bag, I grabbed my books and closed my locker.

When I turned around Memphis cocked a brow. "What are you doing?"

Did I have to explain everything?

"Since fire swallower isn't a good career choice," Still mad at Maw Maw about that one. Way to crush an eight-year-old's dreams. "I'm going to school. And one needs books for school."

"Books yes," he agreed. "Edible underwear no."

I rolled my eyes. "Well, I can't let them go to waste, that would just be rude."

"They aren't a snack that you carry around Nova."

No sooner had those words left his mouth than someone nearby coughed out, "Eat your breakfast whore."

"See, he gets it." I said while scanning the crowd for the insult cougher.

He could be the vandal, in which case he was in desperate need of some spelling lessons.

"The only thing anyone around here gets, is that Gio Mancini hates you." Memphis gave my shoulder a squeeze. "That's not good Nova."

"Thanks for the update." As if I needed one. I was well aware of how Gio Mancini felt about me. Our hatred was mutual.

Memphis pulled me down the hall and muttered, "We need to do something about this."

That was almost funny.

"What would you like to do, Memphis? Kiss his feet?" Asshole would probably like that. "Somehow I don't think saying sorry my brother beat yours to death will help."

Not to mention I didn't want to. I was proud of what Kato did. He was protecting our sister. I only wish I'd been there to see it.

"I know you, Nova."

No, he didn't.

"Don't poke the bear."

Okay, maybe he did.

"Listen, you really need to make up your mind. Yesterday he was a wolf, today he's a bear." There was a vast difference between those two animals.

"It's called a metaphor."

"Well stick to one metaphor," I can't have all these animals running around in my head, on top of trying to correct people's spelling. That was way more work than I cared to put in.

Memphis shot me a dirty look before continuing to lead me around a corner.

The entire time I walked with him I couldn't help but wonder what he was attempting to do. Anytime someone would step in front of us, he would puff his chest out like he was getting ready to block an incoming attack.

Considering I was only five feet and could easily take him down, I wasn't sure what he thought he would block. A ten year old? Rogue banana peel maybe?

I'd seen Memphis lose his footing in the wind. How we made it to my class without him tripping over something was beyond me. The trashcan I knocked over definitely should've got him. It was sickening how nimble he was.

Thankfully my annoying best friend didn't insist on walking

me right into class – he had his own to get to – and I was more than happy to be left alone. Until I opened the door and walked inside.

Guess who was in my first class?

When I said I couldn't wait to see the look on Gio Mancini's face, that didn't mean I wanted it to be this early. My brain was barely awake let alone functional enough to deal with the murderous glare he was throwing my way. And the only available seat was in front of Atlee and right next to him.

Fantastic.

Maw Maw better appreciate these advanced calculus classes.

Ever have that moment when your walking somewhere and theme music starts playing in the back of your head? Well, that's where I was. Except it wasn't some mission impossible spy song. It was death bells that rang with every step I took.

Bong...

He's going to kill you.

Bong...

And eat your heart.

Bong...

Then laugh while you choke on your own blood.

Holding my head high, I made my way down the aisle while trying to ignore the dark glare burning a hole in my skull. Suddenly being a school dropout didn't seem like a bad thing. Plenty of people made their way through life without a diploma.

The shadows on Gio's face were almost as intimidating as the deep tone of his voice, "I thought I told you not to come back."

"Yeah well, unfortunately the truant officer didn't agree with my plans of educational abandonment..." Avoiding his gaze, I quickly slid into the chair. "So, here I am."

It was official. The universe hated me.

Atlee leaned over his desk and sang, "Good morning, Nova."

I didn't need to turn around to see the stupid grin on his face.

"It's Novalee to you." Only my friends and family called me Nova, and he was neither.

"Oh, but I like Nova. It rolls off the tongue." He teased. "Is little Nova upset? Did Nova have a bad morning? Maybe Nova just needs to get fucked."

Why did I ever tell him my name? Don't get me wrong, seeing that girl get slapped was kind of amusing, but the payout, so wasn't worth it.

"No one would fuck her." Gio grumbled.

Oh, fuck him.

"Haven't you heard? I'm a whore." I tipped my chin to roll my eyes over my shoulder towards Atlee. "H O R E."

Why did that bother me so much?

Atlee's brows knit. "That's not how you spell whore."

Thank you.

Now if he could tell that to the uneducated vandal that would be great.

"Let me ask you something, *Nova*," Gio made sure to accentuate the shortening of my name. "Do you want to die?"

Maybe?

"I'm not sure you want to do that. There's an awful lot of witnesses," I looked him right in the eyes and added, "That didn't work out so well for my brother."

Gio didn't like that. A shiver raced up my spine as his expression darkened.

"You don't want to play with me, little girl."

There were those moments in life when the little voice in the back of someone's head told them to shut up. I think mine was broken. "Maybe I do."

Gio's jaw twitched while Atlee snickered, "You're going to regret that."

Oh, please. I had a list of regrets a mile long. This wasn't even in the top fifty. Though I was getting increasingly uncomfortable sitting next to someone who wanted to rip my head off. And probably could with very little effort. Gio's forearms were thicker than my thighs. He may be bigger, stronger and better looking than me, but there was one thing I could do better.

I tipped my head and gave Gio the look I'd been practicing.

To say it didn't go as planned would be a huge understatement. The intensity of his green stare threw me off, turning the condescending part of my expression into one of shock. And the my 'don't give a fuck', suddenly gave all the fucks.

I think I even hiccupped at one point. And my colossal failure didn't end there.

Confusion etched lines across Gio's forehead while Atlee put his hand on my shoulder. "Are you having a seizure?"

Jerking his hand off my shoulder, I hissed, "No, I'm not having a seizure."

I just sucked at expressing myself.

"Are you sure?" Atlee asked. "Because I know sometimes people don't know they're having one."

Oh, my god. "I am not having a seizure!"

The entire class quieted and turned to look at me, causing a trail of mortification to burn its way down my neck.

Bravo, Nova, Bravo.

"Awe, look, she's blushing." Atlee sang in the most condescending tone I'd ever heard. "Are you gonna cry next?"

"No," I sneered back. "I did that last night."

What else was one supposed to do when listening to *Total Eclipse Of The Heart.*

"Wish I'd seen that." Gio muttered.

Atlee's snide comments I could handle. Gio's bothered me. I don't know why, but I wanted to jump up and smack him every time he opened his mouth, while simultaneously hiding from that glint in his eye.

It was a very confusing feeling.

Thankfully the bell rang and the teacher came in, so I could concentrate on something else. Or so I thought.

Ever try to pay attention to calculus while someone was silently murdering you? It's not an easy task to accomplish. Every scratch on the chalkboard or word spoken were muffled. Seconds ticked by like hours, and I swore I could hear Gio breathing.

He wanted a reaction, I knew that. Just like I knew I couldn't give him one. But, eventually I broke and softly snarled, "Do you mind?"

"Yes, I do," He shot back. "Get the fuck out of my school."

"It's not your school." He didn't own St. Agatha's.

He leaned over and whispered, "I'm going to make your life a living hell."

Oh, that was it.

"First off, my life is already a living hell, so good luck with that, and secondly… I hate you."

Take that.

Gio snorted and shook his head, "You don't know what hate means."

"Are you always this arrogant?"

I must've said that a little too loud because the teacher was no longer talking to the entire class.

"Are we interrupting you Miss. Ford?"

He knew my name on day two, that was impressive.

"Sorry sir, I was just telling Gio how inappropriate it was to talk about edible underwear during class."

Gio's eyes locked on mine as the teacher called out, "I believe you know where the office is Mr. Mancini?"

Check asshole.

He didn't say a word, just glared at me and packed up his books. I couldn't help but smile as he stood up and paused to look down at me.

"You're fucking dead."

Chapter 11

NOVALEE

Apparently being hated by Gio Mancini made one popular, and not in a good way. I'd been tripped, had my books slapped out of my hand, and been called names. But my favorite was when demon Barbie *'accidentally'* spilled her coffee on me. That was definitely the icing on a shit storm cake.

Not only did I have a skinned knee and the messiest messy bun on the planet, but there was a big stain on my white shirt – which Maw Maw was going to love. She took personal offence to a stain, like it was there to test her capabilities.

That was one battle she never lost. I had yet to see a stain beat her determination. And to top it all off, I still hadn't figured out the identity of the mispeller, which bothered me more than the assholes walking around this place.

I'd even enlisted Memphis in my search. Of course he thought we were looking for some revenge. And while that was important, it was more important that this guy learned how to spell that word properly.

What if he wanted to send his bitch boss an email later in life? Or what if his wife cheated on him? It wouldn't be a very good fuck off note if half the words were spelt wrong. And yes I was sure it was a guy. A girl would've used something like slut or bitch. Women were evil. Especially to each other.

By the time lunch came I'd come to three conclusions. Hore man was a master at hiding. One should never wear something colorful under a white shirt—a good portion of my English class got to see the smiley faces on my bra. And, this might actually be Gio Mancini's school.

The student body was like a parasite that fed off of his emotions. Pretty sure I was the most hated girl in school. Even Chuck was hesitant to sit with me at lunch.

Memphis was not happy about his boyfriend's reaction, but I got it. Chuck was only trying to protect him. My best friend had a lot of bark with absolutely no ability to bite.

Don't get me wrong, Memphis could act tough and bare his teeth with the best of them. But when push came to shove, he'd just end up getting hurt, which neither Chuck nor I wanted. That didn't stop Memphis from arguing about it.

He and Chuck were in the midst of a fight when I left them in the cafeteria. After all the crap I'd pulled, it took someone else's hatred of me to break the couple's sweetness streak. That was kind of a disappointment, but I was still going to consider it a win. They were arguing about me after all, and that's all I wanted. They were too perfect.

I looked up at the crucifix hanging on the door.

So why did I feel bad about it?

That was almost as confusing as why I was standing outside the chapel. I had no idea how I wound up here. All I was doing was looking for a quiet place to eat and somehow found myself here.

There were worse places to seek refuge I suppose. Like the guys locker room. I made that mistake last year. The smell of sweat and dirty socks followed me around for a week and I was only in there for five minutes.

Still, there was something more appealing about that than eating in a chapel. What was this? Lunch hour with the Lord? Thy kingdom come, your torment will be undone? Hide in thy loving arms and rejoice in the fruit of the cafeteria.

Maybe I could get my ham sandwich blessed, though that might burn going down. Honestly, I was surprised every Sunday when we walked into church and I didn't combust. Come to think of it, eating in the chapel probably wasn't the best idea.

My eyes rolled down the hallway, I could hear voices. Someone was coming. The cross on the door didn't look so intimidating now.

Screw it. I was already here.

Shrugging I pushed open the door and walked in. *Time to get my sandwich on with God.*

The first thing I noticed was how well this room was taken care of. The small church Maw Maw dragged us too had cracks in the walls, shingles falling off the roof, and two broken pews. That wasn't the case here.

There were no cracks in each dark wooden bench and they were freshly waxed, I could smell it in the air. Just like I could smell the cleaner obviously used on the floors and stained glass windows. They were so polished that I could see the various angel images depicted in each pane of glass.

What kind of bullshit was that? Our church had one with the archangel Michael and his sword. The sword was all flaming while his avenging wings were spread out. I loved that thing, then someone threw a baseball through it. That one was on Father John though, I clearly warned him against having me play any kind of sport.

I wasn't the team player type. I wasn't even the player type.

Then again, I didn't consider myself religious either. Yet here I was, hiding from people in a chapel. Talk about tides changing.

"Hello."

"Shit," I screeched and jumped back, causing my food to fly everywhere.

Apparently my situational awareness sucked. Otherwise I would've noticed the small blonde girl sitting in the pew I was standing next to. Literally. She was right there, so close I'd barely have to lift my hand to touch her.

While I didn't notice her, my food sure did. Half of me wanted to laugh at the pile of lettuce sitting on the top of her head like a tiny wig, and the other half of me couldn't help but think of the coffee stain on my shirt and the grief I got over it.

People called me coffee girl, trailer trash, smiley boobs and Jennifer – though I think that one was a case of mistaken identity. I didn't want this girl to receive the same treatment.

Damnit, stupid guilt.

"I'm sorry," I reached out to sweep the lettuce off her head. "I didn't see you there."

"It's okay," She picked a piece of ham off her cheek and held it out like it was covered in the plague. "Accidents happen."

Was it an accident though? I kind of wanted to do it again. There was something about this girl… she was almost too proper. Her part was completely straight without a hair out of place, not even under the black headband that was centered on the top of her head.

The uniform she was wearing didn't have a single wrinkle, and her Maryjane shoes were clean and shiny. Even her white knee high socks were spotless, aside from a few pieces of sandwich that is.

I stood there, watching her brush her clothes clean and tipped my head. This girl seemed well put together. Why was she in here?

"Are you hiding from assholes too?"

Her bright blue eyes snapped up to mine, "You shouldn't cuss in the house of the Lord."

"Uh huh?" House of the Lord? Did Maw Maw have a secret grandchild I didn't know about?

"This is a sanctuary of worship and righteousness, that shouldn't be tainted by foul language."

Where had I heard that before? Oh, right, Maw Maw. She was a big fan of the no cussing lifestyle too. I wondered if this girl would be as easy to change the subject with as Maw Maw.

Only one way to find out.

I held out my hand, "I'm Nova by the way."

If I had a secret cousin I may as well get to know her. Besides, it wasn't like I had many friends here, so I couldn't be too picky. Who was I going to get drunk at parties with when Memphis was busy with Chuck?

She gave my hand a firm shake. "Sutton Alice Barlow."

Her full name, okay, so maybe I wouldn't be getting drunk with her. She did seem nice though.

"Did you come to pray too?"

She came in here to pray? On a weekday, in the afternoon? Who was this girl? Seriously. Maw Maw was the only person I knew who did stuff like that. Or who referred to chapels as houses of the Lord.

The secret grandchild theory was starting to become less of a theory and more of a fact. She looked nothing like Maw Maw, but still…

"Um… No? It's more of a hiding thing."

"Oh," she seemed oddly disappointed.

"Is that why you're here?" Why did I ask that? I didn't care, nor did I want to get pulled into a religious conversation. However, it was still a conversation, and beggars couldn't be choosers.

"Yes" Her gaze narrowed. "You can make fun of me now."

My heart went out to her. Obviously this girl had some experience being picked on. I could relate to that.

I stepped into the pew and sat down beside her. "Why would I make fun of you?"

Sure she was proper, and maybe a little stuck up, but she hadn't been mean. That was more than I could say for anyone else in this place.

Sutton sighed and lifted her gaze to a large crucifix on the wall behind an altar, "Some people think I take my relationship with God too seriously."

"At least you have a relationship," I snickered. "The last one I had ended because he…"

I choked back the words, 'got his dick sucked' – pretty sure Miss. House of the Lord wouldn't like hearing that – and turned my stare to the same spot Sutton was looking.

It was a nice crucifix. Silver with some extra attention to detail, like the thorns in the crown on his head, and wrinkles in the cloth around his waist. They could've done more with his eyes though. That shit looked painful, not peaceful.

Why did churches always do that? Everyone knew the story of Jesus and what happened to him. One would think a tear rolling down his cheek or grimace on his face would be a little more believable.

Sutton whispered, "Jesus hears everything."

Well, he was right there, kind of. In fake form.

"You could ask him for guidance?" the way she looked at me it was like she discovered the secret to the universe.

"Yeah, I don't think Jesus can help with Gio Mancini."

The devil may be an option. At least he could understand Gio. They were both giant evil assholes. I should totally join a satanic cult. Chant in the dark while I danced naked in the moonlight and waited for the Kool-Aid to be served. Now there was a story to tell the grandkids.

At the mention of Gio's name, Sutton's eyes went wide, "You're the girl everyone's been talking about."

"No," I shook my head. That couldn't possibly be me. I got talked at a lot, and tripped, and a couple people threw things at me. But no one was talking about me.

"Yes you are," She insisted. "You're the girl with the sock on her butt."

Oh, "Yeah that was me."

Well, I guess it was better than whore. H O R E. I really needed to find that guy.

Sutton leaned back and gave me a once over. "I thought you'd be taller."

"So did I," I snorted.

Veda had three inches on me, Kato was over six foot, and I was stuck at five foot even like our mom. She was kind enough to give me her freckles too, which were the only part of me that tanned.

Thanks mom.

"You just started yesterday. Why does Gio dislike you so much?" Sutton asked.

"It's just this little thing… with his brother and mine."

How else was I supposed to answer that? Most people didn't take too kindly to the relatives of murderers, regardless of why said murder occurred. It was nice to have someone other than Memphis, even if she was a house of the Lord kind of girl.

"I wouldn't worry about it," Sutton waved her hand dismissively. "Gio and Romeo aren't that close."

"Ah," I breathed, then asked, "who's Romeo?"

"Gio's brother."

He had another brother? Awesome. More Mancini's in the world. Just what I needed.

"Does he go here too?" It never hurt to know one's enemies, and maybe Gio's brother was the elusive mispeller.

"No," Sutton's nose scrunched up, "Romeo is old, he's like twenty-four or something."

If she said that shit around Maw Maw she'd get backhanded.

"If you weren't talking about Romeo, then you must've meant Atlas. How did you know him?" She seemed genuinely curious about that one.

"I don't." Technically I never met the guy.

"But your brother did?"

"Kind of."

Her brows knit, "Why don't you ask your brother for help with Gio?"

"He can't do anything."

"Why not?"

"Umm," I hummed, "he's in jail.

Now she was really interested.

Sutton shifted in the pew so her entire body was facing me.

Maybe she thought she could save his soul or something. She seemed like the kind of person who would get pumped about something like that.

"What did he do?"

"Oh, um…" I rubbed my hand down the back of my neck and softly said, "he kind of murdered Atlas Mancini."

Just when I didn't think her eyes could get any wider, those blue orbs rounded to the size of saucers. "He killed him?"

"Little bit." I nodded.

Kato had good reason, not that I could tell her that. What happened to Veda was nobody's business. Talking about it only made me feel like I was re victimizing her. My sister shouldn't be defined by the horrible thing that happened to her. I didn't want her to be the girl that had her rapist' baby, and I sure as hell wasn't going to contribute to that name tag.

I kept waiting for Sutton to get mad, or slap me and join in with the rest of the hate Nova crowd. But she didn't.

The only thing she did was turn back to the crucifix and say, "I hope your brother finds salvation."

It was weird not being judged, yet being judged. I didn't quite know how to take that. Did I say thank you? Did I get up and storm out, or hug her? I was so confused. Unfortunately I didn't get the chance to do anything.

The door swung open before a single word could leave my mouth.

My heart dropped the second I turned around. Strutting in the chapel were Atlee, his friend Darry I think, and in the lead was Gio. I didn't need to read the smirk on Atlee's face to know that this wasn't a friendly meeting. The dark intent was written all over Gio's face.

His eyes locked on mine, causing a lump to form in my throat. "Did you think you could hide from me?"

That was the intention.

"I don't know if you know this but you're on holy ground." I rested my elbow on the back of the pew and dropped my chin into my palm. "You might want to leave before you catch fire or something."

"I hope you enjoyed your little victory…"

I did. I really, really did.

"Because you're about to regret it."

"You listen here Gio Mancini," Sutton stood up and waved her finger, "this is the house of the Lord and you will not pick on anyone in this sanctimonious place."

I didn't know if she was brave or stupid. If I had to pick one I'd say stupid. Gio was huge, his friends were huge, and all their egos were huge. Sutton was the same size as me. This was like an ant telling the cat to fuck off. It just didn't work.

Proof of which came when Atlee's lips curled. "Well, if it isn't St. Agatha's self-appointed preacher. Who are you trying to save today, Sutton?"

"You should take a good look at yourself, Atlee Fiore," Sutton's eyes narrowed into slits. "God will judge you in the afterlife."

Atlee shot her a wink, that was way too seductive for this scenario, "Don't worry Powder Puff, I already know I'm damned."

As much as I would've loved to sit back and enjoy the show – who didn't like a good girl, bad boy argument – Gio wasn't letting that happen.

He walked up next to me and slammed his hands down. One on the pew in front of me and the other on the back of the one I was sitting in, effectively caging Sutton and I in.

"You made a mistake coming back here."

"This is my first time in here. So *technically*," I rolled my eyes, "I can't come back until I leave."

Was that the best thing to say when staring into the face of death? Probably not, but self-preservation was overrated.

Gio's jade eyes darkened while I sucked in a breath and prepared to meet my maker.

At least I was in the place to do such a thing. Didn't get much closer to the afterlife than a chapel. What I didn't count on was Sutton and her fiery ways. Or should I say insanity.

A crazy little ball of righteousness and fury jumped up on the pew, then threw her hand out, smacking Gio across the face. "Leave her alone."

I heard the slap resound through the room, and watched as seconds ticked by morphing the golden flecks in Gio's eyes into something angry and sinister. If I had to guess what the reaper's face looked like then I'd say I was currently staring at it. I could smell death seeping in the air. And it wasn't my end that was coming.

It was Sutton's.

This girl barely knew me. And what she did know was that my brother was a murderer. For all she knew my whole family could be killers. Maybe we had bloodlust and sacrificed things to our dark god. And yet, she stuck up for me. Clearly she wasn't the brave part of the stupid or brave question.

Unfortunately, neither was I.

Gio opened his mouth, growled out, "You little..." and was cut off as my hand smacked across his cheek.

And now, we were both dead.

There was a second of silence wrapped up in shock, where neither Gio or I could believe I just struck him.

Then he lunged and I swerved.

You know those action movies where the hero ducks under a bullet, does this cool roll, then pops up on the other side unscathed? Yeah, that's not what I did.

I jumped up, smacked the top of my head off the underside of Gio's chin. That knocked me back onto the pew, which I promptly fell off of, and landed face first on the ground with my left leg still propped up on the bench. Apparently grace was not one of my strong suits either.

To make matters worse, little Miss House of the Lord leapt over the back of the bench and landed on her feet like a cat.

I knew this because I saw her Mary-Jane shoes perfectly touch down from my view of under the pew. By the way, this place wasn't as clean as I thought. There were some serious dust bunnies under here.

This day officially sucked. My face hurt, the muscle on the inside of my thigh was being stretched, and I could hear someone laughing. Atlee would be my guess. And did I move from my precarious position? No. I was too busy realizing that pain was a universal language to every muscle, including the one's I didn't know I had.

I couldn't even kick my leg when I felt a hand wrap around my ankle and pull me out. I just laid there letting my cheek drag across the floor, while I silently groaned at the relief from not having my leg propped up in a strenuous way.

I didn't snap back into reality until I heard Sutton's cute little snarls, followed by Gio growling, "Do something about that."

My free foot shot out, kicking him in the shin – which felt like it was made out of steel – but it did the trick. Gio's grip loosened enough for me to rip my ankle out and scurry away.

Or at least try to scurry away. When one was crawling on their belly, one was not too fast.

I made it maybe a foot before I was picked up by the back of my neck. That's when I saw Sutton slung over Atlee's shoulder. And she was putting up a better fight than I was.

Every time I'd throw my arm back, or try to jerk, Gio's fingers would dig in, sending a sharp stab down the side of my neck.

I was trapped and after Darry and Atlee left with Sutton still slung over his shoulder, I was alone. Completely and utterly alone, with no one but the devil to keep me company.

"Tell me something, Nova," Gio leaned in, bringing his lips to my ear. "How would you like to die?"

In my sleep seemed like a peaceful way to go, but if I had an option I'd prefer not to die.

"I'm not sorry for what my brother did."

Apparently not dying wasn't an option.

"You will be." Gio hissed, while digging his fingers in my flesh.

This wasn't a warning like the other day, he was trying to strangle me. And it was working.

I choked and struggled to suck in a breath while reaching back to claw at his arm. Just when blackness was starting to seep into my vision, another voice hit my ears.

"What's going on in here?"

Gio let go, dropping me on the floor where I greedily coughed oxygen back into my lungs. When my vision cleared I could see that Sister Mary of the hallway was standing by the doors with her arms crossed.

"Did he hurt you?"

I looked at her then back at Gio and shook my head. "No."

She cocked a brow, "Don't lie to me child, I know what I saw."

The muscle in Gio's jaw was tensing. It would be so easy to turn him in. He might even end up doing some time for assault. But there was a sad spark on his face that I recognized. My family wasn't the only one that had been destroyed. He lost someone too and I could understand that.

"I tripped and fell, Gio caught me before I landed on the floor." I looked back at Sister Mary of the hallway. "He didn't hurt me, he was helping."

Chapter 12

When this day started I did not see it ending with me parked in a batch of cypress trees across from a trailer park. Yet here I was, staring at the trailer Nova's truck was parked in front of.

I spent my entire life in this city and not once had I heard the name Sault Saint Marie Estates. And now, it was permanently ingrained in the back of my head. Like a big neon sign pointing to a bullseye.

This shitty yellow trailer was where she lived.

Various questions flowed through my mind as I stared at the white screen door Nova disappeared into. What was she doing in there? Was her room one of the windows I could see, or was it around back? And most importantly, was Nova as nonchalant in private?

At school she acted like she gave no fucks, but everyone cared about something. I just had to find that pressure point. Her brother maybe?

"Sister Anne did not appreciate me toting around her little pet project." Atlee leaned back and kicked his feet up on the dash.

An act that normally would result in my fist meeting his face – I kept my shit clean – but today the dirt on Atlee's black Adidas was the least of my worries.

"Fucking Sutton Barlow." He shook his head. "Someone needs to give that girl a good dicking, or slap some sense into her. Could always do both. I can't imagine she'd be that much fun to fuck unless you made her scream a little."

That was comical.

"That girl isn't fucking anyone." If there was a picture beside virgin in the dictionary, it would be of Sutton Barlow.

"You can say that again." Atlee huffed out a snort. "I wouldn't touch her with your dick."

"Stay away from my dick." I leaned in closer to the windshield and eyed the lush green grass in Nova's front yard.

The place appeared well taken care of. It was clean and orderly, but way too colorful in my opinion. Who had that many gnomes? Was it some kind of fucked up collection? There were way too many for a yard that small. Unless they served another purpose? I didn't trust anything the Fords' did.

"She's constantly walking around saying, Jesus this and God that..."

There wasn't anything special or out of the ordinary about the trailer, other than the yard decorations that is. Then again, there was something off with the fence? The white pointed sticks were too shiny to be wood, but not shiny enough for metal.

Plastic maybe?

"Yip, yip, yip," Atlee continued. "Shut the fuck up, bitch. Oh! Then Sister Anne came around the corner..."

It was plastic! Who the fuck would put something like that up? It didn't cost much for wood, nor was it hard to build. Just stick some pegs in the ground and paint that shit. And why the smiling sun flag? What was the point of that? Were they trying to announce some bullshit like 'here lives the happiest people on the fucking planet'?

That was some fucked up deceiving crap right there. They were responsible for my brother's death. Why the fuck should they be happy?

"And I was like," Atlee grabbed his crotch and cupped his balls through his pants. "Suck it, bitch."

"No, you weren't."

"No, I wasn't," he sighed then quickly added, "But I could've."

No he couldn't. Atlee's dad would be less than impressed if he got a call from the school. There was a reason Kendall was a role model student. As far as the public was concerned anyway. She was still a bitch, she just got other people to do her dirty work.

Then there was his baby sister. All she had to do to get shipped off to boarding school was smile the wrong way at a guy. Mind you Alex had always been a bit of a problem. So that one I kind of understood.

"Now I have detention for a month. Fucking bitch. I'll pay Sutton back for that." Atlee turned his stare my way. "How about you?"

"What about me?" My brow arched as some guy stepped out of the trailer next to Nova's.

What the hell?

If crazy had a look then I was staring at it right now. This guy was some kind of mix between mad scientist and trailer trash. His dark hair stood on end while the stained tank-top and tighty whities were clearly visible underneath his open raggedy green bathrobe. Then there was the broom in his hand that he was brandishing like a weapon.

"How much time did you get?"

"For what?" I asked as the guy wildly swung his broom through the air and screamed something incoherent.

What the actual fuck?

"Of course you didn't get in trouble." Atlee flopped his head back and muttered, "I told you Sister Anne didn't like me."

That was never an argument. I don't think any of the staff at St Agatha's liked him. Atlee had a talent for pissing people off. That didn't stop him from complaining about it. According to him, they had it out for him and loved us. Never mind the fact that we didn't do stupid shit publicly, like slapping some bitch in the middle of class.

"It's not because of that."

"Yes it is," Atlee snorted. "Otherwise I'd have a detention buddy."

There was only one reason I didn't get in shit, "Nova covered for me."

"I'm sorry," he sat up and turned my way. "Did you just say Nova covered for you?"

"Yup." I sighed.

"Nova Ford, the girl who you've strangled twice in two days, covered for you?"

Did I stutter? "That's what I said."

He shook his head and held up a finger. "So you're telling me that Novalee Ford, the sister of the asshole who offed your brother… covered for you?"

I didn't need the reminder of who she was, but, "yes."

"Huh?" His eyes rolled over to Nova's beat up truck. "That doesn't make sense."

Tell me about it.

"Why would she do that?"

That was a good question. "I don't know."

My eyes narrowed on the screen door. But I intended to find out.

Nova had the perfect opportunity to get rid of me. One word about what was really happening in the chapel, and I'd have been catapulted straight past suspension and into expulsion. Not only that but Sister Anne would've called the cops.

My dad would've loved that. I could already hear the *'you know better'* lecture, which I wouldn't have an argument with. Because I did know better. Don't do shit in a place with witnesses. It made clean up a hassle. Yet there I was, in the school chapel choking the shit out of Novalee Ford.

I would've killed her, if we weren't interrupted. I wanted to kill her. It was the only thing I could think about while my hands were around her neck. She knew it, too.

There was this look people got when they were about to die. A spark of acceptance that mingled with the horror and desperation on their face. When Nova looked up at me, face red and struggling for breath, I saw that spark.

So why the fuck didn't she say anything? Did she think that would win some kind of favor or brownie points with me? Because it didn't. I still fucking hated her. But I did want to know what her game was.

"Well," Atlee sighed, "that explains your sudden interest in stalking the girl."

Who was stalking? "We just followed her home."

That was all.

Nova was the sister of my enemy, and information was power. For instance, I now knew where Kato's family lived. Sure my father probably had all of that in a file somewhere, but I was collecting first hand knowledge. Like how many gnomes were in the yard, and how they'd probably been collected over a number of years.

Based on the faded colors, I'd say the one with the rainbow hat was the oldest. That wasn't necessarily an important detail, but then again it might be.

"We just followed her home?" Atlee asked.

To which I nodded, "that's right."

"Is that why we're parked in the trees?"

I shrugged, "It was the only place."

"The only place?"

"Yes, Atlee, it was the only place." Just because it was a bit of a bumpy ride weaving through trees, didn't mean anything. "Not all roads are paved."

He leaned forward to look past me and eyed the Spanish moss covering my window like a curtain. "I'm pretty sure this isn't a road."

Everything was a road so long as one could drive on it.

"We fit in here, didn't we?" The arch in Atlee's brow deepened, making me roll my eyes, "Fine, we're stalking her. Happy?"

"Yes," he nodded. "Now that I know what we're doing, I can help."

"Sure," I snorted.

What was he going to do? Pull out a pair of night vision goggles and some camouflage?

"Lucky for you," Atlee twisted and reached into the backseat. "I'm always prepared."

What the hell was this, the boy scouts? The only thing Atlee Fiore was prepared for was his next line up of pussy.

My mouth fell open when he sat back down in the passenger seat and held a pair of black binoculars up to his eyes.

"Alright, let's see what Nova is up to."

"Why do you have binoculars?"

Still looking through the lenses, he muttered, "Why don't you?"

"Because I'm normal." What did he do, walk around with a stalkers kit just in case? And what else did he have in that bag?

"Well Mr. Normal, you sit over there and see what you can figure out from the yard, I'm gonna take a look inside."

I didn't know if I should slap him, or kiss him.

"Huh," he grunted. "Her sister's got a nice ass."

Slap him it is.

I tore the binoculars out of his grip, "Give me those."

"Those are my binoculars." He scowled back at me.

"Yeah, well this is my stalking." Henceforth I should be the one to have a look inside.

"It's not my fault…" Atlee was cut off by a loud clanging.

We both turned to see Nova's crazy neighbor beating the shit out of a trash can. And I meant beating the shit out of. He was whacking that thing so hard I could feel the metal denting.

What in the hell was happening in this place?

"Maybe he doesn't like garbage?" Atlee suggested.

I opened my mouth, then shut it again when the crazy fucker smacked his broom down on the ground, hard. He did it a couple of more times, then ran to the back yard screaming something about bandits.

Neither one of us knew what to say, nor did we notice when the screen door on Nova's trailer opened. The racoon jumping up on the fence had our full attention. Funny thing was, I could've sworn the animal flipped him off before it ran away.

"Hey," Atlee slapped my chest and nodded out the windshield. "There's your girl."

"She's not my…" the last word lodged in my throat the second my eyes locked on the target.

Nova was strutting down the patio steps with her hazelnut hair piled on the top of her head. There was something about a messy bun that got to guys, but it was the dress she was wearing that rendered me speechless.

The teal button up fabric was more along the lines of a uniform, but it hugged her curves perfectly. Every step she took caused the skirt to mold up against her ass. It was a far cry from the mess I'd seen at school. She even had a touch of makeup on her face.

"I'd fuck her."

My eyes snapped over to Atlee. "Don't even think about it."

Not sure why I said that. Atlee was a walking hard on. I'd be more surprised if he had no interest in a girl. Yet for some reason my fists tightened around the steering wheel.

"My bad," he flattened his palm on his chest. "I didn't know you wanted to fuck her."

"I don't want to fuck her!"

Atlee gave me an exaggerated eye roll and sang, "whatever you say, Mr. Normal."

I don't know what he found so hard to believe about that statement. Sure, Nova might've gotten me hard a couple of times. So what? That didn't mean shit. Had I thought about what she would look like bent over with a red ass, maybe. But I also had fantasies about Snow White. That didn't mean I was sitting in my room at night jerking off to cartoons.

"Darry said he'd fuck her."

Good for Darry.

"The football team was talking about her today…"

Was there a point to this?

"Glen Ferguson said he'd…"

"I don't give a shit," I growled.

Jesus fucking Christ would he drop it already.

"I'm just pointing out that there are people interested." I damn near clocked him when he laid his hand on my shoulder. "No one would blame you for wanting a piece."

"No one is fucking her!"

The only interest I had in Novalee Ford was the suffering she would face before her inevitable end.

Atlee shot me a look, "Look at that shit, Gio."

Oh I was. Little Miss Nova wasn't having a good day. Based on the scowl on her face when she hopped back out of her truck, I'd say she couldn't get it to start. Good. I hoped her day continued to get worse.

"You can't tell me you don't want a taste of that."

I shook my head, "Not a chance."

Nothing made me eat my words faster than when Nova climbed up on her front bumper and bent over to inspect the engine. That movement caused the skirt of her dress to ride up just under the bottom of her ass. And the more she moved the more flashes I got. I didn't think cookie monster panties could be so hot.

Maybe a taste wouldn't be so bad?

"Damnit," Atlee muttered while shifting in his seat. "Now I'm gonna be hard when I think of Sesame Street."

What? "Since when do you think of Sesame Street?"

We hadn't seen that show since we were kids, and even then it was sparse. Then again who knew what the fuck went through Atlee's head.

"Well, I sure as hell am going to be thinking about it when I jerk off tonight."

Asshole.

I turned my attention back to Nova just as her arm swung back with what looked like a wrench fisted in her hand. My first thought was that she needed to tighten a bolt or something, but nope. Apparently she needed to beat the fuck out of her engine. Was this some kind of ongoing theme for Sault Saint Marie Estates?

"What in the hell is she doing?" Atlee asked as she brought the wrench down again and again. "Oh God, make her stop."

I would if I could. This shit was painful to watch.

"That's not how you fix a car!" Atlee yelled loud enough to make Nova pause and look around.

Even if I did agree with him, did he have to be so goddamn loud?

The point of stalking was to not be seen or heard. A rule that seemed more painful to maintain when Nova shrugged and continued her assault.

Each ting and clack that rang through the air grated on my

nerves. It was incredibly hard to sit there and cringe instead of storming over and taking that thing away from her. Someone should smack her with it. Not because I hated her – which I did – but because what she was doing was blasphemy.

I'd never felt so sorry for a truck in my life. Call a mechanic or ask her crazy neighbor to help. Anything was better than that.

Eventually she stopped and slammed the hood shut. Though I did have to snort when her chest puffed out like she was satisfied. And I wasn't the only one who found her demeanor funny.

Atlee let out a snicker as she climbed back behind the steering wheel. "There's no way that…"

The loud roar of an engine turning over cut him off.

We both sat there and stared dumbfounded as the truck pulled out of the trailer park and rolled down the road.

"Did that just fucking happen?" Atlee asked.

Yes, yes it did. But I was much more interested in where Novalee was going.

Chapter 13

NOVALEE

*L*et's face it, work sucked. No one liked their job, and if they did then was it truly work? The very definition of that word depicted that one wouldn't find it enjoyable. That was my opinion anyway. And if anyone had a reason to complain about their job, it was me.

There were some serious issues with my place of employment. Like the name for instance. Mae's Good Eats. There was no Mae involved. The owner was a scrawny man named Victor who had no wife and no family that I knew of, let alone a past girlfriend. In fact I'd be surprised if a girl talked to him for longer than ten seconds. And that included possible relatives.

The second problem was the food. It was some weird mix up of what Victor thought Texan BBQ was and Louisiana specialties like Gumbo and baby back ribs. Or pulled pork po'boys with a side of crawfish. But the biggest problem of all, was me. Anyone who would willingly put me in a customer service role clearly shouldn't be in charge of shit.

"What would you recommend?"

I peeked over my notepad at the portly man in booth number two. "I recommend you go two blocks down. There's a great food truck next to the park."

"No," his lip curled in a grimace. "I don't trust food that comes from a truck."

But he trusted the food here? Did he not hear the cook hacking up a lung, which by the way wasn't caused by a sickness. Daryl smoked two packs a day. While he was cooking. Everyone got a little extra spice – or should I say ash – with their meal.

"What's the special?"

Besides for salmonella with a side of E.coli? "Texan chili Muffaletta."

"Oh, you have Texan food?"

"No."

In fact I wouldn't be surprised if the governor of Texas himself took a trip down here just to slap Victor for sullying the state's reputation.

Portly man in booth 2 narrowed his gaze, "But you just said…"

"I know what I said." I also told him to go two blocks down, but he didn't listen to that either.

"Alright," he nodded. "I'll have the special."

"Your funeral," I shrugged while scribbling down his order.

He chuckled when I walked away.

I don't know what he thought was so funny? I was completely serious. Not even I would eat here. And I ate a questionable candy off my bedroom floor… this morning.

Tearing the order off my pad, I slapped the piece of paper down on the window between the front of the dinner and the kitchen. "Here you go."

Daryl's greasy face appeared in the opening, "you're supposed to say order up."

"I'm also supposed to smile at customers."

To be fair I did try to come off as pleasant. I walked up to my first customer with a big smile on my face. He offered me a tip to stop. I was starting to think that facial expressions weren't my forte.

Daryl pointed the lit end of a cigarette at me, "you should smile."

"Uh huh?" My brow rose as a large ash dropped down and floated behind the window. "Are you gonna smile when you die of lung cancer?"

"You sound like my wife," he said with an annoyed eye roll.

Hold up. "You're married?"

Who would want to fall asleep next to that every day? Don't get me wrong, Daryl wasn't hideous or anything, but I don't think him and hygiene were on speaking terms.

"Yes, I'm married," not sure why he sounded all insulted. "Going on ten years now."

Huh. I guess there really was someone for everyone. Go figure.

"If you perked up every once and while, then you might find someone too. A little friendliness goes a long way, Nova."

I didn't ask for Daryl's opinion. When I wanted to know how many cancer sticks I could suck back in a minute, then I'd seek out his professional expertise. Sometime around divorce number two I figured. The alcohol dependency could start with number one. I had to pace out the addictions after all. Besides...

"I'm friendly." I shot back at him, with a little extra snark.

Daryl snatched the piece of paper from the window and gave me a side eye, "telling customers to go to a food truck isn't friendly."

I disagreed. "Rescuing someone from the consequences of their mistakes is a very friendly act."

"Bullshit," his tobacco stained finger pointed at me. "The only person you want to rescue is yourself, from doing any actual work."

Was it my fault that said piece of friendly advice also benefited me? There was an upside to everything after all. And I did actual work. Daryl had no idea how many hours I'd spent trying to scrub that horrible teal color out of the counters. Not to mention the red pleather booths. They were so bright that it physically hurt to look at them.

Who in their right mind would choose that color scheme? Oh wait, it was the Louisiana native who'd never been to Texas, yet somehow thought he knew all about that state's cuisine. Who, by the way, was the same person to employ me for two years.

Obviously Victor wasn't in his right mind.

I still had no idea how I passed the interview. I showed up in a pair of fuzzy onesie pajamas for Christ sake. Mind you no one else applied, so that might've had something to do with it.

Whatever.

Maw Maw was happy about my employment. After all, these were trying times and everyone needed to pitch in. I heard that speech more than once too. It wasn't all bad. Sometimes I made enough to grab a snack from the food truck, which I might've done today if it wasn't for the navy Range Rover parked outside.

Dropping my elbow on the counter, I propped my chin up on my balled fist and eyed the vehicle in the parking lot.

Why was Gio Mancini following me?

I saw him in the trees across the street from the trailer park. He was kind of hard to miss. That shiny new Range Rover stood out like a sore thumb. The fanciest vehicle in that part of town was a Porsche parked behind the burnt out ruins of what used to be a church. And by Porsche I meant the rusted frame of what used to be a Porsche.

Atlee swung his hand through the air while a scowl etched across Gio's face. They appeared to be arguing about something. I wondered what about. If I had to guess, I'd say Atlee was trying to point something out that Gio was getting pissed off about. Then again Gio was always pissed off.

Maybe he was pointing out his stalker flaws? I don't know about Gio, but if I was following someone, I would try not to be seen. Not park in a sparse patch of trees or empty parking lot perhaps? But that was just me.

Other people in this situation might freak out, and start questioning whether they were about to be murdered. Given who the owner of said vehicle was, that was a valid argument. High school should not be the place where one learned what it felt like to struggle for air. That's what drunken parties where one choked on their own vomit was for.

Sister Mary of the hallway saved my life this afternoon. There was no doubt in my mind about that. Apparently witnesses didn't hold a certain asshole back. Which led to the bigger question… Why was I still alive? I could sit here and try to figure out what they were saying, or… I could be the bigger person and take them a drink?

It was hot out and they did look a little parched. Letting Gio pass out from dehydration wouldn't be a good choice on my part. Our families didn't exactly have a great relationship, and God forbid I pissed daddy Mancini off anymore. I might get a first hand look at those cement shoes Memphis talked about.

It was definitely better to be safe than sorry.

Grabbing two cups, I turned around and walked through the swinging doors to the kitchen.

Daryl gave me a strange look when I filled them up with dirty dish water. I know it wasn't the cleanest water but it was still water, but just because someone looked thirsty didn't mean they deserved something fresh. One could argue that this was too fresh for them.

Maybe I should spit in it? Was I that childish?

I glanced down at the pieces of food floating in the cups.

Yes, yes I was.

Daryl did not agree with the rather nice glob I hacked into each cup. "I hope you're not planning on serving those to customers."

Ugh, okay Mr. By the book.

It would still be safer than the food in this place.

"Don't worry," I shot him a smile. "They aren't customers."

So technically I wasn't hurting the business.

That argument went out the window as soon as I walked back into the front of the dinner, and the bell above the door dinged.

Atlee strutted in with a stupid grin on his face, followed by Gio who's eyes narrowed when they locked on mine.

Crap.

"Well, they're customers now," I grumbled while depositing the filled cups on the counter.

My customer service may be shit, and I probably shouldn't be serving people… well, anything. But I wasn't the kind of employee that would sabotage a business. I had some morals. The cuisine drove people away all on its own.

Not to mention if I did mistreat a customer then Daryl would tell Victor, and I might lose my job, which would make Maw Maw kick my ass. And I didn't want the hassle of looking for a new job. Finding another insane boss who didn't care how competent his staff were, was about as likely as Gio deciding to be nice to me.

How weird would that be?

A nice Gio Mancini? Talk about a world ending event. I could ring a bell and walk around with one of those signs saying, the end is nigh. Veda would hide under the table – because she hid from everything.

Maw Maw would be that church lady praying for everyone's salvation while the world burned down around her. There would be children crying in the streets, and dogs with no home to go to. This dinner would probably be fine. I was pretty sure the devil gave Victor his menu choices.

An asshole Gio Mancini was definitely better for everyone.

My chest heaved with a sigh as Gio and Atlee flopped down in a booth to the left.

Damnit. That meant I had to be civilized. What kind of bullshit was that? Did I piss someone off in a former life or something, because no one prepared me for this kind of responsibility. But someone had to save the world.

"Order up," Daryl called out while tapping on his tiny bell.

I hated that stupid bell – which was one of the many things supplied by our so-called cook. Victor didn't like spending money on shit. I had to argue for three weeks for new dish cloths. And by new I meant unstained.

"Order up." He repeated with another ding.

One of these days I was going to shove that thing up his ass. Today however I had other assholes to deal with.

Lucky me.

I grabbed the plate and walked over to booth number two.

The portly man smiled when I deposited it on his table. "This looks good."

I waved him off, "yeah, yeah, whatever." Then slowly made my way across the diner to the glare at the assholes in booth number seven.

Atlee of course grinned, *prick*.

"Hey, Nova."

At least he wasn't staring at me like he could already picture my grave. Unlike some people… Gio.

"Fancy meeting you here."

Really? That was the opening Atlee was going with?

"I don't know if you understand how following someone works. But… you tend to end up in the same place as them from time to time."

Normally I wouldn't think a person my age could be that daft, but someone was walking around that school misspelling whore, so…

Atlee reached across the table and smacked Gio's chest, "told you she saw us."

Did Gio think otherwise? Given their reputation I figured big daddy Mancini would have a stalkers handbook or something.

"I'm digging that uniform by the way," Atlee added with a wink.

Seriously? "You would be the first."

This dress was stiff, itchy, and probably made in the fifties. Not exactly what I would consider sexy.

"You know, Gio and I are big fans of Cookie Monster."

The only thing stranger than that statement, was Gio's response.

"Do you want to get punched?"

Was that a vote kind of question? And if so, could I throw mine in the pot? I'd like to see Atlee get punched.

"Come on," Atlee sang with a twinkle in his eye. "You know you like cookies."

"I swear to God, Atlee…"

If cookies could make Gio grit his teeth like that, then the world wasn't in danger. I'd like to say that this was the strangest conversation I'd heard, but it didn't even make the top ten.

"Anyway…" I rolled my eyes, "what can I get you? And we don't have cookies."

I could wrangle up some arsenic with a side of laxative though.

"Hmm," Atlee tapped his finger off his chin, "what's good?"

"Nothing."

I may not like them, but that didn't warrant making them suffer through the taste of the food in this place. No one deserved that.

"What do you mean nothing?"

What was so confusing about that? "I mean nothing."

With a little luck, they might decide to go somewhere else.

"There has to be something good."

Okay, maybe there was something. "The gumbo isn't bad."

"Perfect," Atlee nodded. "I'll have that then."

Well, that made my job easier, "great, so the food truck is two blocks down. You can't miss it. Just look for the red polka dots."

His brow rose. "You're sending me to a food truck?"

"You wanted to know what was good." He shouldn't ask questions if he didn't want the answer.

"Do you work for the food truck?"

"Pfft no." I wish.

If Atlee wasn't confused before then that shit took hold and pulled his brows together when he picked up the menu. "What the fuck is BBQ rib jambalaya?"

That one was easy. "It's crap in a bowl."

It literally looked like crap.

"Aren't waitresses supposed to pimp the food?

"I'm not your food whore." Mandy had that job, but she wouldn't be out on her corner for another couple of hours. She had a thing for whipped cream.

That's when Gio blurted out, "then why are you here?"

There were so many ways to answer that. "Do you mean, why am I working at a dinner with inedible food? Or why am I here in general?"

"Are you always this smart?"

"Well, I can spell the word whore, so…" That still bothered me.

Gio's brow arched, "why are you working here?"

"Umm… it's called a job?" Maybe he was the mispeller?

When he just stared back, I let out a sigh. "You see, there's this thing called money that most people need for stuff like food and shelter – which I know is a foreign concept for you, Mr. I have a money tree in my backyard – but you know… everybody's gotta eat… but don't eat here."

Seriously. No one should ever eat here. Under any circumstances. If someone was starving with minutes to live, it would be worth it to risk a trip to the food truck.

The muscle in Gio's jaw tensed. "I don't appreciate the attitude."

"Well, I don't appreciate you, so it looks like we're both gonna be disappointed today."

Apparently he didn't like that comment either. His hands balled into fists, drawing my attention to his forearms. There was no denying the power in those muscles. I doubt if he'd even break a sweat snapping my neck. Who was that stacked? Really. What did he do, bench press cars in his spare time?

Great, now that image was stuck in my head.

Asshole.

Fingers snapped in front of my face, "pay attention when I'm talking to you."

Okay, that was too far. I'd already had a hard day – what with almost getting killed and all – I was not going to put up with anymore of his shit.

"Listen here, you tiny little man…" not that Gio was tiny by any means, but that wasn't the point. "I've had just about…"

My lecture was cut off by the sound of the sugar container hitting the floor. Little paper packets rained down around my feet as I glared back at the smirk on Gio's face.

"Oops."

Son of a…

Sucking back my anger, I forced a smile on my face.

"It's okay," I said and crouched down to sweep packets back in the holder. "Accidents happen."

Now I sounded like Sutton. Fantastic. Though I guess that wasn't all bad. The girl did put up a better fight than I did.

Next to fall off the table were the napkins.

I tried my hardest to ignore Gio, but chanting don't kill him silently in my head only worked for so long. When a mug landed on the floor, I had to grit my teeth to stop myself from saying something. I was not going to play in to his game. Instead I'd spit in his food. It seemed like a fair trade to me. Never piss off the cook or the waitress.

As I was about to stand back up, a hand pressed down on my shoulder, forcing me back on my knees.

"Stay down there. That's where you belong."

There were moments in life when something sent a shiver up your spine. See a spider, get a weird sense or hear a creepy story. But nothing made me shudder like I did when I rolled my eyes up to the piercing green stare glaring down at me.

"Are you gonna tell me to suck your dick next?" There were also moments in life when one wished they could take back something they said.

It took everything I had to stay where I was when Gio slid to the edge of the booth. He seemed so much bigger from down here. The light literally disappeared when he bent down to growl in my ear.

"You should show me some respect, little girl..."

Hey, I resented that comment. Just because I was wearing cookie monster underwear, didn't mean... *wait a minute.*

"I could easily turn my attention to other members of your family. Say your sister... or better yet your brother."

A tide of anger boiled through my veins and it took everything I had to keep it from pouring over into my expression.

Especially when he added, "Kato hasn't had a good beatdown in a while."

I lost count of how many times my brother wound up in the infirmary because of a broken bone or mysterious stab wound that no one apparently inflicted.

"Is that an admission of guilt?"

Gio Mancini may think he had the upper hand, but I didn't respond well to threats against the people I cared about.

"Why?" his head tilted to the side. "You gonna snitch?"

If he was hurting my brother, then fuck yes. I would scream that shit from the top of every building in town.

"You didn't say shit to sister Anne."

"That was different." I could take care of myself. Kato was locked up in a cell with nowhere to go, or anyone to help.

"Was it?" Gio's eyes narrowed.

I could feel him sizing me up, as if he was looking for an answer or some kind of explanation for my behavior this afternoon. He wouldn't find one. It wasn't something I could explain. Opportunity was right there staring me in the face, and what did I do? Nothing.

Maybe it was guilt, or maybe I just didn't want the hassle of being pulled into the office. That was never a fun experience, especially when I had to go home to a less than impressed Maw Maw. Perhaps that's why I kept my mouth shut? To save my sister from any further trauma.

Either way it was done now. I couldn't say I'd act any differently if I found myself in the same situation.

"You know what I think, *Nova*..."

Didn't really care what he thought.

"I think you'd do just about anything to save your brother." Gio sat up. "Isn't that right?"

I clamped my lips shut, refusing to respond. We both knew the answer to that question, and I was not about to give him an excuse to torment my brother. Not that he needed one.

"What do you say we test that theory out?"

My stomach sank before he barked out, "crawl." As if I was some kind of pet for him to order around.

I was so far beyond done at this point. Even if I did what he said, it wouldn't change anything. Kato would still be locked up, and Gio would still want to kill him.

"Are you fucking deaf," Gio growled. "I said crawl."

The big bad Mancini family's image was a bunch of bullshit.

They were no different than your basic bully. Which was why I couldn't give in. This wouldn't stop with one demand. There would be another tomorrow, and the next day, and so on. A line had to be drawn in the sand here and now.

So, I lifted my chin, looked Gio dead in the eyes, and hissed, "Make me."

The twitch in the corner of his mouth was enough to make me question my sanity, but when his eyes flared with something dark, a swirling pit of dread began to seep into my bones.

Atlee wasn't helping the situation any. The intrigue toying with his face caused me to think Gio might actually reach out and slap me. My muscles even tensed in preparation.

But that's not what happened.

Instead of the violence I was expecting, Gio ever so calmly slid back in the booth and said, "I'll take some coffee."

Chapter 14

NOVALEE

Two hours, fifty-seven minutes, and thirteen seconds. That's how long Gio Mancini sat in that booth watching me like a cobra getting ready to strike. Although, I did have to give his power of determination credit.

Ten minutes and I was done with my truck's tweed fabric. I'd barely made it home and was already shifting around like a kid on a sugar high. Mind you that could have something to do with the asshole who decided to occupy my workspace.

Prick called me over for every little thing he could think of. This table's dirty, there's a spot on my cup, the coffee is cold and my personal favorite, the service in this place sucks. Know what really sucked? The coffee – that I made sure was extra hot – that I accidently spilt on his lap. If my aim was right, then he wouldn't be getting anything sucked for a while.

Yanking on the steering wheel, I revved my truck over the first speed bump into Sault Saint Marie Estates. The shocks were in desperate need of repair. One little jolt sent a whirling squeak through the cab. I probably shouldn't have let it go this long without some maintenance. Then again, I probably shouldn't have dumped coffee on Gio either. Oh well, *c'est la vie*. It was worth it, and kind of fun.

Someone had to make sure the prick was okay. The booths in Mae's Good Eats were made of pleather. That shit wasn't comfortable on a good day. It wasn't comfortable on a bad day either. Not to mention the horribly padded benches that were impossible to take a nap on. Trust me I tried. Apparently sleeping on the counter was bad for business. Yet Gio didn't seem to have a problem.

For almost three hours he didn't so much as twitch – other than when he called me over for some stupid mundane bullshit. There had to be something wrong with his ass muscles, right? That was the only explanation I could think of. Not that I was thinking about his ass or anything. I was simply concerned for his rear end health, and maybe a little for my ability to continue breathing.

There was something seriously unnerving about a man who could stay that still for so long. On the upside, Gio had a promising future as a living statue. Atlee was another story. He only lasted about an hour, before saying he had something to do.

I assumed the something was someone. Thanks to Memphis, I knew way more about Atlee's reputation than I wanted to. Like details, names, and other things that Memphis shouldn't know. Apparently any part of the body could be tattooed, including the family jewels.

My best friend may have his nose poked in everyone's business, but I had something he didn't. A nice pornographic image that Atlee drew on a napkin and gave me before he left. The idiot did have skills. The attention to detail, like the veins in the dick and shape of a mouth when stretched open were top notch. And slightly disturbing.

I rounded the corner to our trailer and immediately cocked a brow.

There were plenty of things I expected to see on this block. Mr. Garabaldi chasing some vermin in his bathrobe around the yard. Winnie enjoying some moonshine while trying to surf across her fence – which was also made of plastic – or those little pissants Billy and Kyle slinking around in the shadows. What I didn't expect to see was my sister dancing barefoot in the moonlight.

Surprise morphed into confusion as I stared out the windshield, trying to comprehend what I was seeing. Was I dreaming? Did I take something I forgot about? Deluded, drunk or asleep was the only place where my sister smiled anymore. And she certainly didn't twirl around outside in a pink nightgown.

This was the same girl that hid in her room for three days because someone knocked on the door while she was home alone. She'd improved a lot since then. But not singing *Twinkle Twinkle Little Star* in the moonlight improved.

Dumbfounded didn't even begin to explain how I felt. I barely even noticed Veda's friend Rita standing on the deck with her hands on her hips.

My first instinct when I climbed out of the truck was to look for the baby. Even though I knew it was wishful thinking, I hoped to find Knox sitting in the grass. Maybe he wanted some fresh air with his lullaby, or something. That would explain some of Veda's behavior. But the baby wasn't anywhere to be seen. He was probably already asleep.

That did not bode well for this situation.

I'd never wanted to see my nephew more than when I headed for the crappy plastic gate I was terrified to open. What exactly was I walking into? And more importantly how would it end? That was the part that made me swallow down a lump of dread.

"Nova," Veda sang and rushed over to throw her arms around my waist.

The weight of that hug was so suffocating that I missed the pain of Gio's hand around my neck. His hate I could take. Hell, I wanted it. It was easy to ignore that. But this… The bright twinkle in my sister's eyes was more heartbreaking than anything Gio Mancini could do.

"Come dance with me," Veda grabbed my hand and pulled me into the middle of the yard. "It's so beautiful out."

I forced a smile on my face, "yes, it is."

And so was she, all happy and beaming. Oh how I missed that look on her face. It was the one thing that could cheer me up when I had a bad day. And now, all I could think as I watched my sister's hazelnut hair fan out while she spun around was, is this it? Was this the moment I'd been dreading for two years? When there was nothing more I could do for my sister other than watch doctors lock her away.

Veda closed her eyes and tipped her chin up to the sky. "I love how fresh the air smells."

As broken as she was, I couldn't lose her too.

My hand trembled as I reached out to tuck a lock of hair behind her ear. For just a moment she was my sister again. Full of life and ready to take on the world. It was a reminder of what could've been. A mocking glimpse at the woman Veda should've grown into. Like all illusions, this one would fade into hard reality, and this moment was too cruel to bare.

"Veda…" a weight pressed down on my chest when her eyes opened and locked on mine.

That dark void that swallowed my sister up, was still there behind the fake life etched in her expression.

It physically hurt to ask, "what are you doing out here?"

A part of me hoped that Veda would say something to let me know that the girl I grew up with was still in there somewhere. Another part didn't want her to answer. I wasn't ready to face the ramifications of what might happen.

Confusion wasn't one of the emotions I thought would come when she opened her mouth to talk.

"I can smell colors out here."

Smell colors? "What?"

That's when I realized that this wasn't some psycho happy moment, signifying her inevitable breakdown. Veda's pupils were dilated and that hazy smile wasn't mentally induced. It was drug induced. My sister was high. And there was only one person I could think of who would've given her something. Rita Evans, my sister's so-called best friend.

With a sigh, I swung my gaze to the girl standing on the deck. "Did you drug her?"

"Of course." Rita stated like it was a perfectly normal act.

Given the issues that my sister had in the past couple of years, I couldn't really argue that it wasn't called for. But that didn't stop me from asking, "why?"

Rita shrugged, "she freaked out when her phone rang."

Okay, that was new.

"What did you give her?"

She held up a bottle and gave it a shake, "they're called happy pills for a reason."

Why was I not surprised? In high school, Rita was the party girl. She had all the favors and fun. Including one night with my brother. I openly gagged when I saw her sneaking out of his room in the morning. That was the last thing I wanted to know about someone who used to braid my hair. I was so mad I didn't talk to Kato for a week. He should've known better.

Now Rita was more grown up and responsible, but she still had fun on the weekends like anyone else. I used to blame her for not going with Veda that night, but it wasn't her fault. Why would Veda take her best friend on a date? If there was anyone to blame for letting Veda walk out that door, it was me. I was the one that should've stopped her. I knew something was wrong. The way that guy looked at her...

.   .   .

"IT'S NOT FAIR," I huffed and crossed my arms. "How come you get to date and I don't?"

"Because you're fourteen!" Kato yelled from the kitchen.

Were all big brother's this annoying?

"Fourteen is old enough," I spat back at him.

"Like fuck it is. All teenage boys only want one thing..."

Not this speech again. I was well aware of what teenage boys wanted. I was best friends with one. If anything it gave an edge. I had insider knowledge.

"Maybe teenage girls want the same thing." I shot back and chuckled when I heard something clatter against the kitchen floor.

Veda rolled her eyes aways from the mirror and back at me, "you're not helping your cause any."

Would anything help my cause? It was like Kato didn't want me to grow up. Other girls didn't have this problem. Cindy was always going out on dates and to parties. Meanwhile Kato wouldn't even let me wear makeup to school.

It wasn't like I'd cake it on my face or anything. All I wanted was the right to wear a little lip gloss and maybe mascara like the other girls my age. Veda taught me what to do, plus I watched her all the time, like now. She was staring in the mirror while gliding a subtle pink hue over her lips.

I preferred red, it made her mouth pop more. But she liked the less is more technique. Either way she looked beautiful. Sometimes I was jealous of how little she had to try. The natural curl in her hair was perfect and flawless. Much better than my bone straight locks.

"It's not fair." I repeated with another huff. "You were dating at my age."

"Mom was different." Veda set down the lipstick, picked up a bottle of mascara, and muttered, "she didn't really have any rules."

She had rules. "I had to be in bed by nine."

"That was so she could..."

"Veda!" Kato cut her off and appeared in the bathroom doorway. "We talked about this."

Veda looked up at his reflection, "you can't protect her forever."

"Yes I can."

What were they protecting me from? Come to think of it, every time I brought up mom they got quiet, or Kato would change the subject. I just assumed that her death was too painful for them to think about. But maybe it was more than that?

"Did mom do something?"

I wasn't that young when she passed. If something had happened I would've known.

The look my brother and sister exchanged, made me reconsider that thought.

"What are you guys hiding from me?"

"Nothing," Kato said way too quickly.

My sister sighed and turned around to face us, "Kato..."

"Shut it, Veda."

This was ridiculous.

"I'm almost fifteen," I pointed out. "Whatever it is, I can handle it."

"Exactly, you're still a kid." Kato walked away and grumbled, "and you should stay a kid."

Did he have any idea how frustrating it was to be referred to as a kid.

"I'm not a little girl." I said to Veda, who smiled and swept my hair off my forehead.

"I know. But Kato will always see you as a little girl."

Great.

"Now," she straightened her back and smoothed her hands down the skirt of her dress. "How do I look?"

"Beautiful," I grumbled.

She always looked beautiful.

My head tipped when she glanced out of the room into the hall. I'd watched my sister get ready and go out so many times, but this was the first time I'd seen her look... nervous?

"What's wrong?"

Pink tinted Veda's cheeks as she let out a heavy breath. "I really like this guy."

"Didn't you just meet him." She barely knew him enough to like him let alone really like him.

"Yeah," she nodded. "But he's perfect. Charming, sophisticated, and handsome."

Sounded too good to be true if you asked me.

"He called this morning just so he could hear my voice. It was very sweet."

"Or he's stalkerish. But what do I know, I'm not allowed to date."

Veda returned my exaggerated eye roll with one of her own.

"Don't worry," she wrapped her arm around my shoulders and steered me out of the bathroom. "Kato will let up."

"When?" I asked while shooting my brother a dirty look as we walked in the kitchen. "Or do you intend to keep me locked up in this apartment forever?"

"You can date," Kato folded his arms over his chest and leaned back against the counter. "When you're thirty."

Figures.

One of these days I was going to punch him in the nuts so hard his junk wouldn't work. If I wasn't allowed to even kiss a guy then why should he have fun.

"Well I guess it's good for you that Drea's dad didn't make her wait until she was thirty."

Kato's face dropped while Veda gasped. Don't know what she was so surprised about. The walls in this place were paper thin. I could hear them breathing at night.

My brother opened his mouth to say something, but was interrupted by a knock at the door.

Kato, pointed at me, said, "we'll finish this conversation later," then headed over to answer.

Beyond catching the guy's name, I didn't pay attention to the intro-ductions my sister doled out. I was too busy inspecting her date.

Bill looked okay I guess. He was presentable in his suit with his dark hair neatly styled, but there was something off. The way he looked at my sister didn't sit right with me...

VEDA CLASPED her hands on my shoulders and said, "cake would be so good right now."

I stared back into her bright eyes, wishing that I could change the past. If I'd listened to my gut then none of this would've happened. One little word or action could've stopped it all. Kato wouldn't be in jail and Veda wouldn't be lost.

"Let's go make one."

I smiled at my sister. "That sounds great."

We used to bake all the time. Veda and I would sing and dance around the kitchen while Kato played the guitar. This wouldn't be the same as that. It wouldn't even be close. But I'd take it. I'd take the fake façade for as long as it lasted.

A tear rolled down my cheek, filling my fake smile with the bitter taste of hatred. I hated Atlas Mancini for what he did to her. I hated the way she viewed the world now. But mostly I hated myself for not stopping her from walking out that door.

"Come on," Veda sang while skipping for the screen door.

I moved to follow then stopped dead in my tracks as a shiver shot up my spine.

Her date that night... Bill something... he had the same hint of green in his brown eyes that Knox did.

Chapter 15

GIOVANNI

*M*ake me.

Novalee had no idea what those two words did to a man like me. She may as well have dared me to fuck with her. All night long I thought about the day I would *make* her get down on all fours and crawl like a pet. I might even tell her to lick my shoes.

If Nova wanted me to make her, then fine. I'd drag her ego through the dirt and *make* her do every demeaning little thing I could think of. She had no idea who she was messing with. And the first thing I was going to make her pay for was the coffee she dumped on my lap.

"God damnit!" I grunted and shifted my slacks away from the raw patch on my thigh.

My dad paid enough for me to go to that school, one would think the uniforms would be made out of better material.

My fists balled as I stomped across the dark hardwood to the black tiled kitchen floor. "I'll fucking show her."

"I assume you're talking about the Ford girl?"

I was so pissed off that I didn't notice my father sitting on one of the island's black leather chairs.

"Maybe," I murmured while walking around the island to open the fridge door.

As if my morning couldn't get any worse, my brother chose that moment to join us.

"Good morning Little Brother."

Great, a family reunion. Just what I fucking needed.

"What's so fucking good about it." I snarled while grabbing a bottle of OJ.

Romeo strutted over to the coffee pot, "someone's in a bad mood."

Thank you captain obvious.

"What's up your ass?"

"Novalee Ford," my father answered.

"Ah," Romeo filled his mug then looked over at me. "You want to fuck her?"

"No!" Why did everyone keep asking me that? And what the hell were they doing down here anyway? "Don't you guys have some business or something to do?"

"Don't worry Little Brother," Romeo clasped his hand on my shoulder, making my jaw clench. "We're just checking in with you."

Bullshit.

The Mancini's weren't exactly what people would call a traditional family. The only time we sat around a table to share a meal was for Christmas, or when we needed to portray an image.

I spent more time with Darry and Atlee than I did with anyone I was related to. Don't get me wrong, I respected the hell out of my father, but he didn't do idle chit chat or check-ins unless it was job related.

"I'm fine," I hissed through gritted teeth.

Romeo nodded and dropped his hand, thankfully before I punched him in the face.

Thinking that that was the end of my brothers' 'check in', I twisted the top off my bottle, and swallowed down a mouthful of juice. I should've known better.

"How's school?"

The urge to smack my brother around once again balled my fist. "You mean other than Novalee Ford invading my classrooms?"

My father sighed and flipped a page of his newspaper, "she didn't do anything to us, Giovanni."

Chit chat wasn't his thing, but lectures sure as shit were.

"Since when does that matter?" Last week he put out a hit on an entire family because one of them stole from him. Honestly, I didn't know what the hold up was. Anyone else would be six feet under by now.

My father had no one to blame for my bad mood but himself. He was the one that signed off on her scholarship.

"Kato Ford is paying for his crime."

That made me snort. Sitting pretty in a jail cell was not paying for his crime.

"Kato owes us a life debt." As long as he was still breathing, that debt was owed. Though, he probably wouldn't be breathing too good tonight. I made a call after leaving Nova yesterday.

"Yes he does," my father arched a brow over his newspaper at me. "His sister does not."

I huffed out a breath and shook my head, "don't tell me she's still too young."

"Is she eighteen?"

Should've seen that retort coming. My father had certain rules about children. Technically Novalee was a minor, but she wasn't young enough to be considered a child. Then again, I was eighteen and he still treated me like I was a kid. Why else wouldn't he let me take the *Omerta*.

"No." I begrudgingly grumbled back.

"Then you will leave her alone until she is."

He returned to the paper in his hands as if the matter was closed. And as far as he was concerned it was. My father was the boss after all. His word was law.

What I didn't expect was for Romeo to interject.

"I don't know, the Ford siblings are close."

Suspicion tipped my head towards my brother. Did he just argue my point?

Not that my father would listen. "The girl will not pay her brother's debt."

Like I said, his word was law.

Romeo took a sip of his coffee and said, "I'm not talking about her brother."

Then who the hell was he talking about?

My father looked up at my brother, "she's too young."

"Not for Gio." Romeo argued.

That made my father set his paper down on the walnut countertop.

Neither one spoke for a few seconds, and I couldn't help but wonder what I was missing. The only Ford I knew of that crossed us was Kato, but the looks they exchanged said there was something I wasn't being told.

"What exactly are you suggesting?" My father asked.

"The girl could be our way in."

Way in for what?

"No," My father shook his head. "It won't work, she's too paranoid."

"The sister is," Romeo interrupted. "But not Nova. She won't see him coming."

Coming for what? And what did Nova's sister have to do with anything?

"Either of you want to fill me in?" Don't know why I said

anything. Neither one of them seemed to notice or care that I was still standing right there.

"If he pulls it off, let him take the oath."

My heart sped up for half a second. All I'd ever wanted was to join the family business. I was starting to think I'd never get the opportunity.

Then my father spoke. "No, he's not ready."

Our father seemed to have something against me taking the oath. Every time I brought it up, he would say 'you're a kid. Enjoy your childhood.' Atlas and Romeo took it when they were teenagers, yet I was left behind. Like I was too fragile after mom's death to handle that world. If anything I was more prepared than them. They just found her body. I had to listen to her die.

"Yes he is." Romeo argued. "You know he is."

I wasn't sure how I felt about my brother's sudden faith in me. Most of the time I wanted to punch him, but when he added, "It's either that or orphan a child," I could've kissed him.

If that didn't work, then nothing would. My father used to be ruthless and cold. Our mother's death changed him. Now, he went out of his way to keep children out of the line of fire. Someone had to really fuck up for that to happen.

I held my breath as my father folded his hands on the countertop. I could picture the word no coming out of his mouth, but the adrenaline surging through my system hoped for another response.

All I got was a simple nod, before he stood up and walked out. Leaving me alone with Romeo to wonder if that just happened. Did my father agree to let me take the *Omerta*? It didn't seem real.

"Huh," Romeo grunted as he refilled his mug. "That was easier than I thought."

I still wasn't sure it actually happened.

"Want some?" Romeo asked, holding up the pot.

"Ugh," my lip instantly curled. "No."

Just thinking about coffee made my thigh hurt. I should call Nova's boss and get her fired for that shit. Actually, that wasn't a bad idea. I could black ball her for every restaurant in town. Let's see how proud she was when she wasn't making any money.

Romeo shrugged and set the pot back in the back in the chamber.

This all seemed like some kind of dream that would fracture at any moment. I kept waiting for my brother to walk away, but he just stood there eyeing me.

Annoyed by his staring, I barked out, "are you going to tell me what's going on, or hope I figure it out on my own?"

"Careful Little Brother," his brow arched. "I'm your underboss."

Unfortunately he was right. Like it or not, if I took this job, that would make Romeo my boss. The mob had rules, and if I wanted in, I had to follow them. But he was still my brother, meaning I could still hit him if I wanted to.

"So," he took a sip of his coffee then casually asked, "does your bad mood have anything to do with the Ford girl?"

"What the fuck do you think?"

That was the dumbest question I'd ever heard. Why would seeing her face every day piss me off? It wasn't as if her brother killed ours.

"Dad was right, you know. She didn't do anything to us."

My face dropped into a deadpan glance, "and?"

"Do you want to fuck her?"

What the...

"No. It's called revenge, Romeo."

That should be a concept he was well versed in. My brother wasn't all sunshine and forgiveness. I'd seen him do some sick shit in the name of vengeance. When I was eight-years-old he and Atlas broke some kid's arm because he pushed me off the swing.

He lifted the mug to his lips and said, "could you?"

Could I what? Fuck her? What kind of question was that? "I guess."

She wasn't hideous. Actually Novalee was kind of hot. Had I thought about bending her over and taking my anger out on her ass, sure? That didn't mean I had any desire to do it.

"What does that have to do with the job?"

"We need you to get close to her."

My face dropped as he swallowed down a mouthful of caffeine. "Are you fucking kidding me?"

Sounded more like a punishment than a job to me.

Romeo set his mug down on the counter and explained, "her sister's a maid and we need to know if she saw something in the Fiore house."

"So, go to the source." That seemed like the easier solution.

"It's not that simple," Romeo leaned back against the counter and kicked his ankles crossed. "She's paranoid. Shuts down every time I get close."

Sounded like a personal problem to me. "How's getting close to Nova supposed to help with that?"

"She's her sister. And…"

"Girls talk." I finished for him.

God damnit. I was starting to wonder if the Ford family was put on this earth just to fuck up my day. Don't get me wrong, I understood his logic. Sometimes it was easier to get information from someone close to a person than from the person themselves. And girls did tell each other everything. That didn't mean it would work in this case. Or that I wanted to do it. It all depended on how important it was.

"What did she see?"

"Dad and I kill a man."

Fuck. That was pretty damn important.

If Nova's sister did see something, then she could ID them to the cops. Normally witnesses were just taken care of, but given our past connection, taking her out could bring the cops to our door. Not an ideal situation in any circumstance. There was only one problem with my brother's plan.

"Nova fucking hates me," and I hated her. "She'll never let me get close to her."

"Is she afraid of you?"

"Yes."

Nova tried to act like she wasn't, but I could see it on her face. The dread and worry about what I was going to do next. It was sitting just under her contempt. Plus Novalee Ford wasn't stupid. She knew I wanted to kill her.

"Fear can be a powerful tool Little Brother."

"What do you expect me to do, beat the information out of her?" Not that I would argue that method, but broken bones weren't going to make her chatty. She was too proud for that. Nova would happily go to her grave, knowing I didn't get shit.

"I was thinking more like break her, then beat her."

The words *make me* rang through my head.

Ending someone's life was easy, but breaking them… that was tricky. Mind you I was never one to back down from a challenge. Hell, I enjoyed that shit. The possible mind fuckery alone was enough to get my blood singing.

Work Nova was as calm and cool as school Nova. I sat there for hours tormenting her while enjoying the physical signs of annoyance she displayed. I rather enjoyed the frustration tugging at her brow. No matter what I did or said, there was fuck all she could do without risking her job. Which I assumed she needed.

Helplessness angered someone like her, but fed someone like me.

So could I break her?

"Yeah," I nodded. "I can break her."

How did one fuck with someone who lived their life seemingly unphased? Let's face it. Everyone was phased by something.

Including Novalee Ford. I just had to find that pressure point. Kato was a possibility, but seemed almost too easy. Plus, by the time I did break Nova, her sister could have already talked.

"Wouldn't it be easier just to silence the sister?" There had to be a way to make sure she kept her mouth shut. Pay her off, or threaten her. "Everyone has a price."

"If you figure out hers, let me know." Romeo slapped his hand on the island and turned to walk away. "Either way the job will be considered done."

So, I had to either get close to Nova and find out if her sister saw anything, or make sure she kept her mouth shut if she did. I suppose it was too much to ask for a simple task.

"I'll need Atlee and Darry," I said before Romeo left the kitchen.

He paused in the doorway to look back and give me a small nod.

It was time to really start fucking with Novalee, and I'd start by sending Atlee in. He'd broken more than one girl's silence.

Chapter 16

When I woke up in the morning, I thought things were back to the way they were. Veda wasn't dancing in the yard, and the baby was happily shoving fistfuls of cereal and fruit in his mouth. I even got my morning lecture from Maw Maw about not stealing Knox's food.

Considering most of his breakfast was on the floor, I highly doubted he would care about one little piece of strawberry. Not that she thought that was a valid argument. In fact she made me clean up his mess just for mentioning it. All in all it was a very normal morning.

Then I got to school and shit went sideways.

"Hey," Memphis swung his hand, giving my shoulder a playful slap. "Everyone's left you alone today."

That was suspicious all on its own. I was only halfway through the day and pretty sure I'd entered the Freaky Friday zone. Next thing I knew I'd be working with a capable cook and brand new cloths.

"Wait," Chuck held up his palm, "you're telling me that no one's called her a name, or tripped her?"

Memphis shook his head, but his boyfriend didn't seem to believe him.

"Really?" Chuck's head tipped to the side.

"I know." My gaze shifted to the one across the table, "shocking, right?"

Chuck returned my sentiment with an arched brow. Every time the light glinted off his light mint stare, I wanted to smack him. And that was before I thought about the gorgeous hue of his auburn hair that he refused to grow out. People paid good money to mimic those colors and he just woke up with them.

"That is kind of weird." And let's not mention the natural rumble in his tone.

"It's good to know someone is on my side."

At least I wasn't the only one disturbed by this strange turn of events. Now if only Memphis could get with the program, we could put our heads together and try to figure out what was going on. Like the detectives we pretended to be as kids. And we'd probably be much better at crime solving now than back then. I still had no idea who was behind the great candy nabbing.

"Or," Memphis sang, "Maybe they just realized how great you are."

Both Chuck and I shot him 'an are you serious' glance.

"Great is not the word I would use to describe Nova."

I nodded at Chuck, "thank you."

He got me. *Wait a minute... did I step into an alternate dimension?*

Usually that was Memphis's area. The last time Chuck and I agreed on anything was when Memphis dyed his hair black. He said it was goth. It was not. On the upside we now knew just how pale his complexion was.

"Brash, I could see," Chuck popped a cherry tomato in his mouth. "Maybe uncouth, or messy, annoying, lazy, unmotivated..."

Hey now. I was motivated… sometimes.

"Tone deaf…"

Okay I'd give him that one.

"A pain in the ass, unfriendly, the worst waitress in the world…"

"Okay," I cut him off. "We get the point."

If I wanted all my flaws pointed out, I would've gone to bridge club with Maw Maw. There was no one more judgy than a group of old bitties with nothing better to do. Trust me. I once spent three hours listening to the acceptable degrees of skirt lengths.

"We can all agree that I'm not great."

Chuck nodded while Memphis argued, "I don't agree."

"You don't count." I shot back.

"Why not?"

"We shared a crib, which makes your opinion biased."

"I disagree. If anything, that should make my opinion count more." Memphis reached over to pluck a fry off my plate. "I've seen you at your worst."

Pfft, semantics.

"You are kind of biased." Chuck pipped in.

"See," A smile spread across my face as I waved my hand in his direction. "Even your dimwitted boyfriend agrees with me."

Chuck's brow rose, "dimwitted?"

I rolled my eyes, "I'm sure you're a genius when it comes to basketball stats… But we're talking about real world stuff here." I paused for a second to give Chuck a quick scan. "How do you spell whore?"

"Oh my God," Memphis dropped his face in his palm. "Chuck is not the one that vandalized your locker."

"We don't know that. He failed his third grade spelling test."

That could be considered a valuable piece of evidence to a detective.

Memphis groaned while Chuck smacked his lips together and sat back in his chair. "And you wonder why people don't like you."

I didn't wonder about that. I knew people didn't like me. It wasn't my fault they couldn't understand sarcasm. Nor did I care. The less people that liked me, meant less people I had to talk to.

"We're getting off topic here." I narrowed my gaze at the crowd in the cafeteria. "Something fishy is going on. Gio's up to something."

"It's not a conspiracy, Nova," Chuck sighed. "He probably just got bored."

Bored? That was his explanation? "I see there's no need to continue arguing my dimwit remark."

Chuck gave me an exaggerated eye roll, but didn't say a word.

Even he had to admit that bored was a far stretch. People like Gio Mancini didn't get bored. They just upped their game. Which made the way he'd been watching me that much worse. I almost missed that *how am I going to kill you* look he had going on. It was better than the inquisitive spark toying with his expression.

I glanced over my shoulder at the table in the middle of the room where the trio of assholes sat. That's what I'd dubbed them. King asshole returned my stare with a glare of his own. Asshole number two, the golden haired or, 'who shoved a stick up my ass' asshole also looked back at me. But I didn't see asshole number three. The 'I've had too much pussy' asshole.

It was just the two of them at the table. The brown haired twit's chair sat empty. He was there a minute ago, flashing his charming smile at some cheerleader.

Where did Atlee go?

I scanned the room searching for the missing face, but I didn't see it. That couldn't be good. Especially not with that smirk tipping up the corner of Gio's mouth.

"I told you he was up to something."

"Let it go Nova," Memphis said. "He's just sitting there."

"But he's smiling." I pointed out while narrowing my gaze. "Gio Mancini doesn't smile."

"She's right." Chuck agreed.

This would be the part of the movie where the dun, dun, dun, music played.

I turned around long enough to point at Chuck, "you are now my partner in the detective firm," then looked back at asshole one and two.

"Hey," Memphis whined. "I started that firm with you."

"You still haven't found out who stole my candy."

"That was ten years ago."

"But it's still an open case, and have you come to me with any leads?" I gave Memphis a quick side eye. "No."

Case and point.

He grumbled something under his breath while pinching the bridge of his nose.

I couldn't be bothered to try and make out what Memphis was griping about because the air around me suddenly changed.

Ever have the sensation that something wasn't right? Like the twilight zone had invaded your reality, while the world flipped upside down, and gravity reversed itself?

Well, when Atlee appeared and plopped himself down in the chair next to mine, that's where I was.

"Hey there sweet thing."

Sweet thing?

I wasn't the only one confused by the charming smile lighting up his whiskey orbs. Memphis and Chuck sat there with their mouths open, like they wanted to say something, but didn't know what.

"You're looking good today."

No I wasn't.

"I look hungover and sleep deprived."

To be fair I was sleep deprived. It felt like I hadn't slept in weeks. That's what happened when one had to stay up and make sure their high as hell sister didn't run into traffic in the middle of the night.

Thanks Rita.

"Nah, you look great." Atlee tipped his head in a way that made the arch in my brow deepen. "Some guys like the natural thing."

If by natural he meant managed to brush my hair before I was pushed out the door, then sure.

The screech of Memphis's chair sliding closer to me rang through my ears like nails on a chalkboard. "Are you lost?"

The shift in Atlee's demeanor was so quick that if I blinked, I'd have missed the muscle in his jaw tensing. "I wasn't talking to you Blondie."

Blondie? Huh, I now had a new nickname for my best friend.

As much as I was getting tired of my Memphis's protective bullcrap, his question was valid. Atlee should be anywhere else. Like over there next to the brunette with styled hair and make-up.

So when Atlee's expression softened as he looked back at me, I reiterated, "I'm pretty sure you're lost."

He just grinned and threw his arm over the back of my chair, "I'm right where I want to be."

I jerked back from the twinkle in his eye. He was definitely lost.

"Okay, well, you're a little close," I carefully pushed his arm away. "I can smell the last girl on your fingers."

"There's only one girl I want on my fingers."

Not even Memphis knew what to do when Atlee sucked his finger through his lips and made quite possibly the sexiest groan I'd ever heard.

This officially went from weird to what the fuck.

I looked at Memphis who cocked a brow and tipped his head towards Chuck. The silent question of what the hell passed easily between us.

I probably shouldn't have said anything but felt compelled to ask, "did you want something?"

"Yes," he leaned in and hushed his tone. "I want to lick your pussy until you're screaming my name."

Oh wow. Okay, I definitely shouldn't have asked. How did one even respond to that? Somehow I didn't think a simple no thank you would suffice. Could I just tell him to fuck off? Would that end this awkward whatever it was? When Atlee reached up and began twirling a lock of my hair, I opted to go for the distraction tactic.

"I think the girls over there," I nodded at the table of cheerleaders, "are more your type."

They sure didn't seem to be enjoying our interaction. Since Atlee sat down, I'd gotten more than one dirty look.

"I already banged most of them."

Why was I not surprised.

"Besides, why would I waste my attention on them," Atlee slid his chair up so my knees were trapped between his thighs. "when there's a pretty girl right here."

Oh please, not even Maw Maw would buy that load of crap and she loved me.

"Well, maybe you should bang them again." I tried to scoot away but Memphis's position prevented that. I would've turned around to tell him to backoff, but I was kind of afraid to take my eyes off Atlee.

"Sorry sweetheart," Atlee's hand dropped on my knees as his fingers walked up my thigh. "I don't do repeat customers."

Again, not surprised, and why was he touching me?

"What do you say Sugar? Wanna take a ride on this pogo stick?"

That remark seemed to be amusing to Memphis, because he coughed out a quick snicker. I, on the other hand, was just plain confused. What the hell was happening right now? Maybe the alternate dimension theory wasn't that far off?

Then it dawned on me. Well not so much dawned as slapped

me in the face when I glanced over at Gio's table. This was part of his plan. Was this part of Gio's nefarious plan? I didn't know if Atlee was sent over here as a distraction, or if he had something else in mind. But I did know Gio was watching a little too intently for this to be a random occurrence.

"Come on Darlin," Atlee grabbed my chin, pulling my attention back to him. "I'll take you on a wild ride."

Okay, in the matter of a couple of minutes he'd called me three things, none of which were my actual name.

When Memphis twitched behind me, I waved at him to stop. I had this.

"Thanks, but I think I'll pass. I'm not really into the overly used goods."

"Are you sure?" A shadow moved over Atlee's face deepening the smolder burning in his gaze. "Because those big beautiful eyes are telling me otherwise."

Big beautiful eyes? Wow he sucked at this.

"How did you get so many girls into bed?"

Memphis wasn't the only one that snickered at that one. Chuck also let a chuckle out. I didn't get many of those out of him and was kind of proud of it. Most of the time it was uttered grumbles and eye rolls.

But was Atlee phased at all by my comment… not in the slightest. If anything he took it as an opening. "Come out with me tonight and I'll show you."

Oh boy, a date with Atlee Fiore. Was I the last girl on the planet who hadn't seen his junk?

"Sorry, I already have plans to chew broken glass."

That wasn't an entire lie. I did have plans, and they did involve broken glass. Just not chewing on them. Thanks to Maw Maw, it was my turn to help with church yard work.

"Ouch." In the fakest gesture I'd ever seen, Atlee flattened his hand on his chest and shot me a frown. "You act like I have ulterior motives."

"Um, yeah." See unlike the other girls he charmed, I wasn't dumb or desperate. Nor did I care about my social status or dating reputation. Which by the way would only be one thing if I went out with him.

Atlee scoffed out a snort, "is there something wrong with wanting to share your company?"

Memphis, Chuck and I all simultaneously said, "yes."

"Damn," Atlee huffed out a breath and sat back in his chair. "You'd think you were unlikable or something."

This time it was Chuck's eyes that narrowed. "You have talked to her, right?"

Memphis threw a fry at him and shot him a dirty look.

"What, it would explain a lot." Chuck gave him the same look back. "The last guy she went out with was Simon."

I couldn't really argue with that.

"Simon?" Atlee's brow rose. "As in Simon Fisher?"

"Yeah." How did he know Simon?

"Wait," he waved his hands through the air. "You're telling me you dated Simon Fisher?"

Did he miss my answer the first time? "Yes."

"Why?"

Memphis answered that one for me. "She said he has nice hair."

Atlee's lip curled, "so fucking scalp him and keep it as a pet. Don't let him touch you." He paused to cock his head. "Did you let him touch you?"

"No," Memphis snorted. "Cindy took care of that for her."

When did this become gang up on Nova hour?

I turned my glare back on my best friend. "Did you have to bring her up?"

"Technically she went down…" Memphis shot back.

"That's a low blow."

Memphis snickered, "so is Cindy."

Okay, that one was kind of funny. But... "You know I've been dealing with her since birth."

"Which is exactly why you should've punched her in the face in third grade."

"Who the fuck is Cindy?" Atlee whispered to Chuck, who shook his head.

"No one you want to know."

I was much too involved in my argument with Memphis to care what those two were saying. "Violence doesn't solve anything."

"Oh but blatant ignorance does?"

"Who's side are you on?"

"The one where you don't date guys like Simon."

"Can I interject here?" Atlee asked.

Memphis and I both answered with a loud, "no."

"Woah," Atlee held up his palms. "I was just going to say that you are way too hot for Simon."

Okay, now he was just being insulting. "Why are you still here?"

"Well I was waiting to see what time you wanted me to pick you up, but..." Atlee settled back in the chair and his ankles crossed. "I'm kind of enjoying the show."

Chuck knew better than anyone what happened when people got between Memphis and I. He was slicing his hand across his neck, giving Atlee the signal to shut up.

One exchanged look was all Memphis and I needed. The next second our focus was on one thing. Memphis tore apart everything that was wrong with Atlee's style while I pointed out the ineffectiveness of his so-called charismatic ways. At one point he looked to Chuck for help. All he got in response was a shrug.

By the time we were out of things to say, Atlee was just sitting there with a blank look and wide eyes.

"Wow," he let out a heavy breath and stood up. "So I'm gonna go."

Memphis and I cocked a brow at him while Chuck muttered, "Escape while you can."

When Atlee turned to walk away, I called out, "tell your friend to do his own dirty work next time."

Chapter 17

GIOVANNI

It was so hot out I could feel the sun bouncing off my hood warming the air conditioning blowing over my face. I suppose I could've parked under a tree or in some shade, but then I wouldn't have a clear view of the church grounds where Nova was stabbing a sharp stick into the ground.

Based on the trash bag in her other hand, I assumed this gathering of pathetic assholes was some kind of clean up. And I meant pathetic assholes.

The only two men there had been struggling to pick up the same log for over twenty minutes. I had to stop myself twice from yelling at them to put their back into it. They were still doing a better job than Novalee, who didn't appear to be doing her job at all.

She just stood there digging the pointed end of her stick in the ground. Until someone called her out on it, then she was busy for all of five minutes.

Can't say I blamed her. Mundane work was boring as fuck, but it still had to get done. Then again, there were extenuating circumstances in this situation.

The corner of my mouth curled as a pair of blazing hazel eyes rolled my way and a small finger lifted in the air. That was the third time she flipped me off. Each and every time I responded with the same small wave.

Sure, I could've parked somewhere a little more inconspicuous, but then I'd miss that indignant eye roll – which was almost as satisfactory as the way Nova stomped around the yard, huffing out her frustration. That girl redefined the word brat.

I couldn't help but wonder if a firm hand would improve her attitude? Probably not. She was so stubborn that she'd probably flip the reaper off if he came knocking on her door.

Still...

My eyes flowed over the spaghetti straps of her pink tank top and down to the denim cut off shorts hugging her waist. The way the fabric was cradling her ass was making me reconsider my view about jeans on girls.

Typically I preferred a more feminine appearance. Summer dresses, skirts, and stuff like that. But I could get behind the sweaty bored look Nova had going on. Daisy Duke didn't have shit on that. Which rose another question...

How the fuck did a scumbag like Simon Fisher get a girl like that?

Was she the one he offered to trade for his debt? I kind of wanted to punch some sense into his thick skull. For as much as I hated Novalee Ford, I'd still admit that there was no way a guy like that would do any better. And he was going to just throw her away? I didn't know what pissed me off more. His blatant stupidity, or the fact that his fucking name kept coming up.

Simon was starting to become a major thorn in my side. Mind you, Atlee didn't help. Every day he asked if Simon paid his debt. So my opinion might be slightly biased. I had to talk Atlee out of giving him daily reminders. That one I did understand. Mainly because I was tempted to break Simon's face just to shut Atlee up.

Sometimes I think he enjoyed the violent side of life a little too much. But at least he was honest about it. Atlee was pretty much an open book. Darry on the other hand… I loved the guy, but there was something wrong with him. Kind of like the disturbing connection between Simon and Novalee. That was one I didn't see coming.

I looked down to change the radio station when a loud bang rang out. My hand immediately shot out for the glove box where I kept a 9 mm, until I spotted streaks of clear fluid running down my windshield and a plastic bottle rolling across my hood. But it was the image I saw through the wet glass that made me grit my teeth.

Nova smiled, shrugged and mouthed the word 'oops'.

Oh, she wants to play does she?

Resting my forearms on the steering wheel, I leaned in and smiled. When suspicion narrowed her eyes, I tipped my chin at the priest standing behind her with his arms crossed. One look at his stern face made her shoulders slump. She shot me a quick dirty look before stomping off to do her work.

The priest looked over at me but was satisfied with a dismissive wave. I however was getting more and more annoyed the longer I sat here. Those two guys were still struggling with that fucking log.

At this point they should just tie a rope to it and play tug of war. This shit was too painful to watch, but not as painful as knowing that Nova once called herself Simon Fisher's girlfriend.

She hadn't so much as given one guy in school a second glance, and she dated him. Why? What the fuck was so special about Simon Fisher? And could we use it to our advantage? That question was one I intended to get an answer for.

Atlee and Darry were currently doing a little pick up and should be here soon.

I glanced down at my watch at the same time as a familiar engine rev roared down the street. A few seconds later Atlee's cherry red Porsche pulled up beside me. And I wasn't the only one to notice the sports car. Half the heads in the churchyard turned to look. All because fucking Atlee had to drive like he was in the middle of a goddamn race. I'd slap him for that latter. Then again…

My eyes zeroed in on the way Nova's fist tightened on her stick. It appeared as if little miss calm and cool was agitated.

"Hey," Atlee called through my open passenger window. "Did it rain?"

Really? "Yes Atlee it rained, but just on the hood of my car."

His brows knit. "Rain can do that?"

I pinched the bridge of my nose while a hand shot out from behind Atlee and smacked him in the back of the head.

"What the fuck is wrong with you?" Darry grumbled.

"Hey," Atlee looked back over his shoulder. "Strange weather patterns have been known to happen. It's called global warming jackass."

"Global warming doesn't make it rain in one spot." Darry argued.

Atlee retorted with, "But it could."

"No it couldn't."

"Yes it could."

"No it couldn't."

"Yes it could."

"You're not a weatherman Atlee."

"I could be."

"But you're not."

"But I could be."

What the fuck was happening right now? Why were they

arguing about the weather? They were worse than a couple of two year olds.

"Hey!" I slammed my hand down on the dashboard, interrupting their argument. "Did you get him?"

Atlee sounded insulted by my question, "Of course we did. We're not amateurs."

"Really, because I'm pretty sure only an amateur would argue about the weather while they had a hostage in the backseat." Dumbass.

"Oh, as opposed to the master who parked in plain sight." He arched his brow and added, "you do understand the meaning of inconspicuous, right?"

I dropped my gaze to the bright color painted on his car, "you want to talk about inconspicuous?"

"I'm not the one stalking someone."

My eyes narrowed, "neither am I."

"We're playing this game again, are we."

"Shut up," I grumbled. "and just get him in here."

It was time to see what the little fuck knew about Novalee Ford.

Atlee stuck his head out of the window and looked at the church across the street, then back at me. "You do know we can be seen?"

"Do you care?"

He shrugged, "not really."

Darry's blonde head appeared from behind Atlee, "I do."

No he didn't. Darry may come off as the calm silent type, but he would be the first person to crack someone up the side of the head in the middle of a crowded room. He was just being difficult. Probably because I was keeping him from studying for the pop quiz in bio tomorrow.

"Just do it." I growled while turning my phone off.

Carissa didn't like being ignored, and pissy wouldn't even

begin to explain Darry's mood if he knew about the messages she'd been sending me all day. The first day of school was the last time I talked to her.

I told myself it was slip up that wouldn't happen again. But that didn't make it any easier to look Darry in the eye when he begrudgingly got out and opened my back door.

Atlee was a little more discreet about the transfer. He gracefully slipped into his backseat, and kicked open the door, creating a sort of shield with a small gap between the doors. Then Darry pulled Simon out and made him duck down so he wouldn't be seen, while Atlee shot a wink in Nova's direction.

She was watching us intently, probably trying to figure out what was going on. She wouldn't. My windshield was tinted enough that she could see me, but not the backseat. A feature I regretted having installed when I saw Simon's bleeding lip and cut cheek in the rearview mirror.

I wouldn't have minded seeing the look on Nova's face when she saw him. One look could tell a lot about someone. Like if they cared about someone or not. And attachments could be used to our advantage.

I scanned the fresh wounds on Simon's face then shifted my gaze to Atlee's reflection, "Everything go okay?"

I assumed he was responsible for the bruises and cuts. That was until Darry grabbed the headrest of the passenger seat. His bloody knuckles caused my brow to rise.

"Simon wasn't feeling very talkative," Atlee threw his arm over Simon's shoulders and pulled him closer so Darry could slide in and close the door. "But he's okay now. Isn't that right Buddy?"

Simon quickly blurted out, "I have until tomorrow."

"Somehow I don't think you'll have my money tomorrow?" I said while staring at him in the rearview.

"I'll have some of it."

Always excuses with this fucking guy, "do we strike you as the kind of people who take payment plans?"

"N—"

Simon was cut off by Darry's fist cracking off his nose. It wasn't a soft hit. Based on the crunch that followed I'd say Simon's nose was now broken. Which would explain the cry that Atlee quickly clamped his hand over.

I sighed, "was that necessary?"

Without missing a breath Darry stated, "yes."

"Darry's just pissed that he got scratched." Atlee snickered when Darry shot him a dirty look. "Little bitch was feisty."

"She's lucky I didn't punch her in the fucking face." Darry grumbled under his breath.

Honestly, I was surprised that he didn't hit her. Most men drew lines in the sand when it came to women. My father for example, when it came to the fairer sex he tried to make death quick and easy. There were always exceptions of course, but only after all other options had been exhausted. Hence our current job. Darry didn't have any lines.

"Oh come on," Atlee pushed Simon's head back against the seat to look over at Darry. "She was kind of fuckable."

"She'd be a lot more fuckable with a broken jaw."

"That's a waste," Atlee snorted. "You can't face fuck someone with a broken jaw."

"Yes you can." The glint in Darry's eye sent a shiver up my spine.

There were some things I did not want to know about my friends. And his knowledge on the subject of broken face fucking was now at the top of the list. Besides, Simon was trying to say something.

"You mind," I nodded at Atlee, then dropped my eyes down at the hand he had clamped over Simon's mouth.

The instant he dropped his arm, Simon gasped. "Cindy didn't know any better."

Atlee's brow arched. "That was Cindy?"

Who the fuck was Cindy and why were we wasting time talking about her?

I was about to change the subject when Atlee asked, "why doesn't Nova like her?"

Did Nova like anyone other than that blonde pipsqueak she hung around with? Then again, if her dislike for this girl was big enough that Atlee knew about it, then it might not be a bad idea to find out a little more about Cindy.

My eyes locked on the church yard where Nova was giving me an evil stare… she was still trying to see past me. Rising up on her tiptoes to look over people. She should be careful. Curiosity killed the cat.

"I don't know why." Simon shrugged. "It's some ongoing rival crap they've had since kindergarten."

"Nah," Atlee shook his head and said what I was thinking. "There's more to it than that."

The swallow Simon pushed down his throat said one thing to me. Guilt. I knew that look well. I tasted that bitter flavor every time I saw Darry's face. Even now I could feel that heavy pit settling in my gut. My friend's green eyes didn't give me the comfort they used to. They reminded me of my betrayal.

That's when it hit me.

I turned around and looked directly at Simon, "you fucked her."

His eyes widened, "no I didn't."

Interesting how his voice rose a pitch.

"Don't lie to me Simon," I warned.

"I'm not lying," he claimed a little too fast.

All three of us tipped our heads in disbelief.

"I didn't touch Cindy until Nova and I broke up."

Uh huh? I hope Nova didn't buy this load of crap he was trying to sell us.

"And what about Nova?" I asked.

Simon eyed me for a second, before saying "what about her?"

"Tell me everything you know."

It was entirely possible he didn't know much. Every gambler had a tell and Simon was no different. His demeanor shifted when her name was brought up. A dip in the left shoulder and slight twitch on the corner of his mouth. As if he'd been rejected the extra point he needed for a win. Or maybe he was rejected something else?

"How long did you two date?"

He wasn't comfortable answering that question either, "a couple of months. Why?"

"Did you fuck her?"

His eyes locked on mine, "she was my girlfriend."

That was a no. I highly doubted he got more than a kiss from her.

I looked back through the windshield at Nova who now had her hand on her hip. "She's a virgin, isn't she?"

As soon as the words left my mouth I wished I could take them back. There was something deep inside me that ached to hear the answer. Something primal and dark that I didn't want to feed. Not with the sister of the man who killed my brother. I couldn't go down that road. I'd fucked up enough. I couldn't betray Atlas as well. Unless…

My eyes rolled up Nova's bare legs to the scowl on her face. There was more than one way to break someone.

Simon's glare narrowed as he breathed out wheezing breaths through his crooked nose. "Why are you asking about Nova?"

"Because I fucking am!" The why was none of his goddamn business.

I was the only one who needed to know that. I needed to know why I found myself following her. Why did I stare at her in school, and why couldn't I shake her face out of my head? Why was Novalee Ford haunting my thoughts when all I wanted to do was put a bullet between her eyes?

And why the fuck hadn't they picked up that goddamn log yet!

"Ah, I see." Simon smirked. He actually fucking smirked at me. "She turned you down."

Atlee reacted quicker. His fist that cracked off the side of Simon's face. It was a little too hard because the whine he let out attracted some unwanted attention.

When I looked back at the church, Nova wasn't just watching us. She was marching over here.

"Shit, she's coming over."

"Well get rid of her," Atlee said while Darry slammed Simon's face into his knee before he could scream.

Didn't have many options in this situation. We could slit Simon's throat before she could hear his pleas, pretty sure no one would miss him. But Darry and Atlee were seen taking him. Taking out Nova was the other option. While I wouldn't mind that, it was contradictive to the job. Which left only one option.

Sighing, I looked over at the log still laying in the grass.

"Keep him quiet," I muttered and stepped out onto the street. "I have yard work to do."

Chapter 18

Determination coursed through my veins with every step I took. My tolerance level was so far gone at this point that nothing would've stopped me from going over to where Gio was parked. He was up to something.

Memphis could call me paranoid all he wanted, but I knew better. I could feel it in my gut. The feeling was hard to explain. It was kind of like a dark cloud hanging over me that started when I walked into the Twilight Zone version of St. Agatha's.

Not one single person so much as shot me a dirty look. That was just eerie and wrong. I woke up every morning to a scolding either because I was running late or Maw Maw didn't like my choice of outfit. That wasn't much of an issue now.

The stupid uniform hanging on the back of my bedroom door took care of that, but still… I didn't go to school to have an easy time and learn things without being tripped or picked on. I was a teenager god damnit. Make fun of me.

Not to mention my position in the pecking order was way

below invisible and left alone. And it certainly wasn't anywhere close to being hit on by Atlee Fiore. And not well, I might add.

Seriously, how did that guy get so many girls? Was it his spicy cologne or stupid smile, because it certainly wasn't his pickup lines. And after all that bullshit, I had to come here, to church, and clean up while Gio sat across the street and watched.

Asshole.

There I was, trapped under the hot sun, sweating my ass off while he sat comfortably in his air conditioned vehicle. The only cool air that my truck had, came from the little fan on the dashboard that needed a slap to turn on. The water bottle was funny though. Gio didn't like that much.

I could see that vein in his forehead from across the street. Apparently I had a good arm. That was a decent throw. Maybe I'd try out for baseball? I wasn't much into sports, but I wouldn't complain about having a bat to beat Gio with.

My eyes locked on the shiny navy hood as my shoes smacked against the asphalt and I stormed forward.

The icing on my day of disturbing things was when Atlee and Darious showed up and joined Gio. That's when I decided that whatever they were doing, it would end now. I was going to stop it. Nothing would deter me.

I was going to march over there and show them that I would not be pushed around. Even if I had to put my fist through the window to do it.

When the driver's door opened and Gio stepped out, I did falter a bit though. He was a big guy. The sun was literally blocked out by his form. I was a measly little ant compared to him. But I still had fists, and he had nuts. What was that saying? The bigger they are, the harder they fall.

My hands balled at my sides.

I was a strong confident woman… well the strong part might

be a stretch, and Memphis would argue the woman factor, but I was confident that I could do this!

Gio's piercing emerald eyes darkened as he strode forward.

Okay maybe I was a little less confident now. For a second I swore I felt the ground vibrate with his step, but I could still do this. Who needed confidence when they had anger and hatred? Although he did look a little extra murderey today. That wasn't a benefit to my side. Kind of wished I had another water bottle.

Continuing on my march I tipped my head at Gio's black slacks and white button up shirt. He didn't bother to go home and change after school. Would he get in trouble if he had to replace his uniform? My nails were long enough to tear a shirt. Or I could try another tactic. Like distract him with my boobs.

While they were a pain in the ass, boobs were a fantastic distraction device. Men got this blank look when cleavage was visible, including Memphis – who had absolutely no desire to touch them – but he did look. Maybe they had magical powers?

Mine probably didn't have as much magical properties department, and I didn't really have an abundance of cleavage. Not like Cindy. I really hated her right now, with her perky chest and full cleavage. Oh and I couldn't forget her ability to suck, in more ways than one.

Bitch.

Sighing, I looked back at the imposing form coming my way.

Alright, nut punch it is.

I readied myself as the gap between Gio and I closed. Rolled my shoulders back, firmed my balled up fists, and opened my mouth to tell him off. This was it. I was going to stand up to this prick. Except Gio walked right past me. He just went right on by without so much as a twitch in his steady stride, as if I wasn't there.

What just happened?

Why would he do that? Gio knew we were about to have a confrontation, and as far as I could tell he enjoyed those. He didn't walk away from them. I did. Gio Mancini didn't get to use my tactics.

Well, I guess there's only one thing to do.

I spun around, skipped up beside him – which was not easy by the way. Gio had long legs that I needed to jog to keep up with. But that was okay. If anyone was going to walk away it would be me. Not him.

"Was the view not good enough from over there?"

Gio didn't respond. He didn't even glance my way, which pissed me off more. Ignoring was also my thing.

"I could charge you with stalking."

He let out a snort/chuckle that pretty much said 'good luck with that'. At least it was something. Besides, it wasn't an impossibility. I had evidence. Like...

"You sat across the street for over an hour." I knew this because I timed every dreadful second I spent picking up garbage.

"It's a public road." Gio didn't slow down, but his eyes did slide my way. "I can sit there all day if I want."

Not without getting a parking ticket he couldn't.

"You're following me." Was his chest burning too, because sucking in a deep breath was really starting to hurt.

"Looks to me like you're the one doing the following."

Was he really trying to turn this around on me? Of course he was. This was Gio Mancini, king of the assholes.

"Is that why you keep showing up where I am?"

Let's see him argue that.

Gio shrugged, "it's a small city."

A likely excuse.

"It's a town," I panted. "Not a city."

It would also be great if he would stop walking through this town long enough for me to catch my breath.

"A town has a population of under five thousand," this time

Gio's steps thankfully did slow when he looked my way. "Sorrie is over fifty thousand, hence, city."

Technicality. "That doesn't mean you're not following me."

"Yeah," Gio stopped, turned to face me, and folded his arms over his chest. "Prove it."

This mother…

I hunched over, held up my finger, and wheezed in a few breaths, "give me a second."

"What the fuck is wrong with you?"

I'm dying you long legged bastard.

"I'm fine." I coughed.

A deep arch tugged at Gio's brow. "How out of shape are you?"

Hey, let's see how well he could breathe after standing in the hot sun all afternoon.

"That doesn't matter." I forced another breath into my aching lungs and straightened up. "What matters is I can prove it."

"Prove what?" Gio asked. "That you can't jog for more than thirty seconds?"

"That was a lot longer than thirty seconds." It was at least five minutes.

He looked over at his Rover, then turned towards the church. "We haven't even crossed the street yet."

Okay that looked bad. I may need to start some kind of workout in the mornings.

"That just means it won't take you long to get back in your car and leave before I call the cops."

"Is that so?"

"That's right." Defiance lifted my chin with that statement.

"And what are you going to tell them?"

"That you're stalking me." *Duh.*

It didn't matter that I had no proof. I could still file a report.

"Uh huh," Gio pursed his lips and nodded. "And what exactly are you going to use to back this up? Do you have pictures or videos of me parked outside your house, or in your room at night?"

"N— wait… you've been in my room?"

That was a truly terrifying thought. He had to be bluffing. I would know if someone was in my room. Wouldn't I?

Gio didn't say anything. He just gave me the smallest smirk, then turned around and continued walking.

I stood there wondering if this was another one of his games, or if he had actually invaded my personal space? Did he touch anything, or watch me sleep? There was a disturbing image. Gio looming over my bed while I drooled on my pillow.

There was no way he got in our trailer. He couldn't even stalk someone properly. Who parked in broad daylight when they were following someone? Unless they wanted said someone to know they were following them. And Maw Maw did forget to lock the door sometimes.

God damnit, now I was going to have to sanitize everything in my room. There goes my night. Fucking Gio Mancini and his stupid mind games. I was definitely going to punch him in the nuts. As soon as I caught up with him.

That plan went out the window the second I spotted where Gio went. Instead of my fists striking out in anger, my brows knit in confusion.

He was over by the two panting guys who'd been trying to move the same log all afternoon. Not only that, but it appeared as if he was getting ready to lift the heavy piece of wood. I don't know what Gio was up to, but it was not happening on my watch.

I stormed over and slammed my foot down on the log before he could lift it off the ground. "What the hell do you think you're doing?"

"Well," he sighed, "I figured I'd move this over to that wood pile. Why…" He looked up from his bent over position, "are you going to do it?"

"I could," *and die. That thing was huge.* "But by all means," I waved my hand, "Be my guest."

Personally, I had no issue calling his bluff. There was only one problem with that. It wasn't a bluff. Gio hoisted that thing up on his shoulder and I suddenly understood why girls got stupid around some men.

The muscles in his arms tensed and flexed, tearing away all logic thought in my mind until I completely forgot why I was standing there. The only thing that existed were those firm bulges under his tanned skin. I think I even tipped my head at one point to get a better look.

Thankfully Gio's deep tone snapped me back into reality. "You're either plotting my murder…"

Was his smirk always that cocky?

"Or you see something you like."

I snorted, "don't flatter yourself."

Plotting his murder was the only option out of those scenarios. I'd come up with a few ways to end his life. It was the disposal of the body I didn't have a plan for. It would be difficult to move something that big… and hard… and smooth… he kind of smelled good too. All woodsy and fresh.

I noticed that when he bent down and whispered, "you're still staring."

I was not staring. "It's called plotting."

"And what are you plotting?"

I looked him right in the eye and said, "Body disposal methods."

He stared back at me, "you come up with anything?"

"Not yet." But I would.

"Well," Gio straightened up and adjusted the log on his shoulder, once again drawing my attention to his arms. "You know where to find me when you do."

"Yeah, you'll be following me," I called out when he headed towards the wood pile.

I might've went after him to continue the argument if I wasn't interrupted by a stern voice.

"Novalee Nadine Ford."

Crap, Maw Maw.

I heard Gio snicker, "Nadine?"

"Shut up," I growled before turning to smile at Maw Maw.

She did not look happy, that conclusion mostly came from the slap I got to the back of my head, "how many times do I have to tell you to stop standing around?"

"I'm a teenager, that's kind of what we do." That earned me another smack.

"Jesus," I grumbled while rubbing the back of my scalp.

If she kept this up I wouldn't have enough brain cells left to do anything more than stand around.

"Don't you take the Lord's name in vain. We are in a place of worship, little girl…"

Technically we were outside the place of worship, and when did I become the asshole?

"Have you no pride?"

I looked over at the peeling white paint decorating the building and shook my head. "Not really."

Maw Maw's hand swung, killing a dozen more brain cells.

"Ouch, fine. Church is great."

Next to wave through the air was her finger, "Don't you back talk me."

How was that back talk? I said church was great. It wasn't. It was boring as hell. Father John was okay. I didn't mind him so much. Especially when he tried to be hip for the younger crowd. That was entertaining.

Maw Maw shook her head, "I swear the good Lord above decided to test me with you."

"Maybe you should pray more." Just saying. If there was such a thing as a vengeful god and I was her curse, then a little more divine devotion may be called for. I was kind of a pain in the ass.

"I raised you better than this," she grabbed my shoulder and steered me over to a pile of trash. "Now get to work."

A part of me felt the need to point out that she didn't technically raise me, but a bigger part was more worried about the slippers on her feet. Getting slapped with one of those wasn't something someone forgot. And it wasn't something you could run from. I tried that once. All grandmother's seemed to be masters in the art of slipper throwing.

So as much as I would've loved to continue standing around, I grabbed a stick off the ground and stabbed it in the pile.

"I'm watching you, little girl." Maw Maw gave me one last warning look then headed off to check on someone else.

This day kept getting better and better. It probably didn't help that Gio was across the yard chuckling. *Bastard.*

I glared at him and jabbed my stick in the pile while imagining that it was his head. That was how the next hour went. Stabbing things while imagining that it was different body part of Gio's. Every bottle was a leg or an arm, cups and random paper were his head, and everything else was his balls.

Considering he decided to stick around and for some reason help out, it was a fantastic way to burn off some anger. And it wouldn't end with a flying boomerang slipper.

I even managed to ignore him for the last twenty minutes. Mind you, I was working in the back where no one else was. So it made it easy to pretend he wasn't there. Until Gio came waltzing around the side of the building.

Regular Gio Mancini was easy to ignore. He was another asshole student. When the uniform was taken away and replaced with sweaty, shirtless Gio Mancini... the asshole part didn't register in my brain. The wall of flesh and five o'clock shadow darkening his chin sure did though.

I literally felt my jaw drop as my hormones slammed to the surface.

Apparently Gio's arms weren't the only thing that could make a girl stupid. His entire torso was all hard ridges and firmness, covered by smooth skin. The man had a literal eight pack. I'd seen four, and one or two sixes, but eight? I didn't know they came in that size. Simon didn't even have a pack.

"You're staring again."

"I am not staring," I jabbed my stick down. "I'm stabbing you in the balls."

Seriously, who photoshopped him? And where the hell was his shirt? He needed to put that back on right now.

Gio dipped his gaze down the end of my stick, "I think you missed."

I looked down at the cup and sighed. *Damnit, that was a head, not nuts.*

"It was a metaphorical stab. Unlike you…" I shook the cup off in my bag. "I couldn't actually kill someone."

"You sure about that?" Gio braced his shoulder on the wooden wall beside him. "Your brother didn't have a problem."

My grip tightened around the stick. He did not get to talk about Kato. "My brother is a good man."

"Who beat mine to death with a tire iron." The tone in his voice matched the way his jaw clenched. "Pretty sure that negates the good part of your claim."

"Oh and I'm sure you've never done anything like that." I shot back, not really expecting an answer. I got one though.

Gio's shoulder lifted in a shrug, "I never claimed to be a good man."

Did that mean he killed someone? All confrontations we'd had where he wrapped his hands around my neck or threatened me, I never gave much thought about if he would actually do it. Would Gio Mancini end my life? Could he? Hatred and anger made people do a lot of things. But death? That was an entirely different beast. It changed people. Like my dad. There was a void in his stare, as if something inside of him had died. Trauma survivors had the same look.

And so did Gio.

I tipped my head and looked at him. Like really looked at him. It was like I was seeing him for the first time. The arrogant way he carried himself. How he didn't seem to care what anyone thought, or worry when someone called the cops.

There were rumors about the Mancini's and their 'family' business. Words like mob, mafia, and gangster were used. And as much as I would like to pass it off as mere speculation, I couldn't help but think about that day in court. How the three of them walked in and the room went silent. Not even the judge said anything when Gio started harassing me. In fact, I couldn't think of a single time where I'd even heard about someone crossing Cesare Mancini.

Who exactly was Gio Mancini?

"Go ahead," a shiver ran up my spine as his voice dropped an octave. "Ask."

"I don't want to ask you anything." I did, but I pushed down that curiosity and moved to walk away. Some things were better off not known.

Gio stopped me before I could round the corner. He grabbed my arm and pushed me back against the building. "Ask your question, Nova."

"I don't have a question, Gio." I spat back and darted to the left.

His hand shot out, flattening his palm against the building and stopping me from leaving. When I moved in the other direction he did the same thing with his other hand, effectively caging me in his arms.

"Let me go Gio!"

"I will," he stepped in and growled, "after you ask your question."

"I don't have a question."

I did have a problem with this situation though, which I attempted to solve by shoving him back. Not only did I fail epically at that, but now my hands were splayed out on his chest. His very hard and warm chest.

"Yes you do. You want to know how much blood I have on my hands."

It was hard not to notice how he phrased that. How much blood, meant there was some.

Despite the shiver trickling across my skin, I snorted and rolled my eyes. "Why would I care about that?"

"Because you want to know if I could kill you."

One step shattered the small gap of breathing room I did have. And when Gio bent down to bring his lips to my ear, I couldn't breathe at all.

"I could," he whispered. "and what's more, I want to."

He was too close. I didn't like it. I didn't like the heat coming off his body or how I could smell a hint of mint on his breath. And I especially didn't like the intensity of his piercing jade stare when he lifted his head. It felt like he was penetrating my thoughts.

"It wouldn't even be that hard."

When Gio's fingers grazed over my collarbone, I couldn't stop my body from twitching. All I wanted to do was get away.

He raised his hand to my neck. "Just wrap my hand around your throat, and..." Gio twitched his wrist while hissing out a snapping sound. "Lights out."

That alone was enough to cause a lump of dread to form in my throat, but the shadow that moved across his face made me seriously concerned for my safety. It wasn't a game anymore. This was a viable threat to my safety.

I opened my mouth to do the only thing I could think of and scream.

Gio slammed his lips down on mine, sucking up any sound I

managed to make before shock set in. I couldn't move. It was as if my limbs weren't there. For a second the only part of my body that did exist was the patch of skin on my chin that his stubble was abrading.

Gio Mancini was kissing me! He was actually kissing me.

The worst part… he was good at it. I'd been kissed before, but not like this. Not in a way where I could feel him everywhere. From the tips of my toes to the tingling in my scalp, Gio was there. His scent, his hands, and the heat of his breath was all consuming.

And he didn't stop once I'd shut up. Gio growled and pressed in on me while moving his mouth in a way that I couldn't help but give into. My lips parted, his tongue grazed mine and I panicked.

I bit down, catching his bottom lip between my teeth.

"Fuck," Gio pulled back and grumbled down at me. "You bit me."

"You kissed me." I snarled.

"You were about to scream." He took a step back while swiping his thumb over his lip.

I inwardly smiled at the small spot of blood dotting his thumb. "You didn't have to kiss me."

There were plenty of other ways to shut people up. Clamp a hand over my mouth, smack me around a bit. Either of those would've been fine.

Silence washed over us as I waited for him to come back at me. But he didn't. He just stood there and stared. I fought to keep eye contact and not look at his lips, but the longer we stood there, the more I could taste the sweet tea on his tongue.

"Why are you still here!" He needed to go, now.

"Why are you?"

That was a good question. Why was I still here? I could leave. There was a crowd of other people around the corner.

Gio's foot lifted with a single step that caused me to flatten back against the wall. There was something different about the way he was watching me. Something that made the pit in my stomach swirl. I didn't know if he was going to kill me, eat me, or both.

"You should go." I repeated.

He tipped his head and rolled gaze down my body. "You're scared."

"No I'm not." I was totally terrified. Gio needed to go away. A kiss shouldn't feel like that. They should be sloppy and emotionless. A simple gesture that led to other things and then was forgotten.

"Yes, you are," the look on his face darkened. "I can smell it on you."

That was literally impossible. No human could smell that good. Not that that made me feel any better.

"Go fuck yourself," I hissed.

"Novalee Ford!"

Oh crap.

"Maw Maw..." was all I got out before I saw the slipper slicing through the air.

Chapter 19

GIOVANNI

The first thing Romeo said to me when I walked in the door was, 'Got anything?'

Of course, what he meant was did I find out anything, and yes I did. I found out that I was a dumb fuck that made stupid decisions.

I glanced down at the lit up screen of my dinging phone, then slipped it back in my pocket unanswered. Carissa Fiore was one of said stupid decisions. But not the one that had me sitting on the roof outside my bedroom window in the moonlight.

That one was a lot more complicated and not in any way an answer I could give to my brother. We didn't find out if Veda Ford had seen anything because I was too busy kissing her sister.

What in the actual fuck?

Okay, so she was about to scream, but there were plenty of other ways to shut her up. I could've covered her mouth, smothered her, or choked her to death. Hell, a firm slap across the face would've worked. But I didn't go for any of those options.

I didn't use my hands at all. I used my goddamn mouth – which once again brought me back to my original thought... what in the actual fuck?

Kissing Novalee Ford far surpassed any of the fucked up shit I'd done in the past. She was the sister of my enemy, someone I dreamed about strangling, and a royal pain in my ass. And I fucking kissed her.

It must've been the heat. That was the only thing I could think of. I was hauling around heavy shit in stifling temperatures. Anyone would've lost their damn mind, right? I wasn't the only one affected by it. Novalee did kiss me back, so clearly the heat got to her too.

The girl fucking hated me almost as much as I hated her. I don't think she wanted to see me dead, but she glared at me like she did. Henceforth the kiss was nothing more than a knee jerk reaction by two delusional people. That was what I chose to chalk it up to. A mistake that I could move on from – which would've been a lot easier if I couldn't still smell her.

Every time I closed my eyes my nostrils flared with that faint scent. It was sweet and refreshing, like a glass of iced tea on a hot afternoon. My body craved more while my mouth watered at the memory. So I did the only thing I could...

I sat outside in the fresh air with my eyes wide open. There was no hint of Novalee out here. No big hazel eyes glaring at me, another expression I wanted to slap away. There was just the trees in the distance, and lightning bugs flying around.

This quiet view from the back of my house was just what I needed to clear my head. My time was much better spent plotting her murder. It wasn't like I enjoyed it or anything.

She fucking bit me!

The sting in my lip reignited as I gritted my teeth and balled my fists.

Who the fuck did Novalee think she was? Did she have any idea how many girls would've begged to be in her position? I had a new one trying to hang off me every week – anyone of whom would've sucked my dick for a little attention.

And she fucking bit me. Maybe I should bite her? Now there was an idea. I could dig my teeth into the soft flesh of her cheek and tear a chunk out. Bet her blood didn't smell as good as the rest of her. It probably tasted pretty sweet though.

Pinching the bridge of my nose, I let out a long exhale and cleared my mind.

What the fuck was wrong with me? One little kiss and I was suddenly reduced to a scared ten-year-old, hiding outside his window from his father. What was I supposed to tell him? *Sorry I don't have anything yet because I was too busy sucking face with the enemy?*

That would make him take me seriously. I'd been waiting for this opportunity all my life – which Romeo of all people had to convince him to give me – and here I was. Fucking shit up on day one. And why... because she smelled good?

Come on. I had more self-control than that. I wasn't Atlee. I didn't chase after a pretty face and nice ass.

Though, Novalee did have a nice ass. All firm and grabbable. That shit looked great in jeans.

And... I'm thinking about her again.

"Fuck." I slammed my knuckles down into the red clay tiles and dug in until pain radiated up my forearm, making my jaw clench.

Atlas was my brother. He pushed me on the swings and taught me how to not break my hand when I punched someone. And here I was thinking about the sister of the man who killed him. He deserved revenge, not betrayal.

My father and Romeo were around when I was growing up, but not like Atlas. He was the only solid I had. It was my duty to avenge his death. And Novalee was the key for that.

I knew that the day I saw her in court. Kato Ford wasn't very happy when I confronted his baby sister. If he could've jumped over that bench and slit my throat he would've. He would've gladly sacrificed any hope he had of a life after prison to protect her.

We could have Kato beat up, or break his bones over and over again, but nothing would hurt him more than knowing he couldn't protect his baby sister. The suffering and anguish he'd feel while sitting helpless in his jail cell... that was what I wanted. That was what Atlas deserved.

Gazing out at the moonlit trees, I let out a sigh.

The rustling breeze and faint trickling of the fountain used to be calming. Now all I could hear in them was the sound of my brother's voice. A faint whisper of the ghost that used to roam these halls. I could almost hear him calling my name...

"GIO..."

I shuffled my butt along the red tiles, away from my window.

The sound of my name was echoing from the halls and out in the yard, and I ignored them all. I sat up here and watched as my father's men scoured the grounds with flashlights and radios. Why couldn't they just leave me alone?

Saul had gone back and forth in the same clutch of trees six times, like he thought I was hiding in the leaves or something.

"Gio..."

My eyes shifted over to my open window. Atlas was getting closer.

I didn't want to talk to him either. All I wanted to do was sit out here and pretend my father didn't exist. He kept treating me like a kid. But I was a Mancini too, and I had a right to go to Italy with him and my brothers.

"Gio," Atlas called. "Come on, little man, where are you?"

Not going to Italy with you, because apparently I'm too young.

"Are you in here?"

Ignoring my brother's call, I huffed and hugged my knees. Atlas wasn't the first person to come in my room looking for me, but he was the first to pop his head out the window.

"There you are."

Great, I wish I could become invisible.

Atlas tipped his head and cocked a brow. "Not talking, huh?"

Nope.

He folded his arms on the window sill and rested his chin on his hands. "You do know that half the house is looking for you?"

"I don't care," I grumbled while turning away.

I didn't want anyone to find me. Including Atlas.

"What are you doing out here?"

"Dad doesn't like heights." He didn't like me being up here either. He said it was dangerous and I might fall. But I wasn't a baby. I could handle myself. He'd know that if he'd just let me do things on my own.

"Ah, you're hiding from the old man." my brother nodded. "I can understand that."

I lifted my head and looked over at him. "You can?"

"Sure, I want to hide from him sometimes, too."

"You do?" Then why was he always doing what our dad said?

"Yeah, but you know what..."

I shook my head.

"He always finds me."

I dropped my head back on my knees and muttered, "He hasn't found me."

Maybe our dad liked Atlas better. He spent more time with my brothers. They were always doing things together. Meanwhile I was left here with the stupid old moth ball smelling nanny.

"Well," Atlas lifted his head a little further out the window, "that's because you have a pretty great hiding spot."

It was a great spot. No one ever thought to look on the balcony roof outside my window.

"I don't really want to talk to dad either, can I join you?" Atlas asked.

This was my place, but I didn't mind sharing it with my brother.

I nodded and slid over.

Atlas was bigger, so he had a harder time climbing out than I did. He needed to tilt his shoulders and wriggle his hips to get through. It was kind of funny how he flopped down beside me on his back. I couldn't help but giggle at the way his dark hair fell over his face.

"Hey, don't laugh at me." He blew his hair out off his eyes and sat up. "That was hard work."

"I did it."

"Oh, you did , did you?" Atlas threw his arm over my shoulders and ruffled his other hand through my hair. "You little shit."

"Stop it." I growled while slapping his hand away.

Atlas kept messing my hair until I pushed him back and shot him a scowl. I hated when he did that stuff. Now I'd have to brush my hair again. Not that he cared how angry I got. Big brothers were annoying.

"Oh, stop pouting," he propped his arms on his knees and gazed out at the yard. "You're better than that."

"Dad doesn't think so." My chest heaved with a breath as I sucked back a tear. "He won't let me do anything."

"That's because he's scared."

That was dumb. "Why would he be scared?"

I wasn't going to do anything bad. I just wanted to be included.

"Because one day he won't be your dad anymore." Atlas sighed, "he'll be your boss."

That didn't make sense. People couldn't stop being who they were. "He'll always be my dad. Just like you and Romeo will always be my brothers."

"That's right," he looked over at me. "I will always be your brother. I want you to remember that, okay?"

"Okay?" That wasn't something I would forget, like where I put my shoes. We were family. We'd always be family.

"Good." Atlas nodded then rolled his stare out at the yard.

There was something different about the look in his eyes. The way Atlas stared as if he could see something I couldn't, while his forehead furrowed and brows knit. Was he was waiting for something, or planning something?

Maybe he was wondering where all the lightning bugs were? There were usually more little lights flickering out by the pond. I wondered where they were. Were they hiding from someone like I was, or did they just decide not to come out tonight? Maybe they were mad at their fathers? Did lightning bugs even have fathers, and if they did, did their father's ignore them too?

"Atlas..."

"Yeah."

"Do you ever miss mom?"

His dark eyes snapped over to mine. "Why are you asking about mom?"

"I don't know." I shrugged. "I just think about her sometimes."

And hear her screams at night. I'd never forget the sound of her blood dripping down the cupboard door. Each drop echoed through my ears, but it was the silence behind them that was the loudest.

"Don't you think about her?" Did he remember what she looked like? Because I couldn't. Her smile faded more every day.

"Sometimes," Atlas looked back out at the yard and whispered, "But I try not to."

Confusion tipped my head to the side, "Dad says memories are all we have."

He nudged me with his shoulder, "My memories aren't the same as yours, Little Man."

"Because you weren't there that day?"

"Because 'she' wasn't supposed to be there that day."

My brows knit. "Who was supposed to be there?"

"It doesn't matter," Atlas grumbled in response.

I watched the line in his forehead deepen and opened my mouth to ask if he was okay, but Atlas cut me off before I could say anything.

"Come on. We better go inside," Atlas tipped his chin at a beam of light in the yard. "Before Saul starts chopping down trees."

"I don't want to go inside," I huffed and crossed my arms. "I hate dad."
"No, you don't." Atlas said. "But you'll hate me one day." ...

I NEVER DID FIND out what Atlas meant by that. Then again I was only ten. But that look on his face never went away. He changed shortly after that. He got angry and distant. Every time Atlas would walk in the room, I'd silently hope that he would smile at me like he used to.

He never did. Because of that I spent the last three months of his life avoiding him. And now, I'd give anything to see that look on his face.

My gaze trickled over the pond in the distance.

The trees around it had gotten bigger, taller and more full. It kind of pissed me off knowing that Atlas's death had no effect on them. They flourished while I died a little. Everything out here had changed. The shed Atlas helped me build for a clubhouse was gone.

The fountain in the middle of the yard where he taught me how to ride a bike was replaced with a new one, and the garden my mother started never grew back. All the flowers dried out and wilted away. Now it was just another patch of meaningless grass.

It was funny how the world quieted down during certain moments. I could hear the soft rustle of leaves in the night breeze, and feel the hum of Romeo's music in the room below me, but everything else was silent. As if there was a void in this place. There was no voice in the distance calling my name, or footsteps echoing down the hall.

There was just me, the lightning bugs, and the aching betrayal burning through my chest.

It wasn't the fact that I kissed Novalee that was picking at the back of my brain. It was that I couldn't stop thinking about it. I couldn't wash the sweet taste of her out of my mouth, or erase the image of her big hazel eyes from my mind. That spark of fear glimmering across her face haunted my thoughts.

"Fear…" I sat up as realization smacked me in the face.

There was genuine fear in her expression.

I accused her of being scared, but she really was. Novalee was terrified.

Why? What was different? We argued, I laughed when she got in trouble, and I threatened to kill her. That was all pretty normal. There was one thing that wasn't.

My brow rose, "The kiss."

That couldn't be it, could it? Out of everything I'd done to her, it couldn't be a simple kiss that got under her skin. Fuck sakes, I tried to kill her twice. Full on strangulation murder her, and she never looked at me like she did when I kissed her.

I replayed the moment in my mind, going over all of her mannerisms. The way her anger spiked while she hugged herself, and backed away. That's when it hit me… Novalee was hiding. Not from me, but from something else. Herself maybe? I needed to find out.

Chapter 20

After a long day of hard work, there was nothing like enjoying an iced cold refreshing drink out in the cool breeze. It was an almost perfect end to an otherwise crappy day. There was only one thing that could make it better. The slow and painful demise of Gio Mancini.

Swallowing down a mouthful of Maw Maw's sweet tea, I leaned back in the patio chair and kicked my feet up on the banister. The cool liquid flowed down my throat, easing tension out of my muscles. The last time I felt like this was after running a marathon in school. Okay, it was more like laps around the gym but still… Phys Ed was cruel and unusual punishment as far as I was concerned.

Kind of like Gio Mancini. I bet that asshole loved Phys Ed. The athletic genius was all buff and in shape. It was seriously annoying. I found running to the bathroom exhausting. Maybe laps weren't a bad idea.

The key to defeating one's enemy was to think like their enemy.

But did I really want to be one of those people that got up at the ass crack of dawn to go for a run?

That seemed like a monumental waste of time when I could simply have a sharp object on hand. Besides, I was more of an evening person. Everything looked a little magical in the moonlight. The trailer park was a perfect example of that.

I glanced around at the various porch lights glowing in the night.

Sault Saint Marie Estates wasn't what I would call a picturesque place, but in that moment when the sun began to sink below the horizon, I could almost see the beauty that used to be here. It was as if the possibilities and dreams everyone had still lingered in the air, just out of reach, but close enough for hope to hang on.

Of course hope was an illusion. This place, with its potholes and plastic fences, was just as run down as the people in it. Once upon a time Mr. Garabaldi had a wife, or so they said. It was hard to imagine him in anything other than a bathrobe, let alone with a woman on his arm. The fantasy was nice though.

"Nova..."

Speaking of fantasies...

I inwardly grimaced at the sound of my sister's voice.

Was it wrong that I missed the drugged out of her mind version of Veda I came home to the other night? At least she had some pep in her tone then, instead of the dull whisper of a voice she was using now.

Maybe Rita would give me some of those pills? If Veda wouldn't take them, I could always use them. There were a few things I'd like to forget. Such as the taste I'd been trying to wash out of my mouth for the last four hours. Blueberries and sin should not be that sweet. Bastard probably ate healthy too. *Pfft, prick.*

Stupid Gio and his dumb soft lips could fuck right off. He'd clearly lost his damn mind, otherwise he wouldn't have done what he did. And what he did would not be referred to as a kiss. Kisses were small gestures leading up to foreplay.

Or in Simon's case they were bad attempts at cannibalism. Either way, kisses weren't supposed to be soul sucking tingly sensations that left me weak in the knees. But that didn't matter, because said not-kiss would only be referred to as 'the event that shall not be named'—because as far as I was concerned it never happened.

After all, one didn't name a mistake. Unless that mistake came in the form of a child, then it might be called Novalee. Although my mother said I was determined and not a mistake, since I defied all methods of birth control.

"Nova," Veda called again. "Where are you?"

My mother also said that one day I'd want to be around my sister. Clearly her words of wisdom weren't as insightful as I thought.

My teeth gritted as the screen door creaked open.

"Are you out here?"

If I said no, would she stay in the house?

Veda's footsteps smashed that hope to bits.

I took another sip of my drink while Veda shot me a scowl and dropped her hand on her hip. "Didn't you hear me calling you?"

If I said no, would she go back in the house?

"Are you just gonna stare at me?"

Was that an option?

Veda eyed the glass in my hand and took a step. "Are you drinking?"

What else did one do with liquid?

"I could try and chew the sweet tea," I dropped my gaze down to the contents of the glass, "But I don't think that would work very well."

"You know what I mean, Nova." Veda scolded. "There better not be alcohol in there. It's a school night."

"Relax, Mother Teresa, it's just sweet tea." After my last drunken binge Maw Maw declared our trailer dry territory.

"Nova?"

"Ugh, Veda." I shot back.

"Alright then," she crossed her arms. "If you're not drinking, then what are you doing out here?"

"Is there something wrong with someone enjoying the night air?"

"Someone, no. You, yes."

I lifted my hand holding the glass and pointed at her, "I'm hurt by your insinuation."

I wasn't always up to something. In this case I was, but that was beside the point.

My eyes narrowed on the blue trailer down the road as two little boys busted out the door. Billy and Kyle Dunbar. *Little pissants.*

"Hello, are you even listening to me?" Veda sang.

"Of course I am" I stretched my neck to watch as they headed out into the yard.

That's right you little shits, go check on your precious bikes.

They looked pretty worried. I can't imagine why. Everyone around here knew those bikes were their prized possessions. And no one liked upsetting a child.

What kind of person would do that? Perhaps the same kind of person that would make an anonymous phone call warning them that someone was checking out their bicycles. What could I say, I needed a distraction. And as Maw Maw said, neighbors should look out for each other.

"What are you doing?"

Oh right, Veda.

"I'm waiting." I answered.

Her brow rose, "For what?"

Kyle's grubby hand reached out for his bike and my voice deepened, "Revenge."

A cloud of shaving cream erupted as the frantic screams of little boys flowed through my ears in a satisfying rhythm. And now my night was complete.

I sucked back another mouthful of sweet tea and let out a loud, "ah."

Veda's mood however, did not improve. Based on the look she was currently giving me, I'd say it dropped from somber silence to full on irritation. But it was a reaction, and that was more than she normally gave.

"Nova."

"What?" I said in my most innocent tone.

"They're little boys."

"No," I argued. "They're evil spawns of Satan that deserve a lot more than what they got."

Shaving my legs tomorrow wouldn't be pleasant, but it was totally worth it.

"You should show a little compassion."

Why? Because their parents worked a lot and weren't around much? Ours were dead and you didn't see anyone giving us compassion. Besides… "There's no compassion in war."

Veda let out a sigh, "This isn't war."

"Just because you chose not be on the front lines, doesn't mean this isn't war."

Billy and Kyle may not have done anything today. Their last round of ding dong ditch ring the doorbell was a week ago, but it wasn't like I could do anything to the person I was really mad at. What was I going to do? Put a shaving cream bomb in Gio's car?

Huh?

That wasn't a bad idea. Actually the more I thought about it, the more I liked it. Shaving cream made quite the mess. It stuck onto things and snuck into the crevasses. I doubted he'd be too thrilled about having to clean that up. I, on the other hand, would thoroughly enjoy watching him.

I looked over at Billy and Kyle trying to wipe white goop off their faces while imagining it was Gio, and possibly one or two of his friends.

I'm gonna going to need more supplies.

Finger's snapped in front of my face, drawing me back to reality out of my fantasy.

My eyes rolled up to my sister as she huffed an annoyed, "What is wrong with you?"

"I'm afraid you'll have to be more specific than that. As you know, I have many issues." *Such as the event that shall not be named.* "Some might even go as far as to call me a psychiatrist's wet dream."

And by some I meant Memphis.

"I know." Veda sighed and stepped forward to brush a lock of my hair behind my ear. "It might not be a bad idea to talk to someone."

Oh please. "Cause it's done so much good for you."

"I've made progress."

That statement made my eyes roll. She was going on her second year of therapy and Veda still wouldn't leave the house unless it was for work. If that's what she called progress I'd hate to see what she considered regression.

"I know I haven't been the best sister Nova, but I'm trying."

No, she wasn't. I didn't hold it against her or anything, I just never expected to mourn someone who was still alive. I missed my sister. Other than Memphis, Veda was the one person I could talk to and possibly plot revenge with.

Once upon a time I would've gone to her about 'the event that shall not be named'. I'd have asked Veda why I couldn't stop thinking about how Gio's lips felt on mine and what I should stab him in the eye with so he wouldn't do it again. Instead, I worried that the mention of his name would break her.

The sad fact was, I really wanted to tell her. That was all I could think about while I sat there staring back.

Nothing seemed right anymore. I was surrounded by new faces in a new school. Yes I had Memphis, but after this year he'd be gone too. Off to college in a new city, and I'd still be here, waiting for Gio Mancini to kill me.

I needed Veda to hold me and tell me it would all be okay. Even if it was a lie.

A frown tugged at the corner of Veda's mouth. "Are you okay, Nova?"

I was so far from okay that it wasn't funny.

"I'd be fine if Gio would leave me alone –"

My mouth snapped shut too late. One slip of the tongue had terror filling Veda's eyes as the color drained from her face.

Shit, shit. What do I do?

"Gina Thomas is such a bitch." I quickly added and prayed it sounded nonchalant enough.

Veda's brows knit as a touch of color returned to her cheeks. "Gina Thomas?"

"Yeah," I lied. "She's a cheerleader. You know how they are."

Who was Gina Thomas? I had no idea, but someone out there probably had that name. They weren't in my school though.

"I could've sworn you said Gio."

"Pfft," I snorted. "Who's not listening now?"

Damn I was good.

Suspicion still toyed with Veda's expression, but she went with it. Denial was a beautiful thing.

"Okay?" she eyed me quickly. "Well, Kato's on the phone. I thought you'd like to talk to him."

"What?" I jumped up out of my chair, "Why didn't you lead with that?"

Kato only had fifteen minutes to talk and here she was wasting precious time.

"You were busy tormenting little children," she yelled as I rushed through the door into the kitchen where Maw Maw had the phone receiver pressed to her ear.

"There's always time to torment children," I called back while bouncing impatiently from one foot to the other.

Maw Maw's brow arched my way, "Are you picking on sweet little Billy and Kyle again?"

Sweet my ass.

"They started it."

"They are seven years old, Novalee…"

I groaned and rolled my eyes. "That's like twenty-five in demon years, now can we save the set a good example speech for after I talk to Kato?"

For a second I thought she might deny me, until she looked down at my bouncing feet and sighed. "I'd love to talk to you more, my dear boy, but your sister appears to have ants in her pants."

That joke was almost as funny as us having a landline.

I shot Maw Maw a dirty look and held out my palm, where she placed the receiver before walking away. I'd probably pay for that look later, but I was too happy to hear my brother's voice to care.

A smile spread across my face as I held the phone up to my ear. "I hope you haven't dropped the soap lately."

"That's not funny." Kato's unimpressed tone was like music to my ears.

"You're the one who's always saying that we have to be able to joke about the hard things in life." The pun was totally intended.

"I don't know why I talk to you."

"Because you love me." I clarified.

"Yes I do," he sighed. "Even though you're a pain in my ass."

"I'm a pain in everyone's ass."

"The good lord tests me every day with you, child." Maw Maw muttered while digging through a cupboard.

I shot her a look while saying, "At least I'm not late making phone calls."

Kato should've called two hours ago. I was starting to think he got locked in solitary or something.

"Sorry," Kato said. "I just got out of the infirmary."

My face dropped. "Why were you in the infirmary?"

"You know how it is, Nova."

Unfortunately I did. The Mancini's had a lot of friends, some of whom were locked up with my brother. This was the tenth beating my brother had taken this year. He spent more time in the infirmary than he did in his cell. It was ridiculous, and of course no one would do anything about it.

"Kato," I sighed.

"It's okay."

No it wasn't. What if the next time he didn't make it out, or was hurt so bad that he was disfigured or couldn't walk.

That didn't stop him from trying to reassure me. "Things will get better."

"How?"

"I made some friends."

And by friends he meant… "You didn't join a gang did you?"

I'd seen some of those prison shows and knew what friends meant.

"No," Kato snorted. "It's more like a club."

Right, cause that was so much better.

"Is club code for cult?" Because I wasn't going to start wearing robes and dancing naked in the moonlight, unless there was some serious alcohol involved.

"It's not a cult."

"Are you sure? Cause most people don't know it's a cult until it's too late."

Mandy Richards's parents had to hire some guy to kidnap and reprogram her. At least that's what people said. Personally I think she did a stint in rehab. Anyone who ran around naked at a party saying 'I am the lizard queen' was on some serious drugs.

"It's not a cult, Nova! It's a biker club."

"Okay." *Geez calm down.* "Wait… so you're a biker now?"

"Yes," Kato huffed. "I'm a member of The Lost Souls."

The Lost Souls? I think I saw some of those guys when we went to New Orleans. But why would they want my brother? "You've never ridden a bike."

"Yes, I have." Kato argued.

"No, you haven't."

"Yes, I have." He insisted.

To which I challenged, "When?"

"Before I had to take care of you two and trade in for a minivan."

That made me cough out a snort. "You've never driven a minivan either."

"That's beside the point."

"I don't think it is. If you'd lie about one thing, who's to say you wouldn't lie about the other?" I thought it was a valid point.

Kato did not. "Put Maw Maw back on the phone."

"Ugh, I'm sorry, okay?" I twirled the phone cord around my finger and leaned back against the counter. "Tell me more about your *club*."

"All you need to know is they offered me protection so I'll take less beatdowns."

Not sure if the payout was worth it. Less didn't mean none. And what exactly did my brother have to do for this protection? Steal? Hurt someone? Kill someone? That would just get him right back where he was. Whoever these Lost Souls were, they weren't a solution. I wasn't sure if there was a solution.

"Tell me something good about your day."

Good? That was a hard one.

"Some asshole tried to shove his tongue down my throat." Not sure why that was what came out of my mouth?

"I hope you hit him." Kato growled a little more angry than normal.

"No," I smiled. "But I bit him."

"That's my girl."

The hitting I would save for tomorrow. The next time I saw Gio Mancini, he was getting a punch right in the face. And maybe the dick.

Chapter 21

It took less than fifteen minutes to drive to Sault Saint Marie Estates, and even less time than that to sneak up to Nova's yellow trailer. The gnomes decorating the yard were the hardest thing to step around. The little bastards were everywhere. It was like a minefield of pointed hats and chubby cheeks, but I managed to sneak through them without making a sound.

The screen door was closed but the inner door was open, allowing the light from inside to cascade out onto the deck. I could hear the faint sounds of a TV and smell a sweetness floating through the air.

If I had to guess, I'd say someone was baking. I didn't like that scent or the childhood memories they invoked. So I avoided the deck and slinked around the right corner.

The first window I came upon was a modest living room, with an old brown couch and matching chair. To the left of that was a bedroom, which I assumed to be the sister's based on the small crib at the foot of a bed. That and the pictures of a baby with a woman who looked a lot like Nova.

There were a few differences, like the curl in her hair, and lack of freckles. Other than that, it would be easy to mistake them. Nova was younger with a bit more snark in her smile, and she definitely didn't care about her appearance the same way.

Her sister's room was full of pictures of her all dolled up with some blonde girl – a friend maybe? There were typical images one would find in a girl's room. That is until the ones with the baby. Veda Ford didn't seem to care about how she looked anymore.

From what I could tell, the baby didn't look much like his mother. Which made me wonder about Veda. She was in the hospital recovering for a while, so something did happen to her. But why keep the child? He had to take after his father. If it was rape, how could she look at her son every day and not hate him? I didn't get it.

My ears perked at a sound to my right.

I tiptoed around some shrubs and moved in behind the trailer, where the sound was coming from. That's when I saw faded blue curtains flapping out of an open window at the far end. Whatever I was hearing was coming from there.

It didn't take too long for me to figure out that it was singing. And not good singing either. In fact it was downright horrible. I was surprised to recognize any of the lyrics, but I was pretty sure the song was *Hold On* by Wilson Phillips. Who the hell would listen to that?

Novalee, that's who.

I peeked around the curtain to see her laying on her bed with earbuds in her ears next to a giggling and clapping baby. My eyes were immediately drawn to the leg she had propped up on her knee, bouncing in time with the music. She wasn't wearing any pants, just a white tee shirt that barely covered her hips. I couldn't stop staring at her smooth skin.

My tongue swept over the bite on my bottom lip. Would Novalee scream if I bit her? Would her blood taste as sweet as I imagined? I'd never found a tee shirt so hot in my life, nor had I ever been more grateful for the presence of a child.

The baby leaned forward to smack his hands on Novalee's thigh, pulling my eyes away from dangerous territory, but not before I noticed the pink hue left on her skin from the slap. It wouldn't be hard to leave a mark on her.

The baby scooted closer and dug his fingers into her cheek.

Nova didn't seem phased by his actions. She just smiled and said, "You want to hear, Knoxy."

After which she popped out one of her earbuds and passed it to the kid–who immediately sucked it in his mouth.

She wasn't the best babysitter, but there was something oddly adorable about the way she belted out, "hold on for one more day."

How was this kid surviving this? She was so bad and out of tune, that I was tempted to hire a vocal instructor to give her a few tips. Was this what girls did in their spare time? This was really going to put a damper on Atlee's naked pillow fight theory.

Nova's door flew open, making me duck down a touch. Enough so that I was hidden but could still see her sister standing on the other side with her hands on her hips.

"Why are you torturing my child?"

At least the kid had a good mother. If I had to take anymore of her singing my ears might actually bleed.

"I'm not torturing him," Nova shot back. "I'm teaching him about good music."

This was not good music, and certainly not when she was singing it.

Her sister's hand flew through the air, pointing at her son, "He's eating your earbud, Nova!"

"Oh calm down, they have wires. He's not going to choke."

Nova rolled her eyes and tugged on said wire, popping the small bud out of the baby's mouth. "See."

"You're the world's worst babysitter."

That one I agreed with.

"Oh please, Knoxy loves me." Nova picked up the baby and bopped his nose. "Don't you, Knoxy."

He laughed and yanked on fistfuls of her hair.

"Fine," her sister grumbled. "Then you can give him his bath."

She walked away before Nova could do much more than groan and chase after.

I took the chance to look around. If there was one thing I learned from Atlee's sisters it was that someone could find out everything they wanted to know about a teenage girl by searching their room. That place was like a sanctuary to them. All their little secret notes, pictures, and posters were displayed in there. Or at least they should be.

Nova's room was oddly bare. There were the usual things, bed, dresser, and night table, but there was a surprising lack of everything else. There were no posters on her walls, image filled mirror, or little knick knacks laying around.

The only thing she did have displayed were four pictures. One of that blonde twit she hung around with. Next to that was one of the baby, one of her sister, and one of her brother. That one I had to stop myself from climbing in the window to tear up.

The interesting part about the photos was she wasn't in any of them. They were single shots of one person and no one else. The baby and his mother weren't even sitting next to each other. They were separated by the other two, and if I had to guess, I'd say her sister was a couple years younger in that photo.

Why wouldn't Nova have one with her sister and the baby together? It wouldn't be hard for her to get. Veda's room was filled with them. She didn't even have a family picture. It was as if she wanted to have them all there, but not together.

My fists readied when a hand shot out of nowhere and grabbed my shirt to pull me down.

"Get down."

I had to resist the urge to facepalm when I was met with a pair of familiar eyes.

"Atlee," I whisper/growled. "What the hell are you doing here?"

The son of a bitch was dressed all in black and had camo painted on his face, like he was getting ready to go to war.

Atlee pulled out a long stick that had a mirror on the end and started extending it. "I'm stalking her for you."

Could I hit him, I really wanted to hit him.

"Why in the hell would you do that?" I didn't tell him to do shit.

"In case you haven't noticed," he shot me a sideways glance, "you kind of suck at stalking."

I was definitely going to hit him.

"That wasn't stalking." If I wanted to stalk someone, then I'd stalk them without being seen. I was simply observing my opponent.

"Don't worry, Buddy," he smacked his hand on my shoulder. "I got you."

I let out a breath and pinched the bridge of my nose, "Atlee…"

His hand cut me off by clamping over my mouth.

"Shh," he whispered and pointed up at the mirror as Nova walked back in the room.

That thing was useful, that much I'd give him. We had a clear shot of the room and weren't at risk of being seen. We stayed safely tucked away in the shadows and watched as Novalee snatched a towel off a shelf and stormed back out. Guess she was giving the baby a bath after all.

Once the coast was clear, Atlee tugged on my sleeve and moved to the right. "Come on."

"Where are we going?"

"The bathroom is one window down and around the corner."

I almost didn't want to ask, "How do you know that?"

"Her grandma had a shower about forty minutes ago," Atlee paused to look back over his shoulder. "I don't recommend seeing that show."

"I don't think you should be seeing any shows." I growled a little too loud.

We both froze and waited to see if anyone heard us. Once we were sure the coast was clear, Atlee shot me a dirty look and continued around the corner.

Honestly I didn't know where that anger came from? So what if Atlee spied on Nova. She was a job, and he was part of it.

Atlee ducked down, crawled around the corner, and muttered, "Don't worry, I'm not going to fuck her."

"I don't care if you fuck her." I grumbled while following.

"Uh huh?" he stopped below a window with a light on. "Is that why you kissed her?"

What?" "How do you know about that?"

They left long before that happened.

"She bitched about it an hour and a half ago."

She did? "To who?"

"Herself." Atlee answered while raising the mirror.

"She bitched to herself?"

"Yeah," he slid his gaze my way. "She does that a lot."

Maybe the kiss did get to her? Whether or not that information was useful was yet to be seen. I sure as hell wasn't about to start making out with her.

Both of our eyes were drawn up to mirror as the sound of running water cut through the quiet of the night. We watched as Novalee sat on the edge of the tub and swirled her hand in the filling water. I couldn't help but imagine my hands wrapping around her throat to hold her under.

I could almost see desperation fill her eyes and feel her struggle to break free. Then she lifted her arm and used her fingers to moisten her neck, and my mind was filled with another image. One where the wetness on her skin didn't come from water, but sweat and need.

Taking a deep breath, I pushed the image out of my head and attempted to change the subject, "Did she bitch about anything else?"

Something had to irritate her. I'd take anything at this point, so long as it didn't involve me touching her.

"Ah, let's see…" Atlee looked up, searching his mind. "She came home, couldn't find the shorts she was looking for, then bitched about that. Her Maw Maw's chicken was too dry – it smelled delicious to me though – then someone ate the last piece of pie. Her friend Memphis called – they bitched about you. She went to the store to get some milk – two percent because Knox can't handle any higher. Then she planted a shaving cream bomb on some kids bikes – that shit was hilarious. After that she talked to her brother, stomped around her room while grumbling about you kissing her, helped her neighbor chase a raccoon, then she came home bitched about you some more, whined that she couldn't have a tea party with her nephew and started singing."

My brow arched. I didn't know what else to say other than, "How long have you been here?"

He looked down at his watch, "Four hours, thirty-seven minutes and fifteen seconds."

When I just stared at him and didn't say anything, Atlee held up his hand and said, "Don't worry, I've only got one camera left to plant."

"Camera?"

He nodded.

I threw my thumb at the wall, "you put cameras in there."

He nodded again, "Yeah."

As much as I'd love to give him shit, it was actually kind of genius. We might be able to find out if Veda saw anything without going through her sister.

"Do they have sound?"

"I'm not an amateur," he snorted.

"Well," I slapped my hand on his back, "let's go get the last one planted then."

Chapter 22

NOVALEE

The next morning when I woke up, I decided to put all the disturbing occurrences behind me. *All* of the disturbing occurrences. Especially 'the event that shall not be named'. I needed to embrace the new normal day, because normal was exactly what it was going to be. If I had to kill someone to make sure that happened, then so be.

I had a bat somewhere in the truck. There may be a few chunks missing–I vaguely remembered trying to play baseball with a gator–but it was still perfectly usable. A little sharper maybe. If anything that would work to my advantage. Were the cops really going to believe someone when they said they were stabbed with a bat. Don't think so.

Thankfully, whatever weird mood that enveloped St. Agatha's yesterday, was gone when I arrived. I was tripped twice on my way to my locker and someone called me trailer trash. Personally, I thought they could've come up with something more original, but I'd take it.

Plus, I didn't have to dig around for my trusty bat. I wasn't entirely sure what was in the back of my truck, but I think I heard something moving around the other day.

"Watch where you're going, whore," some guy growled when I bumped into him.

Ah, it was good to be back on the bottom rung.

Wait...

He called me whore. My neck twisted as my eyes zeroed in on the brunette head walking down the hall. Could this guy be the mispeller? Nothing really stood out about him, other than a small birthmark on the base of his neck.

Making a mental note of my new suspect, I turned back around and opened my locker. It took a few tried to remember the lock's combination, an action that I blamed entirely on Gio. My mind wasn't exactly running regularly. Then again, it could be from lack of sleep – which was also his fault. Gio plagued my school days, I'd be damned if I was going to let him invade my dreams too.

"Should've bit his tongue off," I grumbled while stuffing books in my bag.

"You don't have Advanced Chem today."

That comment caused me to damn near jump out of my skin. When did Memphis get here?

"How do you know my schedule?" It took everything I had not to curl my lip at the sparkle in his bright eyes. How did he wake up so happy every day?

"I know all your schedules. By the way, your period is due in eight days."

Ha, showed how much he knew. "I got the shot. So, no period for me for three months."

"No, your last shot is almost up," he leaned over to rest his shoulder on the locker next to mine. "You have an appointment to get your next one on Monday."

Damn. "You scare me sometimes."

His shoulders lifted in a small shrug, "You'd be lost without me."

I really would. Memphis was the only person who stood a chance of organizing my chaos.

"So," he sang. "How'd it go yesterday?"

My gaze snapped to his. "Why? What did you hear?"

Did he know?

"I know Kato was supposed to call." He explained while tipping his head. "Why? Did something else happen?"

I huffed out a very unbelievable, "No. "

"Uh huh." He crossed his arms and gave me the look he always did when he knew I was lying.

It was seriously annoying how well he could read me. I guess that's what happened when you shared a crib with someone.

"Nova?"

"Memphis."

"What happened?"

I dropped my advanced chem book back in my locker and calmly said, "Nothing. Kato called, Maw Maw hit me with her slipper. It was a perfectly normal day."

Okay, maybe my words weren't as calm as I thought. But, if I didn't look at him, then he couldn't read my expression.

"You don't really expect me to believe that, do you?"

Kind of.

"Yes, I do." I also expected him to know how stubborn I was. One would think after seventeen years of lost arguments he would've stopped trying. Of course, he would say he won some, but he didn't. I just let him think he did.

"Come on, Nova…" Memphis was cut off by a can that whizzed past and crashed into my locker.

I looked at the soda dripping off my books and sighed. That's about right. Couldn't help but admire the throwers' aim though. He got the can right in the middle of the locker.

"Are you kidding me?" Memphis snarled out at the crowd filling the hall. "Who did that?"

I snorted, "What are you going to do? Beat them up?"

"Someone needs to do something."

And he thought that person was him?

"A trash can has better fighting skills than you." I took off my sweater and used it to sop up some of the mess.

"I took jiu jitsu." He argued.

"You took two classes when you were seven." That was hardly what I'd consider a master.

Memphis puffed his chest out, "I can take care of myself."

Giving up on cleaning up, I slammed my locker shut and shot Memphis a deadpan look. "You can barely take care of yourself."

"I do just fine, thank you very much." He said while lifting his chin.

"Really? How many appointments did you miss last month?" Funny how he always remembered mine but somehow forgot his own. Mind you, most of his appointments were made by his father who thought psychiatric help would miraculously flip his sexual proclivities.

"Without me you would be a pregnant teenage dropout."

"You can't get pregnant without having sex, genius." I shot him a small smug grin.

Sometimes logic had its place. Like when I wanted to win an argument.

"What! You didn't want to do the deed with Simon Fisher," Memphis slapped his palm on his chest. "I'm shocked.

"Hey," I threw my finger up in his face. "Simon had his good points."

"Hair does not count as a good point."

Stubbornness lifted my chin, "I disagree."

"Well in that case, you should date Gio Mancini," his blue eyes slid my way. "He has a nice head of hair too."

"I hadn't noticed." I totally did. "Besides, no one cares how soft his lips are."

I realized my mistake when Memphis pushed off the locker and narrowed his gaze.

"I didn't say anything about his lips."

"I'm pretty sure you did."

Memphis shook his head, "No, I didn't."

"I think you did."

"No," he shook his head again. "You did."

When all else failed, go for deniability.

Giving up on the mess, I slammed my locker shut and gave Memphis the best sardonic snort I could muster. "Why would I bring up Gio Mancini's lips?"

Suspicion narrowed his gaze further, "That's a good question."

It was also one he wouldn't get an answer to.

"What happened yesterday, Nova?"

Damnit.

"As far as we're concerned, yesterday no longer exists."

His brows rose. "It no longer exists?"

"That's right," I nodded. "Yesterday was just a dream. Nothing unusual happened...and even if it did– which it didn't–then it will be one of those things that we shall never ever speak of again. Because yesterday doesn't exist."

"Are you drunk?"

Seriously? "Why on earth would I come here if I had alcohol?"

Who would want to waste their buzz in a place like this when there were swamps to trudge through?

"It wouldn't be the first time you came to school drunk."

"That was one time." I rolled my eyes and headed down the hall towards homeroom.

To be fair, I was *still* drunk from the night before. It wasn't like I went out and got a morning bourbon instead of coffee. Though I was starting to think that might not be a bad idea. Besides,

Memphis wouldn't even know about that if I did have to explain why I got suspended.

Stupid Kenny Fitgerald. It wasn't my fault he lost the tip of his pinky finger. He should've known better than to let me handle the knife. Our home economics teacher banned me from all sharp objects for a reason.

Speaking of sharp objects...

My teeth grit as a familiar face strutted around the corner. Fucking Gio Mancini and his dumb ass friends were moving down the hall like they owned the place. I didn't know what was worse, the way people literally moved out of their way, or how annoyingly well they wore their uniforms. And of course, the asshole trio was right in our path.

"Is there a secret hallway around here we can take?" One could hope.

"It's a private Catholic school, there's probably a dozen secret hallways." *Thank God.* "But, I don't know where any of them are."

Well, what good was he?

Sighing, I stopped moving and looked down the hallway.

They did kind of look like royalty walking through the crowd. Although, my faith in the fairer sex died a little more with each step they took. I'd admit they looked good in those black slacks and white shirts, but that was no reason to fawn all over them.

I looked decent in jeans, but you didn't see guys following me around with puppy dogs eyes, which was exactly what my peers were doing. Atlee had a literal chain of like five girls behind him.

"What is wrong with the female race?" I asked Memphis.

He responded with, "Hormones."

I shot him a dirty look, "Seriously ?"

Why did men always chalk everything up to PMS or hormones?

He shrugged, "Do you have a better explanation?"

I watched Atlee wink at a random girl, and for half a second I thought she might actually pass out.

"No," I sighed. "No, I don't."

"They're clearly idiots." A new voice interjected.

Memphis and I both turned to see a girl with black hair, sneering at the dumbass trio.

"Look at how they all follow Atlee around," she waved at them. "Every one of them thinks they'll be the one to tame him, despite knowing his reputation. It's pathetic."

I couldn't agree more. Who was this girl? She looked familiar. Was she one of the group standing by the door on my first day? A girl like that was kind of hard to forget. The term drop dead gorgeous wasn't strong enough to describe her appearance. Shiny black hair, bright whiskey eyes and the perfect hourglass figure that not even St. Agatha's shapeless uniform could hide. Just looking at her made me question my sexual preferences.

"I long for the day when someone wipes that smug look off his face."

It was pretty obvious who she was talking about. The only other girl I'd seen glare at Atlee like that, was Sutton.

"You seem to have a personal grudge against Atlee." Other than the obvious one night stand scenario. He seemed like the kind of guy that discarded women at a whim.

Her whiskey eyes rolled my way, "That's because I'm his sister."

Oh shit.

Atlee had a sister? "That sucks."

"He's nowhere near as bad as our father."

Did that mean their father was a raging Manwhore too, or was she talking about something else? I got the feeling it was the latter.

"If it makes you feel better, I shot Atlee down yesterday."

"Huh," she gave a small nod. "It does actually."

Maybe I had an ally in this school?

She turned around and ran her gaze over me. I could feel judgment coming off every inch of her face.

"Who are you?"

That's when Memphis stepped in to make introductions. "Nova, this is Kendall. Kendall, Nova."

"Oh," Kendall's brow arched. "You're the infamous, Nova."

She knew who I was? Can't say I was surprised, given who her brother was, but I was a little flattered. Plus, infamous Nova was better than the girl with a sock on her ass, so I'd take it as a win.

"It would've been smarter if your brother left Atlas alone."

Oh, she did not just go there. "Maybe Atlas shouldn't have raped my sister."

"You think your sister was the only one?" She coughed out a snicker. "You're not as smart as I thought."

The question came out of my mouth before I could stop it. "Did he rape you?"

"Please," she snorted. "My father would've killed him."

"Just like my brother," I pointed out.

"Fair enough," her shoulder lifted in a small shrug. "But that doesn't get you off of Gio's radar. You do know they're following you, right?"

Well, yeah. They kind of sucked at stalking.

Kendall's lids narrowed a bit as she turned her attention back to her brother and his friends. "Gio's mother is a soft spot. Feel free to pull on that thread."

Okay, now I was confused, "Why are you telling me this?"

Shouldn't she be on their side?

"I hate them," she sang and walked away.

If anyone could understand that, it was me. My blood boiled just looking at Gio, but it was the voice that got louder with every step he took that made my fists ball.

'I just got out of the infirmary.'

My brother had to join a group of bikers so he wouldn't get

constantly beat up. And even then he would still end up with bruises and broken bones. Because as he said, nothing would stop it. Kato shouldn't even be in prison. Atlas was the criminal, not him.

The whole Mancini family were nothing but high paid criminals. They got away with everything. Beating up helpless guys in prison and kissing girls out of the blue. Well, no more. I'd had enough.

"Nova," Memphis gave my shoulder a squeeze. "Are you okay?"

"I will be." I growled, then stormed away with my eyes locked on my target.

There was a brief moment where Gio raised his brow, but that was all he got before my fist cracked off his jaw. Every ounce of anger I had went into that strike. I hit him so hard that his head twisted to the side and pain radiated up my arm. But I didn't stop there.

I snarled, "That's for my brother," then swung my fists again, this time in his groin while adding, "this one's for me."

There was a moment people had when they realize they fucked up. Where the ground would drop out from under them and cold spike would shoot up their spine. Well, when Gio's dark glare locked on mine, I was in that moment.

He didn't buckle like most guys would when they were hit in the nuts. He just looked really, really pissed off. All I could hear as his fingers gripped my arm, was a tiny voice in the back of my head whisper, "uh oh."

Chaos erupted. Memphis lunged, Atlee and Darry intercepted, and people yelled and ran to get out of the way while I was pulled through a door into a dark room.

Chapter 23

Every emotion had a distinctive scent, but rage… that one had an unyielding beast that demanded to be fed. Oh, and I was going to feed it. I was going to give it all the pain it craved.

That was all I could think when I kicked the door to my left open. I didn't care about anything else. Not the ache in my balls, or the spark of excitement in Atlee's eyes when he knocked Nova's blonde friend to the ground. I didn't even give a shit about the knife Darry pulled out. All I could smell was the coppery tinge of the blood I was going to spill.

Nova jerked back, but I dug my fingers into her flesh until I could feel the muscle underneath and yanked into the dark.

This was a case of cause and effect. She punched me… twice. And now, she was going to die. Plain and simple.

"You better let me go," Nova warned when I nudged the door shut. "I'll scream."

I slammed her back against the wall and hissed, "you better make it a good one."

Cause I was about to shove my fist down her fucking throat. Or…

My hand wrapped around her neck.

It wouldn't take much to snap it. A flick of my wrist and *crack*… lights out.

"Look Gio," Nova flattened her palm on my chest. "Don't you think this is getting a little out of hand?"

Oh, is that what she thought? This shit wasn't even getting started, let alone out of hand.

"You fucking hit me!"

"You had my brother beat up."

Not only could I hear the anger in her tone, but I could see it toying with her expression. There was enough of a glow coming in from the light under the bottom of the door for me to make out the bigger details of her face. Like the way her jaw ticked when she mentioned her brother. Apparently she didn't like the treatment he was getting in prison.

"You're brother's about to have a real bad night." We had scheduled beat downs for Kato, but this one I'd throw in just for her.

I heard the smack from her hand before I felt a sting crawl across my jaw. Whatever thread of control I had was fading fast.

"Hit me again." I tightened my grip until I could feel her pulse pounding beneath my finger, and leaned it to hiss in her face, "I fucking dare you."

I wasn't fucking around anymore, and she knew that. I could feel the fear in the swallow she gulped down.

Most people would do one of two things when faced with death. Shake with fear and beg for their lives, or look for an escape. Not Nova. No. She popped her hand up and sharply jabbed into my Adam's apple.

Instant pain shot down my throat, stealing my ability to breathe. My grip on her slipped as I bent over and coughed through the burn.

Nova used that time to make a break for it.

I saw a sliver of light cut through the dark and quickly slammed my body against the door, cutting off her means of escape. There would be no getting away from me this time. One of us was going down, and it sure as hell wasn't me.

My body barricade didn't stop her from trying to get away. Nova darted off into the darkness, and unfortunately for me, that last strike left me temporarily debilitated. I was too busy coughing to chase after her.

By the time I managed to catch my breath and straighten up, I couldn't see her anywhere. Not that I could see much in here. Even though my eyes had adjusted, I couldn't see anything past a foot but shadows.

"This will be a lot easier if you come out and face your consequences."

Did I think Nova would step out, fuck no. She was way too stubborn for that. But she couldn't say I didn't give her the opportunity. I even gave her to the count of thirty before going on the hunt.

"Alright," I reached behind me to flick the lock on the door. "Hide and seek it is."

Readying myself, I rolled my neck and squared my shoulders. I was actually looking forward to this. It'd been awhile since I had a real challenge. Although my prey was at a serious disadvantage. Nova didn't know shit about this room. But I did.

Atlee, Darry, and I found this unused space during freshman year and decided to use it as a business headquarters of sorts. It was perfect. There were no windows and a closet with a panel in the ceiling that could be moved to hide our books. We were on our way here when Nova decided to attack me.

I knew everything about this room, including possible hiding places. Like say the desk in the left corner, or the metal shelf on the right wall. But if she'd gone for either of those options, I'd have heard it.

It was too dark in here for her not to have bumped into something. My guess was that she was hunkered down somewhere in the dark, listening. I could turn on the light, but where was the fun in that?

"Come out, come out wherever you are," I sang while scouring the shadows for movement.

Aside from the ruckus outside—which was dying down—it was quiet. No frightened gasps or panicked movements. Gotta say, I was a little impressed. I knew Nova was trapped, and she knew she was trapped. Yet she remained calm enough not to give away her position. The girl had balls. Bigger men in her situation would be pissing themselves right about now.

Let's see how long her courage lasts.

I took a step and made sure my foot landed extra hard so she could hear it.

When I didn't get a result, I repeated the action.

Still nothing. There was just me and the dark.

Hmm, it was time to try another tactic.

"You can't hide from me," not in here. "I will find you."

My ears perked at a quiet snort from the left.

There was that stubborn sarcasm.

I sidestepped in that direction, "didn't anyone ever tell you, children should be seen and not heard?"

"Did you just call me a child?" that was followed by a softly muttered, "Shit."

I knew she couldn't keep quiet.

Tsking, I moved closer to the left wall. She was over here, and not far. That softly uttered curse was too clear for her to be across the room. I stopped to listen to the sounds in the darkness. There was my own breathing, echoed footsteps of students in the hall, and something else. I tipped my head, attempting to make it out. The sound was too faint. It was almost like scraping or shifting.

I thought about turning on the light and putting an end to this, but I was having fun. A little too much. My dick hadn't been this hard in a long time. Not necessarily the right girl for that reaction. That didn't mean I couldn't enjoy the game. After all, that's what was getting me off, not the girl.

I let out a small cough, which drew out a squeak that led me to zero in on a darker shadow to the left of me. It was a little over a foot away. I watched it shift to the side and smirked.

Bingo.

"Ready or not, here I come."

The shadow darted, and I lunged.

Nova was fast but not fast enough. A rush of air washed over me as Nova ran past and I reached out, grabbing a handful of her shirt. Her retreat came to a screeching halt. She let out a yelp as I yanked her back. The girl didn't stand a chance. My pinky finger was stronger than her.

The one thing I didn't take into account was the force of the opposite momentum. Nova pulled one way, I pulled the other, and we both ended up toppling to the ground. I hit the hard floor with an 'oof,' but managed to maintain my hold, bringing her body down on top of mine.

Ever been hit with the dead weight of a hundred pound person? It wasn't fun. I'd rather get punched in the nuts again.

"Fuck me," I groaned while throwing my arm over her chest so she couldn't take off again – which she tried to do.

Guess her landing was softer than mine because she jarred up right away. Or at least she tried to. I put a stop to that with one strong clamp of my forearm. I got about a second of reprieve after that before her hands started flying back at me.

I rolled my head out of the way while using my other arm to try and grab her wrists. A task that would've been easier if Nova would stop moving for a second. It was like trying to control a feral cat fighting its way out of a cage. She was not giving up.

"Let me go!" Nova demanded while cracking her heel off my shin.

Now I could take a hit. I'd been fighting with my brothers my entire life, but this wild and savage shit had to stop.

"That's it," I snarled and rolled us over, so *I* was on top of *her*.

That made things much easier. One of her arms got pinned under her chest. The weight of my body made sure it stayed that way and allowed me the freedom to grab her other arm. After that I trapped her legs with my thighs and she was done.

At least, I thought she was done. The hard buck she gave suggested otherwise.

For fuck sakes.

I dropped more of my weight on her back and softly growled in her ear, "Give it up, *Gattina*. You lost."

Nova huffed and twisted her neck to glare back at me. Even in the dark I could see the hatred burning in those hazel orbs.

"Why?" she sang in a sweet tone. "I thought Mancini men liked it when they fought."

Rage ticked through my jaw. She wanted to go there, did she?

"And I thought all Ford girls were sluts that liked to ruin men's lives."

"Fuck you," she screamed while bucking up with her hips while trying to kick out.

Her fight was nothing. It wasn't even a nuisance. I kept her pinned with little effort.

When she finally stilled, I arched a brow and asked," You done?"

She dropped her cheek to the floor and let out a huff. "I hate you."

"Ditto," I snarled back at her.

"Go ahead and do what you're going to do." Nova sighed. "I'll just lay here."

My brows knit, "What exactly do you think I'm going to do?"

"I don't know," she sang in that snarky tone that grated on my nerves. "Your brother did rape my sister."

My teeth ground. I should kill her now. Smash her head against the floor until her brains were leaking out of her broken skull.

"Just do me a favor and put on a condom first, I wouldn't want to catch anything."

I was so fucking sick of this bullshit. Atlas didn't touch her sister, yet she continued to drag his name through the mud.

"You know what," I loosened my hold long enough to flip her over, then hissed in her face, "I should fuck you. Then at least someone in your family would be telling the truth about a rape."

Nova didn't like that. She lifted her head off the ground and snarled, "My sister's not lying."

"Yeah? Then why'd she keep the baby?"

Her eyes stayed locked on mine, but she didn't say anything. I couldn't tell if she'd asked herself the same thing, or if she just didn't have a viable excuse.

"You can't explain that one, can you?"

"Fuck you."

"Nah, I think you'd like that too much."

"You think too highly of yourself," she snorted.

"You're the one that keeps pushing my buttons," I pointed out. "At some point I've gotta wonder if you want me to hurt you."

Her eyes rolled, "Pfft, please."

My head tipped to the side. Her heartbeat just picked up. I could feel it pound through her chest. Did she want me to hurt her? I was just fucking with her, but now...

I tipped my gaze down to her chest just as a knock rang through the door.

"Open the door Mr. Mancini."

Fucking Sister Anne.

Nova sucked in a breath and parted her lips, but I slapped my hand over her mouth.

"One fucking word and I'll gut your friend." I warned quietly.

The glare she gave in response was all the answer I needed. Nova would keep her mouth shut, but just in case I kept my hand right where it was and looked over at the door as the handle jiggled.

This wasn't the first time a member of the staff came knocking. Yet none of them opened the door. I don't think they had a key.

"I told you, they went down the hall."

God love Atlee and his quick thinking.

"No they didn't. I saw Gio take her in there."

Nova's friend was starting to become a pain in my ass too.

"The only thing you saw was my fist hitting your face." Atlee said.

Nova stiffened for a fraction of a second. She tried to brush it off and play cool, but I felt it. Awe, she was worried about her friend. How sweet. Let's hope she cared enough about him to keep her trap shut. Because if that door opened, I'd carry through with my threat.

"You punch like a girl," Nova's friend said, making me grimace.

That was not the right thing to say to someone like Atlee. Proof of which came with the bang that vibrated through the door.

"Stop that." Sister Anne demanded while more bangs and angry words rolled through the air.

Based on the smack and sounds I heard, I'd say Nova's friend wasn't doing very well. But he wasn't backing down either, and the Sister was just getting more and more agitated.

I was so focused on the commotion in the hall that I wasn't paying attention to my captive.

Nova managed to wriggle her legs out from under mine before I realized and pushed my weight back down. One buck of her hips later and we both froze.

Her legs were around my waist, pressing parts of me against parts of her. I could feel the heat from her pussy warming my cock, and suddenly all I could think about was the way she looked on the edge of that tub with water dripping down her neck.

She stared wide eyed at me, "Umm…"

"Shut up," I clamped my hand tighter over her lips. "Don't say anything."

I needed a moment to collect myself. Except my position wasn't helping any. My one hand was holding her wrist over her head, while the other was on her mouth, and my body was stretched out over hers. The lack of light amped everything up. How her breast pressed into me with every breath she took, the little quakes her tiny frame was making, and her sweet scent were all smacking me in the face.

A muttered "Gio," came from under my palm.

"Shut up," I repeated and closed my eyes.

Just when I was starting to regain control, Nova shifted, causing friction for a spark to make my cock twitch.

"Stop fucking moving." I hissed a little angrier than I intended.

It worked. She stilled long enough for me to take a few breaths and reopen my eyes. And that was my mistake. One look at the glimmer in her big wide eyes, and the next thing I knew, my mouth was on hers.

I don't know how it happened, or when I removed my hand, and I didn't care. All I could think about was getting more of that sweet flavor that tainted my mouth all night. I barely noticed Nova dropping her legs from my waist and going still. Something had taken over me.

An urge that I needed to satisfy more than my need to breathe. I craved the taste of her blood and anger. I wanted to feel her hatred while I defiled her in every fucked up and depraved way I could think of.

Feral was the only word I could use to describe it. There was no logic or reason left. Not until her tongue touched mine and my brother's face flashed through my mind.

This was the sister of Atlas's killer.

I pushed myself up and let Nova scuttle away. What the fuck was wrong with me? And what the fuck was wrong with her? Nova should be running out the door, not sitting less than a foot away from me hugging her knees.

"Get the fuck away from me."

"You get away from me." She shot back.

This was not the time for her stubbornness. It was safe for her to leave. Whatever was happening in the hall was over. It was quiet now. Too quiet. The silence in the air thickened the longer we sat there, until I couldn't take it.

"Stop staring at me!"

The scowl I could see through the shadow on her face made me want to grab her and do things I had no business doing to someone with the last name Ford.

"Stop kissing me," she growled. "I don't like it."

Join the club.

"What makes you think you can tell me what to do?"

I was in control here. I decided where she went, who she talked to, and how long she had left to live.

My brows knit.

Since when did I care who she talked to?

"You're such an asshole."

"And you're a pain in my ass." I barked back. "Just get the fuck out."

"You get out."

I pinched the bridge of my nose. Jesus fucking Christ.

Taking a breath, I looked back up and stopped.

There was a sparkle in her eyes. The same one she had yesterday. And it said only one thing… fear. Not of me, but of what just happened.

Suddenly, it all made sense. The lack of anything personal in her room, how she had her photo's placed, and her reaction to this. Even why Nova dated a weasel like Simon could be explained. It was connections she was avoiding. When I kissed her, she felt something. Want or desire maybe. Whatever it was, that's what she was scared of.

And just like that, I had a new plan for Novalee Ford and her brother.

Chapter 24

Well, I think my first week of school was off to a great start. I didn't get suspended until Friday. At least that's how I'd spin it to Maw Maw when I explained what happened. Last year I got tossed out for a week after day two, but I still maintain that it wasn't my fault. I should've never been left unattended in the chemistry lab. This wasn't my fault either.

My jaw tensed as I rolled my eyes over to the other side of the room where Gio and Atlee were busy moving stacks of bibles from one box to another. Their task was almost as monotonous as the one Memphis and I were given.

I grumbled under my breath and clapped two erasers together, causing a cloud of white dust to puff out. Why did they even have these? I hadn't seen a single blackboard. Did the staff just decide to keep these stashed away in case a student pissed them off.

"This is a serious health risk," batting away the cloud, I coughed and looked over at the Nun by the door. "What if I had asthma?"

Sister Mary of the Hallway stared back at me, "You have no health concerns."

Of course I did. No one as out of shape as me was in top physical condition. I would've been able to hit Gio a lot harder if that was the case. My arm still hurt and he didn't even have a mark on his stupid perfect face.

I sneered at the nun and went back to work. Guess I shouldn't be surprised. Sister Mary of the Hallway was waiting for us with her arms crossed, when we came out of the room. And she didn't buy my excuse of getting lost in a secret maze under the school. Probably would've helped if Gio didn't tell her I hit him, so he took me in the room to cool off.

That was such a lie. He took me in that room to kill me. Or to mess with my head. He was doing a good job of that. I could still smell his fresh scent and feel his heaviness weighing me down. What was it with this place? Boys were supposed to smell like dirty socks and sweat.

Yet Atlee was over there smelling like sin on crack, while Gio was all woodsy and masculine. Even Memphis's scent was better here.

Well right now he kind of smelled like blood and defeat, but normally he was a pleasant person to stand next to. We worked well together. His fresh sweetness offset my stale depression.

Sister Mary of the Hallway cleared her throat. "I trust you four can handle yourselves for a couple of minutes."

A voice in the back of my head whispered, 'Don't do it.' But it was too late.

"Okay," I snort/scoffed back at her. "But I'm gonna need more than a few minutes if you want me to handle myself."

I was not prepared for the stick that hit the top of my hand.

"God damnit!" I called out while attempting to shake the burn away.

My outburst was rewarded with another sharp slap on my other hand.

"Son of a bitch." That one was my sore punching arm.

"Nova!"

"What?" I growled at Memphis. "That shit hurts."

Oh crap.

I quickly raised my hands, palms out towards Sister Mary of the Hallway, and said, "I mean it was a well-deserved punishment for my blasphemous words."

Please don't hit me again.

She narrowed her eyes and pointed the stick at me before thankfully walking out. God help this school if she ever got her hands on a whip.

The second she was gone Atlee burst out laughing, "That was fucking great."

Gio had a small smirk on his face, and Memphis let out a snicker while Atlee laughed. And not just normal laughing. It was full on hunched over, clutching his gut laughing. It wasn't that funny but whatever.

"You know what, I hope she comes back in here and hits all of you with her ninja stick." I paused to eye Memphis. "Maybe not you." It would take less time to point out the unmarked parts of his face. "You've taken enough. But Gio should definitely get a few strikes."

A snort came from across the room.

"Sister Anne stopped trying to punish me like that freshman year." Gio's cool gaze slid my way. "That shit doesn't hurt."

I knew he was dead inside. "Yeah… well… I hope you step on a Lego barefoot in the dark."

"Damn girl," Atlee's smile morphed into a grimace. "That's just cold."

"He deserves it. This is all his fault."

"Actually," Memphis interjected. "This is all your fault."

"How is this my fault? I didn't tell you to get in a fight with Atlee."

"No, but you started it by hitting Gio."

Gio pointed at Memphis and tsked in agreement.

"Don't agree with him," I snarled. "He's my friend not yours."

"He should find better friends."

If looks could kill then the one Memphis shot Gio would've struck him dead right then and there. "Warn me next time so I can bring a bat."

"I have a bat," Atlee smirked. "I call her Pam."

That wasn't creepy at all.

I was a little concerned about Memphis's wellbeing. Atlee looked way too happy.

"I think we should accept that we are not fighters."

Memphis's face alone was proof of that. He looked worse than he did when he had the mumps. Meanwhile Atlee was on the other side of the room without so much as a scratch. And I wouldn't even think about how Gio was acting like nothing happened and he wasn't some weirdo that went around kissing people for no reason.

Not that it was on my mind because the room didn't exist. It was gone with yesterday. I wasn't sneaking peeks of Gio's full lips, or rolling my tongue over the lingering taste in my mouth.

Damnit. I should've kicked him in the balls.

I dropped my attention back to the crate of erasers and muttered, "Pricks."

"Don't even waste your time," Memphis said loud enough for them to hear. "They aren't worth it."

Atlee instantly perked up and held his arms out, "You want some more little man?"

And what did Memphis do? He puffed his chest out, "Anytime asshole."

That was all Atlee needed. He jumped up and stepped over one of the desks before I could blink. I barely had time to step in front of Memphis.

"Go back to your corner," I told Atlee, then looked back at Memphis, "and you stop egging him on."

Memphis glared past me, "I can take him."

I was about to be the filling in a kick ass sandwich and all I had for weapons was a couple of erasers. *Fantastic.* I suppose I could smash one in their faces. Maybe they'd choke to death on chalk.

"Atlee," Gio barked when Atlee jarred forward. "Not now."

Not now? What did not now mean, and how did Memphis get an arch nemesis before me? That wasn't fair. Gio didn't count. That was more of a family feud thing. I really needed to put more time into finding Bush Girl.

Atlee shot Memphis a dirty look then turned around to walk back across the room.

"That's right lackey, head back to your boss."

I gave Memphis a deadpan stare, "Really?"

"What?" he shrugged.

"Did you not learn enough last time?"

"I'm fine," he insisted.

"You're one strong fart away from passing out." I tipped my chin at the crate. "Now shut up and bang some erasers."

He folded his arms, "Don't tell me what to do."

"Technically Sister Mary of the Hallway told you what to do." I pointed out.

Memphis's brow rose, "Sister Mary of the what?"

"The Hallway." Duh.

"Okay," he shook his head. "I'm not even going to attempt to touch that one."

"Well, are you going to attempt to do some actual work, or am I the only one who's going to leave covered in chalk?"

"Since when do you have a good work ethic?"

I had a good work ethic... sometimes. Maybe. Okay fine I had no work ethic. But I did have self-preservation, and... "Maw Maw's about to come walking in that door." With her new pair of slippers.

We were all waiting in here for our prospective parents to come and pick us up. I didn't know about the asshole twins, but Memphis and I had valid reasons for concern.

"How are you going to explain this to your dad?"

Memphis's dad was kind of a hard ass. He didn't like me. Said I was a bad influence. Not sure where he got that idea. I was a very pleasant person on occasion, and the only girl Memphis had ever kissed. Considering his view on his son's sexuality, he should love me.

"Please," Memphis rolled his eyes. "He'll just be happy I did something masculine."

Not sure if getting beat up was considered masculine, but okay.

"Are you going to tell me what happened in that room?"

Did he really have to go there? Couldn't we just stand here and slowly cough to death on our clouds of chalk.

"Nothing happened," because like yesterday, the room no longer existed.

Memphis cocked a hip. "You're a shitty liar."

First off, I was only a shitty liar because he knew all of my tells, and secondly it wasn't a lie. Nothing happened. Nothing worth mentioning anyway.

"Humm," I looked down at the eraser in my left palm. "How many years of lessons do you think are in this thing?"

Maybe this eraser was used for something else, like getting rid of a dirty drawing or something.

"You're changing the subject." Memphis sang.

Oh my god, why couldn't he let this go? "Nothing happened. We fought, I punched an asshole in the throat and ran away... the end."

And that was all he was going to get.

"You sure about that?"

Fucking Gio.

I glared over at him, clapped out a cloud of chalk and coughed, "Yes I'm very sure."

"I think you forgot the part where you came on to me."

My jaw dropped. "I did not come on to you. I hate you."

"Didn't stop you from rubbing up against me."

"I was trying to get away from you," seriously. "You're the one that kissed me."

"What?" Memphis's brow rose. "You kissed him."

Damnit.

"Nice," Atlee nodded. "She taste good?"

Did Atlee not see me? I was standing right here.

"Not really," Gio grumbled. "She kind of tastes like shit."

Hey now.

"I'll have you know, I taste great. You taste like shit." I pointed at Gio. "You should eat more fruit."

That was a complete lie, but he didn't need to know that.

Gio's icy emerald glare slid my way. "You couldn't get my dick hard with an extra set of hands and a manual."

What I felt while we were fighting would beg to differ with that statement. But I didn't want to think about that, and I certainly wasn't going to mention it. Then he'd know that I knew and I couldn't pretend that I didn't know, because Gio would know, and he'd want me to know that he knew… this was making my head hurt.

"Hold on," Memphis interjected. "Can we go back to you kissing him."

"*He* kissed *me.*" I corrected. "And I bit him the first time."

The arch in Memphis's brow deepened. "The first time?"

God damnit. Where was food when I needed it. If my mouth was full then I couldn't talk.

I looked down at one of the erasers and arched a brow. I'd eaten worse things.

"Exactly how many times did you kiss him?"

I sighed, "*He* kissed *me*."

It was an important detail that Memphis seemed to not be grasping. Gio wasn't helping any. The prick was enjoying this. Standing over there with a smirk on his face. I should slap him again.

One sentence later and Atlee was my new favorite person. "I knew that mark on your lip didn't come from basketball."

A smile spread across my face as the one on Gio's fell away. *Who's giving away secrets now asshole.*

"Trust me," Gio shot me a dirty look. "A basketball would've tasted better."

That was it. I tossed my erasers on the ground, marched across the room, and grabbed Atlee's face. Let me just say, I was not prepared. One touch of his lips to mine and Atlee had my ass in his hands and tongue swirling in my mouth. He didn't miss a beat.

It was an instant reaction, like this stuff was second nature to him. And he was good at it. I suddenly understood why girls fell for Atlee's shit.

If he could kiss like he was sucking my soul out of my body, then I'd hate to imagine what else he could do. There was a moment where I seriously questioned if a kiss could take away virginity status.

When I pulled away, I was a little lightheaded, but I still had enough logic in my brain to cup Atlee's groin and slide my gaze back to Gio.

"He's hard. Maybe your dick's broken?" Though there was a good chance that Atlee lived his life in a constant hard on state.

Gio glared at Atlee, who stared back at him.

"You're going to hit me now, aren't you?"

He smacked his lips together, "Yup."

Now that would've been fun to watch. However, Memphis's dad–being the kill joy that he was– chose that moment to walk in the room.

Both Gio and Atlee gave him a side eye, while Memphis and I just stood there. We knew that stern state of his dad's well. It was some kind of cross between drill sergeant and businessman. Which was funny because he was a dentist... or it was worse.

"Hi Mr. Blake." I said attempting to break the tension that he always brought with him.

His blonde hair was so stiffly slicked back that hurricane force winds couldn't blow it out of place, and I wouldn't mention the fact that he ironed his jeans. Needless to say Memphis's dad was a great joy to be around.

"Nova," he tsked while tipping his gaze down.

I still have my hand on Atlee's junk, don't I?

I quickly dropped my hand and explained, "This isn't what it looks like.."

"I don't care," he cut me off.

Can't say I was surprised by his response.

"Memphis," Mr. Blake snapped his fingers. "Let's go."

Yeah, that was about right too.

"Call you later," Memphis muttered to me as he hurried past.

His dad promptly spun around and walked out the door, with Memphis following behind.

I raised my hand to give them a wave, "See you later Mr. Blake. As always it's been a pleasure."

"Wow," Atlee snorted. "He seems like a fun guy."

"Doesn't he? I can't count how many times I shared a laugh with that man." Seriously, I couldn't count them, because he didn't laugh. Ever.

The next person came through the door mere seconds after they left, and it wasn't someone I expected.

My brow rose, "Veda?"

The maid uniform she was donning told me Veda came from work, but why was she here at all? Don't get me wrong, in this circumstance I preferred my sister over Maw Maw, but Veda didn't do well in crowded spaces. Or spaces in general.

"What are you doing here?"

"The school called," she stepped back into the doorway. "We should go."

"Don't leave, now Honey," a smolder washed over Atlee's face. "You just got here."

"Seriously?" I gave his shoulder a smack with the back of my hand. "Do you have to flirt with everyone?"

"Yeah."

I mean… was I really expecting a different answer. This was Atlee. Shouldn't Gio be slapping him… Shit Gio! All my effort to keep the mention of his name away from my sister, and here she was face to face with him. No wonder she looked white as a ghost. I had to get her out of here.

"Come on Ve–" I froze as two men walked up behind my sister.

The one in the suit looked vaguely familiar – I may have told him off at some point – but it was the other guy that worried me. The one that could've been Atlas Mancini's twin. Romeo. Veda was going to freak out.

"What the fuck are you doing here?" Gio barked out.

Romeo shrugged, "Dad was busy."

Veda lifted her chin to look behind her and I could visibly see what little color she had drained from her completion.

I rushed forward and threw my arm over her shoulder, so I could both shield her and let her know she wasn't alone. "Let's go get Knox."

My nephew was the only thing that could calm her down, and Veda was seconds away from a full on panic attack.

"Do you mind?" I hissed at the men behind her so they'd get out of the way.

Romeo stepped to the side, but the guy in the suit lifted a brow. "I see you're still rude."

That's where I knew him from. He was the asshole who answered the door when I went to pick up my sister.

"And I see you're still wearing black." I said and pulled Veda around him to go down the hall.

Chapter 25

GIOVANNI

I was halfway through my breakfast when the front door slammed. Not that I thought too much about it. Since my father declared war on the Russians, there were so many people in this house that it was impossible to find a quiet spot.

Security he called it. I called it overkill. No Russian would dare step foot in Sorrie. This town was crawling with Mafioso. They'd be dead before they made it a block. Then again he probably thought the same thing before my mother was killed.

Sometimes I could still hear the crash of the front door being kicked in followed by what seemed like an army of footsteps storming up the stairs. At the time I didn't think anything about the way my mother scooped me off the floor and stuffed me in the cupboard.

It was like a game of hide and seek. But looking back I could recognize the finality in her eyes. She knew what was coming and her only concern was saving me.

'It'll be okay Gio. Be a good boy and don't make a sound, no matter what you hear.'

That was the last thing she said to me. Her murder was credited to the Bratva. That's why my dad hated them so much. I tried to tell him that none of them were Russian, but he didn't listen. He never listened. He said I was a child and children missed things.

I may not have seen what happened to her, but I heard everything. Every scream and taunting phrase said that night were burned into my brain like a scar that wouldn't fade. There was only one accent I heard, and it was Cajun.

Swallowing down another mouthful of eggs, I pushed the memories out of my mind and concentrated on my normal Saturday morning routine of flipping through the newspaper. After this I'd go and workout for an hour or two before Darry, Atlee and I paid a visit to Simon.

His payment was late yet again, and I was feeling slightly murderous after my encounter with Nova yesterday. Simon could stem that tidal wave of rage until the football team's bonfire tonight. Typically I didn't go to those things but Nova was going to be there and I owed her a little pay back.

"Gio." I turned towards the person calling my name and saw Saul waltzing in the kitchen.

Saul wasn't much older than Atlas, but he carried himself like he'd been walking the earth for a thousand years. His face was always straight and shoulders rolled back as if he was expecting someone to jump out and attack. I tried talking to him once when I was a kid, he told me to piss off. Needless to say, we didn't have a friendly relationship.

"What the fuck do you want."

"The boss wants to see you," he answered.

My father was never Mr. Mancini or Cesare, he was always the boss.

"I hate to inform you of this Saul, but *my father*," I flipped a page of my paper, "isn't home."

"He is now."

I arched my brow, although I should've known that the second I saw Saul. My dad never went anywhere without his right hand man. Saul was the only person he trusted to protect him. Can't say I blamed him, Saul was paranoid as fuck.

Sighing out, "Fine," I pushed my chair back and got up to head up the stairs. Saul stepped in front of me before I could leave the room.

"You know the drill."

"Are you fucking kidding me?"

If his lack of expression wasn't enough to answer that question then the little finger twirl he gave me was. That was his way of saying assume the position.

What was I going to do? Kill my dad with coffee breath?

Grumbling under my breath, I held my arms out so Saul could pat me down.

Considering all I had on was a pair of sweats, I don't know what he thought he would find. Once Saul was sure I didn't have a weapon concealed, he waved me on.

I shot him a dirty look and walked away.

I assumed my father was in his office–he practically lived there. Just like I assumed this was about the job I'd been given. He probably wanted to know if I had any information yet, and I did. Veda Ford gave me that when she came to pick up her sister yesterday.

Fear was something I'd seen a lot in my life. My father intimidated a lot of people. But terror was different. People got this desperate look in their eyes. It was the same thing one would see in a doe before it bolted away.

Veda Ford got that same glint when she looked at Antonio Fiore. She definitely saw something. I don't know what, but it was enough to make all the color drain from her face.

I headed up the stairs and rounded the corner for the last door on the right side of the hall. The double doors at the end were my father's bedroom. Those were always closed. My father hadn't been in that room for years. He slept in one down the hall and left his sealed up like some kind of monument.

I wasn't complaining. One look at those golden door handles and all I could see was the blood staining the floor on the other side. Sometimes I swore I could hear my mother screaming inside there.

Why my father kept his office in the room next to it, I never understood.

I did everything I could to ignore the echoed memories crawling through the back of my mind and quickly stepped into my father's office.

What I expected to get was some kind of 'what did you find out' question.

That's not what happened.

My father was seated in his black leather chair while Romeo leaned against one of the bookshelves in the corner.

"Giovanni," my father leaned forward to fold his hands on the top of his mahogany desk. "Explain to me why I had to cut my trip short and come back here."

That made my brows rise. "No one asked you to come home."

"Your school did."

Oh.

I was kind of surprised that he answered his phone when they called.

"It's not a big deal." I got suspended, so what.

"Getting suspended isn't a big deal?"

Was he seriously mad about this? Last summer I was arrested for fighting and he didn't show up for that. One of his men bailed me out, then the paperwork mysteriously got lost so no charges were laid. And that was it. Nothing was said, and he sure as hell didn't call me to his office for a lecture.

I shrugged, "It's only three days."

His dark eyes met mine and that's when realization hit me. He wasn't pissed about the suspension. He was pissed that I got in a fight with Nova. This wasn't about me at all. It was about the job.

"Tell me Gio," the leather chair creaked as he leaned back and let out a breath. "What was the job I gave you?"

I should've known.

When I got in trouble as a child, all my father really did was give me a stern look. And half the time I didn't get that. His men however got their asses handed to them for letting me do whatever it was that I did.

Romeo was the one who stepped up and gave me some words of advice or lecture. So I wasn't surprised when he was the one to pick me up from school. Our father wasn't even home when we got back. Apparently there was some urgent business in New Orleans. Some things never changed.

Sometimes I wondered what it would be like if he actually did show up. What would it be like to be noticed? In that aspect I envied my brothers. He was there for them, I got the hand me down dad's that were ordered to keep an eye on me.

I sighed, "To get close to Nova and find out…"

"That's right." He cut me off. "To get close to Novalee Ford, and you've decided to do this by picking fights with her? That's an interesting tactic."

The look he was giving me was worse than his condescending tone.

"She's stubborn," was the only explanation I could come up with.

"She's stubborn, that's the best you got?"

I didn't say anything because there wasn't anything to say.

There was a time when all I did was search for a way to get a moment like this. When I was nine I jumped off the roof of the garage hoping my dad would take me to the hospital. A year later I cut my arm just to see if he'd notice the bandage. For years all I wanted was for him to see me, then I gave up. Now that I finally had his attention, I didn't know what to do.

After a few seconds of silence my father let out a long breath. "Did you even try to charm the girl?"

"She wouldn't fall for that." Nova was many things, stupid wasn't one of them.

I'd never been more happy to hear my brother's voice than when he lit up a cigarette and added his opinion, "He's right. She wouldn't fall for that."

Though I was pissed that Romeo had obviously been checking up on Nova, I could've kissed him for backing me up.

Then my dad turned his attention to my brother, "Is she attracted to him?"

"She seemed to like kissing him," Romeo nodded.

"Then I fail to see the problem."

It took everything I had not to grind my teeth. I was right fucking here.

"Are you spying on me now," I hissed at Romeo.

"Just keeping a watchful eye little brother."

"I don't need your help, Romeo." Or his watchful eye.

My father rolled his eyes back to me and my stomach dropped. "Yes you do."

"No I don't." Why couldn't he believe that I was just as capable as my brother? "I know Veda Ford saw something."

"You can't know that for sure," Romeo scoffed and shook his head.

"I guess you missed the way she stared at Antonio." He was the one that didn't know for sure. He didn't look close enough to see it. But I did.

"Doesn't prove anything," Romeo blew out a puff of smoke. "The girl's always been jumpy."

"Not like that."

I may not have gotten close to Nova in the way they wanted me to, but I still noticed the change in her sister.

"So she saw something." My father once again folded his hands on the top of his desk. "Do you know what she saw, or who she saw do it?"

Could I say with absolute certainty that she witnessed a murder or that she knew who did it… "No."

"Alright," my father scrubbed a hand down his face and sighed, "Make the call."

It couldn't end this way. My father wasn't right about me not being ready. I could do this. "You don't have to make the call."

"Yes I do. You couldn't complete a simple task and now I'm forced to kill a mother and child."

The disappointment in his tone made me long for the days when I wasn't even a thought in his head.

When his eyes rolled down to a stack of papers my fists balled.

I wanted to hit and scream, 'I'm right here. I've always been right here'.

But I didn't. I just stood there like a pathetic child. I hated him for making me feel like an outsider. I had just as much right to be welcomed in the family as my brothers. It wasn't just my birthright. I'd earned my spot. Unlike my brothers I spent years trying to prove myself, and I was willing to make sacrifices to show him that.

"Veda won't talk. You don't have to kill her."

My father sighed as if I was nothing more than a nuisance. "It's done, Gio."

"Besides," Romeo interjected, "you can't guarantee she'll keep her mouth shut."

"I can if I own her sister."

They both stopped and arched a brow at me. I didn't need to explain further, they knew what I meant. That didn't stop my father from clarifying things.

"You couldn't kill her."

"I know." In order for this to work long term, I'd have to marry Nova. Chances are I'd end up marrying someone I didn't like anyway. Antonio had already started trying for an agreement between myself and his youngest daughter.

My father looked at Romeo who nodded and said, "It could work."

Of course he would look to my brother for confirmation. It was my idea, not Romeo's. Yet he was the one who had to agree. Would my father notice if I died? Would he care, or would it be okay because he still had my brother.

"And if it doesn't work," Romeo added. "We'll just kill them both."

Personally I preferred that outcome, but my father had something against killing mothers. If Veda Ford didn't have a kid or was a man he wouldn't hesitate to pull the trigger. This at least gave him another option.

"Are you sure you want to do this?" My dad asked. "The girl is a Ford."

Did he think I forgot that?

"I can do it."

Can, not want. Being tied to Novalee Ford wasn't exactly something I was looking forward to, but it wasn't as if I had to be faithful. Atlee's dad fucked who he wanted. So did mine and Darry's, it was kind of expected.

"Think hard about this son. Once it's in place, it's done."

I nodded, "I know."

"You'll have to fuck her," he pointed out. "There's no point in having a wife if you don't put an heir in her."

"And a baby would give us extra leverage over her sister," Romeo added.

Fuck, I didn't think about that. I wouldn't deny the fact that Nova–for some fucked up reason–got my dick hard, but I promised myself I wouldn't betray Atlas like that. Then again maybe it wouldn't be betraying Atlas.

I couldn't imagine Kato Ford would be too happy about someone like me defiling his baby sister. And I had some pretty fucked up desires. I could send him pictures and little notes he could stew over in his cell. It didn't get much more helpless than that.

"Yeah," I said, "I can fuck her."

Hard, rough and in every depraved way I could think of. I'd turn her into my own personal fuck toy, hungry for my cock and just as twisted as me. I would destroy Novalee Ford and in turn, her brother.

"Okay," my father sat up. "And how exactly do you propose to get the girl to agree to this?"

That was easy. "She'll trade herself for her brother."

Chapter 26

NOVALEE

Not only did Gio get me suspended, but he got me extra shifts at work. Maw Maw said if I wasn't going to learn then I was going to work.

So I got to spend the first half of my Saturday at the dinner, despite my arguments that it wasn't a regular school day, so therefore work didn't need to replace learning. And yes technically I was the one who hit him, but he dragged it out until we got caught. Meaning the suspension was all his fault.

Thankfully I managed to get out of Maw Maw's home lockdown for a school function. After all, extracurricular activities were important. Did it matter that said activity involved alcohol and dumb decisions? Probably, but Maw Maw didn't need to know that part. As far as she was concerned, I was heading off to support the football team. I even gave her a 'go Holy Rollers,' before I walked out.

After the week I had, I deserved a little fun. Especially if that fun was Gio Mancini free. Games were the only thing the asshole trio bothered to show up to. Personally that would be the one thing I avoided.

I was not a sports girl. Memphis was the only reason I was going to the basketball game tomorrow. He somehow talked me into it. The things a girl would do for a decent chocolate bar.

I pulled up in front of Memphis's white two story and dug my elbow into the steering wheel. His neighbors visibly grimaced at the mangled screech that echoed through the air, which I thought was rude. It took a lot of strength to get my horn to work. My elbow hurt a little. If anything, they should be thanking me. This neighborhood needed a little spice, it was way too suburban.

A few seconds later Memphis skipped out the front door and hopped in the passenger seat.

I grinned at his tight dark jeans and white shirt, "Don't you look dashing."

"I was going more for dapper but dashing works." He turned to give me a once over. "I assume you were going for sex kitten, or is your new look for Gio Mancini?"

My eyes rolled as I groaned and kicked the brake to lift the pedal. "I told you that was nothing."

"If it was nothing then why didn't you tell me about it?"

"Because it was nothing." Hence, not worth mentioning.

My foot pressed down on the gas, as I steered my truck away from the curb and down the street. The quicker we got to this bonfire, the better.

"Nova," Memphis sighed. "You made out with a Mancini…"

I cut him off right then and there. "I didn't make out with him. He kissed me."

He crossed his arms, "And you didn't think that was worth mentioning?"

"No. It was just some stupid bullshit crap meant to get to me." That was it.

Memphis's brow rose, "Did it?"

Yes.

"Of course not."

He tipped his head and I could practically hear the 'who is she trying to fool' roll through his mind.

"I'm fine Memphis."

"Uh huh? Is that why you decided to dress like Cindy?"

"Hey! I look much better in this shirt than Cindy would." She had a lot more in the chest area though. And this sparkly brown tank top I stole from my sister's closet, did redefine the word plunging in plunging neckline. "Besides, I have a reputation to uphold."

"That's right, I forgot about your whore status." Memphis slid his eyes my way then added, "H O R E."

My eye twitched a little. "Nice face by the way. Did you have to use the whole bottle of concealer?"

Okay, that was a low blow. Memphis was sticking up for me, but I didn't ask him to. In fact I tried many times to point out his incapabilities in the fighting department. He did a good job on his face. Most of his bruises were successfully hidden. The swelling under his left eye however... If all else failed he could have a decent career in the make-up industry.

Memphis sneered back at me, "I used less than you did to look like a normal person."

"I'll have you know I'm not wearing concealer." All I had on was some glittery eyeshadow, mascara and a touch of red tinted lip gloss. "And I look fabulous."

"That's what I'm afraid of..." Memphis's eyes narrowed. "What are you up to?"

Why would I be up to anything? It wasn't like I walked around plotting stuff all the time. I did today, but that was beside the point.

"Is there something wrong with looking good?" And I did look good. I even took the time to curl my hair.

He leaned back to once again eye my outfit, "Could those shorts be any shorter?"

"Well, they are called shorts." And the denim material covered my ass, that was all that mattered.

"I like the shirt."

Really? Besides for the black cowboy boots on my feet, my shirt was the one thing I thought Memphis would complain about.

"It's a little low cut though."

There we go.

"Luckily I don't have boobs, so I think I'm good."

Unlike stupid Cindy with her full chest. How was that fair? She shook her ass at any guy who happened by, yet I was the one who got dubbed whore. Oh well. This was one party where I wouldn't have to put up with her petty competition.

Cindy didn't go to St Agatha's and therefore wouldn't be at the bonfire. That kind of made me sad. Who was I going to make snide comments about now?

"Trust me," Memphis grumbled while turning to look out the window. "You have boobs."

"Memphis Blake," I sucked in a fake gasp. "Have you been checking out my breasts?"

He gave me an exaggerated eye roll. "Don't make a big deal out of it."

How could I not?

"I hope you're not switching teams on me. Because that would seriously corrupt the balance of our relationship."

If he suddenly went straight, then I might have to start checking out girls.

"I'm not switching teams."

"Then why are you looking at my boobs?"

"I can't help it," he muttered. "They're this freaky phenomenon that guys have to stare at."

Okay but… "You do realize only girls have boobs, right?"

This was the same man who gave me tips for sucking dick–which I would try out one day. Kind of needed someone with a dick first. Provided that said someone didn't have the last name Mancini, Fiore or whatever the hell Darry's last name was.

Though I did wonder what Darry would do if I walked up to him and dropped to my knees. He was always so quiet. Would it shock him into normalcy, or make him more mysterious?

"Doesn't matter," Memphis shrugged, "There's just something about boobs."

Huh, you learn something new every day. Does that mean I have magical powers?

That was an interesting theory. I might have to test it out. Tonight was as good a night as any, and it would help with my goal.

There was purpose behind my look. I was determined to find someone who kissed as good, or better than Gio. He couldn't be the only one who made my knees weak. Atlee was more of the *I need to take three showers because I'm dirty now*, kisser. But Gio… I needed to wash his taste out of my mouth.

If that meant I had to make out with the entire football team, then so be it. This would be the last night I thought about Gio Mancini and his soul sucking lips.

I steered my truck down a small dirt road and parked next to a group of vehicles behind some trees. Holding a bonfire this close to the swamp wouldn't have been my first choice, but they had alcohol, so who cared. Besides, I wasn't about to plan shit. I didn't have that much school spirit. I barely had school meh.

"Jesus," Memphis muttered when my muffler shot off a bang causing a group of girls to duck for cover.

Not sure what he was complaining about, I thought this shit was great. There was nothing like seeing a bunch of snooty dressed up girls roll around on the ground.

I peeked over my steering wheel at the spot where they dropped down, "How much mud do you think they got on them?"

"When are you going to get this thing fixed?" Memphis shook his head and opened the door.

"Don't pick on my truck." I followed his lead and hopped out onto the grass. "We understand each other."

"Is that because you're both broken?"

"No," I pointed at him then headed down a path to my left. "It's because we both enjoy a good drink."

My truck guzzled through gas like I did alcohol.

Memphis skipped up beside me and sighed, "Why do I get the feeling that something bad is about to happen?"

"Because you're a pessimist. But don't worry," I looked over at him and smiled, "I'll make sure you have a good time."

He pinched the bridge of his nose and muttered, "That's what I'm afraid of."

I put my friend's dour mood out of my mind and weaved my way through a patch of Cypress trees. The crackling of a fire combined with music and various voices led the way to a small clearing. There were people everywhere, dancing, and talking while drinking from red solo cups.

It was kind of pretty the way the roaring flames in the center cast a glow over the crowd. Even the SUV where the music was coming from seemed picturesque. Or disturbing? Give everyone robes and have them chant some eerie phrase, and this would be a very different scenario. One where a virgin might be sacrificed.

"Should I be worried about hidden daggers?

Memphis's brows knit, "What?"

"They do look kind of culty," I waved my hand at the crowd. "And I am a virgin."

He stood there blinking at me for a few seconds before saying, "I'm going to find Chuck."

"That's it, leave the human sacrifice alone." Where was my

gallant protector now?

He pointed at me, "There's something wrong with you."

Did I miss something? I thought we'd established that years ago.

"Go and find your boyfriend," I waved him off. "But don't blame me when my body is found drained of blood."

Memphis shook his head and walked off while I tried to decide which way I was going to go. There was a large barrel on the left side of the crowd filled with what looked like hunch punch, and on the right was a silver keg. Not sure I wanted to risk the punch given the possible sacrifice and cult scenario, so I headed to the right.

There were three guys by the keg. All of whom I assumed were football players based on the varsity jackets they were wearing. One was sitting on a stump with his legs stretched out in a casual manner. Another leaned against a tree with his back to me, and the last one was sitting on the tailgate of a red truck manning the pump.

That was the one I walked up to. "Can I have one of those?"

A curl lifted the corner of his mouth when his sapphire gaze slid my way. "Hey there."

I waited for him to fill up a cup for me but he didn't move. He just sat there staring at me. I could almost feel his gaze sliding over my chest.

"Hello," I snapped my fingers in his face. "Getting parched here."

"Well, we can't have that." He didn't even pull his eyes from my boobs when he reached out to grab a cup. "I don't believe we've met.

"Actually we have." We had English together, which he might know if he bothered to look at my face.

Boob boy's gaze dipped a little lower as he leaned over to fill up my cup, "You want a drink?"

What the hell did he think he was doing? "No, I'd much rather watch you drool."

"Uh huh," he grunted. "You got a name sweetheart?"

The other two guys had now joined in the great nipple stare down.

"Yeah," I snatched the now full cup out of his hand. "It's Boobs McGee."

Gawker number two nodded, "That's a great name."

He only heard the word boobs didn't he? Maybe they really did have magical powers. On the upside, I shouldn't have a problem finding guys to make out with. Not these guys though. Pretty sure they didn't know I had a mouth.

"Nice ass," one yelled when I walked away.

At least that one knew I had other body parts. That was progress.

I melded into the crowd to search for my first test subject. After about thirty minutes of getting the same reaction from every guy I talked to, I came to the conclusion that it wasn't happening tonight. But I did make a mental note to never wear this shirt again. It might even be a good idea to burn it when I got home. No clothing should have that kind of power.

Giving up on my quest to find a better kisser, I made my way through the crowd to the spot where Memphis and Chuck were standing. Or should I say arguing. Chuck did not look happy. He was scowling and waving his hands through the air.

It didn't take long for me to figure out what they were fighting about.

"You always let her pull you into this shit."

"She's my best friend, Chuck."

Awe, they were arguing about me. I was flattered, though technically I didn't pull Memphis into anything. He lunged head first into Atlee.

"You could've been hurt."

He was hurt. Did Chuck not see the swelling in Memphis's eye?

I didn't. I already had a plan for revenge, because that's what best friends did.

Memphis sighed, "What did you expect me to do?"

"I don't know," Chuck threw his hands up in the air. "How about you let her deal with her own shit for once."

As much as I would love to stand back and revel in the tension finally showing up in their relationship, Memphis was getting upset. The way his mouth twitched down told me it was time to break the ice.

So I stepped up and sang, "Do I sense trouble in paradise?"

Chuck's glare locked on me. "This is all your fault."

"What did I do?" Besides for finding the all powerful shirt of man stupidity.

"I hope you're happy."

I shook my head, "Not generally."

I was more of the blah type.

"Chuck," Memphis warned. "It's not a big deal."

"What do you mean it's not a big deal? What if you were hurt worse?" Chuck cupped Memphis's face and dropped his forehead on his. "I don't know what I'd do."

In most cases I would side with Memphis, but I was with Chuck on this one, which was something I was about to point out when Memphis whispered, "Don't worry I'm okay." And they kissed.

I internally gagged.

Didn't they know how to have a proper fight. No one was crying yet. Where were the thrown objects and emotional damage that would be ammunition for future arguments. How did they expect to have a healthy relationship if they refused to destroy each other?

I sighed and took a sip of my drink, "You guys make me sick."

Chuck pulled his mouth off of my best friend and shot me a look, "You're not my favorite person right now."

"Am I ever your favorite person?"

It was a valid question, not that Chuck thought so. His chest heaved with a frustrated breath.

"Do you always have to be so difficult?" Memphis asked.

I was just about to retort his snide remark when a loud voice boomed through the air.

"That's it burn!"

The eerie laugh that followed was coming from a small blonde standing with her arms wide in front of the roaring fire.

"The call is sent forth…"

Memphis and Chuck cocked a brow while I tipped my head at the bag of what appeared to be marshmallows tightly clasped in her hand.

"ALL HAIL THE DRAGON!"

Despite the fact that this chick was clearly crazy – or high out of her mind – everyone around her cheered to her call. "HAIL THE DRAGON!"

Chanting… check. Dancing around a fire… Check. This did not bode well for me.

I swung my eyes back to Memphis, "And you said this wasn't culty."

"You know what… I hope they sacrifice you. In fact I'll hold you down."

Ugh, rude.

"Tell you what," I lifted my hand to point at the blonde. "If you give me whatever she's on, I won't fight the sacrifice."

Memphis's face dropped, "the last thing you need is drugs."

Pfft, killjoy.

"Fine, but I'm not going to stand here and watch you two make out." I walked away while singing, "I'm going to find my own make out partner."

The night was young and I felt a renewed sense of determination.

"Gio isn't here." Memphis sang back, making me shoot a dirty look back at him.

I made my way into the crowd intent on finding someone who's sole focus wasn't on my chest. At this point I didn't even care if it was a girl. And I found that person – or more like walked into them. Unfortunately it was someone I wanted to see less than Gio.

While searching the crowd, I twisted through a dancing couple, and crashed into a hard chest, causing the rest of my beer to splash out of my cup.

"I've been looking for you."

Great, Simon. What was he doing here?

The couple muttered something while I shook droplets off my arm and grumbled under my breath. "Mother…"

The rest of the curse got stuck in my throat when I looked up. He looked worse than Memphis. Simon's right eye was completely swollen shut, his left arm was in a cast, and it looked like there was a piece of his ear missing.

"Did you get hit by a car?" And who was driving, cause I'd like to give them a high five.

"More like a bat."

My brows knit, "What?"

"It doesn't matter," he interrupted. "Can we talk?"

That was an easy, "No".

"You can't still be mad at me?"

I believed I could. In fact I was pretty sure I could stay mad until the end of time. "Did you bring your girlfriend with you?"

Simon's eyes rolled. "Cindy isn't my girlfriend."

"No, she's just the girl you sleep with when you do have a girlfriend."

"Can't you let that go?"

Could I let that go… No, no I don't think I could.

"Have fun Simon, if you'll excuse me…" I turned to walk away.

"I need another drink."

Because someone spilled mine.

"You can have mine."

"No thanks."

"It's bourbon."

I stopped and cocked a brow. I did like bourbon.

"Come on," Simon held up a red cup. "It's the least I can do."

He did owe me…

"Fine," I snatched the cup out of his hand. "But this isn't a peace offering. I still hate you."

His brow arched, "You can't avoid me forever."

Yes I could.

"You'll have to talk to me one day." He called out when I walked deeper in the crowd.

I held up my hand and waved over my shoulder, "No I won't."

The next twenty minutes were spent trying to ignore the fact that my ex-boyfriend was here while I enjoyed his bourbon. Memphis and Chuck had snuck off somewhere – I assumed to make up – and everyone else was too drunk to talk to.

So I decided to just enjoy myself and wave my hand through the music in the air. It was a good beat and the white streaks following my hand were so bright and fluffy I couldn't help but giggle. If only the ground would stop moving.

"Hey there."

I turned to see a pair of blue eyes. It was like looking into the ocean.

"You're cute," something grabbed my ass and pulled me up against a firm body.

I couldn't stop staring at the waves crashing in those eyes. They were going back and forth, back and forth. And they were getting closer. Inch by inch those blue depths moved in until I could feel something warm brush across my lips.

That's when a fist flew through the air.

Chapter 27

High school parties weren't something Darry, Atlee, or I did. When someone grew up in the world we did, gatherings of dancing and debauchery seemed a tad immature. By the time we hit teenage years, our idiotic drunken days were long past. My father gave me my first drink when I was eleven. My brothers were ten.

Atlas once told me it was so I could build up my tolerance and not make a fool of myself when I hit high school, which now that I was older made a lot more sense. The last thing our fathers wanted was for us to draw attention to ourselves and in return, the family. That's pretty much all these things were. Alcohol infused bouts of attention seeking.

Darry followed Atlee and I through the trees and shook his head. "I can't believe you brought up marriage."

Technically all I did was suggest an alternative solution to a problem. Marriage didn't occur to me until after.

"Wait…" Atlee swept a batch of Spanish moss hanging off the Cypress branches out of his way, "this was your idea?"

"Yes," I sighed. "It was my idea."

He better not ask me why. I was still trying to figure that out.

"So, you do want her?"

"No, I don't want her." Of course I didn't want her. It was just a spur of the moment decision. Or temporary insanity.

"Okay…" confusion further embedded in the lines on Atlee's face. "But if you don't want Nova… then why offer to marry her?"

"Who else is he going to marry? Alex?" Darry scoffed out a snort. "That's just asking for trouble."

I was with Darry on that one. Atlee's baby sister wasn't what one would consider a desirable bride. Wives had to be one of two things to survive our world, docile or strong enough not to break. Alex was neither. Chaos followed that girl around like a fucking shadow.

"Hey, Alex is just young." Atlee shot Darry a dirty look. "She'll grow out of it."

Atlee had a soft spot for his baby sister.

Darry did not. "She lit your father's car on fire because he wouldn't let her go out with her friends."

Atlee shrugged, "She was tired of being trapped in the house."

"She was twelve." Darry shot back.

That was bad, and not the worst thing she'd done. Let's just say over the next two years, Alex Fiore amped up her rebellion. So much so that Atlee's dad shipped her off to some boarding school for kids in families like ours. I almost felt bad for Wayward Academy.

Atlee being the protective brother that he was, stopped before we broke through the tree line and spun around to cross his arms at Darry. "You got a problem with my sisters?"

"Yeah, I do." Darry puffed his chest out and squared off with Atlee by returning his glare. "Kendall is always flirting with random guys and Alex is a train wreck. Neither one knows their place."

That wasn't entirely true. Although Kendall was a bit flirtatious, she was also prepared to marry my brother. Being tied to Romeo wasn't a fate I'd want. Couldn't blame her for wanting to feel a bit of freedom before that happened. Not that it would matter to Darry. Nothing Atlee said would matter to Darry.

The simple fact was his sisters were girls and our friend had a special hatred for the female species. Didn't stop him from enjoying them, though I think the girls he'd fucked would argue the enjoyment part. Whatever he did in the bedroom scared them so much that I'd seen girls literally run away when he walked down the hall.

I stepped past them and waved. "Can we continue this debate later?"

We didn't come here to argue the validity of Atlee's sisters as mob wives. A fact that Atlee was more than happy to go along with. He stopped squaring off with Darry and followed me towards the glow of crackling fire.

"Can I ask you a question?"

"What?" I'd say no if I thought he'd keep his mouth shut.

"Well, Nova kind of hates you…"

That didn't sound like a question to me. "And?"

"How exactly do you plan to get her to agree to this agreement?"

"I'm not. I'm going to get her to come to me with it."

Novalee would never agree to marry me, but she would take her brother's life debt. And I couldn't be the one to offer her that option. Her stubborn streak would make her automatically reject anything I said. Meaning Nova had to offer herself up. That was the only way this could work. That didn't mean I couldn't apply a little pressure. Like say, make sure her brother wound up in the hospital tonight.

Atlee's brows knit. "Why would she do that?"

"Self-sacrifice is a beautiful thing," I said as we broke through the tree line.

"Ah," Atlee breathed. "So you're going after Kato?"

"Yup." In fact he should be getting shanked right about now.

Darry's brow rose. "You want her to take her brother's life debt?"

"Can you think of another way?"

He knew there was no other way. He also knew I didn't like it. But we had a job to do and sometimes sacrifices had to be made. My father needed to see that I was willing to do that.

"So you're going to give up revenge on Kato Ford to make sure his sister keeps quiet?"

I understood Darry's question. For the past two years revenge was all I could think of. That was all I talked about. How I would make Kato suffer for what he did. But…

"There's more than one way to torture someone."

Realization sparked across both my friend's faces.

"Defile the baby sister," Darry shifted his gaze out at the crowd of drunken teenagers stumbling around. "That's cold."

Coming from him, I took that as a complement. Atlee was always down to break some bones, but Darry was a twisted fuck that got off on the mind games. He had Simon blubbering like a baby before Atlee broke his arm. Needless to say, Simon paid up. Well, mostly. He still owed us a grand, but after the way we left him, he'd do whatever he had to, to get it.

Atlee snickered, "I like this plan."

The only reason he liked this plan was because it involved pussy.

"Now," Atlee rolled his neck and cracked his knuckles. "Let's find your wife."

God I hated hearing her called that. But it wouldn't last long. Eventually Novalee would fuck up and we could rid the world of the Ford family. Then failure wouldn't be put on me. It would all be on her. And I had no problem pushing her to the breaking point. In fact I was looking forward to it. There would be no leeway. Just actions and consequences.

My eyes locked on a girl in the crowd.

And the consequences would start now.

"What the fuck is she wearing?"

Atlee and Darry both followed my glare. After which Darry shook his head while Atlee let out a whistle.

"Damn, the girl cleans up nice."

What the hell was Atlee talking about? That was not cleaned up. Clean up was a nice outfit and some make up. Not flawless curls cascading down the open back of a skimpy fucking shirt. For fuck sakes, Nova's ass was barely covered in those denim shorts. And there she was, surrounded by bunch of panting fucking jocks, swaying her shit back and forth. Someone was gonna die tonight.

Atlee tipped his head when Nova spun around.

My fists immediately balled. Where the fuck was the front of her shirt? Her tits were practically hanging out. the only thing I couldn't see were her nipples.

"Damn," Atlee clicked his tongue. "That's one hell of a plunging neckline."

I might start the death toll tonight with him.

"That is not a plunging neckline. It's a fucking scrap of fabric!"

Her ass was going to be so red.

"What are you going to do if she's not a virgin?" Darry asked, further enraging me.

Virginity was an important factor when it came to wives. But that wasn't what made the growl rumble out of my chest. It was the possibility that someone else had touched her, which pissed me off more. I shouldn't give a fuck.

If anything I should be praying that some asshole got his hands on her first, because it would negate any possibility of marriage.

Yet all I could think about was finding the motherfucker and ripping him apart until his blood was dripping through my fingers.

When Novalee twerked back into some prick, the only thing that stopped me from charging head first into a full on murder spree was Atlee's reassurance.

"Don't worry, she's a virgin."

He had some weird sixth sense about that shit. Atlee could sniff out a virgin from a mile away. That didn't stop me from growling out, "She better fucking be."

It wasn't until Atlee and Darry exchanged a look that I realized what I was doing. This was Novalee Ford, sister of my enemy. I shouldn't care who did or didn't touch her. She was nothing. A means to an end, and that was it.

And now she's grinding up against that asshole! That's it!

"Whoa, whoa," Atlee stopped me before I could take a step. "I got this."

With that he took off just as that prick grabbed Nova's ass and leaned in.

If it wasn't for Darry clasping his hand on my shoulder, I'd have charged head first into the crowd with Atlee. Thankfully the feel of his fingers digging into my flesh was enough to allow me to take a breath and stem the tide of rage boiling through my veins.

"Remember who she is, Gio."

Blowing out a long exhale, I let Darry's words sink in. Nova was my enemy. A toy to play with for my vengeance. Once I regained control of myself I nodded at Darry, "Thank you."

"No problem," he nodded back then turned his attention to the dispersing crowd.

The party goers weren't too happy about the way Atlee's fists were pounding down into that asshole's face. A few people screamed while others backed away from the fight.

The only people who didn't move were a couple of football players–who seemed to be pondering whether or not to get involved–and Nova. She just stood there, waving her hand through the air as if she didn't notice the fight right in front of her.

What the fuck?

"Just so you know," Darry said, interrupting my thoughts. "It's okay to want her."

My eyes snapped to him, "I don't want her."

"Lie to yourself all you want, Gio, but you can't lie to me," his eyes slid my way. "I've seen how you look at her."

Yeah, like I want to kill her.

"Do you really think Atlas would care who you fucked?"

"Of course he would." I barked back.

Atlas would want me to make the entire Ford family pay for his murder.

Darry shook his head and muttered, "Whatever you say."

"What's that supposed to mean?"

"Let it go."

"No." I was not going to let this go. If Darry had something to say about my brother, then he was going to say it.

He sighed and looked up at me. "You really want to do this now?"

I folded my arms over my chest. "Yes, I do."

"Alright," Darry turned to face me. "Atlas was a self-centered prick. The only person he gave a shit about was himself."

"Watch yourself Darry," I warned. "He was my brother."

"Yeah, and he would've stepped over your body in a heartbeat if he thought it would get him more power."

"You don't know what you're talking about." Atlas loved me. He protected me and taught me things. He didn't ignore me like the rest of my family. "And we're done talking about this."

"Fine," Darry huffed. "But sooner or later you're going to have to snap out of that fuzzy illusion you have of your big brother."

Fuzzy illusion? Darry had no idea who my brother was, nor did he have any right to talk about him. Who the fuck did he think he was? I would've hit him if it wasn't for Atlee dragging Novalee our way. One look at the smile on her face and my anger was instantly displaced.

Why the fuck should she be so happy? What was she thinking, prancing around in next to nothing, shaking her shit at everyone. Let's see how long she keeps that goddamn smile on her face after I get my hands on her.

Atlee's mouth opened and he got out a "Gio…" before I snatched Novalee's elbow out of his grip.

"What the fuck do you think you're doing?" I hissed down at her.

She giggled up at me, "You have pretty eyes."

My brows knit. "What?"

"They sparkle like emeralds." Her hand flattened on my chest as she leaned in and sighed, "I like emeralds. They smell good."

What the hell was happening right now? Since when did Novalee snuggle into me? And she was snuggling. Her cheek was rubbing against my shirt while she inhaled deep sniffs. Where was the anger and hatred? Why wasn't she telling me off. It was creeping me out.

I grabbed her shoulders and pushed her off me. "Stop that."

"Awe," her bottom lip popped out, "But you're warm."

I'm warm?

My brow arched at Atlee, who arched one back.

"That's what I was trying to tell you. I think someone drugged her."

"What do you mean you think someone drugged her?"

"Well, she's all touchy feely," he explained. "And super happy. If I had to guess I'd say it was some kind of Ex and GHB mixture."

If he had to guess? "Do I want to know how you know that?"

Darry shook his head, "Probably not."

The fact that it was Darry who answered made me pause to wonder what those two were doing in their spare time. Whatever it was I was sure I didn't want to know. Besides there were other things to worry about. Like...

"Who drugged her?"

Atlee shrugged, "How the fuck should I know."

"You knew she was drugged." I pointed out.

"That doesn't mean I know who drugged her."

"Did you ask her?"

"Why the fuck would I ask her?"

"Because she would know who drugged her."

"Not necessarily," Atlee argued. "Someone could've slipped it in her drink without her knowing."

"That doesn't mean you don't ask her!" How else were we going to fuck up the asshole who thought he could take my shit.

"Sorry, but I was too concerned with keeping her hands off my junk to ask her shit."

I took a step closer to Atlee, "You let her grab your junk!"

If she put her hands on Atlee again, I'd kill him right here and now.

"She didn't grab anything."

"Oh, but you had no problem letting her try." Of course he didn't because Atlee wanted all the pussy. He worked his way through every girl in school like a ravenous whore. Well, not this time. And not this girl.

"I didn't let her do shit," Atlee wasn't backing down he puffed his chest up and stepped up to me. "She's fucking drugged."

A likely excuse.

"Guys," Darry tried to interject but we both ignored him.

"Just admit it Atlee," my fists balled. "You want to fuck her."

"GUYS!" Darry yelled louder, though neither one of us cared what he had to say.

"Yeah, I want to fuck her," Atlee hissed in my face. "I would tap that shit so hard."

Oh, I was gonna kill him.

"But she's yours, Gio. I would never disrespect you like that."

Those words smacked me in the face like a bucket of ice water. What the hell was I doing? I was ready to tear one of my best friend's faces off for who? Novalee fucking Ford.

"I'm sorry." I took a step back before I did something I would regret. "I just…"

"It's okay," Atlee interrupted. "Let's just get her out of here."

That was a good idea. I could beat Nova's ass in the morning for not taking better care, after I got her somewhere safe.

"That might be hard to do," Darry said while tipping his chin.

We both looked in the direction he was indicating and froze.

Nova stood about ten feet away stroking the grey fur of an animal she had cradled in her arms.

She smiled over at us and sang, "I found a puppy."

"That is not a fucking puppy," Atlee muttered as the opossum opened its long snout and hissed.

Chapter 28

GIOVANNI

Ever try to wrangle a drugged-out girl? It wasn't easy. Especially when that girl was Novalee Ford. She had no self-preservation instincts as it was, otherwise she wouldn't keep poking me – but when her inhibitions were removed, I was left with some 'touchy feely, you smell good and I'm going to say everything I think' version of her.

After I whipped that opossum out of her arms with Darry's jacket, she tried to chase after it. Atlee had to tackle her ass. Then came the headache of getting her in my Range Rover.

She ran around it like we were playing some maniacal game of tag, then climbed on top of it and declared she was the lizard king. I had to use a chocolate bar and lure her inside like fucking puppy.

I wasn't even going to mention what happened when I gave her keys to Atlee, so he could take her truck home. Let's just say it was a good thing Darry had another chocolate bar stashed in his jacket. Thank God for his little brother's weakness for sweet treats.

Now I was trying not to crash while the toddler on crack in the passenger seat kept pawing at me.

"This is so soft," Nova purred while sweeping her palm over my chest. "How did you make a shirt out of blood?"

I'd like to make a shirt out of her blood.

"It's better than the one you're wearing." I was going to burn that fucking thing first chance I got.

Her bottom lip popped out as her eyes dipped down to her chest. "What's wrong with my shirt?"

Besides the fact that her tits were practically hanging out for every jackass to drool over?

A snorted giggle rang through the air. "I have boobs."

"I noticed." I grumbled.

"Oo who's Mr. Grumpy?" She sang while crawling over the center console.

I'd show her grumpy when I tanned her ass.

"Don't be grumpy… you're too warm to be grumpy."

Nova smashed her cheek against me and rubbed up my arm like a cat, making me roll my eyes.

For fuck sakes. "Stop that."

"Why?" She murmured and crawled a little closer.

"Because I'm trying not to kill us." Which was kind of hard to do when she was practically on my lap.

"But you want to kill me."

True, but that was beside the point.

With her cheek firmly squished up against my shoulder, Nova rolled her gaze up to me. "Are you really going to kill me?"

"Maybe," I sighed and steered down the road.

Did I want to end Novalee's life? Yes. I wanted to feel her blood run through my fingers until Kato Ford had nothing left but the endless void of his jail cell. Killing her would kill any hope he had left. But there was something about her.

Or rather a lack of something in those big hazel orbs that

intrigued me. And pissed me off at the same time. Perhaps that was why I offered my father an alternative route. So I could play with my food before I chewed it up and spat it out.

"You're not as mean as you think you are."

I cocked a brow down at her. "If you really believe that then you're stupider than I thought."

She hadn't even begun to see my mean side.

She snorted, "You're stupid," and continued to rub against my arm.

"And you," I pushed her back in the passenger seat, "need to stop pawing at me."

Nova huffed and crossed her arms. "I wasn't pawing."

Oh, please. "You were half a second away from shoving my dick down your throat."

"Pfft," Her lip curled in a childish sneer, "I'll have you know I've never done that before."

Is that right?

Curiosity shifted my eyes over to her defiantly raised chin. "What else haven't you done?"

The second the question left my mouth my hands tightened on the steering wheel. I was ready to kill someone if she said the wrong thing. I could feel the need for blood rise when her lips parted.

"Skydiving."

Really? That's what she was going to come back with? "That's not what I was talking about."

"I don't care," Nova sighed and leaned back over the center console to smash back up against me. "You're too warm to care.

Jesus fucking Christ.

Talking to her was more useless than it was on a normal day. Fuck it, let her do what she wanted. We were almost there. Then hopefully she would pass out.

I rounded the corner and headed down the street for my driveway. My house wasn't the ideal place to take her, but it was better than dropping her off at home. Nova had quite obviously been drugged and given our history, I couldn't imagine any scenario where that would go well. Her sister had a habit of making false accusations. She'd have my ass in cuffs before I had a chance to say anything.

Then again Veda hadn't said anything about what she saw at the Fiore house, which led me to wonder what Veda Ford was planning. Why hadn't she said anything yet? Was she working with someone? Was she too scared of us?

Either way, time was of the essence. If my plan for their brother didn't push Nova to make a deal, then I might have to arrange an accident for Granny.

"You're so firm." Nova flattened her palm on my thigh, making my dick jerk. "And hard… I bet you could hold me down easily."

Hold her down? Did she really just say that? Nah, it was just the drugs talking. Or was it?

It took everything I had to keep my focus on the road when her fingers started inching closer to dangerous territory. I'd never been more happy to see my house than I was when I turned down the driveway.

The tension rolling through my body made those last few feet seem like miles. Seconds ticked by like hours where all I could feel was her breath heating the skin on my upper arm. By the time I pulled to a stop, Nova's fingers were right there, so close to my dick that I could feel every twitch she made.

I couldn't take this shit anymore.

The instant I parked, I opened the door and stepped out onto the driveway, so fast that Nova flopped face first into the driver seat.

"Get out," I growled when she rolled her head to gawk up at me.

And what did she do? She giggled. Fucking giggled like this shit was a goddamn game. Who knows, maybe it was? Maybe she wasn't drugged at all, and was having fun fucking with me.

"Why are your legs so long? Are you part giraffe? Oh, maybe you're a spider."

Nova wiggled her fingers through the air like spider legs and laughed.

Okay so she was drugged, and apparently incapable of getting out. I waited for her to crawl out onto the gravel, but she just laid there looking up at me and laughing.

I sighed, just when I thought she couldn't be anymore exhausting.

"Alright, let's go," I reached in to pull Nova out, thinking that she would walk like a normal person to the door.

I was wrong.

She crumpled on the ground with another giggle, and sang, "My legs don't work."

Really? Ugh fine, guess I was carrying her.

Bending down, I scooped Nova off the ground and threw her over my shoulder. She continued to chuckle as her top half flopped over me like a rag doll. I just rolled my eyes and headed for the door.

"I can see your butt."

A pair of hands slapped down on my ass, making me pause mid stride.

Did she just fucking spank me?

My jaw clenched as her palms came down one after the other while Nova sang, "Bee boop bee do." In time with her slaps.

"Keep that shit up and you'll be sorry."

"Oo, I'll be sorry," she mocked, then smacked both her hands down and dug her fingers into my ass. "Someone has buns of steel."

And someone else was about to have a real sore fucking ass in the morning. The only person here that would do any kind of spanking was me. I didn't give a shit if she was drugged or not. If anything that just added to my reasons for reprimand. When I was done with her, Nova wouldn't be able to sit down for a week.

Thankfully when we walked in the house she seemed to lose interest in my backside.

"The floor is so shiny."

Apparently our hardwood was much more interesting. That is until she saw Saul standing by the stairs.

"Hi," Nova lifted her torso and waved at him, making me clamp my arm around her waist to keep my balance.

Sure, now she can fucking move.

Saul arched a brow at me.

I just shook my head and muttered, "Don't ask," before walking up the stairs.

My first thought was to drop Nova off in one of the spare rooms, but then she tried to grab a bust of the virgin Mary off a table, because apparently she needed a hug, and I decided it probably wasn't a good idea to leave her unsupervised. So I took her to my room.

"Alright, it's time for you to go to sleep." I walked across the room and dropped her into a red loveseat in the corner.

She bounced on the cushions and shot me a frown, "But I'm not tired."

"I don't give a shit." I growled while marching over to sit on my bed.

She might not be tired but I was fucking exhausted.

"Let's play a game!"

"I don't want to play a goddamn game." Unless that game involved making her cry, which was more than likely impossible in her current abnormally happy state.

Nova groaned and crossed her arms, "You're no fun."

She got that right. I was no fun. I was the mean and scary man that wanted to see her suffer. She should be running for the hills. Not laughing on my goddamn loveseat.

Why the fuck wasn't she scared of me? That was the thing that really bothered me. I tried to kill the girl twice and she still continued to get in my face. Did she have a death wish?

I looked over to where Nova was sprawled out.

There was no shaking, no trembling or fear tugging at her face. Just serene comfort and disturbing calmness. She was always calm. Well… not always. There were a couple of times when she freaked out.

I couldn't help but think back to yesterday and the look she gave me when I pulled my mouth off hers. Terror. But of what? Was it what I might do or something else? I had my theories of course.

My brow arched as I tipped my head.

Now might be a good time to test some of those theories out. Nova's inhibitions were lowered meaning that wall she normally hid behind might finally have a crack in it. I might actually get a glimpse into what makes her tick.

I pushed off the bed and made my way over to where Nova was laying.

Her big hazel orbs glimmered up at me as I stood over her.

Neither one of us spoke, we just watched the other in silence. I don't know what Nova was hoping to see, or if she was hoping to see anything, but I was searching for a particular spark. One that I'd seen before hidden in the jade and copper flecks in her eyes.

It wasn't there, but the longer I stared down at her the more I noticed. It was little things. A small twitch in the corner of her mouth or the brief way her brows pulled together. Cracks in her otherwise calm demeanor. Novalee didn't like me studying her, but I think it was the silence that made her uncomfortable. Proof of which came when her pink lips parted.

"Why are you staring at me?"

Interesting.

Not moving an inch, I simply stood there and continued to stare down at her. The moment she broke was nothing short of beautiful. I saw reality smack past her drug-addled mind and flood into her eyes. Lighting up those bright orbs with a prey's fear of danger. That was one instinct not even Nova could fight. That shit would crash through any wall with the weight of impending doom and smack you right in the face.

"Stop that."

That's right, Gattina, squirm under my glare.

"Go away."

The slight squeak in Nova's tone almost made me smirk, but I managed to stay exactly how I was and revel in her discomfort.

"I'm tired," she suddenly declared. "I want to go to sleep."

No she didn't.

The only thing Novalee wanted was for me to leave her alone. That wasn't happening. Especially not when she folded her arms over her chest. That action wasn't done out of anger. She was trying to shield herself from me. Nova didn't like me looking at her, and the more I saw her struggle to keep eye contact, the harder I got.

"Gio…"

I liked the breathy unsureness in her voice way too much for her to be saying my name. Her small trembles had my dick hard as hell, but I was having too much fun toying with her. That didn't stop my eyes from trickling down to her shuttering chest.

And when she whispered, "Please go away," I couldn't keep quiet anymore.

"What would you do if I fucked you right now?"

There was that spark I'd been waiting for.

Her eyes rounded, "You can't…"

"Oh, but I could. And here's the beautiful thing…" Bracing my hand on the back of the loveseat, I leaned in and hissed, "Memory loss is a side effect of the drugs you're on, so you wouldn't remember a thing."

I could plow into her pussy as hard as I wanted, and when Nova woke up in the morning all she'd have to remember it, would be the soreness between her legs.

"You wouldn't do that."

Was she trying to convince herself or me?

"You sure about that?"

"Yes," she nodded. "You're better than that, Gio."

My brow arched, "Am I?"

Her family didn't think my brother was better than that, so why the fuck should I care about consent. I enjoyed overpowering women, that's what half the games Carissa and I played were. Why not do it for real? Could be fun.

Actually the more I thought about, the more I liked the idea of holding Nova down while she begged me to stop. At least then she'd have some truth to a rape accusation.

"Gio..." Nova's pleading eyes met mine. "You don't want to do this."

"You don't know shit about me." I was a sick twisted fuck that got off on making women crawl around like fucking pets.

"So do it then." She challenged, making a smirk crawl across my face.

"You know, the courts," I leaned in to breathe in her ear, "Might consider that consent."

We learned how to play the system at a young age. Why did she think her brother's claims about Atlas's supposed crime weren't allowed to be brought up in court? Everyone was on our payroll.

I couldn't help but snicker when Nova pushed back into the loveseat as if the cushions could save her.

Not so brave now, are you?

"Go away, Gio," she yawned and rolled her face to the right, "I'm bored."

"No, you're scared." I rebuffed.

Her eyelids fluttered as she whispered, "Leave me alone."

The sleep effects of the drugs were kicking in. It wasn't long before her lids closed and her breathing evened out. I should've left then. Just pushed myself off the couch and went to bed myself.

Instead I stood there lazily pulling my eyes over her sleeping form. Over the faint bruises on her neck to the swell of her breasts, and down to the curve of her hips.

When Nova's mouth was shut, I could almost appreciate her creamy completion and firm ass. Too bad her clothes were covered in dirt.

What did she do, roll around on the ground? There wasn't much to that fucking shirt – which was a conversation I would have with her later – but what cloth was there had grass and mud on it.

I should clean her up. Or at the very least change her clothes. Afterall, I didn't want her ruining my furniture.

My feet were taking me over to my dresser to grab a shirt, before I could put much thought into my actions. Next thing I knew I was seated on the edge of the loveseat, removing Nova's shirt. It didn't take much to pull the fabric over her head – though I did pause for a second afterwards.

She wasn't wearing a bra. Meaning I got an uninhibited view of her breasts. They were perfect. Not quite a handful, but full and round with pert little pink nipples that I debated for half a second about tasting. Once I managed to pull my attention off her chest I moved onto her shorts.

That was when I came to a full stop.

Nova's panties were regular navy blue cotton panties. It was the big yellow smiley face sitting right above her pussy that made me cock a brow. What the fuck? Did the girl not own any normal underwear? Who the fuck wore a something like that over their junk, and why did it feel like it was mocking me?

My eyes narrowed on the yellow face. Motherfucker was staring up as if he was saying, 'That's right bitch, I get to touch this shit all the time.' I'd never wanted to punch a drawing more in my life. Then I thought back to something Darry said.

Was Novalee a virgin?

It was an important question. If she wasn't a virgin then my entire plan was out the window. My father would never approve of one of his sons marrying 'used goods' as he would call it. Meaning we could kill them, which I was all for.

Then again, if Nova was a virgin, it would make the defilement of Kato Ford's baby sister that much sweeter. I wouldn't just be taking her from him, I could mold Novalee into my perfect little sex slave and parade her around like a trophy, inducing long term suffering on her piece of shit brother.

But which outcome would I prefer? That was the true question.

Did I want to end the entire Ford family line, or punish Kato through his baby sister? Death was easy, but mental fuckery… that could really mess someone up.

I guess when the time came we would know, one way or the other. My father would insist on an examination to prove purity. *Unless...*

My eyes fell back down to that mocking smile.

I found out for myself.

Sure Atlee said she was a virgin and he seemed to have a knack for sniffing those things out. But that was no guarantee. Sooner or later everyone was wrong.

I trailed my finger along Nova's thigh and dipped the tip under the leg band of her panties. It would be so easy to find out. Just stick my finger in and see if her hymen was still intact. I didn't even have to see her pussy to do it.

My eyes rolled up to Nova's sleeping face and I stopped, because there was one thing I wanted to see.

The look in her eyes when I violated her. I wanted to watch her break when she realized how truly fucked she was. Then I'd taste her guilt when I made her come so fucking hard that she would never stop hating herself.

That's what I wanted.

I wanted to take the one pure thing Kato Ford had and twist it into something depraved and needy. I would take his baby sister and make her mine, just like he took my brother from me.

Chapter 29

NOVALEE

I had no idea what happened last night, but I did know I was extremely comfortable. My sheets were all silky and smelled like jasmine and my bed was cradling me like a fluffy cloud… wait a minute…

My bed wasn't fluffy. It was a lumpy road with the occasional soft spot. And it certainly wasn't warm. This wasn't right. Where was the spring stabbing me in the side and scratchy blanket that smelled like mothballs?

I sniffed the air and crinkled my nose. Was that jasmine and cedar? What the hell? There was something familiar in the scent, but still… Who could sleep like this? All warm and smelling good. It wasn't natural. A person should want to get out of their bed not stay in it. If Maw Maw changed my mattress again…

Alert caused the hairs on the back of my neck to rise.

My head was moving. Not much but enough that I could feel the steady rise and fall, as if someone was breathing. That's when I noticed the heartbeat faintly pulsing under my ear.

Oh God I was on someone's chest.

This was not good. What the hell happened last night? I suppose it could be worse. At least I knew where my pants were. Or did I?

I carefully swept my hand over my hip, searching for the denim material of my shorts.

All I got was the cotton fabric of my underwear. Meaning I once again lost the bottom half of my outfit, this while I was in bed with what I assumed to be some random guy.

Fantastic.

My heart started pounding in my chest as I told myself to calm down. There was a rational explanation for this. Like the person I was laying on could be a jack up woman. Girls came in all different shapes and sizes. Sure the chest I was laying on was abnormally hard, but that didn't mean it was a guy. Of course the lack of breasts might say otherwise... Damnit. Why did logic have to ruin everything?

Wait... I was so dumb. This was obviously Memphis. Wouldn't be the first time we woke up cuddling. Except Memphis didn't really have much for muscles, or tone, or fat for that matter. Then again, he had been talking about working out?

Keeping my eyes closed, I gently patted my hand down on the skin next to my head and froze when my fingers ran over the hard ridges of abs. Yup, this definitely wasn't Memphis. There was no way he would have an eight pack. I didn't even know that was possible. Who the hell was this freak, and could I sneak away without waking them up?

I shifted my hips then stopped when I heard a muffled groan.

Son of a bitch.

This asshole was gonna wake up wasn't he? Ugh, I didn't have the energy for awkward next morning conversation. I preferred to save that for my well-earned walk of shame. At least I'd get to check that off my list. So there was that.

I let out a sigh.

It was probably better if I laid here and pretended to be asleep until this idiot woke up and snuck away from me. Then I could avoid the post sex questions. It wasn't like I could give the guy any tips. I didn't remember anything. I didn't feel anything either. I should feel something, right?

If I did lose my virginity then surely I'd be sore. Everyone was always saying how much their first time hurt – well not everyone… Memphis. And given the hole his virginity was taken from, pain was kind of expected. But still…

I took a second to search my body for foreign sensations. Other than my toes being unusually warm and not hanging off the bed, everything felt normal. Weird but normal.

I thought about opening my eyes, but then I ran the risk of altering whoever I was with to the fact that I was awake. This sucked.

Way to get yourself in a predicament Nova.

It would really help if I knew who was in this bed with me though.

Alright, let's do this shit.

I slowly fluttered my lids open.

Apparently I wasn't just laying on someone, I was under the sheet and they were naked. I knew this because the first thing I saw when my eyes adjusted, was the head of a very large, and very hard, angry looking penis. On the upside there was no way I would not feel any place in my body where that thing entered. So my virginity was still intact. My dignity on the other hand…

There was nothing like knowing the naked man you woke up next to didn't touch you, to crush the ego.

"Talk about insulting."

The dick staring me down did a little jump, making my eyes narrow.

Could that thing hear me? Should I talk to it? Would that calm down that angry vein? What did people do in this scenario? Surely I wasn't the only girl who found herself in this situation. Not that I would know, I didn't have any girlfriends. And Veda's social life was nonexistent. Never thought I'd miss talking to Cindy.

Okay, I could figure this out.

Maybe it was like a rabid animal thing? I could offer that thing a treat while saying stuff like 'who's a good penis', and slowly back away before it bit me. That could work, right?

I eyed the thick head and pondered my options.

That thing was seriously scary. How did guys walk around with something like that hanging between their legs? It looked like it was ready to attack. Then again I was laying on a strange man thinking about talking to his junk so there was a solid argument that I was the crazy one here.

I really needed to stop drinking.

Well, I guess it's time to face the music.

Ever so carefully, I peeled myself off Giant Member Man, hoping he wouldn't wake up. It took some time – I would never again underestimate the complex maneuvers of unwrapping one's leg from another's – but my plan worked. I successfully unfurled my body from his, without waking him up, and slipped out from under the covers.

That's when everything went to hell.

The second I saw Gio's face, I screamed.

Who could blame me? There were a lot of things I could accept–unplanned teenage pregnancy, and a horrible unsatisfying career in the customer service industry–but waking up next to Gio Mancini was not one of them. Especially not a naked Gio Mancini.

And what did my shock get me… a shriek that Gio made when he was jarred awake by my scream. Which would've been funny if it wasn't followed by a angrily grumbled, "What the fuck are you doing in my bed."

After which he promptly kicked me out of said bed.

Now I was used to taking a tumble in my sleep – my bed wasn't big – but Gio's was a lot taller than mine. I had enough time to curse my existence before I slammed down on the floor. Hard. All the air was knocked out of my lungs as my hip clacked off the wooden surface.

However, I did take the bedding with me, leaving Gio uncovered. And that brought a smile to my face despite the fact that I couldn't breathe.

Life was about the small victories.

I think I let out a groan, I couldn't really hear anything past the pain radiating through my hip bone. All I could do was lay there and wait for the fog in my mind to clear. Gio was pissed, that much I could tell. His deep tone vibrated through the air mingling with the ache coursing through me.

When his fuzzy form popped over the edge of the bed, he said something. I couldn't be sure what it was but I thought it was something along the lines of 'What the fuck is wrong with you'. Then again that could've just been me asking myself that question.

"Hello," Gio's fingers snapped in front of my clearing vision. "I asked you a question."

Well someone woke up on the wrong side of the bed. Maybe he was cold.

I groaned and coughed out, "I have the blankets."

There was a moment of silence where I could feel the arch of annoyance that pulled at Gio's brow. He did not look happy. Excellent. I wasn't happy either. But I was warm.

Grinning up at him, I greedily tucked the bedding tightly around me.

"What the fuck are you so pleased about?"

"How's that cold air feel?" I may be on the floor, but he was the one exposed.

He glared down at me and smacked his lips together. "Do you think you won something?"

Kind of.

"You haven't won shit."

I think I did.

Sighing, I snuggled deeper into Gio's soft blanket. I might just have to take these with me.

"You are insufferable."

"Thank you." I took that as a complement.

Apparently he didn't agree because the muscle in his jaw tensed as his eyes darkened. "What the fuck were you doing in my bed?"

How the hell should I know? One minute I was dancing and next I was in the lion's den. A better questions was…

"Why am I in your house?"

Gio wasn't even at the bonfire, was he? What did he do, show up and wait until I was too drunk to argue being whisked away to his lair?

"You want to know why you're in my house?"

"Ah, yeah. That's why I asked the question." Did he not understand how these things worked?

"Do you think you're smart?"

"Clearly I'm smarter than you." It was a fairly basic concept. Someone asked something, and someone else answered it. Not exactly complicated. Neither was spelling the word whore.

My eyes narrowed.

Gio narrowed his.

Next thing I knew his hand shot out and wrapped around my throat. That seemed to be his go to thing, and I was getting really tired of it. Did he have any idea how much concealer I had to use to hide the bruises? Not that I could've told him that. I was too busy choking on his grip while he dragged me back in the bed and slammed me on the mattress.

His angry form loomed over me, "You want to know why you're fucking here?"

Right now, I just wanted to catch my breath. I was beginning to wonder if Gio had a personal vendetta against oxygen.

"Someone fucking drugged you!"

What? Someone drugged me? Why would anyone drug me? That seemed like a waste of time. I wasn't a hard person to lure away. Veda once got me to do her chores for a month for a stick of…

Realization caused a quiet grumble to roll out of my mouth.

Simon.

Slimy bastard. I should've known. He was way too cheap to bring his own alcohol, let alone buy bourbon.

"Who was it?" Gio barked down at me.

I opened my mouth but he cut me off.

"And don't tell me you don't know. I saw that look on your face."

Damnit. Was I that obvious?

"In case you forgot, you tried to kill me… twice." I pointed out. "So maybe whatever look you think you saw was brought on because you once again have your hand on my neck."

Case and point.

"Don't fuck with me, Nova," Gio growled. "Who was it?"

I looked him dead in the eye and said, "Frankenstein."

Gio's emerald eyes visibly darkened, causing a shiver to shoot up my spine.

"You want to play this game, do you?"

I had no idea where Gio got his super speed powers from, but before I knew what was happening, Gio flipped me onto my stomach, pressed his hand down on the back of my head, and smashed my face into the mattress.

"What the—" was all I got out before a heavy hand cracked off my ass.

And I meant cracked.

The sound from Gio's slap rang through my ears while a fiery burn crawled up my tailbone, making me cry out. And he didn't stop there. The onslaught continued while Gio muttered and grumbled over me. I fought back, kicked my legs and swung my arms back to claw at him. Not that it did any good. Gio just carried on hitting me like I was nothing more than a nuisance.

It was agonizing, humiliating, and I had no clue how to make it stop. The only grumbled words of his that I could make out were opossums, smiles and purity. How the hell did those three things fit together? They literally had nothing in common. Gio was making no sense. If I knew what he wanted me to say I would've. I'd have promised my first born if that's what it took to escape his heavy hands.

At one point my ass went numb, either from permanent nerve damage, or from my mind checking out. Either way I gave up. I laid there and took it. And even then Gio didn't stop until I was out of breath and the tears streaming down my face started to dry up.

The few minutes of silence that followed were the longest of my life. I kept waiting for his hand to swing through the air. When it didn't I was pathetically thankful that it was over. Relief washed over me, until I felt Gio's hot breath warm my ear.

"Let's try that again, shall we?"

All I could do was whimper back.

"Who? Drugged. You?"

After an assault like that, any sane person would jump all over the opportunity to confess. I was not one of these sane people.

I rolled my head to unbury my face from the mattress, and peeked back at Gio, "Hit me harder Daddy."

Ever seen someone's mental sanity crack. Like every logical thought in their brain spontaneously combusted at once? Well, it was a sight to see. Gio's head jerked to the side while his eyes went blank for a split second. It was what came after that made me rethink my smart mouth remark.

In one swift motion Gio either swept me under him or crawled over me – it happened too fast for me to be sure – and I found myself once again pressed into his annoyingly soft bed. Except this time it was his weight holding me down, not his hand.

I kind of missed the way his fingers dug into the back of my skull. I could at least try and flail then. Now I was trapped and left with nothing but sad slaps of my hands on the bed. It was pathetic.

I was pathetic.

I was also stubborn.

"I can still move," I sang while flapping my hands around like fins.

Not only did I hear the click of his unimpressed tsk, but I felt it.

"You're testing my limits."

Something in the back of my mind chanted, don't say it, don't say it… but how could I not?

"The limit does not exist."

My brief moment of satisfaction at Gio's gruffly muttered curse was quickly quashed when he shifted behind me. The sensation of something hot and hard poking into my thigh caused every muscle in my body to seize.

Oh my God, his dick is on my leg!

And just like that the air in the room changed.

Gone was the carefree no worry version of me. I was too scared to move let alone talk. If I could've stopped my lungs from working I'd have done that too. The fear of waking that angry thing up was too real to ignore. That's what I told myself anyway. The deep pulse slowly building in my core was much more terrifying.

"Gio," I whispered but he cut me off.

"Shut up!"

I could do that. Speaking probably wasn't a good idea. In fact I'd be as a church mouse. Gio wouldn't even know I was here. I even closed my eyes, hoping that that would add to my nonexistent invisibility powers. It didn't. If anything it made things worse.

I was in a big room with lots of space, yet all I could feel was him. Gio Mancini surrounded me. The bulging muscles in his forearm were inches away from my face, while his weight pressed down on my still burning ass. But the worst part was his scent. That ridiculously addictive aroma got sucked into my lungs with every breath, until it was all I could taste. I didn't like it.

I didn't like it at all.

I tried to think about something else, but nothing worked. No matter where I took my mind, Gio was still there. I could feel his eyes, watching me.

Silence seemed to drag on. Why wasn't he doing anything? My mind was going crazy with anticipation. Spank me, choke me, say something!

"What's wrong Nova?"

Don't say that.

"Nothing."

Was his voice always that deep?

"Really?" his breath warmed the back of my scalp. "Because you're shaking."

I wasn't shaking. Was I? I couldn't think past the dick on my leg.

"You're not scared are you?"

Oh my god why was he still talking to me? Clearly we had other problems to deal with. Such as the churning in my gut and how the sting in my ass was spreading in tingles down the back of my thighs.

My entire body twitched when Gio grazed his nose up the side of my neck and deeply inhaled.

"Fuck," he growled in a way too sexy tone. "I love that scent."

He shouldn't be getting off on fear. But he was. I could feel how much he was because HIS DICK WAS STILL ON MY LEG.

"Come on Nova, you always have something to say."

Oh, I had plenty to say, just not out loud.

Goosebumps trickled across my skin as Gio brushed his lips off the shell of my ear and whispered, "Where's your smart mouth now?"

It left. Fucked off and jumped on the first train out of town.

"Look at me, Nova."

Nope, not happening. His face was way too close to mine for me to risk that.

When I didn't answer Gio swept his hand down my side and purred, "What are you afraid of?"

This, you, everything. The fact that he was able to literally purr out a growl. I could feel the vibrations of it flow out of his chest into my back.

"You know what I think?"

Oh, I had a good idea. His *thoughts* were digging into my thigh.

"I think you like this."

"And I think you're delusional." I tried to add a snort to my response but it came out more like a whimpered garble. It wasn't my finest moment.

"You think I'm delusional?"

Let's see, over inflated sense of entitlement combined with a God complex and violent tendencies so... "Yeah."

Gio's hand suddenly shot between my thigh and cupped my mound, making my eyes fly open as I tried to frantically shoot forward. I didn't make it far. Maybe half an inch before his weight stopped me.

"Nice try," he growled. "You're not going anywhere."

As true as that statement may be, the truly mortifying part of my situation was that I knew Gio could feel the dampness on my panties. His lips were so close to the back of my neck that I could feel smugness curl them.

"It's sweat." It was a lame excuse but it was all I had.

"Sweat?" He leaned over and arched a brow down at me. "That's the best you got?"

Unfortunately, yes.

"Okay," Gio tsked and let out a breath. "This is how this is going to go. You are going to tell me who drugged you…"

Not a chance.

"Or… we're going to play a little game of how sweaty can I make you."

I froze.

He wouldn't. One look at the determination in his eyes told me that yes, yes he would.

"I don't know. I didn't see anything." That was believable, right? Clearly I was lacking in the situational awareness department, otherwise I wouldn't have woken up here.

Gio wasn't buying it. The arch in his brow deepened. "You wanna try that again?"

Not particularly. If I had a choice it would be for Gio to just let it go. Was that too much to ask? I wasn't dwelling on it, so why should he? Come to think of it, that was a good question.

Looking back at him, I asked, "Why do you care?"

What was he hoping to get out of this? Tips?

"Why are you protecting them?" he asked back.

I wasn't protecting them, I was protecting myself. Simon may be a lying, cheating, skeevy weasel, but I trusted him more than I trusted Gio.

Gio tipped his head and warned, " Last Chance."

Refusing to say another word, I stared tight-lipped back at him.

All my bravado diminished with a single finger.

Gio pressed down on my panty clad mound and hit something that shot a spark of electricity through my entire body. Next thing I knew, panic had me blurting out, "Simon."

"Simon?" Gio stopped and looked down at me. "As in Simon Fisher?"

I neither confirmed nor denied said statement, and apparently I didn't have to.

Gio lifted himself off me, sat back, shook his head and muttered "Slimy fucking weasel."

Guess he knew my ex-boyfriend. I shouldn't be surprised. He was in Gio's vehicle the other day. And I had yet to meet someone that didn't refer to Simon as a weasel, or slimy. I really didn't make the best choice in men.

Neither did my body, otherwise my eyes wouldn't be drawn over my shoulder to Gio's well sculpted torso. And it was well sculpted. Everywhere I looked there were hard lines and firm ridges.

Wait a minute... What the hell am I doing?

I shuffled away and sprang off the bed before Gio could stop me.

"You are an asshole," I scowled at him then quickly threw my hand up over my eyes. "Jesus Christ, can you put some clothes on?" It was like his dick was honed in on me or something. I could still see it. "Who sleeps naked anyway?"

Pfft, perv.

"You're the one that crawled into bed with me. I left your drugged ass on the couch over there."

Oh.

I glanced back at the red loveseat on the other side of the room.

"Well... you... changed me."

Ha! I knew there was something. Don't get me wrong, the black shirt I had on was so soft that I wanted to be buried in it, but it wasn't mine.

"You were covered in mud."

Was there something wrong with mud? "I want my clothes back."

Gio firmly stated, "No," and I was so shocked that I almost lowered the hand I was using to shield my vision.

Once that initial surprise was over, I asked, "What do you mean no?"

"I mean no."

Did he know any other word?

"Fine then, I'll drive home in what I've got on." It didn't bother me. The size difference between Gio and me was enough for the shirt to reach my mid thigh. I was covered and that was all that mattered.

I turned to march out the door.

Gio had other plans. "Atlee took your piece of shit truck home, so I'll be driving you."

I stopped with my foot still in the air.

What!

Oh, the shielding hand was coming down now, I didn't care what I saw.

I spun around and sliced my hands through the air. "You let Atlee drive my truck."

"You're welcome."

You're welcome? That's it. He was getting stabbed. There had to be something sharp around here. Unfortunately I didn't see anything within reach. Just a bunch of cherrywood furniture – any piece of which could probably pay off Maw Maw's mortgage – and a way too big bed.

"You know what Gio…"

He crossed his arms and cocked a brow, "What?"

Oh, I was going to tell him what. "I don't need you and your photoshopped abs to do shit for me. I'll get home on my own."

Then hunt down Atlee and murder him. My truck better be in one piece.

"Okay, you do you. If you're still out here after my shower, then I'll take you home."

Gio got off the bed, making no attempt to cover himself or his massive dick from my view and headed over to an open door on the left side of the room.

"Oh," he paused in the doorway to glance back at me, "and my ass could be photoshopped too."

Someone was full of himself, though he did have a nice ass.

No! Stop it Nova.

I gave my head a shake and left the room, but not before I took a pair of red sneakers lovingly placed on Gio's dresser. If he was going to keep my clothes, then I was going to take his shoes.

Chapter 30

The only good thing about my morning was that Maw Maw wasn't home when I walked through the door. Explaining my appearance probably wouldn't go over too well. Especially since I spent what felt like forever walking under the hot sun in shoes three times too big. I didn't know someone could sweat that much.

A couple of times I seriously considered curling up on the side of the road in the grass and mud, but then I'd have to walk down a slight decline, and I didn't have the energy for that.

God I love Veda. All she did when I stumbled through the door was shoot me a look and say she didn't want to know. It would've been nice if she helped me get off the floor though.

It took an hour for me to get enough strength to get up and have a shower – which I wouldn't have bothered to do if I didn't have to work.

Thankfully my truck was parked out front of the trailer, and it looked just like I left it. Minus a few changes I discovered on my way to work. None of which I was impressed about. I no longer had to beat the crap out of the engine to get it to rollover, so my trusty wrench was pretty much useless.

The muffler also didn't fire off a bang anymore. How were people supposed to know when I arrived? And don't even get me started on the radio. If I wanted choices, I would've fixed the knob myself. Atlee and I would have words about that later.

Combine all of that with the fact that I spent the last fifteen minutes explaining to Memphis what happened last night, and this day could bite my ass. On the upside, Sundays in the diner weren't busy. We only had three customers and I managed to redirect one of them to the food truck down the street, leaving me with plenty of time to plan a murder. Mainly Atlee's.

I was pretty sure I could make him fuck himself to death. I just needed a thousand willing girls. That part might be tricky.

"You woke up in Gio's house?"

I sighed.

The only thing worse than after drinking regret, was explaining said regret to your best friend.

"Yes."

"Now, when you say Gio..." Memphis tipped his head. "Do you mean Gio, Gio?"

"Do you know any other Gio?"

If there was another Gio somewhere around here than there was no doubt in mind that I wouldn't like him either. The name alone would guarantee that. In fact I was pretty sure all Gio's were massive pricks.

"Okay," Memphis propped his elbow up on the counter and did a 'hang on' wave with his hand. "So let me see if I'm understanding this right?"

What was there to understand?

"Simon drugged you?"

"Yes." *Damn him and his tempting bourbon.*

"Then Gio Mancini took you home?"

I nodded, "Correct."

"To his house?" Memphis clarified.

"Yes, Memphis, to his house."

How many times did he need to hear it? It wasn't that complicated. I got unknowingly high, woke up in the lion's den, then walked home. Bam done. Mind you I did leave out a few minor details, but Gio's lack of clothing wasn't important information.

Considering some of the other places I'd woken up, this didn't even make the top ten list of worst mornings. Man, raccoons really didn't smell good, and they shed a lot of fur. A year later and I still hadn't gotten that shirt clean.

"Your first mistake was accepting a drink from that slimy bastard."

I mean… "It was bourbon."

All expression dropped off his face. "And you didn't find that suspicious?"

I probably should've, but… "It was bourbon."

"So what? You wouldn't let the Dickson triplets gangbang you for a glass of bourbon, would you?"

I don't know… "Is it good bourbon?"

"Oh my god," Memphis hung his head and pinched the bridge of his nose.

Sure the Dickson triplets gave a whole new meaning to the term white trash, but if they had a bottle of Wolcott, I could look past the missing teeth.

"One of these days someone is going to lure you into a van with the promise of chocolate."

I perked up. "You have chocolate?"

Memphis stared at me.

I stared back at him.

"Anyway," his chest heaved with a heavy sigh. "I'd like to get back to you waking up at Gio's house."

I rolled my eyes, "Do we have to?"

Personally I thought the chocolate topic was much more interesting.

"Gio Mancini took you, Nova, to his house." Memphis's brow arched, "Aren't you the least bit curious as to why he would do that?"

"Umm.." I shook my head, "no not really."

Who cared why Gio did what he did? Maybe he was looking for new ways to humiliate me, or he had some strange obsession with incoherent women? Whatever his reasons were, didn't matter. I got a new pair of shoes out of the deal. They were way too big – I felt like a clown tromping home in them – but the satisfaction I got from taking them was well worth it.

"Unless…" I didn't like the way his eyes narrowed, "you know why he did it?"

"That would require me to understand the inner workings of Gio Mancini's mind." No thank you. I already knew way more about him than I wanted to. Like how his perfect ass moved when he walked across the room naked.

"Did he do something to you?"

That made me snort. "When does Gio not do something to me?"

"Nova?"

"Memphis." I sang back.

He leaned across the counter and whispered, "He didn't… touch you, did he?"

I shot him a deadpan stare. "Really?"

Leave it to Memphis to turn this thing into something dirty. He wasn't wrong, but that was beside the point.

His shoulder lifted in a small shrug, "It's a valid question."

No it wasn't.

"You watch too much porn." I said and went back to wiping down the counter.

"I'm not the one who woke up in some guy's house."

"Listen," I twirled my hand through the air. "Just because you have the perfect boyfriend doesn't mean everyone can... and don't even get me started on your predisposition for PDA. No one wants to see that."

Least of all me.

"Don't change the subject."

Damnit.

The downside of growing up with someone was that eventually they knew everything about each other. For instance, I knew Memphis had a phobia of balloons, he always slept on his left side, had an unhealthy obsession with the color red, and that he refused to eat toast because bread shouldn't be crunchy.

That was why I always gave him a red toaster wrapped up in balloons for his birthday.

Memphis waved his finger at me, "Don't think I'm going to let you avoid this."

And he knew I had a tendency to avoid things. But in my defense, life was much easier that way.

"You're hiding something."

"I'm not hiding anything." I told Memphis everything, including the stuff he didn't want to know. Just last week I called him to describe what I thought a frog's burp would taste like. Animal planet may have been to blame for that one.

"Just like you weren't hiding the fact that you made out with Gio... twice?"

Okay, so maybe I left out the occasional unimportant detail.

"I didn't make out with him." I clarified.

Memphis rolled his eyes, "Fine, you kissed."

That was an important detail of said unimportant information.

"Now," he folded his hands on the laminate countertop and gave me a stern eye, "Are you going to tell me what happened?"

I was not going to tell him. "Nothing happened."

"Bullshit."

"Nothing happened." I tried again.

"No," he shook his head and once again raised his finger. "Something happened."

Why did he keep wagging his finger at me? What was I, two?

"I'm going to find out, Nova."

"There's nothing to find out," I said while continuing to wipe down the counter.

Memphis sat up straight on the stool and crossed his arms. "See, now I know something happened."

No he didn't.

"You're actually working."

Damnit. Foiled by my own productivity.

I stopped and pondered my options. Should I stick to my original story, or...

"I'm not dropping this," Memphis cocked a brow to reaffirm his statement.

I could turn this around on him.

"Okay genius," I dropped the cloth on the counter and turned to face him. "Why don't you tell me what happened? Did Gio Mancini hold me down and spank me then rub his dick up against my thigh?"

There was a second of silence where all I could hear was my own heart pounding, while I thought about how far I'd have to move in order to avoid the follow up questions he'd have. I heard Uruguay was nice this time of year. Thankfully I didn't have to figure out where exactly that country was because Memphis burst out laughing and keeled over.

"That's a good one."

"Right?" *Phew.*

"Gio Mancini spanking you," his palm slapped down on the counter between chuckles. "Can you imagine?"

Actually I could.

"I mean look at you, and look at him."

What was wrong with me? So I didn't have an abundance of cleavage, and I couldn't reach the top shelf without using Knox's stool. But I had good hips and okay hair, when I did something with it.

"He's at least a ten and you're what… a seven on a good day."

Hey now.

"I could be a seven and a half." I muttered.

With make up I could get that up to seven and three quarters.

When I thought Memphis was finally done, he took one look at me and started laughing again. "Gio could have any girl he wanted, but he chose to spank you."

"Alright Chuckles, calm down." *Geeze.* "It wasn't that funny."

My best friend's amusement didn't calm down. It picked up to the point that he was snorting. Great.

Sighing, I looked around at the empty booths and tables wishing for once that I had a customer. I'd hit a new low.

Gio Mancini made me resort to wanting to serve someone. I could always occupy myself with filling up the napkin dispensers. Trixie – the other waitress – had a bug up her ass about the napkins, and she would be here in about fifteen minutes. Then I got to go with Memphis to Chuck's basketball game. I didn't know what activity I was more excited for.

I looked over at Memphis as he swept the tears off his face and snorted out another snicker, then set about refilling the dispensers. Or at least making them look full. A handful of sugar packets behind one single napkin was very deceiving. By the time I was on the last one Memphis had finally quieted down.

"Trixie's going to kill you."

"One can only hope," I sang as the bell above the door chimed.

We both turned to see a lean man in a suit strut in.

It never failed. A customer always had to walk in five minutes before the end of my shift.

Memphis sat up straighter and watched him with a look that I was way too uncomfortable seeing on my best friend's face, while I smacked my lips together and eyed the obnoxiously soft looking waves in his sandy hair.

His steel stare locked on me, "Novalee Ford?"

"Maybe," my eyes narrowed. "Depends on what you want?"

He reached in his jacket and pulled out what I assumed to be a wallet, until he flipped it open and I saw the ID with the letters FBI. "I'm Special Agent Jack Donovan."

"If you're here about a strange package in the middle of the road, I can't help you."

There was no strange package, I just wanted to see what he would do.

Of course Memphis had to ruin my fun.

"Nova," he scolded me then gave Mr. FBI a charming smirk that made my lip curl. "Don't listen to her. She has issues."

Did I somehow get stuck in the middle of one of those romance movies, where the girl's hair would elegantly blow in the wind every time the prince rode past?

"Gird your loins Casanova," I rolled my eyes at my best friend. "The dastardly duke came to see me, not you."

Memphis's face dropped. "You need help."

Says the guy who's two seconds away from twirling his hair.

"You have a boyfriend," I pointed out, then wondered how I became the protector of Memphis's gag worthy relationship.

Mr. FBI cleared his throat, "I hate to intrude, but could I have a minute of your time Miss. Ford?"

Miss. Ford?

"Well you're in luck Jack, my ass is still sore from a rather rough morning encounter, and in about five minutes I have to make the difficult decision on which radio station I want to listen to, while I drive to a basketball game I care nothing about. So…" I dropped my elbow on the counter, propped my chin up with my palm, and smiled sweetly up at him. "Today seems to be the day to intrude."

Memphis facepalmed while Mr. FBI blinked down at me.

"Okay… I'm not quite sure how to respond to that, so I'm just going to bypass it completely."

The man was honest, I'd give him that.

"Fair enough," I nodded. "What can I do for you Jack?"

"I was hoping we could do something for each other."

My brow rose, "Correct me if I'm wrong but isn't it the FBI's job to hunt down guys that do things for underage girls?"

Just saying.

Honest Jack huffed out a sigh. "I'm with the organized crime unit."

"I hardly think stealing a couple of kids' Halloween candy constitutes organized crime." Though I did have a very detailed and intricate plan. Billy and Kyle deserved it. They stole Knox's first.

"I'm investigating Cesare Mancini."

That made both Memphis and I straighten up. I looked at him, he looked at me, then I said, "I don't know how I can help you. I barely know the Mancini's."

But I knew enough not to cross them.

"Well Miss Ford, and correct *me* if I'm wrong," Honest Jack pulled a file out of seemingly nowhere and dropped it down on the counter. "But isn't your brother currently in jail for killing Atlas Mancini?"

"I wasn't there." I sang back.

"And," he reached forward and flipped the file open. "don't you go to school with the youngest son Giovanni, who according to my records has been following you around for a week."

If he wanted to point out facts. "That doesn't mean I know him."

His brow arched. "Is that why you were seen leaving his house at 8:27 this morning."

Look at him being a good little investigator.

"What do you want Jack?" and what else had he seen?

Were there FBI guys sprinkled throughout the entire town? Were there some in here right now, hiding in camouflage?

"I'll be frank with you Miss. Ford."

Alright, Frank it is.

"I've been on this case for three years. We have every avenue covered, except the house."

My eyes rolled up to his. I saw where this was going.

"Let me stop you right there Frank." I closed his file and slid it back towards him. "I can't help you."

Hell would freeze over before I ever set foot in that house again. Let alone to get dirt for the FBI. If I was going to die it was going to be doing some ridiculous thing – like boxing a family of raccoons – that gave Gio Mancini absolutely no satisfaction.

"But I can help you…"

I highly doubted that.

The bell above the door dinged and I nodded as Trixie strutted in, chin all up in the air while her high heels clicked. I might've been annoyed by the snide scowl she shot me if Jack hadn't added…

"Or should I say I can help your brother."

Now he had my attention, and I was guessing by the way the corner of his mouth lifted, he knew it.

"You can get Kato out of prison?"

He shook his head, "No."

What good was he?

"But if you bring me something I can use, I'll have him moved to a federal penitentiary, where there's more security."

Know what else there was more of, organized crime people. So I failed to see how that was any better.

"I understand your brother's had a hard time. He's been in the infirmary numerous times, had countless reprimands, spent time in solitary…"

Exactly my point. How would locking him up in a place with his literal enemy be any better? He'd be dead the first night. Which was exactly what I opened my mouth to tell him, when Jack's next statement caused the world to fall out from under me.

"And he was stabbed in his cell last night."

Kato was stabbed! Why weren't we told? I couldn't breathe. All the air in the room disappeared and all I could see was my brother, cold, alone, and bleeding with no one to look out for him. I wanted nothing more than to hold him in my arms and smell the oil on his clothes. I used to hate that scent, but I'd give anything to smell it again.

A hand pressed down and gave my shoulder a squeeze.

"It's okay, it wasn't a fatal wound." Jack said with sympathy in his tone. "He'll make a full recovery."

No, it wasn't okay. It would never be okay.

I stared back and shook my head, "I can't help you."

I couldn't even help the people I loved.

"Miss Ford–"

"No!" I slammed my hand down on the counter. "Find someone else."

"Alright," Special Agent Jack sighed and tucked his file back in his suit jacket. "But if you change your mind, I'm staying here."

He handed me a card with an address written on the back and walked out.

I stared out the door wondering what I was going to do. Kato couldn't keep going on like this. He said he had protection now, but things were just getting worse. How long would it be before we got the call I'd been dreading? I'd never felt more helpless in my life.

Memphis slid off the stool and walked over to put his arm around me. "It's not a bad idea, Nova."

"It's a horrible idea." I looked down at the card in my hand and tried not to cry, because this was the only idea I had.

Chapter 31

GIOVANNI

When I got out of the shower this morning did I find Novalee waiting for me? No. The suborn little pain in my ass walked home wearing nothing but my shirt and her underwear. And I knew she walked because I had her goddamn phone.

That thing dinged all morning with texts from her friend – he worried about her. Not that I cared to reassure him, or could because that would require knowing her passcode, which was apparently impossible to break.

I tried her birthday, her sister's birthday, the day her brother got locked up and any other date or number combination I thought might be significant to her. None of them worked.

Now it was sitting in my passenger seat staring back at me with a sparkly gemstone YOLO, that was only visible because I cleaned the fucking thing. How she managed to get so much lint on that case I'd never understand.

Only two people had messaged her all day. Memphis and some

company selling long distance. Novalee didn't even send a text to find the fucking thing. Most chicks had their entire lives on that device, and Novalee didn't give a shit who had it.

Even her goddamn belongings made me want to punch something, which I would've been able to do if I could've found Simon. Apparently the weasel had gone into hiding. So I didn't even get that satisfaction. And to top it off, I couldn't find my fucking shoes.

I steered my Rover into St. Agatha's parking lot and let out a breath.

After the game I was going to down a fifth of scotch, or two. At least the rest of my night should be productive. Judging by the number of vehicles here, the rumors about the basketball team were true.

Sorrie was a football town, so we didn't really bother with other sports until closer to the end of the season. And we sure as hell didn't come out for warm up games. This year was a little different. Apparently we had an up and coming star, hence the crowd I could faintly hear before I grabbed Novalee's phone and opened the door to step out.

There was a nice crisp in the air that I might've enjoyed cooling my skin, if I didn't spot a certain truck three rows down from me. Novalee was here? Of course she fucking was. How else would she annoy me?

Then again I could look at this as a blessing. Now I didn't have to hunt her down to beat her ass. Walking home in a fucking tee shirt, what the fuck was she thinking? If she thought that spanking this morning was bad, just wait.

"She'll be fucking sorry," I grumbled and marched across the parking lot.

Atlee was waiting outside the doors, casually leaning back against the wall. When he saw me coming his brow arched, "You don't look too happy."

No shit.

"What happened?"

Where did I start…

"Did you find Simon?"

I stopped on the last step up and glared at him. "Does it look like I found fucking Simon?"

"Hey man," he held up his palms. "I'm just asking."

I stepped up to him and puffed my chest out, "Ask again and see how that goes."

I really wanted to hit something, and Atlee was more than happy to oblige.

"If you wanna go a couple of rounds, I'm down," he pushed off the wall and got right in my face. "But don't start shit with me because you can't find Simon."

Simon was just the icing on the cake of a shitty fucking day that started with Novalee Ford. Though the morning wasn't all bad. I kind of enjoyed the way Nova squirmed under my hold, and the way she squealed…

Atlee tipped his head to look in my eyes, "You okay?"

Not in the slightest.

Sucking in a deep breath, I stepped away from Atlee and shook my head. "Just… find that little weasel."

"We'll find him." Atlee reassured, "Though, I can't say I'm surprised he's hiding."

Neither could I. Simon had to know his little stunt wouldn't go unnoticed. Either he had bigger balls than I thought, or he was stupid. I was going with the latter. He knew Nova was of some interest to us, and his answer to that was to drug her?

"What do you think he was going to do with her?"

I looked at Atlee and ground out, "That's a good fucking question."

It was also one I planned on getting an answer to.

Atlee threw his arm over my shoulder and leaned in, "What did you do to her?"

Did he want to get punched?

"Come on," a smirk spread across his face. "You tapped that ass, didn't you?"

More like smacked the shit out of that ass. I bet Novalee had some nice bruises. Those I wouldn't mind seeing. But that wasn't why we were here.

"Don't you think we have more important things to discuss."

"Ugh," he took his arm off my shoulder. "Why's it always business with you?"

I had many reasons for that. The main one being, I didn't want to hear about Atlee's exploits. I didn't want his tips, or explanation of how much some bitch gushed and what he did after. In fact, I'd die a happy man if I never heard another word about his junk or what he did with it.

"Fine," Atlee sighed when I threw open the door. "But don't think I'm dropping this."

One could only wish.

"How about you just tell me what you found?" I said and walked in the school.

My ears instantly perked as the sound of cheering vibrated down the hall. The crowd was pumped up. That was a good sign, that meant more money for us. No one wanted to bet on a game they didn't care about.

"Darry's in there scoping him out, but I did find out a few things," Atlee skipped up behind me and flipped open a notepad. "Chuck Neilson is a senior, he lives in the east part of town, has mediocre grades, his father is a banker and his mother is a hairdresser..."

I cut him off, "Did you find anything useful?"

Those things were all fine to know, but not exactly something we could use.

"Well, there is one thing."

I didn't like the twinkle in Atlee's eye. That usually meant annoyance for me.

"You're going to love this."

I doubted that.

"Chuck's boyfriend…" the curl in his lip spread as he added, "is Memphis Blake."

I paused with my hand on the gym door, "Really?"

Atlee nodded.

Now that was information we could use. In fact we almost already had everything set up. From what I'd seen Memphis and Novalee were pretty close. Not everyone would take on Atlee for a friend. Can't imagine he'd be too happy when I got my hands on Novalee. Meaning once she offered me a deal for her brother – which she would – everything else would fall into place.

Maybe this day wasn't so bad after all.

"Come on," I pulled the gym door open. "It's time to check out our star player."

The game was in full swing and the bleachers were full of avid fans that cheered as players ran down the court. It didn't take long to figure out which one was Chuck Neilson. The way he dodged and weaved around others, while not losing a beat of the ball bouncing in his hand was hard to miss. He was utterly destroying the other team.

Atlee leaned back against the wall and crossed his arms. "He's good."

Good my ass. Chuck Neilson was a fucking predator on the court. No one could touch him. This game was like watching a cat massacre a bunch of birds. The only question was how devoted was he to basketball? Could he be bribed to shave a few points, or would we have to press a few buttons to convince him?

I crossed my arms and leaned back against the wall, "Think we can get him to play ball?"

Atlee looked out at the court, "Depends."

"On what?"

The look on his face when his eyes slid my way, sent a chill up my spine.

"How much he likes his boyfriend."

Memphis made a mistake when he intercepted Atlee, but he fucked up when continued the fight after he'd already lost. In Atlee's fucked up mind that made him a toy to play with. And he wouldn't stop until it broke. Pain and misery were his drug of choice, but a true challenge… that's what really got his blood singing.

"And there's our leverage now."

I followed Atlee's glare to the side of the court where Memphis was shaking his hips while waving his hands in the air. Why the school decided our mascot needed to be a version of some nineties rap star called Cool Chirs was beyond me.

Though Memphis did pull it off. He didn't look that bad, besides for the ridiculously large gold chains around his neck. And he appeared to be a good mascot. His cheer was infectious. Even righteous little Sutton Barlow was up there dancing with him.

"Look at him over there, smiling like he has something to be happy about." Atlee's eyes darkened as he growled out, "I'm gonna crush your soul boy."

A part of me almost felt sorry for Memphis. Then again I was too busy grinding my own teeth at a face in the crowd to care.

Novalee was seated on the bleachers behind her dancing friend, looking bored as fuck. She was flopped to the side with her head resting against the wall. But it was what she was wearing that caused my fists to ball. Not only did she walk home in a fucking t-shirt, but she fucking showed up here in her goddamn work uniform. Did she enjoy testing my patience?

"What the fuck is she thinking?"

"I know," Atlee agreed. "The guy's gay. She can stop rubbing up against him."

"What?"

"What?" He repeated.

My eyes narrowed, "Who the fuck are you talking about?"

"No one."

Uh huh.

For a split second, Atlee looked like he got caught with his hand in the cookie jar. But that expression was quickly replaced with his normal charming sparkle. "Your girl's getting some attention."

I looked back over to where Nova was sitting and muttered out, "Motherfucker."

The guy sitting beside her was openly eyeing her. And why wouldn't he, the way Nova was leaning caused her skirt to ride halfway up her thigh. And that prick had no problem enjoying the view. Fucker even slid closer. And what did Nova do? Nothing. She just sat there showing her shit to everyone around.

My first instinct was to look for Darry. Maybe he was close enough to rip that prick out of the bleachers, but he was on the other side and three rows up from where Nova was. And he was with Ezra.

I couldn't help but be a little envious of the way Darry pointed out various things to his little brother. Once upon a time that was Atlas and I. Now all I had were memories and painful reminders. All thanks to Novalee's brother.

My eyes snapped back to Nova who was still resting against the wall. My hand itched to teach her a lesson. I could almost feel the sting of her ass cracking off my palm. If she thought this morning was bad, she had no idea what was coming.

All I needed was for her to make the offer, then she was mine. I'd wipe that bored look off her face in two seconds flat. And make her put on a longer fucking skirt!

Did she not see that prick beside her? Of course she didn't.

Because Novalee didn't care about anything, including her reputation. I was starting to think she enjoyed being on the bottom rung of the social ladder. One thing was for sure, the first thing I was going to do once a deal was made, was make her quit that fucking job. I just had to stop myself from killing someone in the meantime.

Taking a deep breath, I slapped Atlee's arm and tipped my chin, "Care to do something about that?"

There would be a lot of blood if I went over there.

I didn't have to explain anything to Atlee. He knew exactly why my teeth were grinding.

"Oh man, that guy's right there." Atlee tsked. "She should really pay more attention to her surroundings."

If looks could kill, then Atlee would've dropped dead. "You think?"

"Don't worry, I'm on it." He shot me a wink then walked away.

And not a second too soon. That idiot was reaching out to touch her when Atlee swooped in, wedging himself between them. I stayed long enough to watch Nova roll her eyes, then spun around and left.

Between Darry's fuzzy memory making and Novalee choice of outfit, I was two seconds away from losing my shit. The ghosts rolling through the back of my mind weren't Darry's fault. He was just being a good brother. But they were hers. Novalee may not have been the one who beat Atlas to death, but she was guilty by default. And yet my dick got hard every time I thought about her tear streaked face.

I jerked off three times and that still wasn't enough. One single thought or sniff of her sweet scent and I was hard all over again. I still wanted to kill her, but I wanted to hear her scream more. How fucked up was that?

Telling myself that this was all part of the bigger goal of

revenge, I rounded the corner and headed down the hall for our makeshift office.

That didn't stop guilt from creeping into my chest. Because while I planned to use Kato's baby sister to torment him, the truth was, I wanted to use her. I couldn't stop picturing her squirming in other ways. Would she cry the first time I fingered her? Would she scream when I forced myself inside her?

But the part I couldn't stop thinking about was the moment Nova realized she liked it. When she looked in my eyes and came so hard hers rolled in the back of her head, that was when my triumph would begin and I could really start to dig my way in her mind. A few things would help with that of course. Like access to her phone.

I walked into the room and shot Atlee a quick text.

> Me: See if you can find out her passcode.

It was a matter of principle at this point.

It took Atlee less than a minute to text me back.

> Atlee: It's 0000

I froze. 0000? Are you fucking kidding me?

> Me: How'd you get it out of her?

She had to be fucking with him.

> Atlee: I asked.

He asked?

> Me: You just asked.

Atlee: Yup.

Me: And she told you?

Atlee: That's right.

Bullshit. There was no way.

Me: And she didn't ask if you'd seen her phone?

Atlee: No, but she did ask me to throw it in the swamp if I found it.

I pulled out her phone and typed in the code. Sure enough the screen unlocked, and just like that I hated Novalee a little more.

There wasn't much to find. Novalee didn't even have a screen-saver, or wallpaper. Everything was original factory settings, except for the ringtones, which was set to a song. There were no pictures, no social media accounts and a total of six contacts.

In other words, her phone was useless. The only thing I did have to search were the mile long messages between her and Memphis, which I wasn't even going to attempt to touch. Not yet anyway.

I'd much rather check our books than scroll through the chaos of Novalee's texts.

Pocketing the phone, I headed over to the closet and reached up to move the loose ceiling tile. I was interrupted before I could pull the books out.

"There you are."

Fuck.

I stopped what I was doing and looked over my shoulder.

Carissa was standing just inside the door. As if my day couldn't get any worse. "What are you doing here, Carissa?"

High school sports weren't exactly her thing. Or sports in general.

"I brought Ezra to the game."

No, Darry brought Ezra to the game. She came looking for me.

"Since when do you care about quality time with the family?"

"Ezra really wanted to come." When her heels clicked on the floor. I busied myself with a stack of papers on the shelf. "You know how kids can be."

Yes I did. I probably knew better than she did. In fact I was pretty sure I'd spent more time with her youngest son than his mother did.

"Well, you wouldn't want to disappoint Ezra," I slid my gaze her way. "You should get back."

Carissa waved her hand dismissively, "Darry's with him."

My point exactly. The only person Carissa came here for was me.

"I thought I'd come and see how you were."

I just bet she did.

"It's been so long since we talked. I miss you."

"No," I snorted. "You miss my dick."

The corner of her mouth curled in a small smirk. "That too."

I rolled my eyes down her full length fur coat. It was way too hot for something like that, and a part of me wanted to ask what she was wearing underneath. But I didn't. I promised myself I'd stay away from her.

So I crossed my arms and sighed, "I'm not in the mood for your games."

"There was a time you used to like my games."

"That's done." That was why I kept blowing her off. One would think she'd have got the message by now.

"Is it?" If I didn't know any better I'd say she was upset about something. Her eyes were narrowed a touch while a sneer tugged at the corner of her mouth. "Or, is your attention on something else, or should I say someone else?"

"Coy doesn't suit you, Carissa."

As much as I wanted to charge over there and shove my dick down her throat, I wasn't about to play into her ploy. When it came to Carissa Barone, everything was a ploy of some kind. But that wasn't what was really bothering me.

"You used to like coy too," she took a few long strides over to the desk in the corner and shot me a smirk. "Did your preferences change?"

I wasn't going to answer her, so we ended up staring at each other. The truth was my preferences had changed. I think they changed a long time ago. I just didn't realize it until now. Don't get me wrong, Carissa was still hot, but I couldn't look at her anymore without hearing someone else's voice.

After a few moments of silence, Carissa ran her manicure fingers along the top of the desk, and sighed, "I saw you looking at that little girl."

So that's what this was about.

"Was that Novalee?"

"That's none of your business."

"So it was." She glanced over her shoulder and I couldn't help but take a few steps closer. "She's pretty."

"She's okay," my gaze dipped down to her bare calves. "What do you want, Carissa?"

She didn't come here to talk about Novalee.

"I don't want anything," she elegantly slid back and sat down on the desk.

Bullshit. Or at least that's what I thought until Carissa's legs began to slowly spread open. Any thought I had fled when the fur coat parted to reveal a small scrap of red lace covering her pussy. She was already wet, I could practically taste her arousal.

"Do you want something, Gio?" she purred while trickling her fingers up her thigh.

Yeah I fucking needed something. I was so pent up that all I could think about was busting my nut. Novalee had me walking around all day with a permanent fucking hard on. It was a problem.

I looked down at the lace fabric and cocked a brow. Maybe I could solve the problem?

"You need to leave." *Before I do something stupid.*

"Why," Carissa snarled. "So you can play with your new toy?"

That was a quick shift. She went from seductive to pissed off in under a second. But it was long enough to remind me of who I was dealing with.

"You should be used to being the old toy by now, Carissa." Not even her husband would fuck her. He had no problem fucking everyone else though.

That really pissed her off. Carissa hopped off the desk and charged forward to spear her finger in my chest. "You do not get to push me to the side."

"Why not? Your husband did. And so did my brother."

Carrissa reared back, confirming what I hoped wasn't true. When Romeo told me it felt like I got punched in the gut. I told myself he was lying, but he had nothing to gain from it.

"Did you fuck both my brothers, or just Romeo?"

Carissa cleared her throat and lifted her chin. "I don't have to listen to this."

"What's wrong sweetheart," I grabbed her arm before she could walk away. "I thought you wanted to play?"

She didn't even flinch when I dug my fingers in her flesh. She just looked back at me and ordered, "Let go of me." As if I would listen to her.

Something had been bothering me since I found out about her and my brother. "Who's Ezra's father, Carissa?"

Her eyes snapped up to mine. "My husband."

"You sure about that?" Last I checked neither she or her husband had dark hair. Even Darry was blonde, yet little Ezra had pitch black hair. Just like Atlas.

"Of course he is." The seductive spark poured back in her light eyes. "Now can we stop this? I hate it when we fight."

Next thing I knew, her hand shot down the front of my jeans and her fingers were wrapping around my cock.

"Let me make it up to you." She purred in my ear, and started stroking my length.

It took everything in me not to openly groan.

Was it really that wrong to let her get me off? She wasn't all bad. When Atlas died she helped me feel like I was in control again. I did things to her that would send other girls running the other way. And she took it. She took every ounce of pain I doled out and begged for more.

Except, it was all fake. The tears, whimpers and pleas she gave weren't real. She wasn't real. Everything out of her mouth was a lie.

"Get the fuck away from me." I grabbed her shoulders and shoved her back so hard she landed ass first on the floor.

And what did Carissa do? She peeked up at me through fluttering lashes and breathed, "are you going to punish me now?"

"For what?" I growled down at her. "More fake tears and phony pleas… no thanks. I'm done with fake Carissa."

I didn't need it anymore.

I didn't need her.

"Now get out," I said, having no sympathy for the look on her face. "Before I decide to have a chat with Darry."

Her eyes widened, "You wouldn't."

"Try me." I hissed.

Did I want to tell Darry what I'd been doing with his mother for four years, or about his brother's questionable paternity? No.

But if that's what it took to get her to leave me alone, then I'd suck it up and take his hatred. At this point I deserved it.

Carissa didn't say a word. She just pulled herself off the floor, brushed her coat off, and promptly walked out.

I grabbed the edge of the desk while the fading clicks of her heels grated on my last nerve. This day was shit. I couldn't find Simon, Novalee was prancing around town in whatever the hell she felt like wearing, then Carissa came in here and riled me up. And I still had yet to get Nova to offer a trade.

"God damnit," I roared while digging my fingers in the desk and flipping it through the air.

The corner of it crashed into a wall, causing the wood to echo with a loud crack that didn't make me feel any better.

"Yeah, fuck that desk. I didn't like it either."

That voice just added to my bad mood.

Without looking back at her, I growled, "Get lost Nova."

I didn't have the patience to deal with her shit. I couldn't guarantee that I wouldn't kill her. Not that she would give me any kind of reprieve.

"I need to talk to you."

"Trust me," my jaw ticked the second I saw her standing there in her waitress uniform. "You really don't want to be here right now."

"I really didn't want my brother to get stabbed either, so…"

Okay, that brightened my mood a bit.

"Did he survive?"

I knew the answer, I just wanted to watch her eyes light up with angry sparks.

"Yes," Novalee hissed.

My lips pursed in a fake frown, "Too bad."

Her eyes narrowed on me.

My eyes narrowed on her.

"Leave Kato alone."

Oh let me think about that, "No."

It was almost cute the way she crossed her arms and stuck her chin out like she could defy me. "He's doing his time."

"Not good enough." I said and headed over to clean up the mess I made.

"What would be good enough?"

"Well, he owes us a life debt, so…" I flipped the desk back on its feet then glanced back at Nova. "His death should about cover it."

His bloody, painful and very miserable death.

"So you're just going to torture Kato for the rest of his life?"

I slammed a drawer shut and nodded, "Pretty much."

If I could torture him in the afterlife, I'd do that too.

Nova's next sentence caused me to stop.

"What if I took his place?"

A smirk spread across my face.

Checkmate.

Chapter 32

NOVALEE

Every fiber of my being wanted to drive down to Louisiana State Pen and have a strong word or two with the warden, but Memphis dragged me to the game instead. He said that it would take my mind off things until Kato could call. I don't know why he thought basketball would do that.

It was just a bunch of guys in shorts running around with a ball. There wasn't even any fighting. What kind of sport didn't have fists and blood?

Ah, let's be real. I wouldn't have cared about those sports either. However, I could now let Sister Mary of the Hallway know that there were sixty-three spots staining the left side of the wall.

She seemed like the cleanliness is next to Godliness type. And I did enjoying seeing Memphis in his mascot uniform. From this day forth I would call him Easy M. That kind of made my suffering worth it.

That is until Atlee decided to join me.

He dropped down on the bench beside me and flashed his

perfect white teeth. "Hey."

"Why are you everywhere?"

Seriously. He was everywhere. I turned left and there was Atlee, turn right and there he was again. Walk into class and oh, guess what… Atlee. I think I even saw him outside my house the other day.

"I'm like God that way. I see everything."

Well I just became an atheist.

"That's great, now if you don't mind…" I rolled my eyes back to the spots on the wall. "I'm trying not to pay attention to the game."

Sixty-eight.

Sixty-nine…

"Hey," Atlee nudged me with his elbow. "What's the passcode to your phone?"

Seventy.

"0000."

Seventy-one…

"0000?" He asked.

Seventy-zero… damnit. Now I had to start all over again.

One.

"That's not a very secure passcode."

Why would I want to be secure? What was someone going to see? My random conversations with Memphis. In fact…

"If you happen to find my phone…" I lost it somewhere between the bonfire and this morning. "Can you throw it in the swamp for me?"

Then I'd have an excuse to avoid calls. At least until Maw Maw got me a new one.

"When you say throw your phone in the swamp…"

With a sigh, I pushed off the wall and sat up to clarify. "I mean grab my phone, and chuck it as far as humanly possible."

If he aimed right, he might be able to hit a gator. Not that I'd ever done that.

He stared at me dumbfounded for a second. "You're a strange girl."

"Thank you." That was the nicest thing he'd said to me.

Now if only his asshole friend would be a little nicer, and leave my brother alone. Kato was already being punished for his crime. He would be locked away from us for another thirteen years. But was that enough? No. Gio wanted him to suffer too.

It felt like the card in my pocket was burning through my clothes. A part of me wanted to take special agent Jack up on his offer. Maybe he really could protect my brother. Then again, maybe he'd just get him killed. There had to be another way, I just had to figure out what it was.

I looked over at Atlee who was avidly watching the game. "Gio's not completely unreasonable, right?"

His whiskey eyes remained trained on the game, "Depends on what you want to reason about."

There was only one thing I could think of. If I let Gio know that his dad was being watched by the FBI, then he'd owe me a favor. At least I thought that was how things worked with their kind of people. Guess there was only one way to find out.

"Is Gio here?"

Atlee nodded, "He's around here somewhere."

"Great," I pushed myself off the bleachers and moved to find a better view point.

"Nova," Atlee called out. "Be careful what you ask for. Some deals can't be broken."

Deal? Weirdo.

I gave him a quick lip curl, then headed off to search the crowd. There were a lot of people here, too many for me to be sure I did a thorough inspection, but that would require possibly talking to people and walking up the bleachers, none of which I was enthusiastic to do.

So I headed out into the hall hoping that I'd get lucky. And if I didn't, at least I'd gotten away from the basketball game. I might even be able to slip away completely. I could go home and immerse myself in a bubble bath while I anxiously stared at the phone waiting for Kato to call. If I was being honest, that's what I really wanted to do.

Sure Memphis would be a little ticked off, but Maw Maw just made a fresh batch of cookies. I could part with one or two. Though two might be pushing it. He did drag me to this game after all. Meaning Memphis should be giving me treats.

Ah the things I do for my best friend.

I left the gym and turned left.

Hearing my footsteps echo off the walls was a little disturbing, but not nearly as disturbing as the empty hallway. I suddenly understood why so many horror movies took place in a school. This shit was so eerie that I missed the feel of my trusty bat.

There was no telling who might be hiding in those lockers. Every time the crowd would cheer, I found myself springing back from the vibrations and eyeing the metal doors. Killers always came from the place you least expected, though.

I jumped around a trash can on the opposite side of the hall and proclaimed, "Ah-ha!"

There was no monster hiding on the other side. That was kind of depressing. So much for having an epic battle with a mythological beast. Guess I'd just tell Memphis about my regular old walk out to my truck.

I looked around at the shadows dancing across the shiny white floor, and suppressed a shiver.

Okay, maybe it wasn't a regular walk.

There was nothing like a bunch of religious decorations to add to the creep factor.

Turning my head, I eyed a large crucifix hung on the right wall. Why did it feel like that thing was watching me?

"Get the fuck away from me!"

My eyes snapped up to the plain white ceiling, "Jesus?"

"Are you going to punish me now?"

Okay that definitely wasn't the son of God. Son's didn't typically have female voices. Although Jesus did seem to like getting punished. What with voluntarily sacrificing himself for our sins and all.

The next statement drew my attention to a door down the hall.

"For what, more fake tears and phony pleas."

I knew that angry tone, and it definitely didn't come from anything divine. Demonic maybe, but I wasn't sure if even hell would accept Gio Mancini. Looks like I found him, and hey he wasn't pissed at me for once. So that was a bonus. Or was it?

My eyes narrowed on the door. Who was this chick he was yelling at? There was no possible way she was more annoying than me. I was a heavyweight in that category.

Gio's voice rolled down the hall, making my fists ball, "Now get out, before I have a talk with Darry."

Now this bitch was just egging me on.

I crept up to the door to peek in at my competitor. The second I looked in the room my blood started to boil. There was a woman sprawled out on the ground as if she'd been pushed, and Gio was glowering over her. I didn't know who this chick thought she was, but that was my murderous intent.

"You wouldn't," she said and her head tipped a bit.

That's when my brow rose. She was more seasoned than I would've thought. Don't get me wrong, the woman was beautiful, blonde hair and perfect facial structure, but a little too old to be wearing something that revealing under her coat. Especially when she was alone in a room with an eighteen year old guy.

Maybe Gio was into cougars? It wouldn't be the worst fetish I'd heard of. Memphis told me about this guy at summer camp that had a thing for cars. And not in the 'I want to drive them sense'. I had questions about that one.

The woman picked herself up off the ground, and I quickly threw myself back, flattening against the wall. As if that would somehow magically hide me. But she was already coming out of the room, so it was too late for me to make a mad dash for another place. All I could do was hold my breath and listen to the slow clap in the back of my head.

Brillant Nova, just brilliant.

Luckily, fate seemed to be on my side. The woman marched out of the room and down the hall, too pissed off to notice me standing there like an idiot.

I watched her retreating form and muttered, "Pfft, pussy."

She gave up way too easily. Gio hadn't even reached death threat status yet.

Once she rounded the corner I let out the breath I was holding and looked back in the room. Gio was really angry. His fists were furling causing the veins in his forearms to stand out. My plan was to try and trade information for my brother's safety, but he didn't appear to be in a negotiating mood. Did I really want to go in there when he was that mad?

"God damnit!" Gio roared and flipped a desk like it weighed no more than a feather.

Yes, yes I did. If for nothing else than to defend my title.

"Yeah, fuck that desk," I said while stepping in the room. "I didn't like it either."

His back went rigid and I could hear his teeth grinding.

Excellent.

"Get lost, Nova." He growled without so much as glancing back at me.

Now why would I do something smart like that? Besides…

"I need to talk to you." Pussy ass pansy face may have walked away before he flipped his lid, but I was here for him.

"Trust me, you really don't want to be here right now."

Oh, but I did. I wanted to push his buttons until he freaked the fuck out. Then he might have a modicum of understanding on how I felt.

"I really didn't want my brother to get stabbed either, so..."

Gio lost his brother, I got it. And I felt for him. I really did. It sucked when you lost someone you loved. But Kato didn't deserve this.

When he spun around anger still toyed with his expression, but so did a twinge of satisfaction. "Did he survive?"

This mother...

"Yes."

If he hadn't survived then I'd be stabbing him with one of those desk legs right now.

It took everything I had not to slap him when his bottom lip popped out in a mocking frown.

"Too bad."

Rage flowed through my jaw as he stood there glaring at me.

"Leave Kato alone."

Gio didn't even give me the courtesy of fake hesitation. He just spat out a flat, "No."

As much as I wanted to follow pussy ass pansy face's lead and storm out, I had to at least try and reason with him.

So I crossed my arms and firmly stated, "He's doing his time."

Justice had been decided. That should be good enough.

"Not good enough."

I sighed as Gio turned around and walked over to the broken desk. "What would be good enough?"

"Well, he owes us a life debt, so..." He flipped the desk back on what remained of its feet and glanced over his shoulder. "His death should about cover it."

"So you're just going to torture him for the rest of his life?"

"Pretty much," he nodded.

Did I really expect anything different? Gio didn't care what my family was going through. It didn't matter how much I missed my brother. All he wanted was our pain and suffering. There was no negotiating with that.

Special Agent Jack's offer was looking more and more appealing. Nothing would make me more happy than watching him lock up the entire Mancini family and throw away the key. But that wouldn't guarantee Kato's safety. It might just get him killed, and possibly myself.

Then what would happen to Veda? Who would she have left? Maw Maw didn't know what to do when she had a panic attack. She didn't know what song helped her fall asleep after she had a nightmare, or when to take the baby away from her. I couldn't risk leaving her alone. But I couldn't leave Kato either.

Atlee's voice suddenly rang through my head.

"Some deals can't be broken."

Deal? Was that the answer? The mafia made deals all the time. At least according to the movies I'd seen. Gio did refer to what Kato owed them as a debt, and debts could be taken on by other people, right? There was no harm in finding out.

"What if I took his place?" The worst he could say was no, and I'd be right back to where I was.

"Why would I agree to that?"

He wanted me to convince him to do this shit? Seriously? Though I suppose he did have a fair argument. He already picked on me, and followed me around – which I was considering giving him lessons on. What kind of stalker hides in plain sight?

So what would he have to gain other than tips? Hell, I couldn't even do anything to stop him from spanking me. My ass was so bruised that I winced every time sat down. And I liked sitting down.

That's when it hit me… "Because I'm not fake."

He told that woman he didn't want her fake tears. I had no shame. I'd give him all the real tears he wanted.

Gio spun around and cocked a brow. "You're not fake?"

"No," I said. "You really want to punish me."

I think my ass was proof of that.

Oh crap the anger was back.

"Were you spying on me?"

"I may have overheard a little," they were being awfully loud. "But I'm not wrong, am I?"

I held my breath and silently prayed that I wouldn't end up like that desk.

Gio folded his arms over his chest and clicked his tongue off the roof of his mouth. "No, you're not wrong."

Phew.

"But you have no idea what you're asking for."

It was fairly simple as far as I was concerned. Gio would take his revenge out on me and leave my brother alone. I thought that was the idea, then again, I could be wrong?

"Will Kato be safe?" I asked, figuring it was better to clarify things, just in case.

"Yes."

There we go. "Then I don't care."

Kato not getting hurt anymore was all that mattered. I'd breathe easier knowing that he was okay. Anxiety was starting to make me twitch every time the phone rang.

"You will care, I can promise you that."

No I wouldn't. I could take his cruelty and hate. I'd been taking shit from everyone for most of my life.

"You already tried to kill me twice, what more can you do?"

"Oh, I can do a lot more." I couldn't help but back away from the shadows that darkened his face. "Trust me."

I believed him, and the sad part was, I was still willing to sign myself over. Kato looked out for me my entire life. He looked out for all of us. It was time someone looked out for him.

"I don't care." I repeated.

Gio took two long strides closer as my back hit the wall. "Think real hard about this."

I never felt more cornered than I did the moment Gio's hands slammed down on the wall on either side of my head. My heart was pounding so hard that I could feel the pulse in the tips of my toes. He was so close the heat from his chest was warming my face.

"Once this deal is done there's no getting out of it. Your life will belong to me."

My chin lifted, rolling my gaze up to his. That's when fear really took hold. I couldn't stop my body from trembling at the glimmer in his jade eyes. Was he going to kill me?

As if he could read my mind, Gio scoffed, "Death is too easy. I prefer to play with my food."

What the hell did that mean? Was he going to eat me? He looked like he wanted to eat me. That predatory smirk on the corner of his mouth, made me realize how much bigger he was than me. His arms were as big as my thighs. Maybe this wasn't a good idea?

"Gio…"

"Rethinking your offer already?" He tipped his head and arched a brow down at me. "I thought you had more balls than that."

I wasn't going to fall for his school yard you can't do that crap. But I totally could do it. "I can take whatever you dish out."

Damnit.

"You sure you want to sign your freedom away?" he bent over, bringing his mouth a breath away from my ear and softly growled, "I will break you down until there's nothing left but a hollow shell."

Pfft, break me down. "Good luck with that."

"Okay," his lips pursed as he gave me a small nod. "Be at my house tomorrow night at eight."

"And if I'm not?"

"Then this conversation never happened." He said, then pushed off the wall and walked away.

Chapter 33

NOVALEE

I yawned and flopped my head back on the patio chair.

Suspension should've meant days off. Where I could lounge around the house and sleep in. But no. I got to spend the night tossing and turning while I went over my options. None of which seemed to have a good outcome.

I could either take the deal with the FBI and possibly put Kato in a worse situation. Or I could make one with Gio and put myself in a precarious position. I thought anyway. Gio wasn't exactly clear with the details.

Bastard.

Memphis might've been able to help me figure it out, but then I'd have to explain the stupidity of my actions. And that was something I'd much rather do when I was already facing the consequences. I did try to ask the doctor about it when I went to get my shot. Pretty sure he thought I was crazy though.

I probably shouldn't have asked him if he'd rather swim with the fishes or strap on a badge. Veda gave me the same look, right before she asked if I was on something. Trust me, I wished I was on something. Then I could blame whatever decision I made on drugs. Not to mention my ass was killing me.

Note to self, needles and bruised flesh did not mix. Try explaining that to a doctor. And a back up doctor at that. Apparently mine had an emergency. He didn't ask questions anymore after the toothpick incident.

I did find the location of said shot weird however. Normally it went in my arm. For some reason this guy needed to give me an exam, then he poked me in the butt. I was pretty sure he was a pervert. So I made sure to let out a nice fart while he was down there. He wouldn't be pulling that stunt again.

Thank God for Maw Maw's chili.

I may not be able to figure out how I was going to help my brother, but I could save girls from pervert doctors. One fart at a time.

Now if only I could quiet my brain long enough to take a nap.

"Nova's all alone again."

I sat straight up and eyed the little boy riding his bike past the trailer.

"That's because no one likes her." Another sang as he pedaled up next to the other.

My eyes narrowed.

Billy and Kyle.

"Look at how she dresses."

I looked down at my plaid shorts. What was wrong with how I dressed?

Billy turned his bike around to come for another pass, as his brother added, "And she smells bad."

Really, that was the best they had. Though I probably could use a shower. It had been a long day.

"Nova is a loser, Nova is a loser," they sang in unison as they rode away.

That's it.

I sprang out of my chair and pointed after them. "You two better watch your backs."

Pissants rushed down the road and ran in their trailer.

That's right. They better be afraid of me.

Another shaving cream bomb was coming their way. Right after I got the energy to go to the store and get supplies.

Taking one last glare at the blue trailer, I sat back down. That's when my day started to get better. A shiny red Corvette was turning into the trailer park, and it was nice and low to the ground.

I sat back and took a satisfying drink of my ice tea as it went over the first pothole.

The crunch and grinding sound it made was music to my ears. As was the loudly bellowed out string of curses that followed. With any luck he'd get stuck and I really get a show. Alas my amusement didn't last long, because the corvette pulled to a stop in front of my truck.

Confusion knit my brows until the driver door opened and Atlee stepped out. Go figure he would drive a Corvette.

"What the fuck?" he bent over to inspect the bottom of his car. "They should have warning signs."

They did. I took them down.

"Do you see this damage?"

No, but I heard it.

"There's a huge scratch on my undercarriage."

"That sucks." Maybe he shouldn't drive an expensive car.

Yesterday I backed into a tree, and he didn't see me stressing over damage. I should probably reattach the bumper though. Pretty sure I had a roll of duct tape around here somewhere.

Atlee continued to fuss over his car while I wondered if I could avoid him by going inside? But I was curious as to why he was here. It wasn't everyday a girl got a house call from Atlee Fiore. Or maybe it was. Maybe I was the only girl in town that he hadn't slept with?

After a few minutes Atlee regained his composure, straightened up and headed my way. That's when I got the pleasure of watching him struggle with Maw Maw's plastic gate. Sure, I could've told him to lift the left corner and kick the bottom, but where was the fun in that? Eventually he gave up and just stepped over it.

"You need a new fence."

I begged to differ. That thing was a security measure. I lost count of how many solicitors didn't knock on our door because they couldn't get it open. If only it would keep out assholes.

I held up my glass as he walked up the steps to the deck, "Want some ice tea?"

"Is it poisoned?"

"I make no promises." I didn't know what was in the water here.

"I'll pass."

That was probably a good call. Our water didn't hold a candle to his filtered fancy water. I bet he didn't even drink out of the tap.

"What can I do for you?"

Atlee reached in his back pocket and pulled out my phone. "Gio asked me to bring this back to you."

Oh crap. I thought I told him to throw that thing in the swamp?

"Thanks," I muttered and tossed it on the chair beside me.

Now I had to answer calls.

Wait...

"Did you say Gio asked you to bring it?"

He nodded, "Yeah."

My eyes narrowed, "Why didn't he bring it himself?"

"He thought you might need to make some calls before eight o'clock."

My face dropped, "You know."

"Of course I do," Atlee snorted.

And they say girls tell each other everything.

He cocked a brow at me, "I told you to be careful what you asked for."

That he did.

My head tilted to the side as I studied his whiskey eyes. Maybe this was a blessing in disguise. I did want someone to talk to after all. Atlee might be able to clarify a few things.

"Can I ask you something?"

"You can ask," he crossed his arms and propped his hip against the banister. "I might even answer."

My eyes rolled. Great another cryptic asshole. Oh well, it wasn't like I had a better option.

"What exactly would this deal entail?"

His brow rose, "What do you think it entails?"

Really? He was going to be that guy.

"Pain, misery, and general dread?"

That sounded right to me.

Atlee sucked in a deep breath, then let it out in a long huff. "Let me put it to you this way… there's only one reason a guy makes a deal like this with a girl."

"Because.. they prefer… killing women?"

He gave me a side eye and a light bulb went off in my mind, making my eyes widen.

Oh… so Gio was going to… do things to me. I didn't like that. Was that even possible? How was something that big going to fit in my tiny little body? I was just one person. This might be too much. Taking beatings was one thing, but this? Just the thought of it caused my body temperature to drop. I could literally feel the blood drain from my face.

Something I assumed Atlee noticed because he tsked and shot me wink, "There we go."

This wasn't right. Atlee had to be wrong. "Gio hates me."

He wanted me dead. He made that very clear.

"Do you have a pussy?"

"Yeah… but…"

"No," he cut me off then repeated, "Do you have a pussy?"

I scoffed out a snort, "It's not that simple."

"Oh, but it is."

"Come on," I shot him a dirty look. "Attraction plays a part."

He shook his head, "It really doesn't."

"Okay, but guys still have to get turned on…"

"Which comes with pussy."

"But –"

"Pussy."

"I mean –"

"Again, pussy."

"There has to be –"

"Nope, just pussy."

"Will you stop doing that," I yelled while throwing my arms down. "You're making this argument very frustrating."

"Hey," he slapped his palm over his heart. "I'm just being honest."

"Well, I don't like your version of honesty."

He shrugged, "Then you shouldn't have asked the question."

Okay, he had a point there. But I think my first mistake was asking Atlee. Men couldn't really be that simple, could they?

"So you're saying all a guy needs…"

"Is pussy."

Why did he keep saying that word?

"And Gio wants my…"

"Pussy."

Oh my god, I was going to hit him.

"What if I say no?" Let's see him answer that with pussy.

"I mean you can say it," his nose crinkled as he tipped his head my way, "but…"

"It wouldn't matter." I finished for him.

"Exactly."

So, I'd essentially be signing up to be a human sex doll. I suppose there were worse fates. Still, I couldn't help but ask, "Are you sure about this?"

His shoulder lifted in a small shrug, "It's what I'd want."

That was my problem right there. Never ask a guy whose favorite word was pussy. Then again…

My mind went back to yesterday and the angry way Gio's dick dug into my thigh.

Maybe Atlee wasn't wrong.

MY STOMACH CHURNED as I took the last few steps. All day I'd been stewing over which way to go and still wasn't sure I made the right call. Would this be better for my brother or worse? I had a record of making wrong decisions, and once I knocked on this door there was no going back. One way or another Kato's fate would be sealed.

It felt like the weight of the world was resting on my shoulders. Every whisp of the wind toying with my hair, and leaves rustling in the distance seeped into my soul. I could hear the two names calling out with every breath.

Jack or Gio?

Jack or Gio?

Which was the right one? Were any of them? And did I have the strength to live with the consequences? Could I actually do this?

I looked over at the brass numbers marking the address and all I could see was my brother's face. He was so broken in that court-room. A far cry from the man I grew up with. The one who threatened my bullies and taught me how to fish. There was nothing left of him but a spark now. I couldn't let that spark die. I could do this.

I had to.

For Kato.

My trembling hand balled into a fist as I reached up and knocked on the door.

Chapter 34

"You were right," Romeo sat down on the edge of one of my bookshelves and sucked back a puff of smoke. "Gio took the bait."

"Of course he did."

Despite what Giovanni thought, I knew my son.

I looked down at the picture of the Ford family I had laying on my desk and ran my finger over Novalee's pretty smile. The first part of my plan was now in motion.

"What about the sister?"

The sister was an issue. Things would have gone better if she didn't stumble into the wrong room. But it wasn't a problem that couldn't be solved.

"Don't worry," I rolled my eyes up to my eldest son. "Veda Ford's day will come."

DRIFTWOOD DAFFODIL 2 BLURB

Family had two meanings for me. There was the one I was born into, and the one I'd been waiting my entire life to swear an oath to. The only problem was my father. He'd been treating me like a kid since my mother was murdered.

My oldest brother was gone, my other brother was now next in line for the throne, and I was still waiting. The forgotten third son of boss.

Then the baby sister of my enemy walked into my school, and waiting wasn't an issue anymore. With one simple knock, knock Novalee Ford gave me my chance to take the oath and get revenge. Only one question remained...

Did I want payment for the life debt her brother owed... or something else?

My name is Giovanni Mancini, and I'm the foot that stomped on the daffodil.

AFTERWORD

Thank you for reading Driftwood Daffodil.
If you enjoyed this book please consider leaving a review. Reviews are always appreciated by authors.

Book 2 will be coming in 01/2024

I'd like to give a special thanks to my beta readers and PAs. You guys are the best and always manage to make me smile. I'd be lost without you.

If you'd like to be among the first to know about new releases and get an inside look into my world join my Facebook group T.L. Hodel's Murder Of Ravens, or my patreon.

Also by T.L. Hodel

The Order Of Ravens And Wolves:
Aftereffect
Scartissue
Happenstance
Accident-Prone
Relapse
Panic-Button

Deviant House:
Innocence
Innocence corrupted (coming soon)

The Lost Souls:
Adversaries
Frenemies

Brothers Of Shadow And Death:
Backfire
Backstab (coming soon)

The Seven Sins Series:
Pride

The Buchanan Brothers
Twisted Abel
Twisting Tallon (Coming soon)

Louisiana Made Men
Driftwood Daffodil 1
Driftwood Daffodil 2(Coming soon)

ABOUT THE AUTHOR

T.L Hodel is a Canadian author, poet and artist. Though coming from a difficult childhood she excelled at writing, having her first poetry published in junior high school. When she's not writing she occupies her self with numerous crafts, hobbies and is an avid gamer. She lives in Calgary with her kids and cat, and may have a slight weakness for horror movies. (Okay, that's a lie, she's probably seen them all)